Critical Acclaim for Robert Carr

"In **Corby Falls** Robert Carr has created a compelling story filled with characters who are both flawed and complicated...He has brilliantly weaved an underlying tone of tension and unrest while raising issues of morality and truth."
Elaine Mccluskey, Author of *The Most Heartless Town in Canada*

"Part thriller, part insider intrigue, and part homage to the melancholy beauty of poetry and all that it inspires, **Corby Falls** is the story of life's entanglements and the consequences of dark secrets."
Rod Carley, Author of *Kinmount*

"(In **Continuums**)...Robert Carr asks age-old questions about the heart in conflict with itself. How do we choose between our life's work and the needs of loved ones? Carr manages deftly to draw us into his characters' lives, such that by turns, we agonize and rejoice with them...A extraordinary debut!"
Joseph Kertes, *New York Times Best-Selling Author*

"(**A Question of Return**)...a terrific, compelling story...not a mystery novel per se, but it manages to carry a sense of mystery over more than a hundred thousand words...and that is called Art!"
Ken Alexander, former editor of *Walrus Magazine*

"Robert Carr...fully honours the dilemmas of his characters, their deep regrets, their fragile hopes."
Jim Bartley, *Globe & Mail*

CORBY FALLS

Novels by Robert Carr

Continuums (Mosaic Press 2008)

A Question of Return (Mosaic Press 2015)

CORBY FALLS

Robert Carr

Library and Archives Canada Cataloguing in Publication

Title: Corby Falls / by Robert Carr.

Names: Carr, Robert (Novelist), 1945- author.

Identifiers: Canadiana (print) 20210105062
Canadiana (ebook) 20210105070

ISBN 9781771615204 (softcover) ISBN 9781771615211 (PDF)
ISBN 9781771615228 (EPUB) ISBN 9781771615235 (Kindle)

Subjects: LCGFT: Novels.

Classification: LCC PS8605.A773 C67 2021
DDC C813/.6—dc23

Published by Mosaic Press, Oakville, Ontario, Canada, 2021.

MOSAIC PRESS, Publishers
www.Mosaic-Press.com
Copyright © Robert Carr, 2021

Printed and bound in Canada.

Cover design by Andrea Tempesta
Cover photo by Paweł Czerwiński on Unsplash

MOSAIC PRESS
1252 Speers Road, Units 1 & 2, Oakville, Ontario, L6L 5N9
(905) 825-2130 • info@mosaic-press.com • www.mosaic-press.com

To Esther, always
To Alexandra and Marty; to Max and Annabelle
To Mason and Anna Jae – so that, one day, they'll rediscover Oji

Engineers' speech is loaded with acronyms. Most of the acronyms found in this book are naturally expanded or explained. Nevertheless, a list is provided here for the reader's reference.

AEM – Ares Exploration Mission. A mission to land a rover on Mars. First and main mission of the Ares Initiative.
CMM – Canadian Mars Mission
CSA – Canadian Space Agency
DLR – German Aerospace Centre (Deutsches Zentrum für Luft- und Raumfahrt)
ESA – European Space Agency
ITT – invitation to tender. Equivalent to a request for proposal.
NASA – National Aeronautics and Space Administration

Chapter 1

December 1970

Saturday turned out to be the slowest day of his life. The planet had barely rotated the entire week, in point of fact. Wednesday, the last day of school, he rang his sister repeatedly after they were let go. It was evening before she answered.

"Why not Saturday?" he asked. "Why wait until Sunday?"

Sarah, who had a mile-long telephone cord, was setting the dinner table; he could hear the clatter of dishes in the background. She was always doing something else besides talking when on the phone. He once saw her correcting tests while chatting with a friend.

"Sunday morning, Miles. Uncle Alvin wants you there on Sunday morning."

"What's wrong with Saturday?"

"Oh, for God's sake."

Thursday, Christmas Eve, had moved along in spurts. Christmas lunch on Friday had been in Millcroft, with Aunt Pearl and Cousin Laura. "Laura is still with me," Aunt Pearl said when her daughter was not within earshot, and then she both sighed and laughed, and Miles was uncertain if she was glad of it or not.

For two years, while a nervous admirer hung around Laura, Pearl had moved in with friends, an older couple needing help. She told everybody she was clearing the young man's path to Laura's heart. But when no marriage proposal was made, she returned. "I'm not going back there, Laura, with those two old fools," were her first words when Laura found her standing at the door with her suitcases. "If Mr. Shy really loves you, he'll put up with me." Miles had heard that story many times. She had things to say, Aunt Pearl, and didn't mind repeating herself. Once, after a visit to Aunt Pearl, Miles asked his father what kind of a man Grandfather had been, because Aunt Pearl had said he'd had a sweetheart he cuddled with in Toronto and would find business down there as often as he could. "Cuddle? Dad?" His father snorted. "There's nothing to tell. Pearl and her tales. Pearl and her mouth."

The only subject one couldn't broach with Aunt Pearl was the son who'd died of meningitis. He'd been much younger than Laura. It seemed to happen in their family, an older daughter and a much younger son. Miles's sister, Sarah, was seventeen years older than him, and Aunt Pearl was nine years older than his father. Aunt Pearl had been a teenager when Miles's great-grandfather, Ellis Rueda – the *alien*, as Pearl sometimes called him – died, and the little anyone knew about him came from her. At times Miles's father would tell her she'd made up or embellished a story. Pearl would pay no attention to him. One evening she told Miles, "With family lore it's the same as with gifts. You take what you get and you don't turn up your nose." When questioned or contradicted by her brother – which was not often – Aunt Pearl would claim that her memory was not reliable anymore. "There are days," she'd say, "when it's all a muddy brew in my head, and days when I'm as sharp as Napoleon."

He spent most of Saturday morning staring at the clock in the sitting room. His father's father, the *cuddler*, had bought it in Toronto, and it had been on the mantelpiece ever since. It didn't keep good time. After Sarah complained about it too many times, their father said, "Think of it as an indoor sundial, roughly thereabout." In the clock's glass case, four chrome balls rotated, slowly and stupidly, one way and then the other. A torsion pendulum, according to his father, a timepiece where the back-and-forth movement occurred along a wire. The kind of clock around which time didn't flow, it snailed. Or crawled, thought Miles, in case *snailed* wasn't really a verb. Yet why shouldn't it be, especially on a day like that?

Mr. Chandos, his Grade Seven science teacher, would frown at either word. No crawling or snailing for him. Nor running, or rushing, or flying, or whizzing by, either, and, oh, how Miles wished any of these wonderful verbs described time that Saturday. Mr. Chandos would pair only the dignified verb *flow* with the noun *time*. Mr. Chandos was awfully fond of time. He thought time was *intriguing*, another favourite word of his, and wanted the entire class to be intrigued with him. He asked them what they thought time was – he energetically shook his bald head when everyone's eyes turned to the clock above the door: no, not what time *it* was – and why time was always flowing at a constant rate. "Practically speaking, that is. For us, on this earth," he added, with a superior smile. Before the silent class, he explained that time was a fundamental physical quantity. Well, thank you, Mr. Chandos, that really helped. He also asked if they could conceive of a world in which time would flow at a variable rate. Did they see a downside to such a world? To which Jim Cowley responded, "I'd like that. Very much. I wish this class would be done in five minutes, or that my father would belt me for no longer than a wink." Mr. Chandos smiled indulgently amid the chuckles. "That would not be possible, Jim," he said. "Not as long as you and your father are anywhere near each other. Maybe if he had an infinitely long belt and . . ." He went on with his explanation, but all Miles remembered was the infinitely long belt. Now, *that* was intriguing.

A day of waiting for the next one. At two o'clock, he put on his winter jacket and went out. Ben's house was closer than Jim's, toward the old bridge, but as at every Christmas, the Paskows had gone to Toronto, where most of their huge tribe dwelt. To reach Jim's place, Miles turned right, and then, past the New Bridge Road, left on Hedge Street.

Disappointment. Jim couldn't make time flow faster, because he'd been grounded. The left side of his face was red and swollen.

"What for?" Miles asked, although he didn't expect an answer. Jim was never sure why he was punished.

They heard Mrs. Cowley's voice. "No talking on the doorstep, Jim. You're letting in the cold air. Your father's due back soon, and he'll thwack you again."

"A Christmas present," Jim said. "When are you leaving?"

"Tomorrow morning. Can't bloody wait."

"God, I wish I could come with you. Get a break from this freaking place."

Miles had never witnessed Bart Cowley's violence but had seen its results on Jim. Bart worked mainly on Jim's skinny body, and Miles was *fully cognizant* – another of Mr. Chandos's expressions – of the marks Bart left on his friend. Jim's mother knew too, of course, and Bill, his older brother, who'd been gone now for almost a year. Jim was belted methodically by his father for sins past and future. It was never done in a fit of anger. Whenever Mrs. Cowley called the school to say that Jim was sick and wouldn't attend for a few days, Miles knew, as did everybody else, that Mr. Cowley had had another go at his son with his belt or fists. Jim reckoned he had five more years before he'd be able to stand up to his father. Maybe sooner, if his brother returned to Corby Falls. Bill was now somewhere near Toronto, working in a CNR yard.

"Does he hit your mother too?" Miles had asked.

"No, not really. Just slapping her."

"He slaps her?"

"Not that often. Not lately, anyway."

He didn't look mean at all, Bart Cowley. Light, sparse hair, almost white, blue eyes blinking at the world as if stunned by what he saw. Not an ugly face, perhaps chopped or unfinished, as if his maker had downed tools for a pee or something and then kind of forgotten and gone on to other things. He'd smile if he saw the two of them together, but then sometimes he'd say,

"Jim will come along with me now," like he was talking to himself or to an unseen confidant, and Jim would follow his father, making faces behind him.

"Can I hang around here?" Miles asked.

Jim shook his head.

"Come on, Jim. I'm about to kill myself."

They heard the phone ring, and Mrs. Cowley shouted, "Jim, pick up the phone."

Jim ran inside, and Miles followed him in and shut the door. He heard Jim shout, "Mom, it's for you," but Jim didn't return straight away. A couple of winter coats were hanging on the wall, with a variety of boots underneath and a large red toolbox. Miles counted five pairs of boots, and then counted them again. Time had resumed its moronic snail's pace. What was Jim doing, letting him wait in the entrance hall like an idiot? Did he think he'd left? He would have, if he had something better to do. He became aware of a whiff of boiled chicken. Boiled carrots too? Beans? That was why dogs had such a heightened sense of smell; they had nothing better to do. He could hear Mrs. Cowley's voice now and then but wasn't able to make out what she said.

A crestfallen Jim returned. "I have to go to the hospital."

"The hospital? In Millcroft?"

"Yes."

"What's wrong with you?"

"It's my father. He had an accident."

"What happened?"

"I'm not sure. Someone hit his van or something."

"Is it bad?"

"He's in intensive care."

On his way to the hardware store, Miles imagined talking Sarah into having Jim Cowley along on their Sunday morning drive to Devil's Elbow. She'd say, as she often did, "Why don't you think before you open your mouth?" It made him say harebrained things to her simply to elicit that reply.

The store was empty.

"Bored at home?" his father asked when he saw him.

"She's going to be late."

"Who?"

"Sarah. Tomorrow morning. You'll see. She's always late."

"She's driving from Lindsay and sleeping here tonight."

Elma Mulligan walked in, followed by Gerrard Bullhop, the new rector of St. Anselm's. Miles's mother had been into churchy things. He remembered numbing hours of sitting beside her in St. Anselm's, fidgeting, or staring at his father's impassive profile on the rare days he came along. He had not been to St. Anselm's since his mother's death. More than a year.

"I saw your lights were on," Elma told his father. "Lucky. Rose Biranek needs new light bulbs. I went to see how she was doing around noon."

"What wattage?"

"I don't know. It's for her bedroom. A light is gone, and she doesn't know where the doctor keeps the spare ones."

"I gather he isn't back yet," Gerrard Bullhop said. The depth of the rector's voice always startled Miles. They all said it was a beautiful voice, warm – as if you could measure the temperature of a voice – and that he was keen on music. They also said he was young. Miles didn't see it. The rector wasn't that new either; it had been almost three years since he'd arrived at St. Anselm's, yet everyone still referred to him as the new rector. Fairly tall, a flat face dominated by an unignorable moustache, a forehead enlarged by receding wavy brown hair, which, to compensate, he wore shoulder length at the back. Apart from the rather more sober outfits the rector favoured, he looked like one of the musketeers on the cover of the book Sarah had given Miles a month earlier.

His father went away and quickly returned with a small box. "Here, Elma, two light bulbs. One hundred watts. Should do." Turning to the rector he said, "Mr. Bullhop, what can I do for you?"

"Gerry. Everybody calls me Gerry, remember? And I like it."

"Yes, Gerry. Of course."

"Are you done here, Elma?" the rector asked.

"I guess."

"How is Rose?"

"Poorly. She came downstairs while I was there. She says the worst is early in the morning, when it takes her five minutes to do it. She gets up at five or six o'clock – always has, Rose – and then makes her way down to the kitchen for a cup of tea. Painful to watch. I said to her, 'Don't do it, Rose. It's dangerous. Or ask the doctor to put in one of those things that slide along the stairs and carry you.' You know what she said? Going down the stairs is her way of knowing she's not just a living corpse. It's easier for her to go up the stairs, but it won't be long before she's stuck on one level. I told her she should move to the ground floor if she loves her kitchen so much. She doesn't want to, because it would mean seeing that slut—"

"Now, Elma, such language."

"I'm repeating Rose's words."

"Rose is a sick, angry woman. Lonely and scared too. I'll go and visit her."

"Why not visit her now, Gerry?" Elma asked sharply. "She could surely use a visit."

"Yes, yes, of course."

Shaking her head, Elma went away.

Miles's father looked expectantly at the rector. Gerry Bullhop had a dark blue winter coat on and a black scarf looped around his neck. He held a cap with earflaps in his hands. Setting it on the counter, he said, "I saw Elma walk in and I did too. We don't see much of you, Joe."

"Oh, you know . . ."

"Not at all, in fact," the rector went on. "You weren't such a stranger once."

"Heather was more into it. One gets busy . . ."

Gerry Bullhop nodded. "Busy, yes, that's what we think we are. Anyway, I'm not here to call attendance. Still, what I have in mind would mean you coming to St. Anselm's again. Not to the service. No, no need to panic. I'd like you to attend the physical plant committee. Somebody like you would be of great help. I'm despairing, Joe. All our money goes in trying to keep St. Anselm's standing, and the structure seems shakier than ever. It's not only you that I want on the committee. It needs many fresh minds—"

Miles said, "Jim's dad has been hurt."

They both looked at him. His father said, "Bart Cowley?"

Miles nodded.

"What happened?"

"His van was hit. Jim and his mom went to the hospital in Millcroft. Jim said his dad was in intensive care."

He walked slowly back home. It was cold, and the daylight was coming to an end. Corby River was mostly frozen now except around the falls. On the radio they'd said it would snow today. What if there was no snow on the slopes? There had been a snowstorm two weeks earlier and nothing since.

A wasted, mournful, endless day. And now this thing with Jim's dad. Intensive care did not sound good at all. Elma Mulligan's husband had been taken to intensive care, or was it to emergency? By the time they got him there, Elma said, he was already dead. Jim's dad wasn't dead, though. Poor Jim. Not that Jim was awfully fond of his father. Still.

It had been centuries since he'd heard his father moving downstairs. It was while lying in one's bed, in the dark, eyes wide open, that time came fully to a halt, or almost. People slept during the night so they wouldn't die of boredom. He switched on the light on the bedside table and picked up his book with a sigh. It took concentration to read about hotheaded musketeers, a queen in serious trouble, and a cardinal who liked harassing her and neglected churchy matters. The chapter he was on now, in which one of the musketeers flirted with priestly ordination, was slow and pointless. When Sarah gave him the book, she said it had been one of her favourites. It wasn't girly or boring – most of it wasn't, anyway – but his mind kept veering toward snow and ski slopes rather than staying with what he was reading. Even thinking of Gerrard Bullhop as a cardinal – ha, Cardinal Bullhop! – didn't make the time *flow* faster. When he switched the light off again, it was past midnight.

When would Sarah get here? She had spent Christmas with her in-laws. His father had said she'd drive to Corby Falls before the day was over, but there was no sign of her yet. Miles had left his door ajar so he could hear her come up to the bedroom across the hall.

How long before he'd be on the slopes? Sarah said they'd get going at eight in the morning. A one-hour drive? Say an hour and a half, with Sarah being late. Nine thirty. An hour of hellos and silly chit-chat with the Westbrooks over a cup of coffee. There was no getting around all that gushing, and the embarrassing comments on his height and his looks. His older cousins would inquire politely about Sarah's family, and Sarah would claim interest in their studies. Thank God his aunt wouldn't be there, so it might turn out to be less of a drag. She didn't ski. She was Catholic, too. Years earlier Sarah had told him that the Westbrooks gave Uncle Alvin a hard time over his choice of wife. Miles had tried to see in what way she was different; all he came up with was that she was more smartly put together than the other women in his family. More *elegant*, to use a word she was fond of.

It was grand of Uncle Alvin to invite him to the cottage the Westbrooks rented near Bethany. He liked Uncle Alvin. His mother's only brother seemed easy-going and somewhat absent. In some way, he was like Miles's father, although a fancier dresser and, at times, chattier. Miles once heard Sarah telling their father that Uncle Alvin felt guilty neglecting his sister's family in Corby Falls.

All right, an hour for coffee and the silly chat. Say ten thirty. Then getting everybody ready to go and into the car, and the short drive to Devil's Elbow. Eleven o'clock. The renting of boots and skis. Eleven thirty. God, not before eleven thirty.

Maybe he couldn't sleep because there was too much light outside. He got out of bed and looked out the window. Almost a full moon. Across the two backyards, the light was still on in Rose Biranek's bedroom. Elma had replaced the burnt-out bulb. The back door was ever so slightly illuminated, which meant Rose had not switched off the light on the top landing either when she went to bed. To the left, at the side of the house, where the patients' entrance to Dr. Biranek's clinic was, the outside light was on too, as always.

It was on that side that Dr. Biranek parked his car, the white Mercedes, and where his patients parked. Dr. Biranek's space, closest to the house, was marked with a metal sign with an impersonal "DOCTOR" on it, as if any physician, not just Dr. Biranek, was entitled to leave his car there. The space was empty. It had been empty for a week, because the doctor was away. With Hollie McGinnes. With "that slut," as Elma Mulligan had told the rector. Hollie's car, the odd-looking Beetle, was there, near the doctor's empty spot.

He'd been, what, six or seven years old when the scandal broke. Although it didn't really break, because Dr. Biranek and his new nurse, Hollie, had not been coy about it. They had not flaunted their affair but hadn't hidden it either. *Scandal* was the word used by his mother, whispered at the dinner table. "It's shameless, Joe, a scandal. They don't even hide it, as if Rose wasn't there or was dead. You can't go on as his patient."

"Heather, he's thirty yards away, and—" His father stopped when he saw Miles staring at them.

Hollie was from Montreal, a nurse at the Hôtel-Dieu hospital, and it was there, on one of his trips, that Dr. Biranek met her. Dr. Biranek travelled often. In winter he took vacations in the Caribbean islands, or Mexico, or Florida – anywhere warm. Rose rarely went with him after she got sick. Miles remembered his mother saying that Rose was alone again. She wasn't strictly alone. Elma Mulligan was at the Biraneks' four days a week, and often came in Saturdays as well, to do house chores and look after Rose. Elma had fallen on hard times after her husband died. She came to the Ruedas' house too, once a week. A splendid monger of gossip, Elma. It was from her that his mother heard the stories she repeated at the dinner table. Some of the stories. With Miles sitting there with his parents, not every story bore repeating, because Elma had a filthy tongue and didn't mind using it. Miles would often creep to the kitchen door when his mother and Elma were in there talking, with mainly Elma carrying on. That was how he learned that Rose had a filthy tongue too.

"It's not that Dr. Biranek is openly nasty to poor Rose," Elma told his mother. "No, never. In fact, he pays me handsomely and always asks Rose if I shouldn't come every day. But he ignores her, wants nothing to do with her. Lately he's been using the sitting room for his thing with Hollie. Yes, that's where he fucks her now, on that couch of his he bought in Toronto. Modern, he says. Ugly, shapeless thing, I say. He calls it a sofa. Part of it is backless, you know. Never seen something like that. Yes, it's on that sofa that they do it. It's stained now, and it's hard to clean it. I pointed that out to the doctor. Was he embarrassed? Not in the slightest. He said, 'We'll be more careful,

Elma.'They do it on the floor too, sometimes. It's because Rose, poor Rose, chased them out of his bedroom. When he stopped sleeping with Rose after she got sick, the doctor moved along the hall into the other bedroom at the back. He used to bring Hollie up there, and Rose would hear them talking and laughing and making noises. She'd get up, hobble into her bathroom, park herself on the toilet seat, and listen to them. She could hear them better from there, because the bathroom is between the two bedrooms. She'd scream at them and bang on the wall, which wasn't easy for Rose, because the bathtub is against that wall and she was afraid she'd fall in. She'd sit on the toilet seat and fill herself with fury. That went on for a while, and then the doctor got his new sofa, and now he doesn't have to go upstairs with Hollie anymore."

His mother didn't mind Elma Mulligan's stories at all. Tired as she was, she'd sit with Elma in the kitchen, shelling peas, or peeling potatoes, or just listening.

"A woman has needs," he heard Elma say. "Body needs and soul needs. And a poor cripple like Rose more than most. The doctor would finish work, have supper, and disappear into that *libery* room of his upstairs. Yes, always in that damned *libery*. That was before Hollie came to work for him, when he had that fat old cow Mabel, or whatever her name was. With Hollie there, he rarely eats at home now. They go for drives, eat dinner who knows where, and then come home and shut themselves downstairs in the sitting room. Rose would drink and smoke in her bedroom, then would stagger out of her room and sit on a chair on the upstairs landing and cry. Cry her heart out, Mrs. Rueda. Now and then I'd be there late, in the kitchen, washing dishes or cleaning or maybe cooking something for the next day, and I'd hear laughter and noises in the sitting room and Rose crying on the top of the stairs. I'd go up the stairs to her and say, 'Come on, Rosie, go back to bed. Why do you do this to yourself?' 'I had such a body, Elma,' she said to me one time. She was sobbing. 'Such a body. Josef couldn't get enough of me. Always having his way with me, fucking and licking every hole I had. Look at me now. Look at me. Are these tits? You call these tits?' She opened her nightgown to show them to me, and there was nothing there. 'Do you hear, Elma, do you hear them going at it down there? What do you think they're doing? Are they fully naked? You think he's behind her, doggy-like? Is she sitting on his face? They don't even shut the light off. He wants to see her beautiful ass and tits. Do you hear, Elma? Do you hear that whore?' And on and on like this, enjoying the foul talk, because, in some way, it made her feel better. And I started laughing and she started laughing, and we laughed together until I convinced her to go to bed."

Had he fallen asleep? He thought he'd heard the noise of car tires on gravel – it meant it hadn't snowed – but he might have dreamt it.

He got up and dragged himself to the cold window. No snow. Dr. Biranek's white Mercedes was parked in the usual spot, the headlights still on. Hollie and the doctor must have caught a late flight to Toronto and driven to Corby Falls directly from the airport. Miles had never been in an airplane. Never been to an airport either. He was twelve years old and there were still scores of things he'd never done. Though by tomorrow night there'd be one less: downhill skiing.

"Shouldn't you be sleeping?"

Sarah was at his open bedroom door. Perhaps she had woken him climbing the stairs. She came close and hugged him. She'd had wine with dinner. Or after dinner.

She was pushing him away from the window when the headlights of the Mercedes were switched off and Dr. Biranek got out of the car. He had a scarf around his neck and no winter coat. He walked toward the side entrance of his house and disappeared inside.

"The doctor keeps late hours," Sarah whispered.

"He's been south with Hollie. He just got back."

She seemed to huff behind him. Then, as if to herself, "Such a dick."

Was Hollie still in the car? Miles waited for the passenger door to open. It didn't. She was probably in the house. They had unloaded their bags already and Dr. Biranek had come back to collect something else from the car. That was why he was so lightly dressed.

The glass panes in the Biraneks' back door were brighter now. No doubt the doctor or Hollie had switched on the lights in the large hall. He wondered if they'd turn off the light in Rose's room, and he watched for her window to darken. But Sarah was again pushing him toward his bed and he gave up.

The alarm clock showed ten minutes past seven. He could hear his father in the kitchen. His father was supposed to wake him up at seven. Not that Miles had anything to do; his bag had been waiting ready for him since early Saturday. He got out of bed and went straight to the window. No trace of daybreak, but the light at the side entrance to Dr. Biranek's clinic was still on. It had snowed overnight. Not much, two inches. Better than nothing. It was still snowing, though hardly at all. He could almost count the snowflakes.

The Mercedes wasn't there anymore. Arrived late, left early. Dr. Biranek didn't seem to need sleep. He must have left soon after he arrived – perhaps called to a patient's bed – because the snow showed no trace of tire tracks at all.

The light was still on in Rose's bedroom.

He crossed the hall and slowly opened the door. His sister moaned, "Oh, go away."

In the kitchen, his father was frying eggs.

"Are these for me?" Miles asked.

"Yes."

"I'm not that hungry."

"No such thing on a skiing day."

"Why isn't Sarah down yet?"

"Miles, it's not even seven thirty."

"We'll be late, you'll see."

A glass of milk and a plate had been set on the table for him. His father slid two eggs on the plate and put a slice of toast on it too. "I'll be off, then," he said.

"Are you going to the store?"

"Tidying up for an hour or two. I left money on the hall table. It was nice of Alvin to ask you along."

"Do you like them, Dad?"

"The Alvins?" This was his father's name for the Westbrooks.

"Yes."

"Sure."

"Did Mom?"

"Yes, of course. They were close in age, she and Alvin."

"We don't see the Westbrooks often."

"They live in Toronto."

"We hardly ever visit them. Ben Paskow is always visiting his family in Toronto."

"It's one of those things, Miles."

"What things?"

"A matter of chemistry."

"Chemistry?"

"That's how your clever sister explains it."

He ate slowly, then he washed his plate and his glass and the cutlery. He went back upstairs to get his bag. Sarah wasn't up yet, and there was no point in rushing back down just to stare at that stupid clock. The window was cold when he pressed his forehead to it. There was daylight now and the sky seemed to be clear. At least they'd have a sunny day.

Dr. Biranek's car was still gone. Perhaps the patient ended up in the hospital in Millcroft and the doctor needed to hang around. *The dick.* Sarah was never one to mince words. Was she angry because the doctor left Rose alone?

The light seemed to still be on in Rose's bedroom, but there was too much daylight now for Miles to be sure. Rose would be up already. She'd have had her cup of tea in the kitchen and would be thinking of making her way back upstairs if she wanted to avoid Hollie. Hollie's small car was still there, beside the doctor's empty spot.

Chapter 2

April 2005

The pasty April sun was mostly behind him now. As he left the expressway, clouds began to gather. Patches of greying snow broke the sullen fields. Horses, always the first let out, seemed uncertain of what was expected of them. He could steer blind on these side roads, yet a day would come, sooner rather than later, when the drives to Corby Falls would end. Dr. Pogaretz's words, a week earlier, had not been encouraging at all. "At his age a pulmonary infection is grave, and his overall condition is poor." And last night Sarah told him she might, after all, move in with Mike. "My heart isn't in it, Miles," she sighed over the phone. "Twenty years we've been together like this – he in Toronto, and I here, in the old house. We're ancient, settled. What's the point? Now that he's retired and bought this place in Caledon, he's insisting. It's quite a spread. For me, he says, so that all my junk can be moved in, and then some. Of course, I wouldn't do it before Dad . . ." She didn't need to complete the sentence. It was a matter of when in the next few months, not if. Their father knew it too. Acceptance was a thread that had run through his whole life, a quiet, often stubborn acceptance which precluded shock or surprise.

Glenarm Road was already wet, and he was soon driving through a cold rain. A strong gale came out of nowhere and the little Corolla became a blunt gauge of wind power. He rejoined the highway to bypass Millcroft. Past the town, the western end of the lake was briefly visible on his right. Clara's Lake had once been called Ghost Lake, the name he grew up with. The locals thought it was putting off tourists and property buyers. He remembered Mr. Moray, whose real estate office was across the street, coming into the hardware store one Saturday with a petition to rename the lake. Miles was behind two rolls of chicken wire near the door, playing hide-and-seek with Jim Cowley. Jim was lost somewhere in the back shed, looking for him between the long shelves. Hank Moray was a big man with a large belly and pants belted low. Bill, Jim's brother, almost twice their age, had told them that Mr. Moray's trousers didn't slide any lower because of his dick. (Bill Cowley said and did outrageous things. He showed them how to masturbate, the mechanics of it; at the age of eight their equipment failed to perform. Bill had nodded his dusty head knowingly and told them to zip up, adding reassuringly, "Never mind, it'll come in handy one day," and, years later, Miles still wondered whether he had intended the pun.) There was nobody in the store, only his father at the counter and Miles hidden behind the chicken wire. He heard the door opening and closing and then heavy boots making their way across the wooden floor.

"I think you should sign this, Joe," a voice said, and Miles recognized it as Mr. Moray's.

It took his father a while to reply. "What's this?"

"It's about the lake, the name of the lake."

It crossed Miles's mind that Hank Moray hardly ever came into their store. If he needed something, it was usually his daughter who'd come and fetch it, or, now and then, his wife, a sickly woman who seemed to do all her errands in housecoats. Everyone knew Hank Moray married her because his father-in-law, still alive, owned much land on the lakeshore.

"I'm not signing it," his father said after some time, and Miles was surprised how sharp and confrontational he sounded.

"Why not?"

"Don't want to."

"Everybody's signing."

"You won't need my signature, then."

"Your store would benefit. Cottage owners tinker, fix things."

"Maybe."

"You're a silly, mulish man."

"I think you should leave now."

"You'll regret it."

"Get out."

On the way out, Mr. Moray kicked the chicken wire with his heavy boot. The roll of wire moved, blocked by Miles's forehead. Miles didn't utter a squeak, and afterward, wiping the blood off, he felt proud of his fortitude. A mark was still visible now, although barely, Mr. Moray's boot having indirectly left a permanent imprint on his forehead.

He had grown closer to his sister during their father's slow decline. Away at university for long stretches at first, and then married, she'd been just another irritating adult to Miles as he grew up, someone who showed up now and then according to an unclear schedule. After their mother died, she came to visit often. She called it "checking on the two orphans," and was always brisk and matter-of-fact with him. She'd been the same with her son too, born seven months after she got married. She said to Miles once, "There are stupid people in the world, lots, in fact, and then there's me, the stupidest. I have no patience for children, yet I became a teacher. And not long after that, to confirm my folly, I married Elliott Grommel, the dullest man in the world, and had a child." A tall, handsome woman, Sarah, sixty-four years old, dressed most of the time in overalls covered in traces of clay or plaster. They were all tall in their family except Heather; the Westbrooks were more moderate in size. His sister had gained some weight lately, and it had not harmed her looks. To Miles, she seemed barely older than he was, which meant either she was aging well or he wasn't. A month before, in Lindsay, a saleswoman had said to them, "You know, you're the perfect illustration that married couples end up looking alike. A subtle resemblance, yet unmistakable." Knowing that Sarah might explode, Miles had joked, "*I* was the one who changed."

The familiar sign for Corby Falls appeared as the highway began veering north after Millcroft. Heading east, Rural Road 41 – Corby Road – ended at a T-junction where it met Market Street, which stretched along the right bank of the river. All the stores in Corby Falls were on Market Street: the drugstore, the IGA, the post office, the hardware store, the LCBO, the barber shop, two eateries – the Gridiron and Bart's Alehouse, the latter more of a drinking place – everything that a small town needed. St. Anselm's Church was on Market Street too, not far from the old bridge, and the bank as well. In the sixties, the false boom years of Corby Falls, there had been two banks. The CIBC lost the competition and closed down. It had air conditioning in the summer, and after running around town Jim Cowley and Miles and Ben Paskow would step in to cool off and annoy Mrs. Beastly, the older teller. That was not her real name. Her face had the colouring of the red walls around her, and Jim said it was because she drank French wine. After finishing with whichever customer she was busy with, she'd come from behind the counter and shout at them, "What do you think this is, the farm shed? I want you beasts out of here before I blink," and they'd run out, screaming, "As you wish, Mrs. Beastly."

The open-air market was on the south side of the street, near a road leading to a long-abandoned sand quarry. Throughout the summer, the vendors set up on Wednesdays and Saturdays. The new bridge, not far, was some twenty yards upstream of the falls. One couldn't exactly see the falls from the new bridge, and the drop was six feet at most. Federica, disappointed by the waterfall on her first visit, said, "This town should be Corby Stumbles, not Corby Falls. It's as much of a letdown as your Rue du Marché." Clara's Lake opened up half a mile downriver, after the waterway's almost one-hundred-and-eighty-degree bend. On the north shore of the lake, on Rural Road 40, wealthy Torontonians had built hefty cottages. The locals called it Slicker Road.

He drove across the new bridge, passed River Street, then turned left on the next street. Without a car, he'd have turned onto River Street, walked along it until the Biraneks' house, strolled by the side door, and crossed into the Ruedas' backyard. Coming from school, he had often done so. He'd always liked River Street, the large, assertive houses on it – now remnants of wealthier denizens and times – the glimpses one had of the river. Parallel to it, Second Street housed the next stratum – not the affluent, yet not the badly off either. And the street behind it, Third, lodged those with lesser means. It was, overall, a perfect reflection of the dwellers' rank in the eyes of the town. Years earlier, River Street had been called First Street, but the more evocative name gained ascendance with time. Aunt Pearl still called it First Street. There was a Fourth Street too, on which the houses were sparse.

Which street one lived on or came from mattered. It had caused the cries and the crises in their parents' life together. With Sarah's help he'd formed a picture of it. That was the advantage of having a much older sister. It wasn't a clear picture, but it provided a few answers. Heather had grown up on First Street, and never forgot it. Her classmate Rose Reaney, the future Rose Biranek, came from Third Street. They hadn't been friends exactly, Heather and Rose – First and Third streets didn't easily mingle in those days – but Heather had both liked and envied the eye-catching and less fettered Rose. During the war, Rose had worked in a munitions factory near Toronto. Shortly before Rose left Corby Falls, in early 1940, Heather married Joe Rueda, her neighbour. Backyard neighbour, because the Ruedas had always been on Second Street. By then, Sarah told Miles, there was hardly anything left of the Westbrooks' former riches. Heather was the youngest of four children, three of whom were girls, and when her time came to get married, she and her mother, long a widow, were living rather modestly in the house on First Street. So Heather joined her husband on Second Street. Temporarily, she thought. The worst part was that the Ruedas' house backed on to the house in which she'd lived until her wedding day. *Her* house. And across the street from it, on the riverbank, was the house of her grandparents. Heather and Joe's bedroom window was at the back of the house on Second Street, and from early on in Heather's married life she'd had a clear view of her social decline.

In 1947, Rose showed up in Corby Falls with her husband, Dr. Josef Biranek. It was shortly after Mrs. Westbrook, Miles's maternal grandmother, died. Heather began to say that her mother's house should be hers, Sarah told Miles. Her sisters, Heather argued, had married when the Westbrooks could still afford to be giving. Uncle Alvin agreed – or did not get involved in the dispute – but the other two sisters didn't. As their mother had died intestate, it was either money in the lawyers' pockets or sell the house and divide the proceeds. Heather asked Joe – begged him – to make her happy and buy the house, but he wouldn't do it. The war years had been hard, and Joe had barely managed to keep the hardware store going. There had been a mortgage on the store when he inherited it. Things got better after the war, but he had only begun to pay back the loan and didn't want to take on a second mortgage. A dreadful mistake, Sarah told Miles. It had been the thing that mattered most to Heather, moving back onto First Street, and her husband refused to do it. She screamed at him, punched his chest, threatened to leave. To make matters worse, the Westbrook family house was soon bought by Dr. and Mrs. Josef Biranek. That Rose Biranek, née Reaney, from Third Street, was now living in her old First Street home struck Heather as particularly cruel. The view from her bedroom became a daily drain on her spirit. Looking across the two backyards to the Biraneks' house inevitably gave her a headache. She became so furious with their father that she chased him out of her bed. It explained, Sarah was certain, the large age difference between her and Miles. Their father moved into the small den downstairs. Sarah suspected their mother didn't miss the intimacy, as she often complained of back pains and migraines. And five years after the Biraneks moved into her former home, Heather shunted Sarah into the larger bedroom at the back of the house and moved into her daughter's smaller room facing the street. There was less light in there, she said, and it helped her cope with her migraines. That's how Miles inherited the larger bedroom when Sarah moved out.

The Czech doctor, as Josef Biranek quickly became known, had been the first physician resident in Corby Falls. Heather and Rose met in the village, of course, although Heather never went out much. Sarah remembered polite words being exchanged, smiles, vague plans of doing something together, with or without their husbands, even parting kisses in the more subdued way of those times. Sarah said that Heather complained to Joe of a constant smirk on Rose's face. And why, Heather demanded one evening at the dinner table, did Rose insist on saying "First Street"? Why did she keep talking about "their house on First Street" whenever they met? The four of them, the Ruedas and the Biraneks, never got together socially for a drink, dinner, or a game of cards. Although Rose invited the Ruedas several times to the house on First Street, Heather always had an excuse – usually one of her migraines. So Rose got the message. Poor Rose.

Had Joe loved Heather? Had Heather loved Joe? "I thought I did," his father said, when Miles, a student already, wondered aloud about it on one of his visits. He'd taken some time before he answered. "Anyway, we had a few good years. And then . . . Rose and the doctor moved into the house your mother grew up in and, well, you know the rest, more or less."

Sarah thought Joe got married to avoid conscription, which everyone knew was coming. "Conscription?" his father repeated when asked. "Yes, it might have been a reason – not to get married, but to do it then." He shook his head. "I had a difficult year or two, and I believed Heather would ease my mind. It turned out that your grandfather had taken a large mortgage on the store just before he passed away. And your grandmother, well, she'd not been well at all, and doctors meant money then. I thought I'd lose the store. The house too."

"When did the cuddler die, Dad?"

His father smiled. "In thirty-eight. I was twenty-two."

They drove to Millcroft in Sarah's car. That morning, Dr. Pogaretz had told Sarah that Mr. Rueda seemed to be responding to the new antibiotic. "He may pull through this time too. Fair odds," Dr. Pogaretz had added. "In a week or two, he'll be back in the old age home. He was here, when, three months ago? He's weak, and at his age he'll have a difficult summer. I wish I could be more reassuring."

Good news wrapped in hopelessness.

The hospital, a soulless structure built at the beginning of the false boom years, had never found favour with the provincial government. The parking lot, at the back, was poorly lit. Beyond it, in the darkness, was the river streaming off Clara's Lake. To think they'd put the parking lot between the building and the river. Inside, he was overcome by a sense of neglect and gloom. The walls badly needed a new coat of paint.

A faint smell of urine and feces greeted them as they entered the room where their father was. His face was grey and he had oxygen tubes in his nose. They sat down by his bed. Sarah touched the cathetered hand and whispered, "Hi, Dad." He slowly opened his eyes, stared blankly at them, and muttered something which, Miles guessed, contained the word *roommates*. Miles turned to look around. The patient in the next bed, tousled white hair and beard, seemed to be asleep. The one in the bed nearest the window was lying motionless on his back. At his bedside, a middle-aged woman in a chair was knitting. A fourth bed was being remade by an orderly.

When, minutes later, their father spoke again – so soft it was hard to hear him – he didn't open his eyes. "Go home now."

They left when an East Asian woman came in and said, "Time for a wash. Who wants to be first?"

In the elevator Sarah said, "This is dreadful."

"It is."

"Dr. Biranek is here too. In a coma, from what Hollie tells me. It's her decision when he goes."

It was colder now. Rain mixed with snow fell on the car's windshield. Sarah's mood was somber. "I have nightmares about ending up here."

"Why would you?"

"Most people die in hospital, Miles. Or soon after having been in one."

The visibility was poor, and he drove slowly. Beside him, Sarah began a gloomy monologue. One thing that made moving in with Mike more palatable was that she wouldn't end up in Millcroft Township Hospital. When their father was there last, three months earlier, she'd witnessed a fight between two nurses. It was about some electronic contrivance they both needed – she wasn't sure exactly what – and there was only one available. They almost came to blows. It wasn't far from the nursing station, and other nurses were snickering. One of them offered odds on the fight's outcome. Dr. Pogaretz and another doctor rushed over and the nurses calmed down.

"She's leaving, by the way," Sarah said.

"Who?"

"Dr. Pogaretz. She's had enough. The government is putting all the money into the big hospitals, so it's Ross Memorial in Lindsay for her."

Back in Corby Falls they had a cold dinner in the kitchen and a lot of wine. He drank much more than Sarah, whose nasty mood had lingered. "Loneliness, discomfort, pain, and humiliation – that's the package death comes with. Young, we don't think of death, it's not on our radar. The longer we live – and we've got very good at it – the larger the package is. By the time we begin to think of it, we've already opened it."

"Jesus, Sarah."

"I'm sixty-four, Miles, and I know what's coming. The brown UPS truck has pulled up on Second Street and I've opened my parcel." She fished for a tissue in her pocket and blew her nose. "Did you hear it?"

"Hear what?"

"It's the humiliation that gets to me the most. 'Time for a wash. Who wants to be first?' I was ready to strangle her, that professional cheer. She wasn't young either. Probably tired of doing that shitty job."

They cleared the table and settled in the living room with a second bottle. Sprawled on the old couch, Sarah insisted on getting news about the "perambulator." She'd had many names for the rover the Europeans were planning to build and land on Mars: the crawler, the buggy, the pram. The mantis too, at first, after Miles showed her a picture of one of the concepts. She said it looked like an insect with wheels for legs. The "perambulator" became her favourite when Miles told her of the heavy British commitment to the European Space Agency's rover.

"It hasn't been going so well," Miles said.

"Subcontractors? The prime? Technical fuckups at Ludwig Robotics?"

Sarah knew the lingo. She didn't really understand what was going on – how could she? – but had a striking command of the lingo.

"No, no, the studies are fine."

"So?"

"An unspoken gag order from high up. No crowing about the perambulator. Even whispering is frowned upon."

"Just between us."

"The CSA mustn't hear."

"Didn't you say . . . Isn't the Canadian Space Agency funding the studies?"

"Indirectly. I'm not allowed to let them know that ESA like what we're doing."

"I don't get it."

"The Canadian Mars Mission, that's the priority."

"Ah, I forgot."

The telephone was ringing. With a groan, Sarah got up and went into the kitchen. It was hard on her – the daily visits to their father, the gloomy thoughts of creeping old age. He could hear bits of what she was saying, words related to their father's health. Probably Mike, the provider of their evening's wine. Mike's stash of good Italian wine, kept under the stairs.

When she came back, she refilled her glass and said, "Elma Mulligan. Yes, still alive. Wants to know how Father is. I know she's been ringing him at the old age home. Christ, into his dying days. She's in a home in Peterborough."

He remembered a weekend in Corby Falls soon after Sarah had left Elliott and moved back in with their father. He met Elma coming out of the hardware store. "Don't go in," she said sharply. "Your father is busy. He doesn't have time for the likes of us. I need help, and he sends me to someone else."

"How are you, Elma?"

"I'm fine. It's your father who worries me."

"He's all right."

"Miles Rueda, your father is – and it saddens me – unforthcoming. Morose. Disinclined to conversation."

"He's always been like that."

"And he's abrupt lately. Not keeping his word either. I'm despairing."

"He's a good man, Elma."

"Even better, I'd offer, with the right woman by him." She sighed. "I should get used already. I was fine for a poke or two . . . Ha, still am, and more than one or two, if I were to count." Disregarding his embarrassment, she took hold of his elbow. "Your stubborn father, Miles, he doesn't have to live alone."

"Sarah's with him now."

Elma scoffed. "Not for long. She's got a beau."

"She said she's here to stay."

"You don't know anything. She'll move in with the beau, and soon. That's what women want. I could keep house for your father – I told him that over and over. Heck, he knows it. You tell him too. Tell him Elma Mulligan still has her strength."

Shaking her head, she left him and walked slowly toward the old bridge. She'd gained weight. She'd had her eyes on his father ever since Joe became a widower. There'd been rumours she'd been sweet on him even before.

"Same Elma. As opinionated and loud-mouthed as ever," Sarah said. "When I told her Dr. Biranek was in the Millcroft hospital too, and dying, she said, 'At last,' and asked if the murderous bitch was still alive."

"Hollie?"

"She still thinks Hollie killed Rose."

"Elma's crazy."

"She said it again, just now. 'Bitch Hollie kept the doctor in Toronto that weekend, and by the time they got back on Monday morning poor Rose was dead.'"

Something wasn't right. He'd had several glasses of wine, four or five, but he was sure his sister had it wrong. "Did you say Monday morning?"

"Huh?"

"Did you say Hollie and Biranek got to Corby Falls on *Monday* morning?"

"I did."

"That can't be."

"What can't be?"

"They didn't get back Monday morning. And you know that as well as I do. You arrived late that Saturday night, saw me standing at the window in my room, and stood there beside me and watched as Biranek got out of his car and went into his house."

It took her a while before she replied. "It's not what Biranek told the coroner."

"What did he say?"

"He said he and Hollie got back to Corby Falls on Monday morning."

"Where you there, at the inquest?"

"Father was."

"Did you tell him what you and I saw?"

"I did."

"And?"

"I'm tired, Miles."

"Come on."

"It was long after the inquiry. Like you, I wasn't here that Monday. Wasn't in Millcroft either. I drove you to Devil's Elbow on Sunday morning because it was on the way to Toronto. I went down there to be with a friend for a few days. That Christmas . . . it hadn't been a good time for Elliott and me. Leaving him and Doug with my in-laws made things worse. When I got back, sure, I must have heard of Rose's death one way or another, but not the particulars. It was less of a story in Millcroft than in Corby Falls. Half a year later, perhaps more, I dropped in here for a visit and stayed for dinner. You must have gone up to your room when Father mentioned what Biranek told the coroner. I don't remember how it came about—"

"What was said about Rose at the inquest? When did she die?"

"They said that she fell down the stairs Saturday afternoon or early evening and died Sunday night."

"And?"

"And nothing."

"Was it Father's idea to say nothing?"

"In the end, yes. He said it amounted to my word against Biranek's. Anyway, Father didn't think Biranek killed Rose. It took him a while, but he came up with something that satisfied him. He thought Biranek came back alone that Saturday night to check on Rose. He found Rose dead in the waiting room and became afraid he'd be accused of pushing her down the stairs. He drove back to Toronto, were Hollie was, and said nothing about his brief trip to Corby Falls."

"The coroner concluded Rose died Sunday night."

"Father thought they were wrong, or that perhaps Biranek thought Rose was dead but she wasn't."

"He's a doctor, Sarah."

"I'm telling you what Father believed at the time. Wanted to believe. He had no stomach for a nasty conflict with his neighbour. And I certainly didn't want to be in the middle. I had other things to worry about."

It was crazy. Biranek had simply taken off and left Rose to die.

"I'm amazed you remember that night," Sarah said.

He had to process what he'd just learned from Sarah, and he was soon in an agitated and noisy monologue, asking and answering his own questions. Why did Biranek hide that he'd been in Corby Falls that Saturday night? It was, of course, not relevant now, with the doctor all but dead. Still, it demanded an answer. Why, unless he was guilty of something? Miles didn't buy their father's explanation. Not at all. Dr. Biranek had found Rose alive, had let her die there, and had driven back to Toronto. And that meant he had killed her. Murdered her. As to Hollie, yes, perhaps their father had been right. They had not seen Hollie that night, and it could be that she wasn't with Biranek and knew nothing about his trip to Corby Falls. Unlikely, but . . .

Miles paced the room, waving his hands. It took him some time to get through it all, with more wine and a trip to the loo. Sarah had kept her eyes closed throughout. He'd been silent for more than a minute before she opened them. She said she was coming down with a cold and was going to bed. He should do the same. Standing up, she added, "As you said, it doesn't matter now."

Another cigarette. He'd gone almost a year without smoking, and this morning it was already his second one. He had a cigarette last night too, after Sarah had gone to bed. Sarah shouldn't have cigarettes in the house. She claimed they were strictly for friends.

He'd slept poorly, his mind whirring. Biranek's callousness was shocking. The first doctor ever to settle in Corby Falls, their infallibly courteous neighbour – erect, elegantly dressed, hair pomaded and impeccably parted – had murdered his wife. A doctor, a saver of lives. A refined lover of books, a man of precise words delivered with a foreign accent which, his father had maintained, hid learning and sophistication.

Growing up within earshot of Elma Mulligan's stories about the Biraneks had made Miles uneasy about his backyard neighbour. It wasn't because of Rose. Only twelve when Rose died, he'd barely thought of her as a real person. She was a source of his mother's headaches primarily, someone who'd changed, in the illogical ways of grownups, from a tolerated companion during Heather's schooldays into a usurper. A diagnosis too, "multiple sclerosis," and as a child Miles had held the belief that the more mysterious the name of an illness, the deadlier it turned out to be. MS was the first acronym he learned, although he didn't know it was an acronym. He heard his parents talk about it, and for years he thought the name of the illness was *emess*. Rose had *emess* and didn't move like other people. At the end, Rose was the sickly wife Dr. Biranek had stopped loving, the sad protagonist of Elma's stories, someone glanced through Miles's bedroom window when, on warm days, leaning on Elma, she'd take a few uncertain steps back and forth in the backyard of the big house to which Heather had dreamt of returning.

The back door of the Biraneks' house opened and closed, and he knew that Hollie had come out for a smoke too. She'd seen him, because she made her way between the sparse bushes where the two yards met and came toward him.

"Better than smoking alone," she said. "Your sister said you'd quit."

"I had. It held until last night."

"How's your father?"

"He might pull through. Sarah told me Dr. Biranek is being kept alive. I'm sorry."

She nodded. "I'm on my way there."

"What will you do?" he asked.

She sighed and blew smoke in the air. Her eyes followed it, as if attempting divination. A grey, dismal sky. "You mean . . . after? I don't know. Might go back home, back to Quebec. I have family there, most of them in Montreal. Two sisters, a brother, nieces and nephews I hardly know." Hollie had thin leather gloves on, and the hand holding the cigarette was shaking slightly. She was formally, almost elegantly, dressed.

"We've hardly seen you in years, Miles. And when you came . . . Josef often said, 'Miles is parsimonious with his visits.'"

"I drive in and drive away," he mumbled. "See Sarah and Father, then back to Toronto. My daughter is with me most weekends."

It had been cold overnight, and the ground under their feet was hard.

"I'll finish this cigarette and go to the hospital," she said. "Don't know why I don't smoke in the house. He's not in there to get upset. Josef was furious if a whiff of smoke got into the house."

A bleak morning. People should die in the summer.

"He spoked a lot about you, Miles," she went on. "God, the way I talk, and he's not dead yet . . . He was so proud of you. Anytime he saw something that mentioned Ludwig Robotics in the newspapers, out came the scissors and he'd run to me with the clipping. 'Look, Hollie. Look what Miles is up to.' He waited for you to drop in and tell him what you were working on. He told friends, and not just friends, 'We have a space scientist in Corby Falls, and he's our neighbour.' He did, yes."

"I'm an engineer, Hollie, not a scientist. Dr. Biranek knew that . . . Knows."

"Do you remember the gathering at our house for the first lunar landing? It was a Sunday, I think. Don't you? Your father was there, yes. Started in the early afternoon, and ended after midnight. We were all glued to the screen for the live broadcast. One of the rare times I saw Josef tipsy. What was it, nineteen sixty-nine? It wasn't *our* house then. Rose was still alive."

Clearly, Hollie would rather smoke and talk than drive to the hospital.

"Hollie, do you remember the weekend Rose died?"

She looked startled. "How could one forget?"

"What did you do that weekend?"

"What did I do?"

"You and Dr. Biranek."

He'd just blurted the question out. He feared she might be offended by it, but she wasn't. It offered her something else to think about.

"Oh, my. I mean, I remember how we found Rose. Poor woman. She was there, on the floor, near the door to the consulting room. We had parked and gone in through the patients' entrance, on the side. Josef had gone in first, and when I went in he was there, kneeling, trying to see if she was still alive. She'd peed herself. I won't forget that, ever."

"Do you remember what you did before?"

"Before?"

"What you did that weekend, before driving back to Corby Falls."

"In Toronto? We were in Toronto."

"Tell me anything you remember, anything at all."

"Why?"

He should have thought of that. "I . . . I had an argument with Sarah, last night. I said that people remember most things around traumatic events, including the little stuff, and Sarah disagreed. She thinks people make things up."

She tried to laugh. "I'm neither. Don't remember much and can't invent. Ah, here's something I remember, we saw hair."

"Hair?"

"Yes."

"*Hair*, the show?"

"Yes."

"Where? Where did you see it?"

"At the Royal Alex. Josef couldn't stop praising it. He loved it. So did I."

"Are you sure that's what you did?"

"I'm sure. Did you ever see it?"

"No. Listen, when did you see it?"

"That weekend."

"I mean, was it Saturday or Sunday?"

She pulled greedily on her cigarette before answering. "Both."

"What do you mean, both?"

"Saturday the first time. And we saw it again the next day. I told you we loved it."

That couldn't be. "Are you certain?"

She nodded.

"What did you do after the show on Saturday?"

"Oh, dear . . . We went back to the hotel, I think."

"You think?"

"I'm pretty sure."

"What hotel?"

"King Eddy. We always stayed there."

"You went to bed?"

"No, I wanted a drink. I liked to drink in those days. Josef wasn't into it, though he'd humour me."

"And?"

"And what?"

"What happened afterwards?"

"Nothing. I had a drink or two and then went to bed. Got up late the following day, with a headache. I had second thoughts about seeing *Hair* again. I wasn't that sure. We were supposed to drive back that day, and I told Josef maybe we should just go. He said we could drive back Monday morning, early Monday morning, so we could open the office in time for the day's patients. And I went along with that. And truth is, I loved *Hair* the second time better than the first. We drove back on Monday and . . . You know the rest."

"Did you sleep through the night? On Saturday?"

"I think so . . . That's an odd question, Miles. How would I remember, anyway?"

"Did Dr. Biranek sleep with you?"

"Really, Miles."

"What I mean is, did he go to sleep at the same time, or did he hang around, read a book in an armchair, go down for some fresh air?"

"How could I remember? Anyway, I'm sure he did. He was there in the morning with me."

So silly of him. How could he think she'd recall what her husband did one Saturday night thirty-five years ago? It was a miracle she remembered as much as she did.

She got another cigarette going from the butt of the old one. "I'd rather chat and smoke than go to the hospital. Might go through the whole pack. Stay a bit longer, Miles. Have another smoke with me. Josef's being kept alive, and everybody's losing patience with me. All I have to do is sign some papers. I don't even know what they say. I've been told it's in case I get nasty with the hospital when he's no more." She pulled gluttonously on her cigarette and exhaled noisily. "It's today . . . I mean . . . if I don't falter. That's why

I got dressed up. One can't sign execution papers with a track suit on. Not classy." She shook her head. "I don't know why it's been so hard for me to sign those silly papers. We had some good times, Josef and I, though he wasn't the easiest man to live with. His way or the highway. And he'd explode out of nothing. He got angry in the bar that Saturday night, the weekend Rose died. It was an unpleasant scene. That's why I recalled we had a drink after the show. We were in the hotel bar, sitting on those silly uncomfortable tall stools, and we agreed we'd see the show again, and Josef felt like sneezing and did, and took his glasses off to blow his nose or whatever, and put the glasses on the next stool, which was empty. Without thinking, of course. And while he was wiping his nose, another man, a big, tall guy, sat on the stool and broke Josef's glasses. He apologized. Josef became upset, although it was his fault, and screamed he had tickets to a show the following evening and how was he going to see without glasses. It took him forever to calm down. Either he did, or I got happy."

She tried to laugh. "It's weird what one remembers. It just came to me now. He got some Scotch tape at the reception desk, and when I went to bed he was tinkering with his damaged glasses. Last time I looked, he'd rigged up something that seemed to hang on his nose. He looked grotesque. And then, when I woke up the next morning, he had good glasses on, not the pair he'd been knocking together before I went to bed. When I asked him how come, he said he'd had another pair of glasses with him, and everything was fine. I never understood why he'd tried to mend his glasses, or why he got so upset the night before, if he knew he had another pair of glasses with him. I presume it was the money, because Josef had expensive eyeglasses. Always did. The lenses were a fortune, and the frames too. Fancy."

Chapter 3

April 2005

He paid the cab driver and watched Katelyn ring the doorbell of her friend's house. She turned and waved, and then the door opened and she disappeared in the eye-catching Annex house. Should he have tried harder? He had painted for Katelyn a jolly evening with Ben and Jennifer, but gave up rather quickly. His own voice lacked conviction.

The restaurant was a short walk away and he got there early. Just as well. He enjoyed the drift of a solitary drink, the coming and the going. He followed the host along the bar, then right and down a few steps. Where was the Absinthe Gempp Pernod poster? On their first dinner there, he and Federica were led to a table under it and she told him that Gustave Gempp married into the Pernod family and created his own absinthe. Where did she acquire that trivia? And why had he retained it after so many years? Perhaps because he'd always liked Le Paradis – the black-and-white photos lining the wall facing the bar as you walked in, the old posters with their whiff of an erstwhile France, the abrupt waiters, the curved-back chairs with worn-out armrests. Federica took him there, and he took to it. They took Laukhin there, and the poet took to it also. He was very sick by then. The evenings he felt better, he'd walk to Le Paradis from his apartment. He'd sit at the bar, on the end, right near the door, slowly sipping his drink, barely touching the food on his plate.

Without Katelyn, he'd end up drinking. He would begin slowly, ease himself into it. He was seated in the lower room and ordered a beer. In front of him hung a photograph he had not seen there before: a middle-aged waiter in a quiet moment behind a closed glass door, peering out onto the street, perhaps waiting for the first customers of the evening. The black vest and the bowtie, the white apron, it was all there, a clean-cut solemn Parisian *garçon* of older times. In some way it reminded him of grave Dr. Biranek. Was it mostly the sleeked parted hair? The doctor's had been sprinkled with dandruff now and again, which he treated himself, and there was an unusual smell around him, not unpleasant, but unexpected. With light hazel eyes that looked straight at you, unblinking, Dr. Biranek made a serious, solid impression.

A correct, meticulous Central European had been Ben's description. Sarah, approaching poetic consonance, had referred to him as "pernickety Biranek." Reserved, that had been everybody's opinion. Even when he began to walk with a cane, in his late sixties, he kept his proud ramrod posture, and people said he had another stick inside him. Sarah was convinced his cane was an affectation, because he used it only when he went out for a leisurely stroll. She'd seen him more than once hurrying without a cane near the hospital in Millcroft. Despite his thin frame, midlife had given Dr. Biranek a protruding belly. He didn't seem to mind and, without smiling, would touch it and say, "The *knedlík* effect. One must put up with some embonpoint if one loves dumplings the way I do." He pronounced the French word with enjoyment, his lips shaped as if to receive one of the beloved *knedlíks*. (*Knedlíky?* Ben might know.) He'd taught Elma how to make the potato dumplings the way he liked them. Miles had once heard Elma mumbling as she was washing the windows in the family room, "There goes Dr. Biranek and his *effect.*"

Miles's father became Biranek's patient soon after the doctor and Rose moved into the house on River Street. A routine developed early on between the two neighbours. Joe Rueda would make a phone call and then walk across the two backyards for a medical consult outside ordinary hours. Afterward, tea was served to them in the doctor's library, the room on the second floor right above the consulting room. The doctor had put in a circular staircase between the two rooms for quick ascent to his beloved books. The tea tray was brought in by Rose, who always used the main stairs. She never hung around, although she always inquired after Heather and her migraines.

Later, when Rose became too weak, it was Hollie who'd come up with the tea. The first time it happened his father described the scene when he returned home. His mother began to cry, and at first Miles thought she was concerned about Rose. "That room," she said between tears, "the room that's Dr. Biranek's library, used to be my bedroom." His father's face turned grey. "Heather, please, don't do this to yourself again." Heather stood up and ran into the kitchen. His father sighed and followed her. Returning alone, he looked at an alarmed Miles and said, "Bloody Westbrooks' house." It wasn't often that Miles heard his father swear.

Except for the entrance portico and the small lozenge window above it, the Westbrooks' former house looked the same from the front as it did from the back. Clad in purple brick, it had ground-to-roof bay windows on each corner with jutting gables above. Heather had been fond of telling Miles stories about the purple house and her happy childhood there. Even before ever stepping into Biraneks' home – an errand from the hardware store – Miles had heard enough to know its layout. Entering from River Street, one came into a long vestibule which opened into the central hall. Not a hall in itself, really, just a crossing of hallways. Straight ahead, at the end of a narrower hallway, was the stained-glass door leading to the backyard. On the left, oak stairs climbed to the upper floor. The dining room had been on the right, through wide folding doors usually kept open. It became the waiting room for Dr. Biranek's patients, and it accommodated filing cabinets and Hollie's small desk as well. The Biraneks carved out a new side door for patients' access in the eastern wall of the house. There were four gravelled parking spaces outside. A small sign was affixed atop the door: DR. J. BIRANEK.

He had learned from his mother that a large kitchen was on the left, past the stairway, and that the room in which Dr. Biranek had set his consulting room, at the front, had been her father's favourite place, where he'd seek refuge from his children's noise. As you entered the house from the street, it was immediately on the right, and Dr. Biranek added another door to it from the patients' waiting area. The room across the entrance hall from the doctor's consulting room became the new dining room. It was more awkward to reach from the kitchen, but then the Biraneks never entertained much. The large living room, facing the backyard, was across the back hallway from the kitchen. He knew from his mother that her parents' bedroom had been on the second floor at the back of the house, on the western side. It became the doctor's and Rose's bedroom, and then Rose's alone once she became sick and Biranek no longer slept with her.

He remembered the first time he had a good look himself inside the Biraneks' house. At the grandly named Millcroft Collegiate Institute, their English teacher, Mrs. Davidson, had run a sputtering book club, attended mainly by girls. Miles had joined – Ben was the only other boy – and he became a target for jeers from his schoolmates. He told himself he did it for the girls, mainly for Thula Angstrom, who had long red hair, a freckled neck, and unsettling breasts. They read works that were not on the curriculum, mostly long, heavy tomes, because Mrs. Davidson's taste ran toward the gigantic novels of the previous century. In Grade Thirteen, it had been the long-winded Russians, and Miles had knocked on the Biraneks' front door to borrow *War and Peace*. He followed the doctor along the entrance hall, then up the stairs and past the master bedroom (after a U-turn on the landing) and the railing alongside the stairwell. They turned again, then stopped in front of a door to the left, not far from the lozenge window facing the street. The doctor had looked doubtfully at Miles's sneakers and asked him to take them off. The library had thick wall-to-wall broadloom and floor-to-ceiling bookshelves. Two leather armchairs, each with a side table, faced each other near the bay window. A bookcase ladder forlorn in a corner. Nothing else to distract a reader, and Miles assumed the doctor never had more than one visitor at a time in his holy of holies. Dr. Biranek picked up two thick volumes and, handing them to Miles, said, "I know you'll take good care of them." He marked down Miles's name, the title of the book, and the date in a black binder.

When it was just him and Ben, their talk often drifted to Corby Falls. Laukhin cropped up too, particularly when Miles drank to excess. This time it was Ben who first mentioned the poet, when he complained about the third symposium. Ben had not been at all for it. "Laukhin deserves a rest on the fifteenth anniversary of his death," he said. "There was the small gathering in Toronto after five years, and the rather large one in Moscow after ten. Enough, I've argued. Twenty years, okay; twenty-five, even better. You should've heard the outcry. 'You, of all people!' To make matters worse, funding is hard to get."

It was Saturday, and Le Paradis was full and noisy. Ben was disappointed to see Miles had come without Katelyn. "Jen so wanted to see her."

"Some sort of party with sleepover," Miles said. "Not sure I understand. I was told boys were not involved in part two."

They had a drink while waiting for Jennifer, and then another one, and then ordered a bottle of wine. After some head-scratching they had ordered a plate of cheese and some bread to nibble. Jen rang Ben every fifteen minutes to say she'd be there soon. "Well, we'll have another glass," Ben said after each of his wife's calls. Unusual for him.

"What's keeping her?"

"She had to run downtown. An office emergency. Something has to be ready for somebody who's flying somewhere tomorrow. How is Mr. Rueda?"

He told Ben about how depressed he and Sarah had been visiting their father in the hospital. He was back in the old age home now, but the doctors were not holding much hope he'd last beyond the summer. Sarah was being pressured by Mike to move in with him in Caledon. She wasn't keen on it. If she did, the old house in Corby Falls should be sold. Miles could do with his half of the money, but Sarah wanted to delay the sale in case living full time with Mike didn't work out.

"And if the house is sold, Ben, we should sell the shack on Clara's Lake."

"It won't fetch much. Wrong side of the lake."

"Hang on to it, then?"

"I don't know."

"You own half of it. I need your consent."

"Whatever you do is fine with me."

"You haven't been near it in a decade. Sarah says she's got too old for it. She wasn't there last summer at all, and returning after such a long period of neglect makes her uneasy. I'm the one who goes there every May, chases the mice out, cleans up the shit, mends what can still be mended."

"We'll sell, then."

They ordered *pâté de campagne* and more bread.

"Federica's favourite restaurant," Miles said. "The no-nonsense waiters remind her of France. She wants to take Katelyn away."

"What do you mean, *away*? And for or how long?"

"Three years, perhaps four."

"What?"

"She's full of surprises."

"Where to?"

"Paris. She's always dreamt of living there, and husband Greg was offered a position that's hard to refuse. She sees it as an extraordinary opportunity for Katelyn too, expand her horizon."

"What are you going to do?"

"I won't allow it. She talks about going back to Dr. Dermer."

Ben looked at him surprised.

Miles nodded. "She thinks we might be able to have a civilized conversation in his presence."

"Dermer did fuck all for your marriage."

"He made it limp along for a few more years. An earlier divorce would have been much harder on Katelyn."

"So you say."

"She's also bribing me. Trying to, anyway. Splitting the proceeds from the sale of the house on Montgomery, business class flights to France, fancy hotels."

Ben raised his eyebrows. "It's worth considering."

"She fucked my trip last week," Miles went on. "Another surprise. I was about to fly to Germany from the UK, and I had to return to Toronto."

A month earlier he heard from Katelyn that Greg was considering a few years in Europe. "They want him to lead some sort of a task. I think that's what he said, 'task.' Taxation, of course. Mom is quite taken with it." And when Miles didn't say anything, she added, "I don't mind the thought either." Slowly, he learned more about it, and it was madness. "Greg said it would be three, possibly four, years in Paris, with an organization doing work for . . . some other organization. I don't remember their endless names. We'd have a big apartment, and a maid and a chauffeur." Katelyn conceded that Greg had not been entirely sure a chauffeur was included. She'd like to go with them, yes, and Miles, as a good father, would visit them often. "Don't dismiss it, Dad. You always said Paris was your favourite city."

It was Federica's favourite city. He hadn't selected one yet.

"Paris, Miles, Paris!" Federica said when, two days later, he confronted her. "A huge apartment in the *seizième*, and—"

"It's Katelyn, Feds. She's only fourteen. You can't drop her in a new school in a foreign city. A new language too."

"You know I've dreamt of this. Don't deny it to me, Miles, because I'm not going without Katelyn."

He said he couldn't be away from Katelyn for so long, and Federica accused him of selfishness. "I won't be working in Paris, Miles. I'll have all the time in the world for Katelyn. A lot more than I have now. And far more than you've ever had or will have here, in Toronto." There were long arguments about what was best for Katelyn, the extraordinary opportunity, as Federica saw it, for their daughter to be in a different country, to learn and *live* new things. Katelyn was asked who she wanted to be with if her mother did go. Not wanting to hurt either parent, she said she was fine whichever way, but Miles knew she'd rather be with Federica in Paris. Extravagant images of Federica's life in France invaded his mind – dinners with brilliant and amusing friends, weekends spent in glamorous châteaux, or under the sun at Longchamp. He knew such thoughts were unworthy of him.

That quarrel came as they were still arguing about the house they had bought together on Montgomery Avenue. Miles had gone on living in it, paying half of what they agreed was a reasonable rent to Federica. Because she had contributed significantly more to its acquisition, Federica wanted the house sold and the proceeds split accordingly. The law was against her, but Federica would not concede and kept the lawyers busy. Miles's lawyer, Emma Levitsky, warned him it was a ploy to wear him out. That might have been the intent, but because Miles's consent was needed for Katelyn to go to Paris, Federica became amenable to splitting the income from the sale evenly. "Only three years, Miles, and then we'll be back and Katelyn will be back," Federica said. "Greg has no intention of staying any longer than that." Miles said no, and it was then, on the phone, that Federica cried for the first time. Between sobs, she proposed they resurrect their weekly sessions with Dr. Dermer. Miles said he'd give the matter more thought while away on a business trip in Europe. The crying always got to him.

He was three days in Stevenage, with Mohan Upreti, the technical lead on ESA projects, and a younger engineer unafraid of driving on the wrong side. Before they could fly to Munich for the second part of their trip, he had to return to Toronto because Federica had complained of "the other side's foot-dragging" in an unexpected application to court.

"A surprising motion," said Emma Levitsky, and Miles, holding the phone to his pulsing ear, imagined Federica approaching the judge with an odd yet convincing sequence of steps.

"I had an agreement with her before I flew over here," Miles said.

Emma Levitsky's sigh and the explanation that followed were barely audible to him. In her motion, Federica gave Miles's absence as a typical example of the demands of his job and compared it with what would be her constant presence by Katelyn's side in Paris.

"Bitch," he whispered.

"It may have been her lawyer's advice," Emma Levitsky said three thousand miles away. When he asked her to speak louder, she said her office was being repainted and she was in the boardroom speaking into a device with little holes in it that might not, in fact, be the microphone. "Catch the earliest flight back to Toronto. I'll see you tomorrow. It's late, and I ought to get home. I called earlier too."

"Would the judge make a decision in my absence?" he asked.

There was a long pause – both the delay in the line and sober consideration. "Why take a chance? I want the judge to see you. I want you to appear in front of her and convince her that when it comes to your daughter you'll leave an important business trip on the other side of the world without hesitation. Your former wife is trying to depict just the opposite – that in the middle of your dispute regarding Katelyn's best interests, you flew to England."

The clock by his bed showed ten minutes past one. He got up and looked outside. Across from him a row of drab townhouses with dark windows watched a deserted street. "Terraced" houses here. He should have bowed out earlier, should not have agreed to the last two rounds. He remembered Mohan's look of disapproval as he left the pub early. Relatively early. In a good mood, Miles had remained. God, the Brits could drink. Why on earth had he stayed so late? He had a ghastly headache, the combined result of the drinks he'd ingested that evening and being suddenly woken up with unpleasant news.

When at four o'clock in the afternoon of the same long day he took a seat in Emma Levitsky's boardroom, his first words were pointless. "How could she do this?" "When it comes to ex-couples . . ." His lawyer didn't finish the sentence, as if what she was going to say was obvious. Exhausted, he stared at the painting of a naked young woman playing a cello anchored between her parted legs. Her eyes were big, the pupils dilated, as if before she settled herself in that simple wooden chair and seized her bow, she'd applied drops of belladonna. She had a serene, belle-laide face, unaffected by the music or the effort of playing. He read in her expression both contentment and gravity. Unruly hair, long and brown, in ringlets. Solid thighs and calves, and full shoulders and arms. It was a sensual, private scene, made more so by some intimate items of clothing visible on an unmade bed in the background. Undoubtedly, this was a musician who could not properly perform unless freed from vestimentary constraints. The large upright canvas seemed ill-suited to the long, low-ceilinged room.

In the end, Federica's motion failed. Emma Levitsky portrayed Miles as a father for whom his daughter's interests were central to his life. She demanded the dismissal of the other party's frivolous applications. Emma Levitsky was old and sounded tired, and her words seemed to have weight with the judge, a short, stout woman who maintained a skeptical smile throughout.

Another call from Jen, and Ben listened, covering his other ear. "On their way," he said. "She's with her boss, VP of something."

"Banks are full of VPs."

"She's bringing her here."

"What?"

"Well, one needs to make friends at a new place."

"Have you met her?"

"Once, briefly. Lyn Collins. Seemed pleasant."

"How does Jen find in-house work?"

"Less drama and stress, more regular hours. Tonight is an exception. And the work is stimulating enough . . ."

Ben was looking at the ceiling now, and that was the hint that he was feeling the effects of the alcohol. Oddly, it was Jen who had pointed out this telltale sign to Miles. Jen would not be happy and would fault him. A good wife never blamed her husband. Ah, there they were, Jen and Ms. Collins. Ben waved to catch their attention. Miles stood up and hugged Jen. Polite handshake with Lyn Collins. She was rather thin, wearing a dark pant suit which contrasted with a light-coloured scarf and her dyed blond hair. She dressed well, Lyn Collins. Her clothes were understated but clearly expensive. He surmised the advice of a fashion consultant paid by the bank. Image consultant? Her face said early sixties, but she seemed younger and fitter. A personal trainer as well?

They small-talked for a while. Lyn had a low, husky voice. She was intrigued by Miles's profession. Working on "space things," as he'd put it, sounded both vague and exciting. Had he always wanted to build these "space things"? What "space things," anyway? And, without waiting for his answer, she smiled and added, "My son is an engineer. He works on what he calls clean energy. He says it's the future, but right now I help him with the rent."

While they ordered, Jen kept looking at Ben, who was beginning to fade. "You two are quite loaded," she said. "Ben definitely is. How much did you have to drink? Miles, you know that Ben is a quick drunk."

"Sure, it's me."

"It's not what I mean."

"Ben is drunk because you weren't here. He drank because he has a Russian soul. He drank because we reminisced about our youth and Corby Falls."

Jen explained to Lyn that Ben and Miles had grown up in Corby Falls, a small town two hours' drive northeast. "It's a mystery to me, always has been: although nothing happened in Corby Falls, these two talk of nothing else."

"Jennifer exaggerates," Miles said to Lyn.

"Plenty of things happen in Corby Falls," Ben said, suddenly alert.

"Like what?"

"The township has a woman mayor. The first time that's happened. She was the red-haired beauty of our high school. Miles knows a lot about Thula Angstrom. He dated her in Grade Thirteen, and once freed her breasts. So he claimed, so he claimed."

"I don't know if 'dated' describes it," Miles said.

"Come on, Miles, we were all jealous of you."

"No, I wasn't for her. She married another local boy. Perhaps for the better."

"Anyway, that's Millcroft Township, not Corby Falls proper," Jen said.

"She's the mayor," Ben said.

"Face it, nothing happens there."

"The school principal had a heart attack in the washroom," Miles said. "Heard it from my sister. Wasn't easy to extricate him."

"Big news."

"St. Anselm's Church is about to collapse."

"Ancient," Jen said. "I heard that the first time I went out with Ben."

"Murder," Miles heard himself say triumphantly. "There was foul murder in Corby Falls."

Over more wine and beef bourguignon, Miles told them what he'd seen the weekend Rose Biranek died. He quite enjoyed listening to his voice, and gave the story ample colour and drama. He made the point several times that there was no reason for the doctor to hide his brief trip to Corby Falls unless he'd done something terrible to his wife that night.

His audience was quite taken with his story. But in the silence that followed, Jen suggested Miles had made it all up. "It's the wine talking. Ben? You've never said a word about this before."

"It's news to me," Ben said.

"What do you think, though?"

"Miles is drunk, no doubt."

"I didn't make it up. And Ben remembers Rose Biranek's death."

Ben nodded judiciously several times. "I barely do. It happened long ago, and there was no talk of murder then."

"How old did you say you were?" Jen said. "Twelve?"

"Some things stay with you."

"Thirty-five years later?"

"It wasn't just me. There was another witness . . ."

"Ah, a sleepover," Jen said, enjoying herself. "How cute. Wasn't Ben, so who was it? Jim Cowley? Jim was their inseparable buddy in Corby Falls," she explained to Lyn.

"Jim knew everything there was to know," Ben said. "Nothing escaped him."

"No, not Jim," Miles said. "It was an adult, and—"

"I need to pee," Ben said. "Miles is very, very drunk. Don't listen to him. His stories are too long and I need to find the washroom."

"Who's the other witness?" Lyn asked.

"Can you make it?" Jen asked Ben, who hadn't moved after he declared his intention.

"It doesn't matter now," Miles said, standing up. "The murderer is dead. I'll go with Ben. Keep him straight and steady."

"Alleged murderer," Ben said.

"Oh, he killed her."

Chapter 4

August 2005

Their father's death at the end of August was both a relief and timely. "We ran out of options," Dr. Pogaretz told Miles and Sarah. She added that several organ systems had been failing, and later Miles wondered what she had marked down on the medical certificate, with so many causes of death available to her. Were there little boxes one ticked? Was there one at the bottom for "all of the above"?

The morning following Sarah's summons – "Come up. They are saying it's a matter of days" – Miles had driven to Corby Falls, the third time that melancholy month. On the ride to the hospital, Sarah said their father had been unconscious or unable to communicate for several days and was likely in discomfort, because he'd suddenly groan as if in pain or frightened by something. He departed at a reasonable hour, in the middle of the day; not for him late-night or early-morning dramatics. "Any moment now," the doctor told them, when they arrived at the Millcroft Township Hospital. They sat facing each other across their father's bed and traded a few whispered remarks. Sarah sighed from time to time. The other beds were empty – it was the only time Miles had seen his father alone in a hospital room – and he surmised that the other patients were kept away when one was dying. Shortly before noon, they went down to the ground floor for a stretch and a cup of coffee, and when they returned Dr. Pogaretz was there and their father was dead. So typical of him, Miles thought, waiting for his children to be momentarily away, causing the least amount of fuss. Later they followed their father's body to a small room which had a plain bed, two armchairs, and a large painting of a northern valley with a meandering river. Sparse coniferous trees grew on the banks of the river, and mountains with triangular patches of grey snow formed a foreboding background. Two candle holders and a wooden crucifix occupied a low narrow table set against one wall. A portable Jesus, in case the mourners objected to his presence. Miles sat alone with his father's body in the designated room while Sarah looked after the funeral arrangements. Before she went, she told Miles the hospital workers had several names for that antechamber of sober recollection and last goodbyes, the most popular being the "Departure Lounge." How apt. It was from there that the river gently carried the soul toward the immense ocean of nothingness. His father's gaunt face had relaxed in death and taken a contented look, as if proudly announcing he'd done it, found rest at last. As it had often been when he was alive, his message was voiceless.

A timely death too, for Miles. He'd been given clear hints he should avoid coming to work for a few days. Let the storm pass, that was the best interpretation of Geoff Simmons's words. Sarah's phone call had come on a Monday night. That day, he had arrived at work near lunchtime after an unpleasant hour and a half in the dentist's chair. Touching his still numb chin, Miles listened to a rather impatient message from Cecil Fowler-Biggelow requesting him to come at once to the boardroom, where a meeting on Mars exploration had been called without prior notice. He rushed to the boardroom and was surprised to find the top brass and then some around the huge table. Even Ted Ludwig, the big boss, the head of Ludwig Space, had flown in from Vancouver. Rather short, always well-pressed and dapper, Ted inhabited a world where perspiration and crumpled suits were banished. So unlike Geoff, the general manager of their division, sitting on Ted's right. Most of the chairs lined against the walls were occupied. The discussion, clearly well under way, was heated and noisy, and no one paid attention to Miles as he sat in an empty chair by the door. Near him Mohan was leaning back, eyes closed, as if unwilling to be a witness to the folly around him. The stale air hit Miles's nostrils, a mixture of male sweat and triangular sandwiches. Geoff said, "We are down to two landing sites." Then Marc Garneau's name was mentioned, and someone Miles couldn't identify said, "The president wants it yesterday. The dollars are beginning to worry him." Another voice wanted to know the amount of risk included, and Miles surmised that CSA had urgently requested updated cost inputs. On the Canadian Mars Mission? The slide on the screen displayed CSA's budgets for the last five fiscal years, a question mark beside the amount for 2006–2007 and blanks and question marks for the following four fiscal years. He should have ignored Cecil's call. He found it hard to concentrate, the anesthetic still present in his right maxillary. Seeking clarification, he leaned toward Mohan and asked, "We're not back to the risible CMM, are we?" He was loud, aware his numb jaw might slur his words. It was just as an unexpected lull fell upon the room. Briefly he hoped no one had paid attention to him. No such luck. The long silence and the heads turned his way told him he had been heard by all. Geoff Simmons cleared his throat and in his deep voice said, "Perhaps now is a good time to break for lunch. Ted? Yes, half an hour, not more."

Miles hurried out, but Fowler-Biggelow caught up to him. "A word. Now."

He followed Cecil into his office, and as Miles was shutting the door his boss exploded. "Risible? Did I hear *risible*? Fuck! Have you lost your mind?"

Cecil's elongated body waved when agitated. Every part of him was long and thin: the arms, with joints that seemed to have no limits; the shoulder-length hair, with much grey in it now; the pointed nose. Under stress, Fowler-Biggelow's lordly manner became abrupt and foul. It was an accident, Miles explained. He'd rushed into the meeting. He hadn't been told what it was about. His question was meant to be whispered, but he'd been injected full of lidocaine at the dentist. Cecil knew how that made you feel. Well, *not* feel; you couldn't properly form a sentence. He'd blurted the words louder than intended.

Geoff Simmons slowly opened the door, a paper plate in one hand piled with sandwiches, making the manoeuvre awkward. Munching, he put the plate on Cecil's desk and sat in a chair beside it. Massive and predisposed to rotundness, with abundant short hair, both cranial and facial, Geoff looked like a gigantic dark-feathered owl. Perhaps it was the fixity of his stare, or the brusque way he turned his head as he sought opinions. He'd lace his fingers behind his head when weighing his options, revealing patches of sweat in the underarms of his shirt. Miles had the impression that the damp blotches shrouded a pair of complementary sensors, organic lidars unique to Geoff. Possessor of an unctuously grave voice, Geoff would say, "I did this," and, "We failed that." He liked to be called Geoffrey, would accept Geoff, and was upset when he got emails that began "Hi Jeff," never failing to correct the guilty correspondent.

Still in grovelling mode, Miles pointed to his mouth and said, "Dentist. I'm an idiot, Geoff. Didn't expect the sudden silence, and with the anesthetic, you know."

"What's troubling me, Miles," Geoff said, after staring at him as if at a peculiar rodent never devoured before, "is that you really think it's a farcical mission. Or risible. It isn't. The Russians will provide the launcher and the lander at an affordable price."

"Promises. And then the price will escalate and CSA—"

"That's not your worry. Mind the tiny ESA projects you are playing with and let us mind the big programs. I don't want discussions and arguments. Not from you, anyway. And Miles, the old man wants it. Do you understand?"

"The old man?"

"Old Ludwig."

"Dear God, is he still alive?"

"Don't be impertinent," Cecil said.

Geoff shook his head. "The damage is done."

"Damage?" Miles asked.

"CSA will think twice before funding the mission if Ludwig's own people are calling CMM risible."

"It was just us in there, Geoff."

"There were twenty-five people in that room, Miles. Each has friends or colleagues, even acquaintances, who work in our field. People they talk to and exchange gossip with. They in turn have their own colleagues. Don't you think a Ludwig employee calling CMM risible is good material for some chit-chat over a couple of beers? You can't be that naive not to know that language like that would reach CSA. It's a small world, ours, Miles. Ludwig is the premiere space company in this country. Every day there is at least one meeting in which Ludwig and CSA people talk and mingle and gossip."

Geoff got up, picked up his plate, and opened the door. Without turning, he said, "Cecil, I don't think Miles is needed back in there after lunch. And shouldn't he go on a trip or something? Visit Astrium? See his ESA friends in Noordwijk? Perhaps a vacation."

He sat in the small room where his father lay, feeling guilty because he wasn't thinking exclusively about him. The large painting caught his eye again, then Sarah's brutal words returned to him. "Loneliness, discomfort, pain, and humiliation – that's the package death comes with. The longer we live . . . the larger the package is." Sarah seemed to think her package had arrived already. Had his been sent too? Was it being prepared? He imagined an immense warehouse not unlike an Amazon shipment centre, where clever little robots were busy putting together his parcel. Several assembly lines? Prostate cancer here, colon cancer there. That line, the busiest, handling nothing but coronary diseases, a whole bunch to pick from. Also bustling, the lines for hip replacements, dementia, incontinence. Giant computers reading billions of genetic codes and sending out appropriate instructions.

They should provide alcohol in this room, because dark thoughts were bound to stalk anyone here. He forced his mind to stray again, and it veered back to work, to Geoff Simmons's owlish stare and his parting suggestion that Miles take "a trip or something." If Geoff wanted him away for a while, he couldn't be far from wanting him away for good. A permanent trip. More worrying than the prospect of dismissal for Miles was that, despite having hardly any money in the bank, he viewed it without alarm. It was irrational, but when he imagined his life without what he lately couldn't stop himself from calling the *space crap*, he did so with senseless equanimity. The very thought of the Canadian Mars Mission brought a grimace to his face; hundreds of millions of dollars spent to put a couple of sensors on the surface of Mars. Such pretentiousness. Mohan had renamed it the Canadian Thermometer Mission. The words *planetary exploration* made Miles cringe too. They shouldn't, yet they did. The last time he uttered them at home, trying to impress Katelyn one Saturday morning, they'd come back to bite him. Katelyn repeated what he'd told her at school, and two weeks later her science teacher was on the phone asking him to speak to the students about his "enthralling work." He couldn't. There was no enthusiasm in him, no thrill, and to fake it in front of thirteen-year-olds was unthinkable. He asked Mohan to replace him. Somehow Fowler-Biggelow got wind of the invitation and said he'd take care of it. Soon afterward, Cecil went to Katelyn's school with a *Toronto Star* photographer. Judging from the colour picture on the front page the following day, the audience was far larger than just Katelyn's class. The caption read, "Dr. Cecil Fowler-Biggelow, VP of Business Development at Ludwig Robotics, describes the excitement and challenges of planetary exploration to mesmerized students."

He remembered his father telling anyone who cared to listen that his son had been accepted into engineering in Toronto. A garrulous spell so unlike him. Yet Joe had seemed disappointed that the hardware store would not stay in the family. He had considered briefly keeping the store, finding somebody to run it. Not easy, as it had never been a gold mine. He had not been particularly good at it. No business acumen, never mind enthusiasm. They turned out to be similar, father and son, disliking what they did for a living. Still, what excuse did Miles have? How could he have been so wrong? His father got stuck with the store on the premature death of his own father, and in the village of Corby Falls in those days ... Though Joe had wondered what turns his life might have taken had he been less willing to accept what came his way. For a decade, he had toiled at putting memories of his childhood and youth down on paper. He'd planned to cover his later years too. Miles first heard of it from Sarah, and in one of his rare letters to his father he asked if it was true. "It's daft, I know," his father wrote in reply. "Big-headed too – recollections of a life in which nothing happened. We leave no trace in this world, Miles. I want to leave a part of me, to Sarah, to you, to my grandchildren and their children. We are what our thoughts are. Even if it's only a sequence of silly sentences, you'll have something from me, or of me, that's more than an object or a photograph." Seven years ago, his father had changed his mind and burnt what he'd written. "It's better like this," he said, when Miles asked him why he'd done it. "In the stove, all of it. I was hoping to eventually see a pattern, a line aiming somewhere, however faint and twisting. Nothing. A life must make sense, and I'm too old to make sense of mine. Even my marriage with your mother was botched, and I kind of accepted it. Heather and

I, well, I don't need to tell you. She wasn't easy, your mother. I thought I'd be wiser after all these years. Sadly, I'm not. I did nothing with my life, Miles. In the end, I was left with Sarah and you. That's all. Perhaps it's not that bad – two children, and both good people – but there's no need for hundreds of pages to say that." Miles had never heard his father make such a long speech. Worried, he protested. "No, don't give up. If going back over your life upsets you, then focus on something else. Write about the *alien*, your grandfather, the first Rueda on this continent, about his Irish wife, the uncles who died in the First World War. Aunt Pearl is a great source of stories about the Ruedas. She'll talk and you can write everything down. Write about Mother's family, even if you never liked them. Don't give up. I want to read it, Sarah does too, and your grandchildren will eventually." His father made a dismissive gesture with his hands.

His bed was in one of the two small front-facing rooms. He slept poorly, awakened by imbecilic dreams. Across the narrow hall he heard his sister's faint snoring.

The day before the funeral, he wandered into the adjacent bedroom. His father had used it as a study in the years he worked on his recollections. The room seemed untouched since the day, two years earlier, Joe had moved himself to the old age home in Millcroft. The table on which Miles had done his homework was set against the window. Pens of various colours congregated with thick highlighters in a pewter stein. Pads of paper – white, yellow, light green – were neatly piled up and aligned with the right edge of the table. His father must have been fond of inspiring colour combinations. A *Collins English Dictionary* – the 1976 Australian edition, yellow sale sticker still on the dust cover – lay close to the pads of paper, mute sentinel of correct wording. Aimlessly browsing through it left Miles with an impression of dust in his nostrils. The last person to touch these pages had been his father, now lying in a coffin in the funeral home.

The other furniture in the room were the old Morris chair in which his father had dozed off mulling an appropriate turn of phrase, and a tall chest of drawers used, Miles discovered now, as a filing cabinet. Folders with old newspaper cuttings, flyers, brochures, a battered soft-covered *Roget's Thesaurus*, a thin guide to Millcroft Township, an envelope with his parents' birth certificates, his mother's death certificate, a couple of old passports – though Joe and Heather had never travelled – maps, a history of Corby Falls poorly printed on now yellowed paper. In binders with coloured sheets covered with his father's handwriting Miles found what were probably early drafts or attempts. His father had not burnt everything, or, when he'd said he did, he meant it figuratively, to leave no doubt that he was done with his attempt at revisiting his life. Should he read what his father wrote? It would be against his wishes, wouldn't it?

In another drawer he found letters neatly tied up in bundles. Letters that Sarah wrote home when she was a student, business letters with the address of the hardware store on the envelopes, letters Miles had sent as a child to his father, though not many of these, since he'd rarely been away from home before high school. Some timeworn letters seemed to have been written by his father's uncles during the First World War. He wasn't entirely sure. He'd have to get back to them later, but who else's could they be?

Sarah said on one occasion, rather irritated, that their father discovered writing late in life, "because beloved son Miles had gone away for his studies. He never wrote to me while I was away. Not once." Their mother was still alive when Sarah went to college, and it was she who, although not a keen letter writer, had kept the correspondence going. During Sarah's difficult last years with Elliott, she had expressed her annoyance at their father's late epistolary interest, because Joe, distressed by what was happening in her marriage, was letting Miles know about it in his letters. "I'd rather you heard about it directly from me, not Dad," she complained to Miles. "Damn. How on earth does he know so much? Could Elliott be whining to him?"

Miles had been surprised by the stream of letters from his father. They were short at the beginning, bits of news, as if Joe had fallen unexpectedly upon a language he was trying his hand at. Little by little, longer letters arrived. Musings on his life, plans for retirement, thoughts on part-time helpers, gossip heard at the Gridiron, the latest from Sarah and her family. Especially Sarah and her family, how worried he was because of her. He didn't expect a similar outpouring back from Miles and made that clear to him. "A word or two is fine, so I know you're all right, passing your exams." It had been a discreet preparation for his late and ambitious undertaking. He'd warned Miles he wanted his letters back. "Letters are like gifts, Dad," Miles had said. "You can't have them back." Only later did Miles understand the reason behind that request.

His father's letters to him were in a lower drawer, tied up in yearly bundles. He picked a letter at random from a bundle whose rubber band had snapped. Written in October 1985, it was the usual rambling dispatch, with overuse of parentheses.

I'm writing after lunch. The Gridiron was full – the Sunday churchgoers need sustenance. The special was shepherd's pie again, almost as if the cook believes that the more often you offer it the better it tastes. She is new and young, and lacks imagination. When I expressed a mild complaint, Herb told me that her husband, or partner (or whatever one has these days), had disappeared recently, leaving her with two children. It's sad, of course, though what does that have to do with bland, repetitive cooking?

(Herb, by the way, is getting old and can't hear a thing. We don't talk, we shout, and my mild complaint was heard by all lunchtime customers. He's been trying for years to sell the restaurant. None of his children are interested in taking over.)

It's sunny today around here, and the strong light cheers the autumn heart. I took a long walk this morning toward the lake. The path along the river was dry and I had a pleasant hour.

I need this light and cheer because Sarah worries me no end. Willful Sarah. I'm afraid this is serious, not one of her flare-ups. Yesterday she brought in more of her stuff from Millcroft, and is now re-settled here, in your old bedroom. You'll have to move to one of the smaller rooms now. She said, "I'll be here for a while, a long while, and Miles won't. He can sleep elsewhere the couple of days he spends here now and then. Unless you want it, Dad."

(I don't want it. I'm fine in the small room on the first floor. No point in moving back after all these years.)

In a way, I don't mind having Sarah back because I'll be less lonesome. Still, leaving a husband after twenty-two years, just like that. She told me that she was having an affair. (I'm sure she opened up simply to deter me from trying to talk her out of the divorce.) I can't say I was that surprised. Twelve years ago (more than twelve?) Sarah had a fling with a colleague of hers, an art teacher at her school. Do you remember him, Pace or Rice, something like that? You might have had him as a teacher, although he wasn't there long. He was younger than Sarah. She took sculpting lessons from him, and one thing led to another. He left the school, quietly, once rumours began spreading.

(Come to think of it, this could be news to you. Old news.)

Thursday night, at dinner (yes, several times a week we have dinner together now), Sarah said she was "beyond fed up" (her words) with Elliott. I don't really remember a time she did not berate him, and I recall your mother telling me, "I don't know why Sarah's getting married." I don't think Sarah knew either. She told me Thursday night she was divorcing Elliott, there was no changing her mind. I tried. As she got up to clear the table, she said, "I love you, Dad, but butt out. I'm forty-four." She said she's been at ease with herself since she made the decision. She also said, and it hurt, that she did not want to follow my example, mired for years in a marriage which had never worked.

She wants to give up teaching, your headstrong sister. I'm telling her, stay for three or four more years, until you have twenty-five years of teaching and a better pension, and then you'll be free to sculpt to your heart's content. She says she'll give it more thought, for my sake, but she has little time to waste. It's this rashness that worries me. She mentions part-time teaching, or working in the store with me for half a day so that she has time for her fixation. I'll put off selling the store if she'll help me a little.

He remembered the rumours about Sarah's affair with Harrold Mace, the art teacher at Millcroft Collegiate. At fourteen, he had not been happy to have Sarah teach at his high school. It was bad enough to have his sister there every day, and he was always edgy hearing her name mentioned, so when Jim Cowley said he'd seen Mr. Mace and Sarah behind the bus station, Miles didn't wait for Jim to finish what he had to say, and Jim didn't wait for Miles to get to him. He ran away laughing, delighted both by his story and the effect it had had on Miles. "They *were* sucking face, I'm telling you, Mr. Mace and your sister."

There was a PS.

I met Hollie Biranek the other day on Main Street. She complained it had been too long since they saw you, and Dr. Biranek is convinced you are avoiding their house. "Miles wouldn't do that," Hollie said, "not to Josef. He knows how much my husband enjoys his visits, but young people are often preoccupied and mindless of others. Please tell Miles to drop in for a visit. I know he's been in Corby Falls a number of times without ringing our bell."

It was quiet in the house. He'd miss that, the stillness of the small town, the kind of quiet that made one feel immersed, soaked in silence. It reminded him of the shack on the southern shore of Clara's Lake. Federica had never taken to it, even when they were staying in Corby Falls and just driving the three kilometres to the lake for a swim on sweltering days. Neither did Katelyn. The realtor had shaken his head when Miles drove him there in June. "It's just the land," he said. "The rest is worthless. And the land itself . . . You'll do better waiting a few more years. The other side of the lake is getting crowded, you know, and people will begin to look in over here. But not yet. Patience."

That morning, before Sarah left, he asked her how long she wanted to hang on to the old house.

"How long?"

"The trial period with Mike, living with him. A month, three, six, a full year?"

"I don't know."

"I could do with the money."

"Less than a year, that's all I can say."

Federica and Katelyn came up the morning of the funeral. Katelyn had not seen her grandfather often, and when she had, his reticence made things awkward. Miles wasn't sure how his daughter was taking her grandfather's death. What did fourteen-year-olds make of death anyway?

It was unseasonably cold at the cemetery. The wind and the threatening clouds seemed to hurry everybody. Katelyn gripped his hand when she saw tears on his face. He didn't know why he was crying. It could have been the dark clouds, the windy day, the inept, rushed words of the young rector, the wheeled-in residents of the old age home. One of them, who kept repeating "groof" or "roof" while staring at the ground, seemed to have no idea where he was or why he was there. Sarah and Miles were told that he had often been seen chatting with their father, and so they had driven him to the cemetery with the others. Maybe he knew where he was and was muttering "proof, proof," a plea – no better place or occasion – for a sign of the afterlife. Wouldn't he be looking up, though?

Elliott came to the cemetery with his wife. She was much younger than he was, or so it seemed. Miles watched him talk to Sarah, who laughed warily at something he said. Later, Elliott approached him and offered condolences. He was his usual awkward self, aged, and thirty or forty pounds more of him.

Miles's nephew Douglas had flown in from Vancouver. He apologized for not bringing his family – "It just didn't work out, you know, with the kids in New Zealand with their mother" – and moved cautiously between Elliott and Sarah, unwilling to hurt either of his parents. Eventually, he settled near Miles and whispered, "It's a difficult day." Miles said, "Stop this Switzerland act of yours, Doug. It's been almost twenty years since your parents divorced. Katelyn, say hello to your cousin. Give him your other hand and see he doesn't let go." Miles admonished himself afterward – he shouldn't talk to his nephew like that. He was, after all, only five years older than Doug. Sarah had often been testy with her son and couldn't hide her impatience with him. She once confessed to Miles that she felt guilty about it, hoping, Miles guessed, that he would find something soothing to say to her. "He looks exactly like his father. Looks and behaves. What's wrong with me, Miles? How can I talk this way about my own child?"

Mike Ancona had arrived the night before. At the cemetery, he revolved around Sarah, looking at his watch. His hair was fully white now, and he seemed to Miles to have lost some of his height. He would be driving back to Toronto directly from the burial in order to catch one of his grandchildren's birthdays. "Which grandchild?" Miles asked Sarah mindlessly. "I forget," she said. "He's got oodles of them and I lost track."

Aunt Pearl, who should have been near him during the ceremony, arrived late, just as they were preparing to leave the cemetery. Pushing her mother's wheelchair close to him, his cousin Laura whispered, "We had a difficult morning. She's better now, although I'm not sure she knows where she is."

His aunt was both cheerful and confused. When he greeted her, she said, "Dear me, you came!" They all stared at her, and she looked at them, and then again at Miles, shaking her head. "Oh, you aren't him, are you? No . . . For a second I thought he came back to be here, with the family, for this get-together. I thought it was so nice of him."

"Who, Aunt Pearl?" Miles asked.

"Him. Grandpa Ellis."

"He'd have chosen a merrier time."

"It's not a good time? Who are you?"

"It's me, Miles, your nephew."

Laura rolled her eyes. It was at least a year since he'd last seen his cousin, and she looked shockingly old to him. "Uncle Joe's son, Mother," Laura said. "Joe, your brother. The one who's finally resting now."

"He was a jolly, cheerful man, Grandpa Ellis," Aunt Pearl went on. "Happy." She pointed an unsteady finger at him. "Are you happy? Miles? Did you say, Miles?"

"I'm not all gloom."

"You're so much like him. He was tall too, even taller than you. The same eyes. The hair too. It was mostly white, true, though I'm sure it had been light, like yours. I can't see that well. Same smiling mouth, yes, same as Grandpa Ellis. He used to twirl with his wife. Just like that, without warning, he'd get near Grandma Caitlin, pick her up, and twirl. A brief dance without music. He was very strong. Grandma Caitlin would beat his chest to be let down, but she didn't mind. I *know* she didn't mind. He'd let her down and laugh and go back to doing whatever he was doing. Do you twirl with your wife, Miles?"

"Not lately."

"You should. Wives like that. My husband wouldn't do it. Wouldn't dance either. A fool, a sad fool. Not Grandpa Ellis, no. He was a happy man, yes, happy with his life, happy with his family. It was his way of expressing that, to thank his fate. I mean, before the older boys died in the last war . . ."

"It wasn't the last war, Mother," Laura said.

"Here is Katelyn, Aunt Pearl," Miles said. "You remember my daughter, Katelyn?"

"Who? Yes. What's her name again?"

"Katelyn, your grandniece."

"Maybe."

"Katelyn Anne. We called her Anne when she was small. She now insists on Katelyn. That's why you don't recall her name. Katelyn, after Grandmother Caitlin. Only different spelling."

"Ah, yes."

After the cemetery they drove to the house. The kitchen, where the drinks were, was crowded. Getting through, he was told how solid Joe had been. Dependable, quiet, solid. Well, they said traits often skipped a generation. When at long last he got out of the kitchen, a glass of wine in his hand, he made his way to the family room, the addition at the back built by Joe, hoping to placate Heather after the Biraneks' arrival. With sliding doors leading into the backyard, and easy access to a shed not far away, the room had long been transformed by Sarah into her *atelier*. Wire frames, clay models wrapped in damp cloths, plaster casts, had been pushed against the walls, and traces of an energetic sweep-up with a broom were still visible on the floor. Federica, a plate in her hands, was staring at the plaster of a heavily stylized charging bull. When she saw him, she said, "An overload of vigour, isn't it? What else to expect from Sarah?" They exchanged appropriate, banal words – the sadness of the event, Federica's regret at not having known her father-in-law better. She had gotten along well with Joe. She used to say he was a dear old man. What was to dislike about an undemanding and quiet father-in-law living almost two hundred kilometres away?

Black had always suited Federica. She said to him, "The only one I really liked in Corby Falls is now gone."

He accepted her words as a terse eulogy. It wasn't strictly true; she had dismissed everybody and everything in Corby Falls, though she'd liked Sarah, or not minded her. She'd liked him too, for a while. He asked her how Greg was. He'd seen Federica's husband at the cemetery, holding hands with her, whispering in her ear. And then, as usual, acrimony crept in – a mild expression of it in a day like that – with Federica asking if he had given more thought to their disputations.

"Not now, Federica."

"Sorry. I should go and look for Greg. He's been cornered by the St. Anselm's rector. Tax advice, not sins."

Disputations. He imagined the two of them facing Dr. Dermer again and trying to be civil to each other, as if arguing academic points in front of a genial arbitrator. And he remembered Erwin Dermer's perplexed reply to Miles's suggestion that he and Federica resume their sessions with him. "Look, Mr. Rueda, Miles, I fix couples, that's my specialty, try to keep them together. I don't often counsel divorced people on how to stay amiable afterwards. Have you run this by Federica? She came up with it? I don't know. Really don't. Perhaps at the summer's end. I'm going away for six weeks now. Yes, that long, a National Geographic trip. Galapagos, turtles, speciation. Never took such a long time off in my life."

Ben Paskow approached him. "That was quick and simple."

"He'd been quite forceful about it – no speeches and no service. The rector was offended."

"It's ten years, more, since I was last in Corby Falls. I hardly recognized Jim. How's the paper rover?"

"We have an engineering prototype now, scampering among sand dunes in an abandoned hangar. Serious young people get dirty and come up with fancy measurements of mobility. We lock the place when we finish the work, but every time we return for new tests we spend half an hour clearing raccoon shit. No one can figure out how they get in, the beasts, yet we want to go to Mars."

"The beasts don't want you in their shelter."

"I'm not in favour these days. Not with raccoons, not with Federica, not with my bosses. Especially my bosses. I was told to disappear."

"They fired you?"

"That's next. I'm to keep away."

"Can they do that?"

"Father saved me. A death perfectly timed. I should stay away a few more days."

"Come to Laukhin's third symposium."

Miles shook his head doubtfully.

"I remember you at the first symposium," Ben went on, "ten years ago. You seemed to enjoy it."

"I came for the free drinks at the end, and because Federica insisted. She claimed to love Laukhin's poetry."

"Join us. Drop in at the opening reception. Free drinks again. Dinner too. I'll give you an impressive tag. Tell stories about Laukhin – you've done major pub-crawling with him, after all – or make them up. Everybody will love you for it."

Jim Cowley, holding a bottle of beer, waved his free hand at him. Miles would have to have a few beers with Jim before he drove back to Toronto, otherwise his friend would be hurt. After a couple of drinks, the induced bonhomie usually untied their tongues and they fell into silly reminiscing and laughter, but it was getting harder and harder. Federica had found Jim boring and uncouth and had scoffed at Miles's guilty efforts to keep the friendship going. "I doubt he's keen either," she'd said often. "Face it, Miles, you two have nothing in common now. The roots are dead, and no amount of beer will revive them."

Sarah and Doug had joined Jim, and Miles was ambling toward their group when he almost bumped into the back of an older woman. When she turned, he realized it was Hollie Biranek. "I'm not here for you," she said. "I'm here because Josef would have wanted me to be here."

"I'm sorry for your loss, Hollie."

"You were not at his funeral, Miles. Your sister was there, but not you."

"I was away."

"Away? I saw you here the day he died."

"I had to fly to the UK two days later, then on to Germany. Well, was supposed to get to Germany . . . Work, you know. Couldn't get out of it."

"Josef was so fond of you. Proud too."

"I'm sorry I couldn't make it."

Hollie had left. He'd watched the former beauty walk out through the opened sliding door. He leaned against the wall near a clay model covered in a dark, wet cloth. To think that he had masturbated with Hollie's body in mind in his adolescent days. Ha, following Bill Cowley's instructions. She'd be what now, early seventies? Less. Late sixties? He remembered Elma Mulligan telling his mother that Hollie claimed she was fifteen years younger than Dr. Biranek, but Elma thought the age difference was bigger.

"You mean she's younger than that?" his mother had asked.

"She is."

"Elma, that's daft. What woman wants to make herself older?"

"She's a sly one. Heed my words, Heather Rueda, heed my words."

Jim made his way toward him. "Your neighbour seemed unhappy with you."

"I wasn't at the doctor's funeral."

"Do you still dream of her milky-white ass?"

"I do."

The summer before Rose's death, Jim and Miles had happened to catch the doctor and Hollie going at it. Miles had told Jim Elma's story about what the doctor and Hollie got up to on the Biraneks' sitting room couch, and the boys often crept to that window on nights they saw the light on. The curtains were always drawn, but one July evening they had been left open, and a floor lamp was on behind the entangled pair. Hollie was straddling the doctor, and Miles, breathless, had gazed at a profile view of Hollie's upright body, her smooth back, her rounded buttocks, her breasts, lower and ampler than he'd expected.

Jim had gained more weight. He had heft now, and the suit he wore left little spare room for him. To think he'd been so skinny once. His brown-grey eyes seemed smaller under the now heavier lids. They now looked around the room, perhaps in search of something to comment on. There wasn't enough booze in either Jim or himself to temporarily smooth away the passage of time.

"It's nice of you to come, Jim."

"I liked your father."

"I liked him too. How is your lovely wife, the girls?"

"Fine, fine. The girls aren't girls anymore, and are wild."

"Wild? That's Jim Cowley talking?"

Jim laughed.

What now? Why was it so difficult?

"A suit, Jim, I'm impressed. Beyond the call of duty. Last I saw you in a suit was at my wedding."

"I'm getting used to them. Barry wants to see me in suits these days."

"Ah, dad-in-law Barry Matlock has given the order."

"He thinks I'm good at gabbing with clients, entertaining them. I can hold my drink too. I suspect he doesn't think I'm good at anything else."

"How is the B&M Construction scam?"

Jim sighed. "We could be busier. In fact, we could be a lot busier. It's not so bad now, because it's summer, and people don't mind that much."

"What's Barry saying?"

"He's not happy. There's the hospital, though, coming up."

"The hospital?"

"The one in Millcroft. It's a big job, millions."

"Ah, Biranek's money, isn't it? The world is abuzz with it."

"His money, yes."

"You've got it already? I mean, did B&M get the contract?"

"We'll get something. We pay taxes in this township, Miles. And we keep a lot of people employed, directly and indirectly. There'll be some work in Corby Falls too. The church, St. Anselm's, there's money to fix it now. Saint Biranek of blessed memory."

Katelyn, Federica, and Greg were the last to leave. After he walked them to their car, Miles stepped out into the neglected backyard for a cigarette. He was leaning against the shed and staring at the Biraneks' house when Sarah came out and strolled toward him.

"She's pissed with me," he said, nodding at Hollie's place.

"That was obvious."

"You noticed?"

"She'd told me too."

"What's with her? Did Biranek leave her broke?"

"Hollie was left well provided for."

"How do you know?"

"Everybody knows. Can't keep such things secret in a village. Anyway, she told me she didn't know what to do with all the money Dr. Biranek left her. She said she'd never expected to have to write a will, and her family were going to be pleasantly surprised after her death."

He lit a cigarette.

"I hope you're not going to keep smoking," she said.

"I won't."

"I'll have one too."

Miles lit another cigarette and passed it to her. They smoked in silence.

"This is it, the beginning of oblivion," Sarah sighed.

He nodded.

"That's why Dr. Biranek would have a hospital named after him," she went on. "I saw Thula Angstrom yesterday in Millcroft. Another woman pissed at you."

She was Thula Locksley now – had been since she married Tom Locksley. Sarah, who had taught the township's new mayor for a year, still called her Thula Angstrom. Two months earlier, Thula had rung Miles at Ludwig Robotics. She was direct, as if they had recently talked to each other. "I heard you'd be in Millcroft to see your father. Come to see me at Township Hall, Miles. I got your number from Jim Cowley."

"Thula Locksley! I can barely breathe," he'd said. "How long since I last saw you? Thirty years?"

"Less. You were at our wedding."

"I was? I block out bad memories."

"Drop in, Miles. We'll have lunch and talk about the township. Corby Falls too."

"Ah, it's the mayor calling, not Thula. Heartbreaking."

"Don't be silly."

"I should congratulate you. Mayor . . . Wow! Sarah told me you're doing fine. But then she thinks any woman would do a better job than the men they've had in the past."

They had lunch together in the mayor's office the following Saturday, when he drove to Millcroft to see his father. Pointing at sandwiches on paper plates, Thula said she had a budget meeting later and that they'd have more time to chat if they didn't go out. Yes, she was often at her desk on weekends. It became clear to Miles that he was simply one item in a busy day, and that the mayor had little time to waste. She was hard working and efficient, Thula, always had been. She'd been direct and efficient too when, in the last month of high school, she dismissed him for Tom Locksley. She liked Tom, Thula said, when he pressed his case. Miles was going to Toronto and would never come back. Tom was going to Trent, and so was she. She was a country girl, and she liked it there, in Millcroft.

Most of the mayor's office was occupied by a couch and a gigantic desk. Holding his plate Miles sat on a chair in front of the desk. Thula made an apologetic gesture with her sandwich and said she'd be getting a much smaller desk soon. "There'll be place for a table and a couple of chairs too, once I get rid of this monstrosity," she added. "Next time you come, we'll have lunch sitting at a table." She knocked on the desk. "The ex-mayor's taste. Bloody male egos. He didn't take his defeat well. What a useless man. And that," she pointed at the couch, "that will go too. It opens into a bed, you know. Why? I mean, why did he need a bed? His house is three minutes away."

"How is Tom?" Miles asked.

"Going through some adjustments."

"Adjustments?"

"You know, with me being the mayor and so busy these days . . ."

Sarah had been right – Thula was a broad woman now, with an ample bosom.

"It's about Josef Biranek, Miles," Thula said.

"Oh?"

"Biranek's will. He left twelve million dollars to the township. A major windfall. I'm sure you've heard already, it's the talk of Millcroft these days."

She told him that Dr. Biranek had made a fortune from stocks and other savvy investments. An early holder of RIM shares – and that, Thula commented with enthusiasm, clearly showed how astute the doctor had been. The details of his bequest would be in the newspapers soon, so she might as well reveal them to Miles. Dr. Biranek had left most of his money to the hospital in Millcroft – with which he'd been associated for his entire medical career – provided it changed its name to the Josef Biranek Hospital. He also left money for repairs to St. Anselm's Church in Corby Falls, which, as Miles undoubtedly knew, had long had a major crack in its wall facing the river and a leaking roof. Dr. Biranek had stipulated in his will that his bequest would be managed by Joe Montanari, his lawyer, and by the township's mayor.

The sandwich was surprisingly good. Thula said she'd ordered their frugal lunch from a recently opened Italian restaurant not far away. Things were changing in Millcroft. Not as fast as she'd like, but they were changing. Biranek's bequest could not have come at a better time. She nodded several times to underline her words. The township was grateful to Dr. Biranek and wanted to do something to honour his memory. Several ideas were being debated, and the one thing everybody agreed on was to commission a book about the doctor. His life, his work in the township. Did Miles know he'd been active in township affairs after he retired from his medical practice? Even before. The book should have all that, for sure. It should cover his early years too, his childhood and youth in Czechoslovakia, his studies there – two years of medicine in Prague – whatever could be dug up. The writer should consider a trip to the Czech Republic. Hollie Biranek might be able to partially fill in details on the doctor's life before Canada. What else? Yes, his years at the University of Toronto, and his year of internship. And, of course, his life in Corby Falls with first wife, Rose, and then with Hollie. Research was needed, Thula was aware of that. Hollie said her husband had left several boxes of letters. Boxes of personal papers too. The township would consider having a local do some initial research into Dr. Biranek's life in Corby Falls and take a first look at the doctor's papers. He or she, whoever they'd hire, could also tape preliminary interviews with Hollie Biranek. The local hire would work around the writer's timetable and needs. She looked at Miles and smiled. There was no one better suited to write the book than Ben Paskow. Born in Corby Falls. Wrote about people for a living. Might have been a patient of Dr. Biranek before the family moved away.

"And you, Miles, will help him."

"I'm an engineer, Thula."

"Ben will do the writing. You knew the doctor much better than he did. You'll push his hand this way or that way."

"I wouldn't know—"

"Why so modest, Miles? Whose essays did Mrs. Davidson read aloud in English class? Yours. You were her star."

"Did you approach Ben?"

"Wasn't interested. He needs prodding by a friend. You are the one to do it. Biranek was your family's neighbour for decades. He was your doctor too, and Hollie said he enjoyed no one's company as much as yours. You also know Hollie. I'm sure she'd be glad to help. It doesn't have to be a huge book, Miles. Basic facts. Of course, its length is up to Ben. Anything around a hundred pages would do. Even less. The commission comes with a fee – from the township, not from the bequest. Something to cover expenses too, of course."

It was the last thing he'd expected. "It's not going to work," he said.

"Why not?"

He sighed and said he was living in Toronto and wouldn't be able to find the time for it. Katelyn was with him most weekends. His job kept him late at work every day, projects which had fallen behind. Embarrassingly, preposterously behind. Moreover, he doubted Ben would change his mind. He'd hardly known Biranek.

Thula made a disappointed noise. "Talk to him, Miles." She stood up, and as she was pushing him out the door, she added – her voice acquiring the mocking tone Miles remembered from the few times he'd been allowed to free her breasts – he should stop being difficult and so ridiculously self-important.

A week later he received an email from Thula wondering whether he'd talked to Ben. She also wrote of plans for a memorial evening in which Dr. Biranek and his gifts for the township would be celebrated. She wanted Miles to say a few words. There would be a main speaker, and other speakers too, but something about Dr. Biranek's beginnings in Corby Falls would be a fitting complement. Miles's sister Sarah might help him.

Miles didn't answer her email. Some days later, he received a letter from Thula, on the letterhead of the mayor of Millcroft Township, with more or less the same content. And two weeks later, she phoned him. Why was he not answering her correspondence? She sounded annoyed. He lied that he'd been extremely busy at work. After a silence following his childish explanation, he added that it was the end of a project for the European Space Agency, hoping that the impressive sounding name would derail her.

"You couldn't find a second to type a simple email?" she asked.

He said his father's illness had made him despondent and he wasn't functioning properly.

"Come on, Miles. It's the way life ends. You father had a long one."

He got angry. Why was she refusing to get the message? "I can't do it, Thula. I won't do it. I will not talk to Ben about a book on Biranek, or give a speech about the doctor at the celebration you're planning. I have neither the time nor the inclination." It came out more abruptly than he intended.

She hung up on him, though not before she said, "Fuck you, Miles."

"She apologized for swearing at you. Did she really?"

"She said, 'Fuck you.'"

"Why won't you do it?"

"You know why, Sarah."

His eyes returned to the Biraneks' house. It was for sale, he'd seen the sign in front of the house, on River Street. He wondered if Hollie was near one of the bedroom windows, peering down at them. She and Dr. Biranek moved into Rose's bedroom days after her death. At least that was what Elma Mulligan reported, after Dr. Biranek told her that, with Rose gone, her services would not be needed anymore. "As if the house needs no more cleaning or tidying up," Elma had complained to his father. "It's that whore, Hollie, who pushed the doctor to fire me. They'll soon have someone else, for sure. Hollie won't do the chores herself, mark my words, Joe Rueda."

Sarah said, "Thula told me she's given up on Ben and you for the book. She's already found someone else. But she can't understand why you won't speak at the commemorative gathering."

"She should find somebody else for that too," Miles said. "A former colleague, for example. A doctor or two who met Biranek during his early days in the township might still be around."

"Thula said they'd raise a statue for him."

He chuckled. "Where?"

"In front of the hospital. It's twelve million dollars, Miles – huge for the township."

"On a horse?"

She rolled her eyes. "Not an actual statue, a bust on some sort of a pedestal. She said I could have it."

He looked at her. "Have what?"

"The commission."

"Ah. A modest one, I assume."

"Provided I change your mind and you agree to speak at his memorial."

"You're joking."

"I wouldn't mind doing it."

"She's blackmailing me. She's using you to blackmail me."

"I know."

When Miles remained silent, Sarah laughed softly. "Well, nothing will come out of it. The bequest has run into problems it seems."

"Problems?"

"Technical ones, as per our Thula. I'll show you."

She went inside the house. It was warmer now, and the wind was gone. Or almost, although the clouds had stayed. Odd that it had not rained the entire day. The sumacs, shorter and sparser than he recalled, would soon turn crimson. He thought of Sarah's words – "This is it, the beginning of oblivion" – and then of his own oblivion, and imagined Katelyn saying the same words to her husband or a friend, and he found it melancholy that everyone was so accepting of others' deaths, of the sudden slamming of the giant gate.

Sarah came out of the house and handed him a copy of the *Millcroft Gazette* from two weeks earlier. "Read this," she said, pointing to a column called Township Alert. The title of the alert was "Biranek's Bequests." It was signed "Eddy B."

It has been three months since the news about Dr. Biranek's large bequest to the hospital in Millcroft and the smaller one to St. Anselm's Anglican church in Corby Falls. At first, for a month or more, Township Hall was buzzing with excitement and plans for the work. All we've heard for the last two weeks, however, has been silence, a deafening silence. Everyone has been quiet, even tight-lipped. Clearly gag orders have come down from high up. Mayor Thula Locksley refuses to answer our questions. When we caught up with her last week she said, "There are complications, and we'll sort them out." "What kind of complications?" we asked. "Technical," she replied.

We are not giving up. Because the status of Dr. Biranek's bequests becomes more and more mysterious every passing day. Township Hall continues to be silent, although Mayor Locksley did say yesterday, as she left in the evening, that they were "faced with unexpected complications." Thus, the technical complications are also unexpected. Now, complications are always unexpected; otherwise they wouldn't be complications, only anticipated steps. We don't like the sound of this at all. We earn our living dilligently with hard work, and we'll dig deeper.

The director of the hospital in Millcroft declined an interview with us. There is nothing more worrisome, since everybody knows Peter Burlington is fond of the press.

We have also talked to Jonah Helm, one of the churchwardens at St. Anselm's. He said Township Hall was silent as to why the delay in making the funds available to the church. They were distressed beyond description at St. Anselm's because, concerned by the precarious structure of the building, they had already hired an architect and paid him an initial amount from the church's meagre funds.

The rector at St. Anselm's was in a dark mood: "There seem to be some people doing evil work, whether knowingly or not."

We will not give up until this mystery is solved.

"Was there a follow up?" Miles asked.

"No."

"Maybe there's no mystery – just delays, boring delays."

"Eddy's been told to drop it."

"How do you know?"

"I have a friend at the *Gazette*."

"Who is this Eddy B.?"

"Tom Bryson's son. He's been working at the *Millcroft Gazette* for close to five years now."

"Tom Bryson from B&M Construction?"

"Same."

"Who told Eddy Bryson to keep quiet?"

"The editor, but he'd have been told himself that the paper was to drop it. Stern orders. Poor Eddy. He thought he had a big story. He told everybody it would let him make the big leap."

"Big leap?"

"A big city daily."

He waved the copy of the *Gazette*. "Can I keep this?"

Chapter 5

August 2005

Miles called Ben on Monday morning to say he'd show up at the opening reception that evening.

"All set for the literary event of the year?" he asked him.

Ben snorted. "It was touch and go until the last moment. The dean used his weight to get two rooms in Hart House but otherwise refused to contribute a dime. Having the opening reception in the quad turned out opportune. There was a wedding reception there yesterday, and for only a few dollars more we were able to keep the tent over the patio and some tables and chairs on the lawn for another day. It was the Bakers, Laukhin's faithfuls, who opened their purse again. I'm sure you remember the Bakers. You might see them tonight. He had a stroke a year ago and is a tad lost."

Miles had not forgotten the Bakers, or their huge house on the Bridle Path. He remembered very clearly the launch they hosted for the second volume of the journals – a May evening in 1988, one year before Laukhin's stroke – and the savage drinking that went along with it. Even Federica got plastered toward the end, when most of the guests were gone, and Laukhin seemed to have his hands all over her while nodding at her literary opinions. Although as to the exact positioning of the poet's hands Miles had never been sure, having reached by then – he was told – a state of complete stupor. Later, when bitterness came between them, she would say he'd always fitted in with the drunks, but on that May night Miles had impressed his wife with how seamlessly he mingled with the literati. It was because of Federica that they followed Ben to many of the bookish congregations he attended. Her undergraduate years had been in languages and letters, and she missed that world. Likely disappointed with her middlebrow engineer husband, she kept pushing books of poetry into Miles's hands and testing him with taxing fiction – Proust in particular, which she thought should be read in the original French. She and Ben insisted Miles read each volume of the journals as it came out.

They had met Laukhin through Ben. At their wedding, the poet made a brief speech which fell between amusing and insulting. Following that, he proceeded to get drunk and noisily cantankerous. The newly married couple would ask Laukhin to join them for dinner or a drink with Ben and Jennifer, and more often than not the poet would come, confessing he needed the company of young minds. For an hour or two he'd be delightful. The drinking would bring him down, though, and he'd say something about Audrey and sink gloomily in his chair, hardly listening to the general banter. The only one who kept pace with him was Miles, and Federica would exchange glances with Ben and hit her husband under the table. Miles felt the poet liked him, although Ben reminded him that Laukhin was fond of anybody who held his drink. "And, Miles, he enjoys Federica's presence at least as much as yours. He listens to her views on poetry. It's not a good sign." Federica herself acknowledged she was flirting with Laukhin. "It's so easy, and I adore him. Don't worry, darling, it's nothing. That dead love of his, Audrey, is still with him."

Miles didn't go to work that Monday. Mohan assured him on the phone that his absence would not be felt. They would be having a conference call on the rover payload in the morning with the Italians and the Germans, he said. It was about the mass budget and interfaces. There was sarcasm in Mohan's voice, an insinuation that things would go smoother without Miles there. Cecil Fowler-Biggelow sounded preoccupied when Miles rang him next to say he'd be absent for another two days. "Yes, yes, a father's death is hard. Of course, be away as long as you need to be. Geoff is still mad, by the way. He usually gets over such things quickly, or forgets about them, but this time, I don't know . . ."

Cecil's voice was gloomy and distant. "Anything the matter, Cecil?"

"No. Probably not. Difficulties with the Mars mission. Minor ones."

He took the subway to Bloor and walked west from there under a still-strong sun. Before the Royal Conservatory of Music, he crossed the street and strolled south on Philosopher's Walk. He was early, and past the music school he lingered on the path. He had once wooed Federica there, on one of the benches behind the law school's Flavelle House. Was she still a student that summer or already articling with Brook Lemmings and Nitschke? BLN. Just BN, after Greg Lemmings left. She had come up from downtown to pick up something from Flavelle House. She had seemed absent-minded, claimed to be tired, and soon left. Left him wondering, too.

A large number of Russian academics had come to the symposium, Ben told him, after he freed himself from a group standing in the shade of the canopy. It seemed the Russians were determined to fully repatriate the scholarly work on Laukhin and his father. Many of Laukhin's past friends and collaborators showed up too, some elderly and needing companions. Two of his

English translators had come, one with a brand new wife. His former literary agent had arrived the night before, much aged and not well. At the opening session that morning, he'd talked at length and fondly about Laukhin, and, Ben said, in the attentive room his inward breaths had an ominous whistling sound. At the end, exhausted, he alluded to a "tickling worm" in his chest. No one had been brave enough to ask what he meant.

A few steps led down from the patio to the lawn, which stretched all the way to the western end of the long quadrangle. The several tables left over from the wedding the day before had been lined up in the shade of the southern wall. At the far end, unflinching, Soldiers' Tower bore the heat of the now fading sun.

With a solemn gesture that reminded Miles of Olympic ceremonies, Ben hung a lanyard with a name badge around his neck. "A few former lovers are here as well, and it's only fitting." He delivered the meatier gossip with a smirk: "Ewa Kucharsky, a former student in our department, is one of them. Her liaison with Laukhin caused a scandal in the early eighties. She drove in from Chicago, where she now teaches. There, the third table, blond hair, talking with Joan-Geraldine Page, an ex-lover from the poet's Soviet days. She's a Brit, studied in Moscow once. Her oldest, a daughter, lives in Toronto. It made Joan-Geraldine's decision to attend the symposium easier."

"What do I tell people, Ben, if they ask what I'm doing here?"

"Tell them you were a presence during Laukhin's last melancholy years. Add 'drinking buddy' if pressed."

Presence, yes. *Presence* was all right. He should pencil it on his name badge. It left room for interpretation.

His friend went on. "The old man at the second table, bent, red-faced, sitting with a middle-aged woman, is Viktor Zhelenin, once a well-known name. He flew in from Paris this afternoon, and the woman is his daughter. Zhelenin spent five years in the gulag. Later, until the fall of the Communists, he published a literary magazine in Paris called *Sintesy*. He knew Laukhin well and was keen to have his poetry. Tetchy, always getting into fights. Despises academics."

There were only a few faces he thought he recognized, and hardly any name he remembered. What was he doing here? "I don't see Helen."

"Probably near the bar," said Ben. "She said she wouldn't come, but I saw her earlier."

"Wouldn't come? You said she worked hard to make this happen, and that without her—"

"She's in bad shape, Miles."

"Why? What's wrong?"

"I'd rather let her tell you."

The bar was inside, in the long hallway, its low, timbered ceiling clashing with the gothic archways leading into the Great Hall. The crowd around the bar counter sounded Russian. Helen, her back to Miles, was listening to a short man who made much use of his hands. A woman in a flowery dress approached the two and addressed the man, in English, as Professor Varlamov. A warm handshake followed, with Varlamov briefly using both hands. Miles ordered a beer, the day still too hot for anything else.

"Miles, it's been ages," he heard Helen say behind him, and he turned around. "Ben said you'd be here. You must be desperate."

"I'm not sure why I came."

"I didn't think I'd be coming either."

"A former student of Laukhin shouldn't say that."

"I shouldn't have come."

The woman in the flowery dress seemed to have a long story to tell Professor Varlamov, who kept looking in their direction. Undoubtedly at Helen.

"What's wrong, Helen?" Miles asked.

"It's Ben who insisted. Ben the psychologist. Said it would do me good."

"He told me you did all the work."

"I'm not up to it, Miles. One week before the flattening."

"The what?"

"My boobs are being removed. It seems they are intent on harming the rest of my body."

"Oh, Helen . . ."

"I don't have the patience and the smiles."

She began speaking fast, clearly to avoid words of sympathy. She'd been close to finishing her book of recollections about Laukhin, and she finally had a title, *Studying with the Poet*, not entirely satisfying, but it would do if nothing better came to mind. Her intention had been to have it done and printed before the symposium, but things had not worked out that way. Still, what she'd done for the symposium had been a welcome distraction. She'd finish her book after the surgery and all the chemical crap that followed afterward. At the opening session that morning she'd read an excerpt from it. She forced herself to come in order to hear how it sounded, feel what the participants thought of it. Vanity. She had read poorly.

There was more to Helen's pain. After gulping what was left in her glass and ordering another one, she sighed and said she'd talk about anything except her forthcoming surgery or "that bastard Bleidd." But then she began talking about her husband. A few days earlier, she'd learned he was having an affair. Bleidd, who had been catching a flight to Calgary, called from the airport to say he'd left his phone at home and was sending an underling to bring it to him. She found the phone in one of his jacket pockets, and also a recent billet-doux.

"Fine timing." She laughed bitterly. "He's known for some time I'm going to be mutilated."

"Don't say that."

"What the fuck should I say?"

"Are you sure that's what it was?" Miles asked. "I don't see Bleidd—"

"She explained what she'd do to his naked body in Calgary. Handwritten, almost a whole page. All it lacked was diagrams. She works with him. Red hair, young, thin, pale. Comes to our house, all laughter, the slut."

His mind pictured a faceless slender female body causing erotic frissons to Bleidd's rather large and formless bulk. "Did you confront him?"

"He's not back yet, and I haven't called him. I can't deal with both this and . . . I don't want him around me, but I don't know how to do it without telling him I know. And if I don't tell him, I'll have to put up with his concerned face, 'Oh, dear Helen, we'll face this together,' hypocrite shit like that. Fuck. Sorry, Miles. Why do I . . . Silly me. Got to go to the loo."

Watching her moving cautiously away, Miles remembered another evening many years before during which Helen had purposefully got sloshed. It was a New Year's Eve party at her house. Laukhin called from Stockholm shortly before midnight to wish his students a happy New Year. A volume of his selected poetry was being published in Swedish, something considered essential in bending the academy's choice for the literature prize. Laukhin – and his agent – had been baffled by the difficulties the translator seemed to be having with his poems. Time was of some essence and Laukhin's agent had asked him to drop into Stockholm on his return from a poetry event in Frankfurt. Helen, collapsed intoxicated on a sofa, had handed over the phone to Ben, saying the line was bad and she'd had too much wine. Laukhin was frustrated at not being of much help to the translator or able to judge his drawn-out effort, Ben told the gathering after the conversation was over. The poet's words came through slurred. It was early morning in Sweden, and Ben guessed the difficulty was Laukhin's post-revelry discomfort rather than technical glitches on the line. He thought he'd heard a female voice. "Are you alone, Artyom Pavlovich?" he asked. The answer, enigmatic, came after a long pause. "Yes and no." There was unanimous merriment and nodding of heads when Ben told the room Laukhin's answer.

In the first minutes of the New Year, Federica, pressing against Miles, said she loved him. She was tipsy and she lied. She lied effortlessly, Federica, and

Miles loved to hear her lies. It might not have been an outright or conscious lie. Perhaps an enthusiasm, a warmth brought on by being briefly out of law and taxes, of being with people who shared the passion of her undergrad years, of being in the entourage of a future winner of the Nobel Prize in Literature. Not far from them, Helen was singing softly. The top button in the front of her bravely low-cut dress had come undone. "Helen is almost frontless," Federica whispered. "One abrupt move and we'll see nipples." Helen's rich husband, Bleidd, chatting with someone across the room, kept glancing at her. Helen had been emotional and giddy the whole evening. Her thesis was finally going well, after a couple of "wasted years," as she herself recognized. The subject was Pasternak – the origins of his famous novel. It was a danger-ously well-beaten path, and Helen was aware of that, but the journals Laukh-in's father had kept contained numerous entries about Pasternak and the long gestation of his novel. Trying to get up from her sofa, Helen said, "Magnet to my ass, this couch. Ooooh . . . I'm pissed, yes, but I have the right to be. You know why, Miles? Because I'll stop drinking today. No more. No, not for ever, don't be silly, but for a long while. You know why? Do you want to know why, Miles? And you, Federica, do you want to know? It's Federica, isn't it? I'll tell you, yes, I'll tell all. Confession time. I'm pregnant. Yes, pregnant. *Post coitum* pregnancy occurs. Wait till I tell my straitlaced husband. There he is, watching me. Didn't tell him yet – he wouldn't have let me drink tonight."

He hesitated at one of the doors leading back to the tented patio, then walked out and crossed to the steps down to the lawn. Another woman had joined Ewa Kucharsky and Joan-Geraldine. Her striking turquoise dress stood out among the rather drab outfits around her. He'd seen her as he came in, on the steps to the entrance, chatting with a man in a baseball cap, and briefly he thought it was Federica. He had stopped and feigned looking around while glancing at her. A petite version of Federica. The same colouring too. Yes, petite, which perhaps explained the ambitiously high heels.

Professor Varlamov approached him and read his name badge in an exag-gerated friendly pantomime. It was clear he was trying to remember Miles's name and the institution he was associated with. "Ilya Varlamov," he said, pointing at his own badge. "I remember you, don't I? You are with, with . . ."

"I'm Miles Rueda."

"Ah, yes, Professor Rueda."

"Miles, please."

"Remind me—"

"That woman, Professor Varlamov, the one sitting with her back to us, with two other women. The third table, turquoise dress. Who is she?"

Varlamov switched to Russian, and from the direction the professor was looking in, Miles knew he was answering his question.

Miles said meekly, "My Russian, you know . . ."

"You don't speak Russian? Who are you again?"

"Miles Rueda."

"Yes, yes. And what do you do?"

"I'm . . . I was a presence."

"A what?"

"A presence, during Laukhin's last melancholy years."

"What does that mean, to be a *presence*?"

"We had a special rapport."

"What kind of rapport?"

"A drinking one."

Varlamov exhaled. "Ah, yes, of course." He laughed and shook a finger at him. "You know, for a second . . ."

"I'm a friend of Professor Paskow."

"Professor Paskow invited you?"

"He insisted."

"Russian," Varlamov said with satisfaction.

"Sorry?"

"The woman you asked about, she's Russian. Attractive, yes. Good eye, Miles Rueda."

"Are you sure?"

"Yes, of course. The last love."

"I'm not following."

"Laukhin's last love in Moscow. Before he forgot to return. The last, how do you say, last fling. Writes poetry too. Yes, a poetess. Meagre output, here and there, rather weak. Wrote some drivel after Laukhin left. Hurt, of course. Too much sentiment, if I remember. She lives in Russia, in Saint Petersburg. Come to think of it, she wasn't at the second symposium, in Moscow. Yes, she disappeared, and no one remembered her. It took me a while this morning to realize who she was. I asked her why she was not seen at the Moscow symposium, and she said no one invited her. They were not in Russia at the time and heard of it too late. Big symposium it was, the one in Moscow. Huge, far bigger than this one. Better organized too."

Three former lovers of Laukhin, and all three at the same table. Who knew, there might be others.

"What's her name?" he asked.

"Pripogurina. Anna Pripogurina. I didn't expect her here, in Toronto. It was your friend who found and invited her. Interesting, actually. Observe her reaction tomorrow. There is a paper to be presented in the morning by one of my former students, a good paper, yes, claiming that *Poems for A*, you know, Laukhin's last verses before his stroke, was not about Audrey Millay or whoever his lover here was, but about her, that Anna you're looking at, an earlier love of the poet."

"That might be stretching—"

"Only a Russian woman could inspire such touching poetry. I'm joking. It's just being republished in Russia, *Poems for A*. Why the interest, Miles Rueda?"

"Oh, I don't . . . You know, Laukhin talked about her, if she is who you say she is. Often and fondly."

"Did he now?"

"His last year or so. After the stroke."

Varlamov grabbed his arm and shook it. "She's married, you know. Immensely rich husband. Forget it."

A tall, dark-haired man approached them and exchanged greetings with Varlamov. *Stanford University* was readable on his name badge. Miles mumbled his name, then pointed toward the bar and walked away. Strange to see them together, he thought, those former lovers of Laukhin. Did they know one another and their histories with the poet? Likely, otherwise what were the odds of finding themselves at the same table?

With his second drink, a glass of wine this time, he walked back out and stepped onto the lawn. Noise and shouts came to him from a large group gathered around Zhelenin's table. Ben left the group and, shaking his head, joined Miles.

"What's the argument?" Miles asked.

"A Russian academic's paper presented this morning, 'The Definitive Version of Laukhin's *Poets in Heaven.*' Zhelenin wasn't there, and someone had the unfortunate idea to tell him about it. The old *zek* – everybody knows this – has always claimed the definitive version of *Poets in Heaven* is the one published by him in the last issue of *Sintesy*."

Miles left Ben and joined the noisy group. A woman close to Zhelenin said something in Russian. Zhelenin shook his head without replying, and his daughter provided a brief answer, which led to some general merriment.

"The English translation was made from the version published in *Sintesy*," Zhelenin said in English. "I'm certain of that. It should count for something."

"Unauthorized," the tall professor from Stanford said.

"You didn't even read the paper," a young man with a French accent told Zhelenin.

"I don't have to."

"How can you dismiss it unseen?"

"On sent toujours la merde. Gros caca."

"You and your version," the young man said, shaking his head.

"I'm proud of it," Zhelenin shouted. "I'm proud of the version I published. *Sintesy* went out with a bang. The *definitive* version."

"It surely isn't," the Stanford man said to Zhelenin. "You yourself told me last year, Viktor Efremovich, that Laukhin stopped everybody from publishing *Poets in Heaven* while he was alive."

"So?" Zhelenin said.

"He was unhappy with the poem. Never wanted it published."

"So?"

"The version in *Sintesy* is an early one too."

"So?"

"He worked on the poem for years afterwards."

"How would you know?"

"Professor Paskow told me."

"So?"

Each "So?" from Zhelenin sounded more and more threatening. His daughter gently touched his arm.

"Stop saying 'So?' all the time," the Stanford man said, clearly aggravated. "Try making an argument."

"It doesn't mean he was happier with the silly tinkering of his later versions. There, that's an argument. I need somebody worthy of one, though."

The women at the third table were laughing. Should he ask Ben to walk over with him? They seemed to be having such a good time, they'd likely resent him. Laukhin once told him, "Never break into a merry group if you wish to make an impression." A Russian poet's counsel, likely made up on the spot. Where had they been? One of the three or four watering holes where Laukhin had been a habitué, sitting at one end of the bar with drinks in front of them, the constant in their outings. Laukhin, red-faced and red-eyed, more affected by the alcohol than he was, carrying on about his imminent death. To drive the poet's dark thoughts away, Miles had suggested joining the two women laughing together at the other end.

Back inside, and holding another drink, he ambled along the lengthy hallway. The cooler air was a welcome relief. He turned back, uncertain whether parading with a glass of wine was the thing to do. The door to the Map Room was open, and he sat down on a red couch below the painted plan of the university. He imagined the woman in the turquoise dress walking in and sitting right there beside him. A poet – careful, a *poetess*, according to Varlamov. What would he say to her? That he'd lived for six years in the apartment in which her former lover spent the last three years of his life? That he'd gone pub-crawling with him? That his former wife, Federica, had not been happy about it? That his good friend Professor Ben Paskow had been Laukhin's closest collaborator? That he had read some translated Russian poetry, albeit pushed to do so by Federica and Ben?

He should ask Ben about Anna Pripogurina in case he came face to face with her. Ben might know what would hold her attention; he had invited her to the symposium, after all.

Another glass of wine? His drinking had been under control now – more or less – for several years. Still, he should be careful. On the other hand, he wouldn't be working the following day, and Federica was no longer on Montgomery Avenue. His pub-crawling with Laukhin had driven her to screaming tantrums. He'd tell her Laukhin was in a pitiful state. "He needs friends. He needs help." "For God's sake, Miles," Federica would shout, "he has other friends, closer ones. His Russian comrades, they all drink. Let his agent, whatever his name is, save him. Let Ben get reeling with his mentor." And she'd explode with rage when, coming home past midnight and stinking of alcohol, he'd noisily fumble his way to bed and feel for her body. Often he slept what was left of the night on the living room couch. Katelyn, an early riser, would find him there and say, "Dad has been naughty again."

It was only after they got married and moved in together that Federica realized how much Miles was actually drinking. She was a junior lawyer then, working long hours. In front of Dr. Dermer, years afterward, she claimed that most times she got home late at night in those early years, either she found Miles drinking at home or he arrived sozzled after her. That was an exaggeration, he'd say in his defence, trying to catch Dr. Dermer's eye. Lawyers always exaggerated, and Federica excelled at it.

She must have known what she was getting into with him. After all, they had been together for almost three years before they got married. And lawyers, her professional milieu, were ardent drinkers. Not arguments he could throw in, but listening to Federica's complaints in Dr. Dermer's office, he silently went through them. The get-togethers at BLN, and there seemed to be one every other month, ended with half of the firm completely pissed. He'd seen them eyeing beautiful Federica, and heard the silly comments wrapped as compliments that her presence induced. He felt they knew things about her he didn't know. Of course they did; they spent all that time cooped up together in their black towers. Who knew what took place in those plush offices? From what Federica told him once, *obiter dictum* and mildly amused, a considerable fornication effort was always under way at their firm. It was secretaries and articling students who traditionally raised the general libido, but with more and more female lawyers joining the firm, habits changed, and collegial humping was becoming a trend. "Don't worry, darling," she told him. "I don't fancy any of them, or approve of flings at work." She had lied, though, or he thought she had, because Greg Lemmings had been a tax lawyer at the firm before the teaching load at Osgoode and the work he undertook for various governments made him quit. She articled for and then worked with him for two years. Might have been his summer student too. Office sex at lunchtime and, with Miles, domestic snuggles at night. Bordering on nymphomaniac, Federica. No, that was an exaggeration, a lawyerly one. Unworthy of him, born of spite. But she'd always been a bit of a tart. He'd often thought that, with both admiration and dismay. Another lawyerly exaggeration. Well, she had the looks and inclination to be. The fabric of a tart. Yet he'd never caught her at anything untoward while they were married. And when she started or restarted her affair with Greg Lemmings, things at home were bad already.

He had met Greg Lemmings at the first party he went to with Federica at BLN. It was one of the get-togethers where spouses and partners were included. Greg told Miles that evening that he might be coaxed into more government work, thus having to leave the practice of law. He expressed regret at no longer working with such a talented young lawyer as Federica. "A future star of taxation law," he added, pointing his finger at Federica's breasts. Thinner in those days, Greg had a ponderous way with words, which Miles attributed to the precision needed to unscramble tax rules and implications. Greg's then wife, slightly taller than him, struck Miles as haughty. When he shared that impression with Federica, she startled him. "You're wrong; she's just shy. She was bred for looks, children, and conversation. She's failed the last subject." A comment which, later, made him suspicious. For how would Federica know? She might have met Greg's wife a few times before, yet such a definite diagnosis could only have come from Greg. And Greg would not have offered such information unless . . .

Truth be told, he had fond memories of the parties at BLN. He joined in the robust drinking with gusto and took delight in the rowdy, swaggering talk. He'd had an easy time inserting himself into the general merriment. His drinking and their drinking helped, of course. He knew that Ben's warning about Laukhin applied to boozing lawyers too: they liked anybody who liked them and drank with them. They warily studied him. He felt their probing eyes. How could smart, sophisticated, beautiful Federica fall for this penniless engineer, this small-town nobody? He had asked himself the same question. That and another one, twinned to the first. Why would she stay with him for almost twenty years?

A young couple, students no doubt, walked into the Map Room and looked crossly at him. They wanted him out, and he obliged. His glass was empty anyway.

Replenishing his glass at the bar, his mind went back to Federica. His drinking was the reason their marriage went awry. That was what she had always told him. That was how she explained their fights to Dr. Dermer; that was what she declared during their divorce. There had been more, though. Federica's feelings for him never equalled his feelings for her. When they met, she was still pining after the older and married Darius Milo, the star performer during her years of undergraduate enthusiasm for French. Darius Milo who, between embraces, had filled Federica's head with Proustiana. Darius Milo who, despairing of obtuse Ontarians pronouncing his last name as if it rhymed with "silo," began writing it "Miló."

Yes, she had *liked* him. He could be mildly amusing, especially with a couple of drinks in him. He could even fudge his way through a conversation about books and authors. His friendship with Ben had provided him with the smattering of literary talk that at first had impressed Federica. And seventeen years was a respectable stretch for a marriage. Their thing began to come undone around the time Federica became pregnant with Katelyn. *Their thing* was Federica's term for what had brought and kept them together. After she told him she was pregnant, she asked, "This thing of ours, Miles, what exactly is it?" He remembered being taken aback, questioning himself. "We feel good in each other's company," he told her. "Affection. Admiration – yes, I admire you. Love." "Love?" she asked. "I do love you, yes," he replied, and added, "You know, of the two of us, I'm the one who keeps mentioning it." She stopped to think, and then she quoted Proust: "It is the one who is not really in love who says more tender things." Applied to them, though, Proust's observation was dead wrong. They persisted with *their thing*, hoping newborn Katelyn Anne would somehow extend it, help mend the cracks. And she did. Katelyn, the joy she brought them, was the reason they stayed married a dozen years longer. Perhaps Dr. Dermer was also responsible for some of their bonus years. *Bonus years* was coined by Federica too.

Fucking Proust. Always quoted by Federica. She'd often add the source of the proffered wisdom, as if to remove any doubt about its weight. After their separation, Miles told Ben Paskow, and only half in jest, "Without Proust we'd still be together." Federica had managed to turn him from a puzzled, page-skipping reader of Proust into a denigrator. "You can't be lukewarm about Proust," she declared, the first time he confessed only a mild affection for the famous writer. You either love him fully, without riders, or you hate him." Miles let it pass; they were still fresh lovers, and most outrageous things were left unpunished. Not later, though, no. Later he'd rise for much less.

Ben was talking with Professor Varlamov. "Yes, yes, of course," Varlamov was saying, as Miles approached them, "the journals *are* the work Pavel Laukhin is most admired for. Yet his spy novels have seen a resurgence in Russia, read for," and here Varlamov began counting on his fingers, "their economical style, irony, minimal adherence to the party line, and, why hide it, a certain nostalgia. And while we fully agree that the journals are literary masterpieces—"

"The journals as published are," interrupted Ben, "not as written or kept by Pavel Laukhin. Pavel Laukhin brought compelling stories and material, but rough, compressed, unpolished. Couldn't have been otherwise, of course; afraid they'd be found. It's like comparing the finished *Red Cavalry* with the author's 1920 diary. Only Art Laukhin transformed his father's journals into the jewels—"

"In Russia we credit the father far more than the son. There are good arguments for this view," Varlamov hastened to add, seeing Ben shake his head. "Read again volumes four and five, which, while of no lesser quality than the earlier volumes, were less worked on by the son and came out after his death. Well, you of all people should know." Varlamov's English was good, and he seemed keen on using it. "There's such interest in Laukhin in Russia now. The Laukhins, I should say, father and son. I personally have three, how do you say, *aspiranty* . . ."

"Graduate students."

"Yes, graduate students. I have three working on Laukhin. On the Laukhins, to be more correct. And I could easily have others. They are more interested in the father than in the son."

His friend took a deep breath. He looked probingly at Miles, as if wondering if any help would come from him to stop the nonsense. Yet Varlamov had offered Ben a perfect out with his indirect compliment. And Miles knew better than get into a dispute between two academics.

"The work Artyom Laukhin did on the journals was immense," Ben said, "and that included the last two volumes. My part was finishing touches mainly. And you forget the poetry—"

"Poets are no longer celebrated in Russia now. Not as before, anyway. That's what you, the West, did to us. Ha. A joke, of course, but with a melancholy kernel. I too remind my students that, as literature, the son's work is head and shoulders above the father's. A hard case to make, though, if one has no interest in poetry. Just before I left, one student told me that Pavel

Laukhin should be the only name appearing on the journals' covers. Strictly the father."

Ben's face was turning red. "Strictly Pavel Laukhin, when his son was so instrumental in making it the triumph—"

Varlamov chopped the air in front of Ben's chest with his hand. "You in the West make too much of Artyom Laukhin's contribution. We believe, too, that the English translations of Pavel Laukhin's novels – three or four, I'm not sure – are of a deplorable quality."

"I never heard Art Laukhin complain," Ben said.

"I doubt he read them. I mean, in English. Did you?"

"No."

"Don't. You should read the Russian originals." The hand that had chopped the air was waving around. "The next symposium – in Moscow, of course – should be a *Laukhins* symposium, both of them. Pavel and Artyom. Yes, father and son. They are inextricably, symbiotically, linked."

"Of course, the journal linked them. The son, in preparing his father's notebooks for publication, elevated them to another level."

"Here you go again. I don't think the son's contribution was that significant."

"Surely you can't—"

"If anything, it was the other way. One of my students is working on a thesis showing the influence of Pavel Laukhin's journals on his son's poetry. It's all there to see."

"See what?"

"Each one of his son's major poems is a reflection of one or several passages in the father's journals. Why the face, Professor Paskow? It shouldn't be such a surprise."

Miles's friend seemed too dumbfounded to say anything. Varlamov raised himself on the toes of his shoes and asked, staring intently at Ben, "How many graduate students do you have?"

"On Laukhin?"

"Yes, yes."

"One. She's been sick this year . . ."

"Ah, a woman." Varlamov took two steps away, then changed his mind and turned back to Ben. "How's the biography going?"

"Art Laukhin's?"

"Five years ago, in Moscow, you said you'd write one."

"It's slower than I expected. Still gathering material. I'm going to spend my sabbatical at it, next year, most of it in Russia, talking to people, chasing things."

"Have you written anything?"

"Notes mainly."

"Kryukov, you know, he's doing one. Keeps it secret."

"Are you sure?"

"Ask him. See what he says." He pointed somewhere behind Ben. "There he is, talking to that impossible man from Stanford. You better hurry. I was tempted too, but I'm too old for grand undertakings like this. Anyway, for me, the father is more interesting."

The table where the three women had been laughing together was empty now. Miles looked for the turquoise dress but couldn't see it anywhere.

Varlamov left them. Staring after him, Ben said, "I like Varlamov, although he demands a lot of patience. He begins every conversation as if we've just been introduced." He sighed. "I'm having difficulties lately with gatherings of this nature: show delight at meeting old acquaintances and colleagues; make plans for future academic undertakings; appear enthusiastic to the eager youth; smile. To make matters worse, there seem to be few new stories. Old ones are rehashed, and if they change at all it's likely due to forgetfulness. The same controversies keep being relived too, and with the same spite and fury. It's hard to understand. Shouldn't age mellow us?"

"Helen is in bad shape," Miles said.

"Did . . . did she tell you?"

Miles nodded.

"Bleidd too?"

"Boobs and Bleidd, in that order."

"Not lucky, is she?"

"Not lucky."

"Look after her, Miles."

"What?"

"I mean, tonight."

"How on earth would I do that?"

"Make sure she gets home all right. She seemed set to get drunk, and I've got to stay here to the end. I doubt she'll stick around for the dinner. She knows she won't miss much. The meal, I fear, will be a disappointment. We ran out of money, you see."

One of the companions of the turquoise dress, the older woman – Joan-Geraldine? – joined them. Ben made the introductions, and she said she loved his keynote speech that morning. Ben asked if she was joining them for the dinner in the Great Hall. Joan-Geraldine shook her head. "I promised my daughter I'd babysit. Ewa offered to drive me back to my daughter's house. It's not far, and Ewa will return. Very amusing, Ewa."

"The other woman who was with you earlier," Miles asked, "the one in a turquoise dress, is she gone?"

"Anna? Yes. Had a flight to catch. An interesting woman. She knew Laukhin in Russia. Intimately. She said that after her father killed himself, her mother married Laukhin's first cousin. They both disapproved of her fling with Laukhin." Looking at Ben, she added, "I'm glad I came, you know. The three of us had a grand time – fond recollections of the poet."

"Would you write them down?" Ben asked.

"Sorry?"

"I mean, write down what you remember about Laukhin. I'm gathering material for a biography, you see."

Joan-Geraldine looked merrily at him. "Ben, it would be a dozen pages of porn."

Startled, Ben mumbled, "Surely there was more . . ."

"I'll think about it." She waved and went away.

"'A dozen pages of porn.' Superb," Miles said, following Joan-Geraldine with his eyes.

"Interested in Anna Pripogurina?" Ben asked. "I can tell you more about her. A lot more. Born Lyutova, and writes poetry under that name. Laukhin was very fond of her. Before he left the Soviet Union they were, briefly, lovers. In his last years he tried, without success, to reconnect with her. It took me years to find her, and I'm glad she came."

Shouts or screams reached them from the Zhelenin table. "They are going to kill the old man," Ben said. "I better go and see what's happening. Where is that dinner? Why haven't we sat down yet?" He went away.

Helen appeared beside Miles. If she had drunk a lot, she covered it well. "Are you staying for dinner?" she asked.

"I thought I would."

"That's too bad."

"Aren't you staying?"

"No. I hoped you'd keep me company."

"Oh? Well, sure, why not? . . . Where do you want to go?"

"Say, my place."

He exhaled. "Your place?"

"You heard me."

"I mean, Helen . . ."

"A last fuck with boobs."

"Jesus."

"It's a simple proposition, Miles. No need for miracles."

"Helen, you know, males are easily persuaded, we are animals."

"Good."

"You're . . . you're sure?"

"Yes."

"I . . . I don't know. It's so unexpected."

"I'm not asking for a lifelong commitment, Miles, just a one-night fuck. I can't ask Ben. Thought of Varlamov before you showed up."

Chapter 6

September 2005

It was Don Verbrugge, the volatile marketing man and reader of the *National Post*, who brought the article to his attention. Friday after lunch, he came grinning into Miles's cubicle, waving the main section of the daily. "Ah, the dramas of small towns. Dusty drawn curtains, abuse and incest, fortunes hidden in barns, smoldering hatreds. Scandal in Corby Falls – who would have thought? Read this and then the blog. You must read the blog." "Scandal" came out as *scandale*, the French way, as if to underline the refined nature of his delight. Stressing the last syllable sounded more ominous too, hinting at larger dimensions. "I have a meeting now, but I'd love to learn more," Don added, pointing to the newspaper he'd placed on Miles's desk.

As he picked up the newspaper, Miles reflected that *scandale* suited Don. Previously employed by Airbus in Toulouse, he had arrived at Ludwig Robotics with the rumour he'd hit a colleague in a meeting and that there was "unexpected" damage as a result. Miles had queried him about it, and Don confirmed the story. "It was in a pub, not in a meeting, and I had to leave quickly and quietly if the incident was to be forgotten. So I came home to Toronto. A mistake." Somehow, Fowler-Biggelow heard a star salesman was available. There were protests, of course: the proper selection process was not followed, and there were more critical positions to be filled. Within a month, though, Don Verbrugge was hired. It turned out, too, that Don was a distant cousin of Geoff Simmons's wife.

He found the item that got Don all worked up on the fourth page of the main section, the headline, "Bequest Entangled," circled with red ink. The writer's name was underneath: Lyle Blanchard. Miles was too busy to read it then and there. There was a short note at the bottom which explained Don's allusion to a blog. "Lyle Blanchard is a contributor to the *Post*. His website is lyleblanchard.ca."

He read the article as soon as he arrived home. Oddly, there was no baiting lead paragraph. The beginning was mild, about Dr. Biranek – described as a war refugee who found another home in Canada – and about Millcroft, the township, the town, its rundown hospital. It mentioned Dr. Biranek's long association – almost half a century – with the hospital and his medical practice in Corby Falls, the nearby village he'd resided in since his arrival in the township. There was a brief paragraph on Biranek's first wife, whom he'd met in Toronto during the war, and more on his second one, who survived him. It went on with his not-unexpected death at the end of April, at the age of eighty-seven, and the generous bequests contained in his will.

Dr. Biranek left $12 million to Millcroft Township Hospital and $300,000 to St. Anselm's Church in Corby Falls. For a small hospital, such a large sum of money is the door to a bright future. Quoted in the *Millcroft Gazette* soon after the bequests were made public, Peter Burlington, director of the hospital, said, "Dr. Biranek's donation will do for our hospital what the provincial government has failed to do throughout decades of neglect."

Dr. Biranek's bequests were gratefully received four months ago by the township. The province also expressed its appreciation. A spokesman for the Ministry of Health said (*Post*, Wednesday, May 22) that Ontario took pride in people like Dr. Biranek and that the provincial government would also make a contribution to the hospital. He did not provide more details but said he had hopes for a matching amount. Interviewed the same day, Thula Locksley, the new mayor of the township, said a memorial gathering for the township's benefactor was planned. Asked whether the donation was conditional on the hospital changing its name, Mayor Locksley said it was. She added that it was an honour to do so. She revealed that a commemorative bust of the doctor was also planned, to be placed either in Millcroft or Corby Falls.

That was four months ago. It is a different story now, one of enforced silence. Nothing seems to have happened since. Attempts by township residents to find out more have been unsuccessful. A spokesperson for the provincial Ministry of Health will state only that the township needs more time to finalize its plans. Mayor Locksley, Peter Burlington, and the rector at St. Anselm's Church all declined the *Post*'s requests for interviews.

And that was that, a rather abrupt end of the article.

Katelyn walked in as he was preparing a simple pasta dish for dinner.

"Your mother's not coming in to say hello?"

"She was in a hurry. They are off to some sort of a fancy do, she and Greg. She looked quite swanky, Mom. Ornamental."

"Ah, a taxation ball."

He sat down to eat with Katelyn, and squabbled with her because she planned to spend the following night at her friend Martha's house, and he insisted on driving her there.

"It's a ten-minute walk from the subway," she said, as they were finishing their meal. She held up her hands, fingers spread. "*Ten minutes.* Look, if it makes you feel better, Martha will wait for me at the station."

Relentless, like Federica. "Don't you see her at school?"

"It's not the same thing."

"I'll drive you."

"I'm fourteen."

"I know."

"I've been on the TTC by myself before. Many times. I'm sometimes dropped at the subway and walk here."

It was true; it was time for him to let go.

"So?" she asked, exasperated.

"I'm having a sudden attack of anxiety."

"Mother wouldn't do this to me. She's less clingy, you know. Fathers are not supposed to be clingy."

Clingy? Where did she get that from? Did Federica put the idea in her head? A sly, sticky word to describe him while Paris plans were being discussed. "It's a treat for me, Katelyn – being with you. I only have the weekend."

It was a losing argument. She was bored with him. What amusements, what stimulating activities, did he offer her? She was clearly at an age when parents were or were becoming a nuisance. Especially a *clingy* parent like him.

After he cleared the table, alone – Katelyn had gone upstairs without a word and slammed the door to her room – he dialled his sister's number. She wasn't home.

Another banging noise came out of Katelyn's bedroom. She'd been four years old when they bought the house on Montgomery, and Miles felt Katelyn had never liked living there. It wasn't the kind of thing a four-year-old would say, but after they moved in Katelyn kept asking when they'd go back to the home with elevator and the wide balcony from where they "saw the world." Her wish had come from him. He used to take little Katelyn into his arms, walk onto the big balcony of their nineteenth-floor apartment on Prince Arthur Street, and whisper to her, "See, Katelyn Anne, from here you can see the entire world." She seemed fascinated by the view, or by the concept of having the entire world right there for her to contemplate, and would be happy to stay there with him for a long time, in his arms, gazing at the city. Those had been moments of great happiness for him.

The apartment had been Laukhin's during the last three years of his life. The poet had moved onto Prince Arthur Street at the beginning of 1988. He could afford the high rent because the royalties from the first volume of his father's journal had exceeded all expectations. "My windfall," Laukhin liked to tell visitors, in love with the word. Often he'd add, "From my father's tree, plucked by mighty European gusts," because the sales in Europe had been particularly strong.

After Laukhin's death came the surprise of his will. Surprises. The lawyer's name was Sokhanyuk, and in his somber office on Steeles Avenue West, his deep reading voice had carried echoes of merriment. "'I leave my Chemakoff ink and watercolour – which Audrey used to call *The Mannequin Birds* – to Miles Rueda and Federica Leigh, because they grandly pretended to find it both intriguing and uplifting the few times they were in my apartment on Prince Arthur.'" Sokhanyuk's wide, fat face laughed happily and loudly. His pink jowls swung at a slight delay with each nod of his head as he repeated "grandly pretended" several times. Miles looked incredulously at him and asked, "Are you sure? To us?" Sokhanyuk, who wore intimidating dark glasses indoors, raised his round shoulders. "Why ask such questions? Enjoy, enjoy. The other chap, the young professor, your age, had the same reaction when I read to him that the royalties for the fifth volume of Pavel Laukhin's journals were to go to, hang on, ah, here it is, 'my best student, and now collaborator and friend, Dr. Benjamin Henry Paskow.' There was this proviso, of course, that Dr. Paskow would continue working on the publication of the journals. It was Laukhin's way to make sure he'd do it. He was a clever man, Laukhin. A poet, and a clever man." There was more jollity for Sokhanyuk in the will. "He left you his drinking box too. Where is it, yes, listen, 'I also leave to Miles Rueda the art deco liquor cabinet now in my living room. He is to think of me every time he pours a drink kept in there.'" Miles had never met Sokhanyuk before, but he'd heard about him from Laukhin. The poet told Miles that Leo Sokhanyuk was recommended to him by a friend who was in construction. "Construction, Miles, building permits, that's where the sharpest minds are," Laukhin had said, chuckling, obviously taken with the idea that his lawyer also looked after the interests of shady clients.

The moment she learned of Laukhin's death, Federica paid the first and last months' rent to get the poet's apartment. A bribe too, because the building had a waiting list. Miles had always liked the apartment and its location. He wasn't sure, though, they could afford it, and Federica was two months pregnant. "We both love the apartment," Federica said, "and you can't beat the location. The drive for you is longer, true, but you'll be mainly against the traffic and I won't need a car living there."

"Feds, have you told them you're pregnant?"

"Not yet."

"When are you going to?"

"Leave it to me."

"What if they don't like it?"

"They won't like it."

"What if they let you go?"

"I don't think they will. If they do, I'll get another job. Miles, I have no intention of living on an engineer's salary."

He poured himself a drink, and with the main section of the *Post* under his arm he went upstairs to his den. Blanchard's website had typical navigation headers: Home, About, Top Stories, Notes, a Search box. He expected to see a picture of Lyle Blanchard when he clicked on About, but there were only words. Born in 1938, a respectable sixty-seven-year-old. Worked for a Kitchener newspaper, for a radio station in London, for the *Globe* for many years, and for the *Post* until 2003. Interested in local stories. Unhappy with the limitations and constraints of mainstream journalism, finding personal blogging liberating. The Notes section had relatively short entries displayed in reverse chronological order. Quickly scanning a few, Miles found them personal and gossipy, almost a diary. He went down a few months and found nothing related to Biranek or Millcroft. He was thinking of typing "Biranek" in the Search box but instead clicked on Top Stories. And there it was, at the very top of the drop-down list, "Bequest Entangled," posted two days earlier. He clicked on the promising title and then printed out the rather long entry.

With the printout and the newspaper, and still carrying his drink, he went down and stepped outside onto the back porch. The view from it spoke of neglect and helplessness. The lawn had dead spots and badly needed a haircut. In the vegetable patch, which Miles planted every May and was now overgrown with weeds, a few ripe cherry tomatoes hung reproachfully on wilting vines. "Why do you do this?" Katelyn had asked him in May. She'd come out of the house to help him in the garden. "You clean up this patch every spring, you plant it, and then you never step in it until the following year." "How do you know?" he asked. "I know, Dad."

It was still warm, although the sun was diving somewhere to his left. He sat down on one of the canvas chairs. He liked that time of the day. Federica had liked it too, once. They spent many summer dusks sipping a drink and chatting on their high-up balcony on Prince Arthur. Federica had called it "our verandah in the clouds." It had a soothing effect on them, and somehow they never quarrelled there. They had tried to recreate that serene mood, that sense of ease and peacefulness, on the back porch on Montgomery Avenue. It never worked.

The beginning was almost word for word the article in the *Post*. The uncomfortable part came next. Blanchard wrote that he'd spent several days in the township hoping to learn more about wonderful Dr. Biranek and the reasons his bequests were no longer a subject on everyone's lips.

I ended up in Corby Falls, in the local watering hole, Bart's Alehouse. After sipping a pint alone I supplied a round to the few stool-hoppers, and, in a roundabout way – fearing they'd clam up otherwise – inserted Dr. Biranek's name in the ensuing chat. Someone mentioned the bequests the doctor left. I supplied another round. The tongues got looser, but there wasn't much in what they said. I ordered something to nibble and sat down at a table. An older couple were sharing a late lunch nearby. The woman leaned toward me and said, "The doctor had a murky side to him." Her companion muttered, "Hilda, don't. He was a good doctor." I told them I wanted to know more. The woman whispered something to the man, who shrugged. She turned back to me and said that if I really wanted to know more about Biranek, I should talk to older people, closer to his age. "Like who?" I asked. "Try Elma Mulligan – I hear she's still around somewhere. She wasn't fond of the doctor, though, or of his second wife, Hollie, and might massage the truth."

I tracked Elma Mulligan at the Restful Nest, an old age home in Peterborough. She was in a wheelchair, bitter, difficult, still sharp. She told me from the beginning that she'd been very attached to Rose, Dr. Biranek's first wife, and had not liked Hollie McGinnes or the doctor. "Never liked him, not at all. And I didn't like her, Hollie. She killed Rose, you know. Of course she did. They said they'd return to Corby Falls on Saturday and didn't. Then they said they'd return early on Sunday and didn't either. They showed up on Monday morning. Too late. Rosie died on Sunday night, with no one to help her or hear her."

Some of the words Elma uttered were unprintable. I told Elma that Hollie Biranek had survived her husband and I'd have to filter what she said. She laughed. "At my age, I don't care." I told her Dr. Biranek died in late April. She shrugged. She'd heard that from her niece, only weeks after his funeral. She'd heard of his money and largesse toward the township too. "That's what rich people do," she said. "Cover their sins with gifts."

She told me she was eighty-one years old and was at the Nest because her knees gave up on her, both of them, one after the other. Elma's husband died in a hunting accident when she was thirty. "He was a hunter and a fool," she said. He left her with a rusted van, a rifle, a shotgun, and little else. A mortgage too. She had to sell the house and buy a small bungalow, and began working for people. Five days a week in the Biraneks' house once Rose got sick. Sometimes six. She was let go after Rose's death. She knew it would happen. "It was because of that bitch, Hollie."

Almost every day there, she knew what was going on. "Rose had MS. She liked to chat and had plenty of time for it as her illness got worse. Dr. Biranek spent less and less time with her. Poor Rose, she had no one to talk to and would follow me, slowly hobbling, as I was doing the chores." She stopped, looking past me, as if trying to reconstruct the image in her mind. When she focused again, she asked, "Which newspaper did you say you were with? Oh, don't bother – it matters not. I'll tell you all you want to know. More than you want to know. Like Rose, I have no one to talk to." She laughed at herself and went on. "Rose was born in Corby Falls. I was two years younger, and I remember her from primary school – friendly, good looking, loud, hotheaded. Tall, with a strong body – such a joke. Men leered at her. She left Corby Falls soon after the war began, looking for *more life*. That was what she said to me when I asked her why she'd left Corby Falls. 'I looked for *more life*, Elma.' She worked in a munitions factory in Toronto. It was at a dance hall that she met Dr. Biranek, who wasn't a doctor yet. She said his English made her laugh and that he was a fancy dancer. He was a catch for her, a doctor. They got married in Toronto, at the end of the war, and in forty-seven or forty-eight they moved to Corby Falls. I remember even now how startled I was the first time I caught sight of Rose back in Corby Falls."

She sighed, and I thought she was reliving that unexpected reunion, but when she began to talk again she mentioned Rose's daughter. Two years before she married Dr. Biranek, Rose had given birth to a daughter. The father was a soldier, a young boy from Port Credit, who died in 1942. Rose knew he died, because he'd stopped writing and her letters to him came back. As they weren't married or engaged, she was the last to learn about the death of her daughter's father. Her beau's parents didn't want to have anything to do with her and refused to tell her what they knew. They chased her away when she told them she was pregnant with their grandchild. Her daughter's name was Mary, and Rose had to give her away before she married Josef Biranek. She had no choice, because he wouldn't marry her otherwise. Mary was two years old at the time.

The couple who took Mary, the Lamberts, had not been able to have children on their own. They were neighbours of a second or third cousin of Rose, an older woman who looked after Mary while Rose made munitions. The cousin died soon afterward, and the Lamberts moved to the other side of Toronto. Elma thought the daughter became Mary Lambert and that she grew up in Toronto. As she talked, Elma's eyes filled with tears. Rose would say that her illness was God's punishment for abandoning Mary. She never saw her again after she gave her away. Dr. Biranek had been opposed to any contact or even receiving news about her. He said the less Rose knew, the better for both her and her daughter.

Because the doctor wanted to practice in a small community, Rose returned to Corby Falls with her new husband. She was diagnosed with MS in the late 1950s. Dr. Biranek began neglecting her and took up with other women, eventually settling down with his office nurse, who became his second wife after Rose's death. The doctor would make love – Elma used a ruder word – to his future wife within the earshot of sickly Rose. "On purpose," Elma said. "That's how they killed Rosie – loneliness and bitterness. He went for women, Dr. Biranek, one of those men. He'd tried to have his way with me too. I was doing the laundry one day in the basement, and he came from behind me all of a sudden and grabbed my titties. Pushed himself onto me, yes. He was already hard. I got angry and butted his chin with my head. He didn't like that and let go. Yes, he came on to me with Rose upstairs, and Hollie too. I might not have been let go had I been more accommodating. But I couldn't do it to Rosie. No, I couldn't."

Driving back to Toronto, I reflected on what I heard from Elma Mulligan. If half of what she said were true, then there was more than a murky shade on Dr. Biranek's white coat. Could that explain the silence at Millcroft Township Hall? Could the Millcroft hospital be renamed in honour of a murky character? Should any of this matter if the millions of dollars left by the doctor were for a good cause – the badly needed expansion and modernization of the township hospital?

Back in Toronto, I found a Mary Lambert in the Toronto telephone directory. I called and left a message to call me back. She didn't. Next time I called, she picked up the phone. When I told her who I was, she said she had nothing to say to me and hung up.

Something else has reached my desk as I am close to posting this material, and it may be a better explanation for the widespread reluctance to speak in Millcroft: the death of Dr. Biranek's first wife might not have been an unfortunate accident. Sounds far-fetched, yet I will look into it. Because, if indeed Rose Biranek's death was not a tragic accident, and if Biranek was somehow involved, then clearly the hospital name will not have "Biranek" in it in the future. And without the name change, there may not be a bequest for the hospital.

I will try to get a copy of the coroner's report on Rose Biranek's death. I will keep trying to talk to Mary Lambert.

It was getting dark. He went inside and poured himself another drink. Somebody had gone to the *Post* and told them what he or she knew about Dr. Biranek. The *Post*, probably, asked Lyle Blanchard to look into it. And Blanchard found it much to his liking. So much so that he spent considerable time on it. The newspaper must have been willing to print only the more factual beginning of Blanchard's entire material. And because Blanchard had alluded to the murder of Rose Biranek on his website, the somebody who had alerted the *Post* to the story was either Lyn Collins or Hollie Biranek. Jennifer could have done it too, even Ben, but it was absurd to think it was either of them.

Hollie? If anyone else knew about Rose's end it would be Hollie, though when she had come out of her house to have a smoke with him back in April she seemed to have no clue that her husband might have had something to do with it. Unless, of course, she was a superb actress. Had Biranek told her he'd driven to Corby Falls that Saturday night? Had he confessed, or had she somehow put two and two together? Had he told anyone else of his deed? Had she?

Yes, definitely, Hollie could have been the source. With the doctor leaving the bulk of his money to the township, she decided the story needed airing now. Did she, though? Hollie had told Sarah she didn't know what to do with the money Biranek left her. She even half joked she was worried she'd have to write a will. Still, twelve million dollars was huge. Greed gave wayward counsel. If the bequests were to fall through, the money would revert to her, unless there were additional stipulations in Biranek's will. Who would know? The lawyer, Joe Montanari, would, of course, and Hollie herself. Thula would too.

No, he was the guilty party, himself. It all began with the story he told at Le Paradis several months earlier. But how had it reached Blanchard's ear? Through Lyn Collins? Why would Lyn Collins do it?

He rang Sarah's number. She didn't answer and he left her a message: she should read the article about Biranek in that day's *Post* and then get on the author's website for the first of the Top Stories.

As soon as he put the phone down it rang. It was Don.

"Well?" Don said.

"Well what?"

"The article in the *Post*. And the blog, of course. Is this an old story for you?"

There were voices around Don, and it was hard to hear what he was saying. "I knew of the bequests."

"That's all you have to say?"

"It's Friday night, Don. Why this interest?"

"I know you. You're my friend."

"Ah."

"I know the writer too."

"The author of the article? Lyle Blanchard?"

"Old Lyle, yes. Friend of my parents. Lyle is my father's generation. Perhaps not quite my father's ancient age, a bit younger. Whenever I see his name above an article, I tell myself, there's old Lyle, still at it. For him, this Biranek thing is bespoke work, stubborn digging, talking to people. And now, on his website, without the newspaper's constraints cramping his style, he's in full flight. I see him now and then, you know, at my parents' place. Big fellow, with a huge capacity for drinking and quarrelling."

A woman's voice asked Don, or someone else, if he was coming.

"Where are you calling from?" said Miles.

"A pub. Join us. There's girls."

"Katelyn is here."

There were always girls with Don, and in his stories. He had a narrow face and grey, dissipated eyes. Married once, briefly, or so Miles had gathered. Don kept saying that now, at well over forty, he should give it another shot. He was always meticulously attired, with carefully matched shirts and ties, which he renewed, he'd told Miles, out of a catalogue from an outfit somewhere in New England. He considered the three years he'd spent with Ludwig a waste. "I'm squandering good years of my life," he once told Miles over a beer in a bleak hotel lounge during a trip to Huntsville, Alabama. There were peanut shells everywhere on the floor and the end of a football game on a giant television screen. The hotel, a long walk within the airport itself, was faded and grim. A faint smell of beer seemed to hang everywhere. "I must have been blind. At my age. How glamour lures the feeble of mind. This is not *real* work, Miles. I don't have a *real* job. You don't have a *real* job. These are not *real* people we work with and deal with. These are people trapped in a black hole created some thirty years ago with the Apollo landings and the contest with the Russians. What the hell am I doing here? I'm a marketing man. I sell things. What do I sell here, Miles? Space? Good Lord. Everybody is making a buck these days, Miles, everybody except the space boys. And who do I choose to be with? The space boys. And the places we get to travel. Houston and Huntsville and then Houston again. The thing that really gets to me, though, is the arrogance of the people, their hubris . . ." That evening in the hotel lounge, while watching beefy young men clad in strident colours clobber each other, Don had continued venting his frustration long after Miles stopped listening.

"Did you know this Dr. Biranek? Of course you did. Corby Falls is a hamlet."

"I knew him."

"Well?"

"He was a neighbour and my father's physician." Miles immediately regretted saying that and added a lie, or a half-lie. "I didn't know him well. If I met him on the street, we'd pass the time of day. Not much more."

He cut the article out of the *Post* with a pair of scissors and stapled it with the printout from Blanchard's website. He added the stapled sheets to the blue folder where he'd put the piece from the *Millcroft Gazette*, then wrote "Biranek" on the outside with a thick black pen. It was like having a vague idea for a research project and putting away one or two relevant notes or technical articles. Time and again, they would be forgotten or abandoned.

Not in this case, though; this research would have to be worked at, an investigation into his own gargantuan stupidity.

No doubt the material on Blanchard's website would slowly trickle into the mainstream media. It was the kind of thing journalists dreamt of, both scandal and substance. A large bequest for a hospital was a story of import. That the donor was a baddie, forcing his future wife to part with her two-year-old daughter and later behaving appallingly when the wife fell ill, magnified the interest. And, to top it all, he seemed to have been implicated in her death. A villain.

Sarah called him back shortly before ten. The entire township was talking about the piece in the *Post*, and she'd already read the related write-up on Blanchard's website. The big shock, of course, was Mary Lambert. Most people didn't believe Rose had a daughter. They said somebody must be posing as her daughter to get hold of *their money*. "It isn't Biranek's money anymore," Sarah laughed. "It's our money now." She wasn't as surprised as many in the township, because once – in her mid-teens – she'd heard Elma Mulligan mention the child Rose had had before she got married.

"You knew Rose had a daughter?"

"I think I heard it. Once. I hope I'm not imagining things. Miles, it's fifty years back."

What Sarah found odd was that Elma hadn't told other people about Mary, though it was possible she had and no one believed her. And Hollie, oh, poor Hollie. At the bank that afternoon, the talk in the queue was all about Hollie. She might not yet have seen the article or the story online about Biranek's bequest. Her windows were dark, which meant she was away.

He interrupted her again. "Sarah, did you tell the story to anyone? Ever?"

"Tell what?"

"What we both saw the weekend Rose died. What once you told Dad."

There was a brief pause. "No one."

"You're sure?"

"Yes. Why?"

"Did Dad?"

"Dad? I doubt it. Why?"

"I'll read you one sentence from the blog. 'The death of Dr. Biranek's first wife might not have been an unfortunate accident.'"

There was silence at the end of the line. "Do you think it's related to what we saw?" Sarah said.

"How could it not be? Have you heard anybody else saying Rose was killed?"

"Elma Mulligan."

"I'm serious, Sarah."

"So am I. Anyway, I think it's a shot in the dark."

"It's the crux of the whole piece, its core. Don't you see?"

"Who's this Lyle Blanchard?"

"A former *Post* journalist. He writes for them now and then."

"Blanchard himself doesn't believe it. He says it sounds far-fetched, doesn't he?"

"Then why put it in there? Why include something that would make him look ridiculous later? He's like a clever novelist, ending a chapter with the promise of exciting things to come."

More silence from his sister. She was digesting what he'd said.

Might as well confess to what was really upsetting him. "The thing is, Sarah, well, your brother is an idiot . . . *I* told the story. I did."

"You mean . . ."

"Yes. I shouldn't have, I know. I never thought . . . I had several glasses of wine, true. They loved it."

"They?"

"There were four of us."

"Christ. Where?"

"In Toronto."

"When was that?"

"Three months ago, in a restaurant."

"Who were you with?"

"Ben. His wife, Jennifer. Lyn Collins, a woman who works with Jen at the Bank of Nova Scotia. Jen's boss, it seems."

"No one else?"

"No."

"This woman, Lyn or whatever, was she particularly interested in your story?"

"No more than the others. Jen seemed to enjoy it a lot . . . Ben liked it too, undoubtedly because he knew or had heard of the people involved in it."

"What do you know of Lyn?"

"Nothing. Big shot at Scotiabank, from what Ben says."

"Did she ask a lot of questions?"

"I don't remember . . . I had a lot to drink."

"It's either her or the Paskows. One of them spread your story."

"What a fuckup. Jesus."

"Relax, Miles."

"Relax? The story about Rose's death suddenly gets spread around. And it reaches . . . I don't know who it reaches, but clearly Blanchard heard it. I have no idea how. And he knows I'm the source."

"Not a given."

"You'll see. Some people in the township know too, or they'll soon find out. And they'll lynch me when that happens. I won't be able to show my face up there again. I'll be the Toronto asshole who suddenly remembered something he imagined thirty-five years ago as a child. The bastard who robbed them of twelve million dollars – no, more than that, if you count the money the provincial government promised to kick in."

"It will never come to that."

"They'll lynch you too."

"Me?"

"The thing is, Sarah . . ."

"Yes?"

"I might have mentioned you too."

"What?"

"I'm not sure. As I said, I had a lot to drink. Jen was late, and Ben and I had many glasses. And after I finished the story, someone said, 'Oh, something seen thirty-five years ago by you, a twelve-year-old boy, it has no weight at all,' and I said there was another witness there, an adult . . . and . . . and I might have mentioned you."

"Miles! You keep me out of this!"

"Well, it's not as if—"

"You keep me out of this, do you hear?"

"I'm not sure I mentioned you. Not sure at all. I don't remember. I think it was Lyn, yes, it was her, who asked me who the other witness was, but Ben needed to pee, and he was kind of legless, you know how he gets when he drinks, and I went with him, and . . . I simply don't remember if I told her."

"Would Ben remember?"

"I doubt it. Perhaps Jen."

"You better check with her. You're right, they'll lynch me. And, unlike you, I live in Corby Falls."

"Aren't you in Caledon now?"

"I live here!" she shouted. "I'm keeping the house and live here!"

The following evening he drove an annoyed Katelyn to her friend's house.

"Is Mom still talking about the move to Paris?" he asked on the way.

She stared reproachfully at him. "Yes."

"A lot?"

Katelyn shrugged.

"With Greg?"

"Yes."

"What are they saying?"

"You know I can't tell you what they talk about."

"Help me, Katelyn."

"Not this way."

She was more mature than he was. More principled too.

"Do *you* want to go?" he asked.

"To France?"

"Yes. Do you want to live for a few years in Paris?"

"Dad, I've already told you. I don't care."

"When you first mentioned this to me you seemed taken by the idea."

"I'm less now."

"I don't believe you."

"Whatever you and Mom decide is fine with me. Strict neutrality."

He laughed. "Where did you get that, *strict neutrality?*"

"From a friend."

"Who?"

"A friend of Martha's. Her parents have split too, and she swears by it. Never take sides, she says."

"What do *you* want?"

"You heard me."

"Say Mom and I were back together and I was offered a job in France, and Mom was keen on going provided you were too. Your decision. Would you want to go?"

"You won't trick me."

"I think you'd like to. You'd like to live there."

"If you know already, why do you ask?"

Yes, he knew. Federica had filled her mind with notions about the beauty and charm of Paris, but his daughter didn't want to hurt him. Didn't want to hurt her mother either.

"I don't want to be away from you, Katelyn."

"You can visit. Paid visits, from what I heard."

That was it, a clear statement of what she really wished. "Does Greg know?"

"Know what?"

"About this offer of paid visits."

She seemed puzzled by the question. "I guess . . . I don't know."

"What kind of person is he?"

"Greg? Is that why you didn't let me take the subway? To ask me about Greg?"

"No, of course not. I just want to know."

"Why?"

"I'm curious."

"You've met him."

"It's always polite drivel between us."

"Mom says you've known him for years."

"I've never talked to him. I mean, proper talk."

"Why don't you ask Mom?"

"You know why, Katelyn."

She sighed, exasperated. "Greg's all right. Like you, I don't know him that well." After a while, as if relieved she'd found something to say, she added, "I think he bores Mom."

He nodded as if he had expected that. Stupidly, it made him feel good. He wasn't still in love with Federica – well, not much anyway – and they'd been living apart for two years, yet he was glad she found Greg dull. Such vanity.

"What makes you think so?"

She shrugged. "Perhaps not bored. Sometimes, you know, her face . . . gets tense when she listens to him. It's not what he says, more at how long-winded he is."

The traffic was slow, and he was glad. At home, it was hard to pin Katelyn down for such a conversation; she'd fly to her room claiming she had work to do. But now, unexpectedly, she carried on. "I don't know. Perhaps I'm the one that's exasperated and think Mom is too. All that fiscal policy stuff . . . He's not often there, anyway. He works long hours, and Mom too. And on weekends he's at the cottage. And not just summer weekends."

"With you and Mom."

"Not always. He's there throughout the year. Works better there – gets the necessary solitude, he says."

"What does he talk about?"

"Sorry?"

"Well, what does Greg talk about? At the dinner table, for example, when the three of you are together."

"I don't know, Dad. His work. Taxes. Golf. His students. His cases – well, his former cases. The cottage. Music. He likes music. He's very clever, you know."

"Do they talk about books?"

"Books?"

"Yes, books to read. You know – literature, writers. Proust. Mom was deep into Proust once."

"Not usually."

"Does he bore you?" She'd already told him that, but he wanted to hear it again.

She touched his hand lightly. "Poor old Dad. Why is Greg so much on your mind?"

Yes, he thought on the drive back, poor old Dad. Poor old Dad, who got a kick hearing that his former wife's husband was, in the opinion of a fourteen-year-old, a bore. Embarrassing. Proust must have said something about having such an absurd reaction. He'd said everything about everything. Or had he? Could it be that he, Miles Rueda, had serendipitously landed on the one topic on which Proust held no opinion? He'd win a prize of some sort if that was the case. Federica might know. He should ask her. "*Federica, chérie, est-ce que Proust a ecrit sur le plaisir qu'on a . . .*" Mordant. A pity his paltry French wouldn't let him finish the question. He should work on it, complete the sentence, and then try it out next time he drove Katelyn to Federica's mansion. Preferably within Greg's hearing.

It was Ben who picked up the phone. Yes, he'd seen Blanchard's write-up in the *Post* and had duly read the related entry on his website. "I was going to call you, Miles. Your silly story at Le Paradis seems less silly now." Ben's voice contained a note of irony. "Odd coincidence, wouldn't you say? Such imagination. I had too much to drink, true, but I enjoyed listening to you. Some doubted the memory of a twelve-year-old, if I recall, but not me. What's the point in querying a good yarn? I didn't remember how the argument ended. Jen had to remind me. Jen, by the way, is quite excited."

"Listen . . . you didn't repeat my silly story, by any chance, did you?"

"Tell others? No."

"Good. Keep it that way. You mustn't repeat it, Ben. I was drunk and didn't know what I was saying. All right? Let me talk to Jen."

Jen remembered the end of Miles's story and his mentioning another witness, a grownup. But no, he had not named him. Or her. She wasn't entirely sure why. "So, Miles, who was this adult witness of yours?"

"No one."

"Come on, Miles."

"I made it up, Jen. I drink and make up stories."

"Oh, I think there's more to it than that. Ben showed me that blog – Blanchard's, or whatever the name was. Too much of a coincidence."

"A product of my disturbed mind."

"I don't believe you."

"Jen, do me a favour, a huge favour. Forget my story and don't talk to anyone about it."

She was silent for a while. "You're serious, aren't you?"

"I am. That boss of yours, Lyn Collins, did she say anything?"

"Like what?"

"Did she comment on my story? Say, the next time you saw her."

"No. Well, she said it had been an interesting evening, but otherwise, no. She wondered whether you drank a lot."

Three days later the *Globe and Mail* had a short article on Dr. Biranek's bequests. For Katelyn's sake, Miles had kept an old subscription to the *Globe* since his days with Federica. One of Katelyn's teachers told Federica, who in turn told him, that children needed a newspaper at home. He rarely spent more than ten minutes reading the *Globe* the evenings he picked it up. Don called him a news troglodyte. Yet now he was getting the *Post* as well as the *Globe*. Every weekday morning on his way to work he'd stop on the drive to the highway to get the *Post* from one of the orange boxes on Eglinton. He'd have dinner scouring both papers for anything related to the Biranek bequests and did the same sipping his Saturday morning coffee after running out to get the *Post*.

He was more worried about Blanchard's website, checking it two or three times a day. And exactly two weeks after Don pointed to him the article in the *Post*, a new entry appeared on the website. It was just what he had feared. The new entry had an ominous heading: "Now Murder." It repeated some of the material of the earlier entry and ended with the dreaded blow.

The facts leading to the death of Rose Biranek, Dr. Biranek's first wife, are now in doubt. When she died, thirty-five years ago, her husband, Dr. Biranek, had been away with Hollie McGinnes, his office nurse and future wife. Alone in the Biraneks' house in Corby Falls, Rose – long a sufferer of MS – had a fall on the stairs leading to the ground floor. According to the coroner's report (quoted in the *Millcroft Gazette* at the time), Rose was badly hurt, suffering severe fractures as a result. The folding doors to the doctor's waiting room happened to be open, and she managed to drag herself in there. She died twenty-four to thirty hours later, alone, unable to move any farther or call for help.

Rose died late on Sunday evening or on Sunday night, and her body was found by Dr. Biranek returning home the morning of the following day. He'd been expected to get back to Corby Falls early on Saturday; unfortunately for Rose, he had delayed his return by two days. Here is the startling news: someone has recently surfaced whose recollections of that weekend suggest foul play. I don't know who this someone is or the exact nature of the foul play. Not yet.

For a week now I've tried to talk to Mary Lambert, the daughter Rose gave away for adoption before she married Dr. Biranek. My calls were not returned, and when I waited for her in front of her house she shouted she had nothing to say to me. Meanwhile I've learned – more startling news – that Mary Lambert drove to Millcroft and talked to the mayor of the township at least twice in the last three months. I went back to Millcroft to make inquiries. Alas, Mayor Locksley wasn't willing to answer questions regarding either Mary Lambert or Dr. Biranek's bequests. (Should we begin talking of a Biranek Affair?) I cornered her in Millcroft Township Hall as she came out of her office, and told her I knew that someone, a witness, had new facts about Rose Biranek's death. I asked her if she knew who this someone was. "A madman," she snapped. "Only a madman could have such allegations after thirty-five years, someone desperate for notoriety. It's absurd, laughable." I asked her for a name, and she didn't answer. I asked how she knew it was a man. She said she knew nothing about any witness and had meant simply that only a mad person, man or woman, could pretend to have any new information after so many years.

As the mayor was moving away, I shouted, "I know you've met with Mary Lambert. And not just once. What have you discussed?" She stopped briefly, clearly startled, then said she had no time for silly questions. She was not in a good mood, Mayor Locksley, and had some spicy words for me before she disappeared into another room. I'll spare my readers.

This investigation will continue. I'll look for this unknown witness and find out what he or she saw or heard. I'm certain the "someone desperate for notoriety" was a witness to the events – or some of them – surrounding Rose Biranek's death. I think the mayor knows who the witness is, and from her initial outburst – "a madman" – I'm beginning to think the witness is a man. I'm not entirely sure, of course, but it's a good assumption. He is, obviously, someone who, at the time of Rose's death, lived in Corby Falls and knew the Biraneks.

The whole interaction with Thula rang false. Would she have been such a fool? Did Blanchard take some liberties with what he reported was said in the exchange? He clearly knew a lot more and was taking his time, revealing it gradually, unhurriedly, like a cat playing with a mouse before devouring it. He knew who the witness was, the *someone*, and was holding back. He'd fully exploit his so-called search and clever deductions.

A photo of Mary Lambert accompanied the entry. A slightly plump face, with the sad half-smile of one who knows full smiles are not for the likes of her; straight dark hair, almost shoulder length, parted somewhere atop, covering a corner of her right eye. In the photo, Mary Lambert was a thirty-something-year-old woman, though by Miles's calculations she would now be over sixty. Where on earth did Lyle Blanchard get it? Underneath, he read that Mary Lambert worked as a dental technician somewhere on Queen Street East, was divorced or separated from her husband, and had a son, now thirty years old or thereabouts. Rather sparse information, clearly not obtained directly from the subject.

The first reader's comment on the "Now Murder" entry was posted three days later.

> You are right to describe the new facts as startling. What's harder to believe, though, is that those trying to block Dr. Biranek's bequests are helped by one of us, someone who lives or has lived in Corby Falls. One of us who doesn't want a better hospital for our township, or a safe roof over the heads of St. Anselm's churchgoers. We don't know who this *one of us* is. We will. No doubt something is terribly wrong with him and needs correcting.
>
> D.N., Corby Falls

Was D.N. one of Mayor Locksley's friends who wrote at her dictation? He should ask Sarah whether she knew of a D.N. in Corby Falls; the last sentence was clearly a warning addressed to him.

Another comment appeared the following day.

> The Millcroft hospital desperately needs the funding from Dr. Biranek's bequest. Our daughter gave birth in the hospital recently, and it reminded us of a third world country. We don't understand why there seem to be doubts as to the availability of funding from Dr. Biranek's bequests. This is distressing.
>
> Melinda Chu, Millcroft

He printed the two comments and put them in the blue folder. He wished he could read the coroner's report from Rose Biranek's death. How did one get a copy?

On Sunday evening, with Katelyn gone, he felt low. He wished he could talk to someone else about the jam he was in. Sarah had been relieved when he repeated to her the conversation he'd had with Jennifer, and showed little patience for his worries now. She kept dismissing them, a habit undoubtedly born of dealing with a much younger brother she'd had to endure. For a brief moment he considered having a drink with the always available Don. Ludicrous.

He rummaged for a drinkable drink in Laukhin's liquor cabinet and found an almost full bottle of *vieille prune* in the lower part, behind the dusty remnants of the sweet crap Federica had favoured. It must have been there for years. He tasted it. *Vieille prune* wasn't bad at all, though perhaps not ideal for achieving quick numbness. The night before, he'd downed the last four fingers of whisky.

An empty liquor cabinet, effectively. Laukhin would have choked. Would Ben join him for a drink? No, not Ben. One couldn't properly drink and talk with him; Ben would fall asleep, not to mention his censorious stares and head-shaking. He would not approve of Miles's excess. And it was excess that Miles needed, besides empathy.

The *vieille prune* was growing on him. He'd been rash doubting it. A golden, refined liquid which made the future interesting and vaguely comic. It wouldn't be long before his name would be in Blanchard's blog. And from there in the *Post* and all the newspapers. They'd soon zero in on him, a neighbour of the Biraneks at the time of Rose's death. Who else could have seen something that weekend? Only a neighbour, and the Ruedas had been neighbours then and were still now.

What of the other neighbours? The house to the right of the Biraneks' as one looked from River Street had been empty for years. Miles remembered playing with Jim Cowley in the overgrown backyard and being caught there by an angry Hank Moray who had been trying to sell that property. Mr. Moray's father-in-law owned that property. And the house to the left of the Biraneks'? A blank, or almost. Miles vaguely recalled an older couple and the intermittent presence of some small children. Across River Street? The Collards. Yes, he remembered them. How could he not? Hank Moray's in-laws. Jeremiah Collard (Jeremiah? – something biblical and long) was the richest man in Corby Falls and lived in the large buff-brick house built on the river by Miles's Westbrook great-grandfather. Another daughter of the Collards, a sister of Hank Moray's wife, lived with them now and then, a periodic refugee from an abusive husband.

No, this speculation of his didn't matter, because Blanchard knew already – had always known – who the "one of us" was, the one who had something "terribly wrong with him."

In the end he did ring Sarah. She came on the line as he was leaving her a message.

"I didn't think you were home," he said. "What took you so long?"

"I was sorting out my babies – what to take with me and what to keep here. I'm tempted to go by weight."

"Have you seen the latest entry?"

"Seen it."

"The comments too?"

"Yes. I'm surprised there were only two."

"The town must be buzzing."

"There aren't heaps of blog readers here."

"Anything in the *Gazette*?"

"No."

"Are people still talking to you?"

She laughed. "A couple."

"They're preparing the lynching, stealthily. I mean my lynching."

"Don't be silly."

"What startled me are Mary Lambert's trips to Millcroft. How does Blanchard know?"

"Somebody in the mayor's entourage is talking."

"Things are unfolding the way I predicted. Exactly. Slow disclosure until my name is revealed. I'm sure everybody knows by now that the *one of us* is me."

"Miles . . . How would they?"

"How did it go? Let me read it, I have it handy. 'One of us who doesn't want a better hospital for our township, or a safe roof over the heads of St. Anselm's churchgoers . . . No doubt something is terribly wrong with him and needs correcting.' *Him*, Sarah. D.N. has no doubt it's a man. What correction do you think they have in mind?" When Sarah didn't answer, he had another question. "Who the fuck is this D.N. anyway?"

"Are you drinking, Miles?"

"I'm sipping *vieille prune*. Wait. Something called Vieille Prune Bertrand. Highly recommended. Who's this D.N., Sarah?"

"I don't know."

"Can't you think of anyone with those initials in Corby Falls?"

"I've tried to figure that one out. The only person I know is Dave Nicholls, and he's eighty-two years old and has Alzheimer's. His wife's name is Donna, and she's not any younger. I doubt she reads blogs. I've asked around and I'll keep on asking."

"What a disaster. What an utter calamity."

Sarah's silence told him she thought he was making too much of the whole thing.

"How is permanent companionship?" he said.

"Trying. I'm finding reasons to return home. Five days is the best yet."

"You've travelled with him, and for longer than that."

"It's not the same. Oh, Jim wants to talk to you."

"Jim Cowley?"

"We bumped into each other in Millcroft. He still calls me Mrs. Grommel."

"All he has to do is ring me."

"He wants to sniff you over. He wondered when you'd be visiting Corby Falls next. A good question – when are you driving up?"

"For the lynching?"

"Yes."

"I don't know. End of the month? By then my name will be everywhere, the *one of us* fully identified."

"Jim said you must give him a call when you come up."

"Did I ever fail to?"

Vieille Prune Bertrand – who on earth brought that bottle? He held a short pious thought for Laukhin, as the poet's will requested of him, and then wondered if the bottle of *vieille prune* could have been one of Darius Milo's old offerings to Federica and left in Laukhin's cherished cabinet together with her limoncellos and Drambuies. Would it have lasted so long?

He should be grateful to Darius Milo, because it was thanks to him that he was in a better mood now. He had to concede that dutiful Bertrand met all the requirements. The temporary peace, the illusion of sharp insights, the mawkishness. The invasion of absurdity too, although this whole mess *was* the peak of absurdity and Bertrand's contribution wasn't needed. Ha. For thirty-five years he hadn't even known what he knew.

Chapter 7

September 2005

Moving stealthily in the dark, he tiptoed into the bathroom, carefully shut the door, and then switched on the light. The habits acquired during almost twenty years with Federica were not easily discarded. It took him a while before he fully opened his eyes. As he brushed his teeth – "always from the root to the tip, to prevent stripping the gums off," had been the dental hygienist's edict – he remembered that he'd be meeting Dr. Chu that morning. Would Dr. Chu approve of his newly acquired technique?

Dr. Chu had ended his last email with "one tiny request." After his visit to Ludwig Robotics, Chu would be flying to Montreal to see an aunt he was fond of. Would Miles have a useful contact at the Canadian Space Agency, somebody interested in the sampling of planetary soil? If he was already going to be in Montreal, Dr. Chu would like to make a demonstration at the agency.

Miles first became aware of Dr. Chu from a voicemail message four months earlier. After he repeated Miles's name several times, Dr. Chu introduced himself and mentioned his affiliation with the Hong Kong Institute of Technology. He had got Miles's name and phone number from Larry Barsoum at the Jet Propulsion Laboratory. Dr. Chu said he would be travelling to North America soon – demonstrations in Pasadena again, and Houston – and would like to stop in Toronto as well. The last time Dr. Chu was at JPL, Larry Barsoum had told him that Ludwig Robotics might be interested in the work Dr. Chu was doing in grasping tools for planetary exploration. "Special, delicate work," Dr. Chu had added after a pause, and Miles was left uncertain whether the last words were the end of Larry Barsoum's opinion, or Dr. Chu's own views. Dr. Chu proposed the date of June 15 for his visit. "Smack in the middle of the month," he had shouted excitedly. Would Miles confirm his availability? The message was broken up by what Miles took to be traffic noises, as if Dr. Chu were speaking from a phone booth on one of Hong Kong's crowded streets.

He ignored that first message from Dr. Chu. The following Monday there had been another one. In a wounded tone Dr. Chu reminded Mr. Rueda that he had only a few days before flying over and needed to make the final travelling arrangements.

Miles had called George Szetes. "A Dr. Chu from Hong Kong is pestering me for a visit here on the fifteenth. I'm away that day, George, and so is Mohan. Could you entertain the good doctor? I'll ask Don Verbrugge to support you."

"I'm busy, Miles. This impossible proposal—"

"It's at most an hour."

"Why me?"

"The proposal you're working on, the Canadian Mars Mission. He's into tools for planetary exploration. There is definitely an overlap."

"What kind of tools?"

"Soil sampling."

"You don't say. We might have enough money to land a flag. A small one at that."

"Be positive, George."

"You'll talk to Don?"

"I will. He'll do the talking. You know how marketing men are."

Don was interested in any potential development, however remote or miraculous. That, he claimed, was his mantra. He would also, Miles reflected slyly, offset George's surliness.

A stocky man with a white ponytail, George was fond of bow ties. He told people he was a "fifty-sixer" – a description that mostly aroused confusion or grins and comments like "à *chacun son goût.*" Although in Canada since a relatively young age, he retained a resilient, if light, accent and bizarre lexical choices. His favourite topic of conversation, besides managers as arrogant dimwits, was the Austro-Hungarian Empire and the tragic effects of its collapse on the course of European history. There was no doubt George was deranged. A volcano of rightful indignation smoldered continually within his broad chest, and it often erupted. This, and his sarcasm, had stalled his career. He was in charge of the CMM proposal because he was organized, careful – some said nitpicking – and technically brilliant. Yet his views were often disregarded.

The sight of George in the cafeteria the day Miles came back from his trip reminded him of Dr. Chu's visit. George was eating a sandwich while reading a stapled sheaf of papers. He brought his own sandwiches, always with a red-brownish layer of something between slices of rye bread. He claimed that the concoction filling the sandwich, whose composition Miles once knew, had a soothing effect on his ulcers.

"Tell me about Dr. Chu, George," Miles said, setting down the tray with his lunch across from him.

George lifted his eyes slowly toward Miles. He minded being interrupted, and Miles could sense the hot lava making its way up George's throat.

"Dr. Chu?" George looked around as if weighing his chances of hitting Miles without witnesses. "Did you already talk to Don? No, I think not."

He set the papers on the table, took his glasses off, wiped the corners of his mouth with a napkin, put his glasses back on, and leaned forward. "It was a seminal visit, Miles, one of those meetings that turns a company around. And we know, don't we, this company needs turning."

George leaned back and began to rock in his chair as if waiting to be prompted to carry on.

"Well," Miles said gently.

"He's a dentist."

"Huh?"

"A dentist, Miles. Dr. Chu is a doctor in dentistry. Oh, I presume he's affiliated in some way with whatever university in Hong Kong he claims he is. His wares are surgical pliers, claws, forceps, and suchlike. Mind you, with a heavy and not fully surprising bias toward teeth-pulling. He spends his free time devising monstrous claws, probably meant to extract entire jaws. That's how he gets his jollies. Not dangerous. He thinks that by enlarging some of his tooth forceps, he'll get tools that would come in handy in space. You should have seen the pamphlet he had with him. Good God, you would have thought that planetary exploration was a branch of dentistry. How exactly was he found, this Dr. Chu of yours, Miles? Who discovered him? One of the imbecile members of the board of directors? A consultant, somebody from Ernst & Young? I mean, if empowerment was a flop, let's give dentistry a try."

The leek soup was still hot and Miles twirled the spoon in it. "Do you still have Dr. Chu's pamphlet?"

"Now, why would I keep it, Miles? Why would I keep a dentist's pamphlet? Give me one good reason. No need to worry, though, he will send us another one. He promised – yes, he did – updated with Canadian content. You know why, Miles? I'll tell you why. Because Dr. Chu is now doing some technical consulting for us."

George paused skillfully, and Miles sighed and nudged him along. "Go on."

"He's gaga about space, your doctor. He wants to make something, a contribution, however minute, toward – yes, I know this sounds jejune – the advancement of planetary exploration. I say *he*, but he often said 'they' – *they* wish to do this; *they* are finishing that – so there might be an entire gang of unhinged dentists out there in Hong Kong. I didn't exactly ask for clarification. He begged us to give him, them, whoever, something to do. So I did."

"You what?"

"I did. Don't worry, we don't have to pay him. I don't think he's after our dollars, although I did not directly query him on this delicate subject."

"What, for heaven's sake, did you ask him to do, George?"

George Szetes duckbilled his lips, delighted by Miles's distress. He produced strange noises in his throat. "Hmmm. Let's see. Hmmm. You remember the 'alignment lever' interface? Surely you remember it, Miles, the one I worked on until NASA's idiot-savants turned their thumbs down on it. I gave him a couple of drawings and told him it's not working as well as we would like it to. I told him that we were at an impasse and might drop the concept altogether. 'Fix it, Dr. Chu,' I said to him. 'Make it work.' Yes, yes, Miles, I know, it's been abandoned. I have to say, humbly, that it was mainly Don's idea; he suggested it. A brilliant thought. Everybody is happy. Dr. Chu was ecstatic. He did not know how to thank Don. He felt less indebted to me, I think. Mind you, I might not have been very friendly toward Dr. Chu. He got on much better with Don. Oh, he loves Don. You think Don's angling for a trip to Hong Kong? Never mind. Have a chat with Don Verbrugge."

The light from the bathroom dug a bright shaft in the darkness. Near the bed, fumbling for his wristwatch, he stumbled on the book he'd left open on the floor the night before. A book – with Federica's words written on the title page, "Bon anniversaire, mon amour" – about the consequential sixteenth century and Fernão de Magalhães, the Portuguese explorer known to his crew as the *capitán-general*, who became famous among English speakers as Magellan.

Federica used to complain about Miles switching the light on and the noise he made getting up. His morning ablutions, therefore, were performed with the bathroom door strictly shut. Afterwards he would get dressed in the dim light drifting by the door left barely ajar. With Federica still in bed, Miles would then switch off the bathroom light before leaving the bedroom, though not before imprinting into his brain the location of the doorknob he'd have to reach and twist, ever so delicately, in order to leave. Most times, he found the knob spot-on and was dumbfounded by this bizarre gift of his. At his funeral – Miles was convinced he'd die first – Federica would lean toward Greg and say, puzzled, "He had an uncanny ability to locate doorknobs in the dark."

On Eglinton he stopped at a *Post* box and scooped a paper. Back in the car, he quickly scanned the main section. No new piece from Lyle Blanchard. On the way to Allen Road, he tried to guess when and where the next blow would come. Likely on the website first. The newspaper seemed reluctant to follow up on the story of the bequests from Dr. Biranek. Hard to understand. The speculation on Rose Biranek's death apart, there was a good story there, with the discovery of her daughter and her recent mysterious trips to Millcroft. Her cruel abandonment at a tender age too. And the interview with Elma Mulligan, perhaps pared down, had plenty of draw in it. Plenty of punch as well. Perhaps the newspaper needed more time to decide what was publishable from Blanchard's blog, with the necessary editorial tweaks. It didn't matter much now, anyway, as the *Post* readers attracted to the story already knew that Blanchard's website was the place with the juicy parts.

That early in the morning the highway was empty. Night still draped the city, punctured at intervals by the high-mast lights. The Corolla seemed rejuvenated by the cool air and made an encouraging swishing sound. He might get another year with her. On CBC, an Australian rebroadcast was prattling on about deficit worries, aid to Indonesia, and a new shearing device less traumatic to sheep. Hallelujah.

Miles was at his desk shortly after five o'clock. A parking spot close to the back door was one benefit of arriving very early. The geese were also sleepy, or less agitated, and the poop-avoidance trip was shorter. Although always an early riser, he had a particular reason to arrive at work with the cleaning crew today. He'd leave Ludwig at three thirty in the afternoon so that by four thirty he could be in Dr. Dermer's familiar office, entrenched in one of his armchairs. Federica would already be there. She'd always been there first, either waiting for Dermer's previous session to finish or already in his office. It was their first reunion in front of Dr. Dermer after giving up two years earlier. For three years they had tried, and for a while there was an inkling of progress. Dr. Dermer told Miles from the beginning to cut down on his drinking, and he had. He'd been drinking less anyway with Katelyn growing up. The doctor tried to convince him that there was a factual truth and an emotional truth, and that the latter was likely behind what Miles called Federica's exaggerations. That minor progress in their relationship, though, turned out to be a "sessions placebo" effect, and in the last of their three years of counselling Miles had just gone through the motions. He had sat there in Dr. Dermer's office, side by side with Federica but not reaching her. *Side by side* might not be quite right. Their armchairs were at a slight angle to each other and their sights converged on Dr. Dermer. Conducting the weekly sessions from a swivel chair, Dr. Dermer pursued his task of healing their marital hurts, although mostly he had seemed adept, in a soft spoken and smiling way, at producing venom. For, as Federica catalogued Miles's failures, the bitterness accrued in a disappointing marriage would pour out through her lips and hit Miles's ears – he had always thought of it this way, otherwise he could not explain the pain – in a solid, rock-like state, as if Dr. Dermer had a strengthening influence on intermolecular forces.

The first thing he did was check his voice mail. He also nudged his computer mouse a fraction of an inch so that the fishes – he might be the last man on earth with this Jurassic screensaver – disappeared to reveal that he had seven new emails. Meanwhile the voice messages were beginning to spill out. From Mohan, a confirmation of a teleconference the next day at 9 A.M. with Astrium. That meant 2 P.M. in Stevenage. Also from Mohan, a request to postpone the teleconference on teaming with Alenia on a minor study for the Sample Retrieval Mission, the lesser or later mission in ESA's Ares Initiative. In a discursive message, Enrico Viale, the lead at ESA for the Ares Rover, wanted to have a chat on wheel-walking and suggested as an afterthought that Ludwig might be interested in the work being done at DLR on wheel flexibility. He ended by saying he'd send him an email. Someone whose name Miles didn't catch, in a *laboratoire* in Toulouse, had thoughts or software on rover navigation. Both? He too said he'd send an email. The personnel department had left a voice message as well, and so had Federica, reminding him of the session with Dr. Dermer that afternoon.

Then Miles read the email messages, many of them responses to responses to responses, and by the time he finished, with some answers, it was already seven thirty. He leaned back in his chair, gazed at the ceiling with arms stretched up, and then with a sigh picked up the draft invitation to tender on the Sample Retrieval Mission. He'd have to make up his mind on this one by the end of the day. Fifty thousand dollars, and a lot of work for that paltry amount. Ludwig would not make money on it; they might even have to fork out a few coins And going with Alenia on this? Astrium would wrinkle their nose. Ah, the slow round of dances with different partners every time a new invitation to tender was released. Same groups of dancers, showing various degrees of vigour and poise, all depending on the amount dropped in ESA's purse by their governments. Not worth it, this retrieval mission, unless it was an investment in ESA's Ares Initiative. Get some benevolence for the rover mission. Fat chance, with Ludwig betting on the Canadian Mars Mission pipedream.

Dr. Chu's pamphlet arrived two months after the conversation with George in the company cafeteria. It came with a short letter and a wooden proto-type. In the letter, Dr. Chu talked about the "improvements to the alignment lever concept, already tested and incorporated within the prototype." Dr. Chu hoped that "your scientists will quickly assess the improvements we have made and give it the go-ahead." He also hoped the prototype was not sent too late and that "the alignment lever interface will now find a home with the Space Station boxes."

The pamphlet was large, three feet by four; it was printed on both sides and unfolded like a city map. One side announced, in large letters, the "Chu-Zhao Space Grasphold* Concept." The asterisk sent the reader to a footnote explaining the portmanteau word through an equality: "grasphold = grasp + hold." It also told the reader that the concept has been patented. Dr. Chu and Dr. Zhao were, Miles inferred, the principal investigators. Other team members contributed, all doctors of some sort. Professor K.L. Chan, a Nobel Prize winner for physics, was the "Scientific Adviser." The two principals and the Nobel laureate appeared in a small photograph. Dr. Chu's hands seemed to be forming a scoop, while the Nobel Prize winner was keenly listening. Dr. Zhao, who likely had seen the scoop before, was staring somewhere into space. And above the photograph, yes, there it was, the "New Alignment Lever, designed for passive anchor and lock onto cargo boxes delivered by Canada arms."

A large heading explained what most of the illustrations were about: "Mars End-Effectors, capable of precise telerobotic rock/soil sampling for return to Earth." There were pictures of Mars I, Mars II, and Mars III grippers, grim looking, as if designed by brooding medieval minds. On the side, vertical golden words advertised the quality of "Persistent Gripping." There were pictures captioned "Gripping Large Rocks," "Gripping Medium Rocks," "Gripping Small Rocks," and "Gripping Rocks of Any Shape and Size."

Miles's favourite caption, the one that stopped his breath for a moment, had a serene, almost campestral quality: "Picking Samples While Strolling on Mars." The photo showed two simple claws at the end of a long stick, with a rock between the claws. Miles pictured himself arm in arm with Federica, picking rock samples on a pleasant stroll on Mars. Federica carried a picnic basket with goat cheese and a bottle of California zin. She wore an off-white dress, loose, mind-teasing, under which, Miles was convinced, her body swayed for him. Federica's allure made Miles miss some fine rock specimens, although his job was effortless; he didn't even have to bend, thanks to the nifty device provided by Dr. Chu. Behind them, also arm in arm, were Dr. Chu and Dr. Dermer. Dr. Chu gave Miles brief instructions and made encouraging sounds. Dr. Dermer was more intent on Miles's and Federica's body language. The places he had to travel, poor Dr. Dermer, for his patients.

The theme on the other side of the large pamphlet, again proclaimed in vertical golden words, was "Under Zero Gravity." There must have been two hundred small photographs – each with an explanation – of medical instruments

and devices. Some devices turned out to reside already on-board the
Russian Mir station, hanging, if Miles understood the caption properly, from
the belts of the station dwellers. After some search for a common thread
Miles decided that most of the devices were meant to simplify life for the
crew up there in space. They allowed the "attachment of things" so that they
didn't "float or get lost" and were "handily available at the opportune time."
The best was the "Watch Adapter," which, as the caption said, provided "a
transparent suction cup – reading unobsoured [*sic*] – for attachment to astronaut watch." Scanning further, Miles found attachments to finger rings. Ear-
lobes were opportune mooring points too. One ear accessory was called the
"Ear Lobe Removable Mini-Carrier." Under the picture of a red and hairy
earlobe, the advantage of the mini-carrier was simply explained: "Nikolay
Kalchev, Russian cosmonaut, pierced his ear. The most secure removable
mini-carrier on Mir." These Russians, Miles mumbled with admiration, they
really went all the way. There was no stopping them.

At eight o'clock, Miles walked to the cafeteria to get a cup of coffee. The
week's choice was a blend from Kenya. He wondered whether he should mix
it with a dash of the Irish Cream variety but decided against this unmanly
mélange. Back at his desk, he plunged into a report comparing Ludwig's
own Scene Modeller, still being worked on, with similar navigation software
developed in Europe. The report was long on words and short on facts, and
he was wasting his time.

At eight thirty-five, he rang Don Verbrugge. Don was at his desk and
sounded pressed for time. It quickly became obvious that Dr. Chu's visit
was not on Don's schedule for that day. With a sigh, Miles reminded Don
of Dr. Chu's return that morning and that he was counting on his support.
Don complained that he had to finish his belated capture plan for satellite
servicing. Then he paused, laughed, and added that he deserved a break and
talking again to the delightful Dr. Chu would be a pleasure he could indulge
in for a short while.

Don's availability turned out to be irrelevant, because Dr. Chu simply did
not show up. It was a relief, although Miles felt annoyed. Dr. Chu should
have called. Common courtesy.

At ten thirty, Miles went to an R&D planning meeting. He couldn't wait
for it to be over, yet it dragged on with endless chatter over the lunch hour and
broke up close to one o'clock only because there were other meetings to attend.

He grabbed a sandwich and arrived at his desk in time to listen to Mohan's
complaints about the work piling up. With two ESA studies coming to

a critical end, the new cycle in CSA's Space Technology Development Program, and with the expected ESA's invitations to tender for Phase B of the Mars rover, he was drowning or soon would be. Miles assured him that they'd get more resources if the invitations to tender were to show up soon and that he doubted their imminent arrival since the commitments of various countries to ESA's Mars projects, including Canada's, were far from being firm.

At ten minutes to two, as Miles returned to his office with a cup of Kenya blend, the receptionist called him. A visitor, Dr. Chu, was waiting for him in the lobby. After he checked the available conference rooms, Miles left Don Verbrugge a begging message for support urgently needed in room 2103. "Dr. Chu, to my immense dismay, has somehow materialized. Help." On the way to the lobby Miles uttered a soft succession of four-letter words.

Dr. Chu wore thick eyeglasses and a beard consisting of black strands timidly scattered on his chin. Perhaps all Chinese doctors were required by tradition to sport a beard. Only tradition could lead to such dismal results. Dr. Chu's moustache had more vigour. He was in his late thirties, short, plump, ruffled, and sweaty, clearly tired from a long trip.

"Dr. Chu?" Miles asked, his right hand extending in front of him as if it had a life of its own. "Miles Rueda."

"Mr. Rueda, finally meeting. I am glad, so glad. Coming from airport, directly, you know. I missed an earlier connection. Sorry for being bit late."

Bit late? Miles was ready to correct him, but Dr. Chu laughed, a laughter replete with good will and international friendship.

"You can leave your luggage here," Miles said, pointing to Dr. Chu's large, silvery suitcase, which seemed more suited for transferring bullion.

"No, no, impossible. My work here, most successful prototypes. I show them to you."

"Ah. Well, then, let me take it for you," Miles offered, expecting an amused refusal from the younger Dr. Chu. After all, Miles's hair was turning white in places. But Dr. Chu nodded and picked up a travel shoulder bag.

Miles could barely lift Dr. Chu's case – made of aluminum, he realized, when he banged his knees on it – and by the time they reached the conference room, one flight of stairs up and at the other end of the building, he was struggling for breath, his legs were shaky, and the fingers of his right hand showed red and white blotches. He began rubbing them, and Dr. Chu observed merrily, "Keeps you strong, doesn't it? Good thing. May not be good for back, though, to appear fair. I am carrying for more than a week, dozens of airports, hotels, institutions. I take any chance of break. A miracle planes don't plunge. I mean, overloaded. A joke. You all right? You look white. Like my patients look when I drill their teeth. Another joke. Can't stop myself. Too much, how you say, verbal energy."

The large conference table sported an empty coffee cup, a half-eaten dark-brown cookie that lay on a paper napkin like a giant, asymmetric cockroach, and some stapled handouts from an earlier meeting. There was no sight of Verbrugge. Miles was not sure how to start and tried to gain time by clearing the table and tempting Dr. Chu with coffee. Dr. Chu was not interested.

"Dr. Chu," Miles began gingerly, sitting down across from his visitor, "you see me at a loss . . . I am not sure what brings you here, apart from the fact that you were in the neighbourhood, so to speak." He projected on Dr. Chu the most engaging smile he was capable of. "What I mean . . . I'm not sure what else we should explore, besides what you already saw and discussed with George Szetes on your previous visit."

"George, yes. Rather sour man, not given to lateral thinking. Mr. Verbrugge, Don, is man with open mind. Mr. Rueda, your words are cloud-carrying winds. Surely there must be something we can do together. The prototype, what of the improved prototype I sent back to you? Professor K.L. Chan himself worked on the improvements. He won Nobel Prize, you know. Big scientist. Very, very big. He took quick look at drawings Mr. Szetes gave me and immediately saw what was wrong. Three improvements he made, just like that, in few hours. Raised hinge level, included an angular freeplay for the lever head, and spring-loaded the locking pins. Raising hinge level was not obvious. He did calculations – on back of envelope, ha, ha, as you engineers are fond of saying – and immediately knew where main problem was. He is very busy man, you know, low temperature physics, he can't spend much time on alignment levers."

Don Verbrugge walked in, bouncing, clearly in a good mood. With one foot out the door at Ludwig, he had become less guarded about what he said. As he and Dr. Chu beamed at each other like the best of friends, Miles became apprehensive.

"It's so good to see you, Dr. Chu," Don said, radiating joy. "How is the science of claws?"

Dr. Chu's face glowed with delight and he initiated a vigorous shaking of hands. "I was telling Mr. Rueda – oh, I call you Miles, like in America; you call me Larry – about some improvements we make to design of alignment levers. Have you incorporated them?" This last question from Dr. Chu was addressed to both Miles and Don.

Don turned to Miles. "Yes, Miles, what of it? I saw the prototype that Dr. Chu sent. Works flawlessly. You yourself had mentioned it to me the other day."

Miles sighed and inwardly swore to break Don's knees at the first opportunity. "Dr. Chu," he said, "the alignment levers have been dropped as an interface for our boxes. NASA was never comfortable with them. If there was, or there still is, some misunderstanding as to the status of the alignment levers, I apologize. They will not be used. Your improvements, and I have no doubt that the new prototype is working better, are . . . are academic."

Miles made the awkward confession with what he hoped was a disarmingly soft voice and waited to make sure that the message had sunk in. Clouds indeed were gathering on Dr. Chu's forehead and Miles feared disagreeable moments ahead. He looked at Don for help – after all, this awkward moment was his creation – but Don ignored him. Miles, desperate to fill in the heavy silence, carried on, not exactly knowing where he was going, with a lot of mumbling and repetitions. "Dr. Chu – Larry – I am somewhat perplexed . . . Let's assume that the alignment levers are revived, that there is a sudden renewed interest in them. It can happen; nothing is impossible. Unlikely, though. Right, Don? And let us assume that your improvements, say at least one of them, are retained in the final design. What then? What are your expectations? Let me be even more direct: Is it money? Because if it is, you are with the wrong company . . . no, wrong industry. It's hard to make a living building things for space. I'd say next to impossible."

Dr. Chu stared at him with incomprehension. "Money? No, not money, I assure you. Besides, you could not afford us. You could not afford me. In Hong Kong, salaries four times higher. Four times!" He held up four fingers and thrust them toward Don and Miles. "I make more money in one day drilling teeth than you pay for one week of engineering consulting here. No money. It's space, the exploration, the thrill, the flight to the planets, the flutter of alien wings. The unknown. You people don't know how privileged you are. All. You build these wonderful devices that go up there. Money, Miles? Oh, this is so silly. One of silliest things I ever hear. Who needs money in Hong Kong? No, give us chance to work on your work. Give us task – small task, anything – on some mechanical item. A screw, a humble nut even. We want contribution, however small. So far, all we do is watch TV. There are few of us, dozen, yes, around academia, interested in space. I spend my own money. This trip, paid from my pocket. An old lady, fortune teller, once said my life is connected with Mars. I know is true, must be true. One day, Mars rover will pick up sample rock to be returned to Earth with end-effector based on my design. My gripper."

The man was consumed, Miles reflected, a space fanatic. Could he be wired with explosives? What was in that heavy suitcase of his, anyway?

"I obsess," Dr. Chu went on, as if reading Miles's mind. "I am freak, space freak, as you say in America. Of course. Forceps freak too. My father tells often, 'No future in forceps.' He laugh at me. I prove him wrong." Dr. Chu paused while another cloud landed on his forehead – probably briefly confronting his father's conventional mind. "I think of space all time. Always. When I drill teeth, when I make love, when I sit on loo. Should any of my grippers make it to Mars, I die happy. Why not? Why wouldn't they make it? They are best. Look."

He lay the silver suitcase on the floor and opened it. Miles stared at a jumble of hardware and rocks of various sizes. Out came a short stick with an oversized handle at one end. What looked like an electrical motor and some transmission elements were mounted below the handle. A Black & Decker label was affixed on the motor cage. Also out of the suitcase came several grippers with sharp teeth or edges. One of them was inserted by Dr. Chu with a sturdy-sounding click into the other end of the stick. The handle had a toggle switch that Miles assumed was for opening and closing the gripper. Dr. Chu connected one end of an electrical cable to the stick and the other to one of the outlets in the room. He then began to scatter an assortment of rocks on the floor. He took a pan out of the suitcase and then a plastic bag of sand, its neck tied up with wire. He opened the bag.

"Soil," Dr. Chu said, as the sand poured into the pan.

The room had a vaguely Martian look now, and Miles prayed briefly nobody walked in. Don watched intently, mesmerized by the magician with the stick.

Dr. Chu made a final survey of the room and began his demo. "First, the rock end-effector. It pick rocks of different sizes with secure grip. The jaws, you notice, remain parallel during their travel. I'm particularly proud of this feature. The automated curvature compensation provides wraparound action. The jaws of gripper have jagged knife edges, razor sharp. Don't get your fingers caught in there! Ha, ha."

Dr. Chu gripped the nearest rock with ease and walked his catch over to the silver suitcase. He dropped the payload – by pressing a small switch on the handle, Miles guessed – and repeated the drill with a second, larger rock. He then replaced the end-effector with another one, less ominous looking. "Here, the two ends of the gripper are dishes, hollowed sphere segments, with small interlocking teeth on edge of dishes. This one grasp rocks of different shapes. Also trap soil when the two dishes are together." As he said these words, Dr. Chu dipped the end-effector into the sand with the dishes almost two inches apart and then brought the sides together. He extracted the end-effector from the sand and opened the dishes, letting a small amount of trapped sand fall back into the pan. Miles thought that war trophies were never dropped with more pride by victorious generals. "This third prototype" – and Dr. Chu inserted a new device – "can grasp rocks embedded in soil. Mind you, medium size rocks. Only one jaw moves, as you see. Other one is fixed. Tip has enough sharpness for easy penetration of soil. And, not least, our small group is working now on design to allow the functioning of a similar pick-up stick under the gloved hand of astronaut. Without bending!"

He stopped, beaming at Don and Miles. "Did same demo in Pasadena last week. Talked to Arnie Beckham, you must know him, the lead of Trailfinder III. I hope he use one of our secure grippers. Yesterday I was in Houston and talked to manned flight people. Great interest in concept of rock picking from standing position. I also send one of my prototypes to Russia . . . Well, another story. Sad story. Now I fly back through Moscow, to pick up. They say no money to ship it back to me. Can you believe that?"

Dr. Chu poured the sand back into its bag and carefully secured the neck with the length of wire. He stowed the pan and the bag in the suitcase, took a quick look around, and, finding no stray Martian props, shut and locked the case. He straightened up, stared at Miles and Don, and said, triumphantly, "Well?"

Driving to Dr. Dermer's office that afternoon, Miles wondered whether Dr. Chu had an insane streak in him or it was dentistry that made him desperately eccentric. Passionate, no doubt, which was another way of saying obsessed. He'd be called a triumphant dreamer if one of his claws found its way to Mars. A visionary – on a small scale, of course. Focused. Entrepreneurial. If he didn't succeed, people would mutter that he was a nutcase. Had not Magellan been obsessed by the idea of finding a passage to India around the American continent? And in the end, against all odds, one boat out of the five that started the voyage – true, without Magellan – made it back to Spain by sailing westward. The startling assertions and sheer boosterism in Dr. Chu's pamphlet were laughable, yet had not Magellan also exaggerated, even lied? Hadn't he told the king of Spain and his counsellors that he knew, and knew exactly, thanks to secret maps no one else had seen, where the passage to India was? Had his passion led him to believe that he was telling the truth? Was it still a lie when chance and obstinacy made it irrelevant? In his pathetic and, yes, endearing way, Dr. Chu was as obsessed and passionate as the *capitán-general*.

What passion did he, Miles, bring to this world? The painful question, the sad corollary of that day. He, who believed Dr. Chu was mad. He, for whom work no longer held any appeal. What had Dr. Chu said? The flight to the planets, the unknown, the flutter of alien wings. Christ, he had not had enough passion to make Federica happy, never mind work or grander obsessions. She might have called it ambition that he lacked, but it was the same: passion, ambition, obsession. She had always maintained his drinking ended their marriage, but what Federica saw as his lack of ambition had always been a factor. To her, judging from her oblique remarks, ambition meant getting to the upper rungs of the ladder. But to him it meant doing interesting work. Stimulating. Work that didn't cause him to glance at his watch throughout the day. But in time, and it took him, alas, many years, he realized he wasn't interested anymore in interesting work.

What was wrong with him, only forty-seven years old? Was it a midlife crisis, or some other nauseous cliché? *Space crap.* It was work that others were passionate about. Work Dr. Chu would kill for. True, apart from an early engineering prototype of the rover, now going through mobility tests in a raccoon infested hangar, the ESA stuff he'd been in charge of for the last three years or so had been all plans and feasibility studies. And meetings, and costing exercises, and costing options, and pricing meetings, and trips abroad with more meetings, and evenings in pubs or restaurants, with him trying to be companionable and affable, wishing he could be elsewhere. Perhaps engineering had never really been his calling. He'd had a certain affinity for math – not a talent for it, only a fascination with its succinctness and power in the rare times these were revealed to him. Delight, too, in the glimpses of beauty he was allowed. It had led him to engineering, had carried him along for a while – perhaps combined with the vague glamour of space work – and had veiled the depressing truth that engineering proper had no real appeal for him. He should have heeded the warning he once received from his grad school thesis adviser: "A liking for math does not an engineer make." The archaic order of the words had made them memorable, but the message itself had not sunk in.

He didn't know, and probably never would know, whether he had deluded himself all along or his profession had simply become tiresome to him. Likely the former. Mohan Upreti, now there was a born engineer. Not the most nimble with math, true, and laborious in his writing, but he had creativity and a belief in what he liked to refer to, unselfconsciously, as his *snout*. It was what others called gut feeling, yet Mohan did have a rather fleshy, bulbous nose, and he reached his solutions or came to his concepts the way a dog found his way to meat. When unhappy with an idea proposed around him, he'd wrinkle his nose and even move it laterally, not much, but enough to rivet Miles. Mohan was equally good at coming up with rover concepts based on a set of dry requirements and constraints, or assessing the details of some students' proposal for a two-axes drive mechanism that would allow for both steering and walking of the rover chassis. Difficult to deal with, though, Mohan, a bit cracked in the head. While rarely losing his temper with his underlings, a model of patience, in fact, he had to fight to keep it in check when dealing with his superiors. Not conducive to a glittering career. He and Miles had periodic arguments, now and then coming to the brink of real conflict. Most of the time Miles gave in. A teetotaler too, Mohan, so Miles couldn't say, "Let's talk about this over a beer." With customers, Mohan would have a Coke and be the first to leave the pub. He once told Miles, "I already have a boozy nose, Miles. You can do the drinking for both of us."

The traffic heading east on Highway 401 was bumper to bumper, and around Allen Road it came to a halt. In the car behind him – he could see it in the rear-view mirror – the driver and passenger promptly began necking heavily, as if all they'd been waiting for was a lull in the general migration. Those two, Miles thought, were briskly approaching the final phases of foreplay. Horns were blown, envious encouragement from the surrounding cars.

The traffic was no better on Bayview Avenue, and by the time Miles reached Dr. Dermer's office he was twenty minutes late. One look at Federica's face and another at Dr. Dermer's concerned look were enough for him to know that rocks were piling up around his waiting armchair. It was as if they'd last been in that room only a week before. Dr. Dermer gestured silently to Miles to take the empty seat while he scribbled furiously in his notepad. Dr. Dermer was fond of notes, and his pen was always hovering over his pad. Three years earlier, Miles had wondered whether Dr. Dermer was really making notes at all. Maybe he was merely doodling, or writing a comic play. What would an audit uncover in Dr. Dermer's notebooks?

"While we were waiting, Federica explained what the conflict was about," Dr. Dermer said. "I'd like her to go through it again so that you can hear what she thinks and feels. We'll then reverse roles, and it will be your turn to make your case, reveal the roots of your objections, and you, Federica, you'll listen to Miles. Agreed? We'll then take it from there, one step at a time."

Federica sighed and began. As expected, there was nothing new in what she said. Miles asked himself again why he had agreed to this. Why did he think the presence of another person in the room would lead them, miraculously, to an agreement? How could he be that stupid, that soft? He was like putty with Federica. Slowly, he lost track of what she was saying. Dr. Dermer's office was on the first floor of a two-storey house shared by four soothers of marital grief. Post-marital grief in their case. The windows looked out on a quiet street. A few brown oak leaves were already scattered on Dr. Dermer's lawn. Miles had a good view, because his chair – he'd always sat in that chair – was near one of the windows, which that day had the blinds pulled half-way down, like a flag at half-mast. A middle-aged woman in a business suit and sneakers was being pulled by a huge dog on the end of a leash. The dog veered onto Dr. Dermer's lawn, squatted, and did his thing. Another brown daub. Her thing? The woman pulled out a plastic bag, enfolded her hand in it, and, bending, deftly scooped up the sizeable pile. She straightened up and spent a long time studying the contents of the bag, then patted the dog. Here was another application for one of Dr. Chu's grasping and holding devices. Scooping dog poop without bending. A mild adjustment for handling softer objects might be needed. Accommodating a plastic bag and tying a knot to secure its contents might be tricky, yet nothing that competent engineers couldn't resolve.

Federica's voice – a soft and woeful background noise, heard but not comprehended – aroused in Miles a surge of desperation. He knew it would pass, it always did, in ten or fifteen minutes, at most several hours. Why, and here he quarrelled with his genetic makeup, did this happen to him in a day of extreme hilarity, one in which, furthermore, he saw a supreme – granted, bizarre – example of irrepressible struggle against one's lot. He felt utter, helpless, desolation. Numb with pain. *Pain* was not the right word. Nor *grief*. The words in English were too bland, not suggestive enough. *Dolour?* Yes, *dolour* would do better, had more length and suffocation and despondency. He was trapped by his failures, by creeping old age, by the realization that, even if he could, he did not know what to change. It was lucky, Miles thought, that *dolour* was a weightless product of the soul and not the material output of some gland – in which case his dolour would ooze out of his pores, spread out, glistening like marmalade, all over his body, accumulate in thick layers under his clothes and, ultimately, make a mess of Dr. Dermer's armchair.

Chapter 8

October 2005

He had in mind an early pub dinner across the street and then driving to pick up Katelyn. It was his ironical daughter who had phoned on Thursday to tell him Federica and Greg were flying to London Saturday evening. "I won't come up on Friday," she said, "but I'll be with you a whole week from Saturday. You'll have to fetch me before Mom and Greg leave for the airport. A business and pleasure trip – Greg's business, Mom's pleasure. They have theatre tickets for Sunday, the day they arrive, and for four other nights. Mom's doing, of course. Greg was not happy at all. He said he'd be falling asleep either during her shows or his meetings." Miles had been glad – an entire week with Katelyn – yet irritated; Federica should have let him know about it, and weeks earlier.

The phone rang while he was in the kitchen, contemplating a drink; two o'clock was an advanced enough hour for what Laukhin had called "the wake-up blast." It was Cecil Fowler-Biggelow. Miles was to drop everything and attend a get-together at Geoff Simmons's house in Kleinburg.

"Sorry, Miles. Yes, I realize it's rather sudden. Work obligations, you know how it is."

"I'm never asked to such functions. Haven't been to Geoff's house either."

"It seems your presence is needed."

"Geoff can't do without me?"

"Don't be difficult."

"What's the occasion? The Russian visitors?"

"Yes."

"I was told to avoid them."

"There are a few snags, and there may be a plan B. I'll tell you later, if it comes to that. The CSA people will be there too. Marc Garneau and his assistant, Louis Gandarax."

"Cecil, I'm picking up my daughter tonight."

"Drop that."

"I can't. Her mother is going away for a week."

"When?"

"Before seven."

"Plenty of time. A big Russian chief has flown in. A long impossible name, immensely rich, one of the nouveaux riches in the former Soviet Union. A buddy of Ted Ludwig, from what I hear. The two of them concocted this Mars mission of ours, and everybody's rushing in to save it. He landed in Toronto from Saint Petersburg with a couple of Lavochkin engineers and – that's the surprise – with wife in tow. Geoff has asked his wife to put together an ad hoc cocktail party for this afternoon, prior to a more intimate dinner. Ted Ludwig has descended from Vancouver and Marc Garneau is flying in from Montreal. Gathering of big shots."

"Are things that bad?"

"Pripogurin may bring more flexibility."

"Sorry, who?"

"It's come back to me. Pripogurin, the big Russian chief. Get yourself ready, Miles. A car will be there in half an hour. It will take you home as well. It's a three o'clock start. Early, yes. The idea is to get our Russian friends pissed, and that takes time."

Big chief Pripogurin, with wife in tow. He hoped she turned out to be Anna Pripogurina, the woman in the turquoise dress he'd got a glimpse of in the Hart House quad that summer. Likely not a common last name in Russia, but what did he know. In the rear-view mirror the uniformed driver seemed to be smirking. At him or at the dull suburbia lined up on both sides of Islington? Where did Fowler-Biggelow find him? With a uniform like that – he looked like a discharged army marshal – he was fit to drive presidents and queens and oligarchs, not an indigent engineer who had to fetch his daughter in a few hours. Were there oligarchs in Saint Petersburg, or were they all bunched up in Moscow? More to the point, was Pripogurin an oligarch? A minor oligarch, subsisting in the grey lands where they became confused with successful businessmen? The name Pripogurin had been a shock. A pleasant one, and it had silenced his protests.

Kleinburg wasn't far from the house in Caledon in which Sarah was now, on and off, with lover Mike. The last time he'd been in Kleinburg, five-year-old Katelyn had thrown up in the car over Federica, who'd sat in the back seat with her, and the two of them had spent half an hour cleaning up in the restroom at the McMichael gallery.

The limo pulled in shortly after three thirty. The house was huge, with gables upon gables protruding from the steep roof. Vaguely Tudor revival without the false timber, Federica would have whispered for his education. Cars were parked in the street and in the wide driveway. A smiling woman dressed in black ushered him quickly through a hallway and into a large room full of people and noise.

Cecil Fowler-Biggelow looked as if he'd spent a difficult half hour. He rushed to meet Miles and interrupted his words of greeting with impatient nods of his head. "Yes, yes. I was told to entertain Pripogurin's wife. Dorothea insists on talking to her in high school French. I don't understand why and I don't understand French. It's given me a concussion. Never mind. Come and talk to Pripogurina, the wife. Relieve me. And don't lose sight of her." Short, precise instructions to one of his vassals, Miles thought. Was the assignment a way to muzzle him?

Before Pripogurina, though, there were introductions to the two Russians who'd come to Toronto for the talks. Alexey Kuragin, whose card said – Miles put his glasses on – "Myachkin Design Bureau, Landing Systems," seemed to be on his way to happy intoxication. And, from the famed Lavochkin, Mikhail Tamm. Lavochkin built everything from rocket upper stages to satellites and interplanetary probes, and could practically put together the entire Canadian Mars Mission. Kuragin, red-faced, shook Miles's hand energetically. Tamm, thin and white-haired, smiled sadly. Miles explained what he was doing at Ludwig Space, and in reasonable English Kuragin said that he and Miles might work together some day, as, after all, rovers needed a landing craft. Tamm touched Kuragin's elbow and said softly, "Perhaps another time, Alexey Vladimirovich."

Fowler-Biggelow pulled him along. Miles had hoped to get a drink at last, but his boss stopped near a group of women that included Dorothea Simmons. Dorothea said she was delighted Miles could make it on such short notice and was sure he'd look after her guest in the language of Pushkin and Lermontov. Then she introduced Miles to her guest, Anna Pripogurina, who smiled at him and inquired, in English, if he spoke Russian.

Miles winced. "Alas, I do not."

Dorothea laughed. "Now, why did I think you did? Still . . . here is Millicent, my nonpareil friend."

She was tight, Dorothea. The stress of planning the day's amusements on short notice, no doubt. Millicent was a silly name, although it had a quaint resonance. She had a pleasant face and carried with her a vast roundness, masked by loose, overflowing fabric. Her white forehead seemed waxed. Behind Millicent, some ten feet away, Geoff Simmons was talking to someone Miles guessed to be Pripogurin. Geoff turned his wide back to Miles the moment their eyes met. Of the two, Simmons looked more oligarchic than Pripogurin, but it was a flippant observation to equate oligarchic with thuggish. Ted Ludwig joined the two men and said something that extracted laughter and a circular hand gesture from Geoff.

Men and women dressed in black tempted them with intricate canapés. Champagne – a drink at last – was placed in his hands by a waiter resentful of Fowler-Biggelow's dismissive hand wave. The large crowd and the Russian presence reminded him of the parties held at the home of the Bakers for the launch of Pavel Laukhin's journals. The Bakers, in fact, were at the Simmonses' too; he'd noticed them as he followed Fowler-Biggelow through the room.

Millicent told Miles her husband was a scientist who went a long way back with Geoff Simmons. Two years earlier, she and her husband had been guided around Saint Petersburg by Anna Pripogurina herself. "Poor Anna," Millicent said loudly, wanting to be heard by all, "she must have really suffered, putting up with us, but she held up well." She smiled at Anna, who smiled back. Miles told Pripogurina that Anna was his daughter's middle name. He told himself he had to do better the next time he opened his mouth.

Dorothea Simmons excused herself and went away. In hesitant English, Anna Pripogurina said she felt like a relic. "Nowadays everyone speaks English. I learned French from my mother and then in school. My English is a struggle. I'm often in London – we have a small flat there – yet one wouldn't think so listening to me. There are languages one has affinities to, don't you think?"

Her English, apart the accent, was fine. She was his age – he knew that – and petite, with dark hair and a luminous, kind face. No eye-catching turquoise for her that afternoon but a simple black dress and high heels. Her jewellery was confined to a thin silver necklace and a pair of discreet diamond earrings. She had a quiet, contented way of talking, and her thoughts came out in fully formed sentences – even in a language foreign to her – as if she had given ample consideration to whatever subject arose, and recently too. He told her he had heard she wrote poetry.

"People make too much of it," she said, shaking her head. "I know it's because of Grisha, my husband; he loses common sense when he talks about me. It's odd, because he is a scientist, and a brilliant one. I'm a minor poet, if that. Negligible. Twenty-five years ago a slim volume of my poetry came out, and nothing since."

"Nothing in twenty-five years?"

She hesitated. "I still write poetry, if that is what you are wondering. And this month I will have a volume of new poetry published. Thin, seventy pages – all I could gather after serious dithering and doubt."

"You're being modest."

"Not at all. It is being published privately. Grisha practically forced me to agree. He wants his wife to have another book of poetry out there, no matter what. When I mentioned it wasn't easy to publish poetry in the new Russia, he said, 'Don't even try, Anna. Leave the publishing houses to the young and the poor.' The thing is, I wasn't happy with what I wrote, and I'm not happy with what I write. It's overworked; I try too hard. I don't know why, but the magic sounds are gone. It's supposed to be effortless, isn't it? They say it comes back – a dry period, and then the floodgates open again." She lifted her eyebrows as if doubting what she was saying. "It's been years, though. It's of no import – only to me."

Pripogurin joined them, and after shaking Miles's hand he inquired politely of his role at Ludwig Space. He listened, nodded, then, in Russian, said something to Anna. Turning toward her husband, she was soon laughing.

Fucking Grisha. It was absurd to be annoyed, yet he was. He looked around him, aware of his task to entertain the poetess. Not far away, Millicent separated abruptly from an older man and cornered a girl with a tray of canapés. Miles joined her, and Millicent said, "I spent five minutes with a perfectly deaf man. Unnerving. I had to run away. Dolly must have been really pressed."

"Dolly?"

"Dorothea Simmons. She hates *Dorothea*."

The canapés were tartines with something brown-grey and fluffy on them surrounded by a hint of greens and a delicate slice of spring radish. He brought his face closer to the tray to identify more clearly what was being offered, a rather unsanitary gesture that earned a stern rebuke from the girl.

"How can I help you, sir?"

"Sorry."

He turned to Millicent and smiled. "Vanity makes me keep my eyeglasses in my pocket."

"It's a mousse," Millicent said. "Foie gras and spinach, if *épinard* is spinach. I'm not sure what *veloutée* means. The odds are it's edible. I was shown the menu earlier by Dorothea. The Simmonses' caterer is a real chef, famous for his canapés. I wouldn't worry, the grub here is excellent. The wine as well. Geoff is, they say, a connoisseur. I suggest you get rid of that horrid sparkler. Shouldn't you put on your glasses?"

He smiled. "I'll be fine."

"Are you sure? You won't bump into people?"

"I do function without eyeglasses. I wanted to be able to tell my daughter all about this splendid place and what they are feeding us. Do you think I can pinch the menu somewhere?"

"It's expected. I'll see what I can do."

The poetess was again alone, and Miles, gently steering Millicent, rejoined her. Millicent suggested they try the quail tartines. She described the minute wonders – small slices of smoked quail breast on a bed of lettuce with a trail of pink sauce and silk-thin lard. A blueberry and a microscopic orangey mushroom completed the marvellous aggregate. To think that this had been a gathering quickly put together. Dolly Simmons had unusual powers. And where did she find thirty – more than thirty? – people on a Saturday afternoon on short notice? Desperately summoned neighbours? The kind of arm-twisting phone calls he had been subjected to?

Millicent departed toward an old couple that received her with enthusiasm.

"I saw you at the symposium," Miles said.

"I'm sorry?"

"I saw you at the Laukhin symposium in Toronto not long ago. It was the opening reception."

She raised her eyebrows quizzically. "You were there? I don't think I saw you."

"You left early, before the dinner. You were sitting with two other women at a table in the quadrangle, and seemed to be enjoying yourself."

For the first time, she paid more than polite attention to him. "I'm lost," she said. "Didn't Mrs. Simmons say you are an engineer at the company her husband is with?"

"She did, yes."

"What were you doing at a literary symposium?"

"I had a free and somewhat upsetting day, and the evening seemed of a similar cast. A good friend of mine invited me. You know him, I'm sure: Ben Paskow. Professor Paskow."

"He's a good friend of yours," she said, not as a question but as confirmation to herself that she had heard him properly.

"We grew up in the same small town."

"It was your friend who sent me the invitation to the symposium."

Miles scooped another glass of wine from a server walking by with a tray. It was time for his best ammunition. "I knew Laukhin, you know."

Again she looked surprised. "You did?"

"Through Ben, of course. Didn't know him that well, only the Laukhin of the last two or three years. Federica and I . . . my wife . . . former wife, that is, we're divorced . . . younger people made Laukhin less melancholy. He wasn't happy at the end, even before the first stroke."

"Yes, your friend told me."

"I went pub-crawling with him – with Laukhin."

"Pub-crawling?"

"Drinking. Migratory boozing."

"Ah."

"It upset Federica, my then wife . . . Can't blame her . . . I wasn't someone to be with after a night of drinking with Laukhin." Clearly his mind was not working. It was the second time he'd mentioned Federica to a woman he wanted to impress.

Anna the poetess smiled. "I imagine you weren't."

"He left me his drinks box."

"His what?"

"His drinks cabinet. He called it his *drinks box*. It was in his apartment, an outrageous piece of furniture, and we'd all comment on it. He claimed it was genuinely Soviet, a restricted model he acquired at great expense, though no one believed him. I kept it."

"I'd like to see it."

The wine was indeed delicious. Millicent was right; Geoff might be a thug, but he knew his liquor. He should be careful not to get carried away, although a limo with a chauffeur was waiting for him, and afterward he could always jump into a cab with Katelyn.

"I lived in his apartment for a few years, with my wife and daughter," he said. He was keen on keeping her interest in him. "After Laukhin died, of course. We rented the apartment – it just so happened. Did Ben show it to you, the street, the building? Not far from the university."

"There wasn't time. I'd like to see that as well." Anna smiled, and he felt buoyed. The wine had made him insightful; he thought that the smile of some women had the ability to make one feel unique and admirable. "You must have known Laukhin rather well," she added.

"We got along."

Millicent and Dolly Simmons reappeared near them. "I was just talking with a Swedish count," Dolly said. "Did I invite a Swedish count? A Swedish count in Kleinburg?"

Fowler-Biggelow had been circling around them for a while. Miles left Anna with the two other women and, light-headed, stepped toward his boss.

"Did I see Kees Vermaak here?" Miles said.

"Yes, of course."

"George Szetes too?"

"The Russians insisted. For some reason they like him. He was a nuisance at meetings. A mistake to have him with us."

"He's the proposal manager, Cecil. He had to be there."

"Proposal coordinator. Kees is the proposal manager."

"I thought he was the proposed program manager for CMM."

"That too. How is she?"

"Sorry? Who?"

"Pripogurin's wife."

"You've met her."

"We didn't speak much."

"Did you try, Cecil?"

"I couldn't barge through Dorothea's French. How did she get sozzled so quickly? Never mind. How is the wife?"

"Pleasant woman. Interesting too."

"Good. Good. Does she like Toronto?"

"I didn't ask."

"How long are they going to be here?"

"Didn't ask that either."

Fowler-Biggelow gave him an impatient look. "That's a criminal lack of initiative."

"I'm sure Geoff or Ted Ludwig would know."

"Ask, Miles. Ask, assess, suggest. And keep in touch with her."

"What?"

"It's important. Stick with her while she's here."

"That's what I've been doing since I arrived."

"I mean, while she's here in Toronto."

"Cecil, she's with her husband."

"Rise to the task."

"Kind of a Ludwig gigolo?"

"Don't be frivolous, Miles. Geoff thinks it might help. He's been watching you two."

"First, I'm detailed to her by you, and now I'm pushed into her arms by the big boss. Is Ludwig Robotics in such dire straits?"

"CMM is," Fowler-Biggelow said. "The Russians have jacked up the price. Significantly. And CSA . . . they have no more money, or so they say. Last night on the phone, Garneau wasn't encouraging at all, and . . . You better go back to her – she's alone."

He turned abruptly and went away, a signal that further chatter was superfluous. The order had been passed on down the ranks.

A scowling Kees Vermaak came toward him.

"Having a nice time, Kees?"

"I'd rather be elsewhere. Bloody Russians."

"Not easy to deal with?"

"They practically doubled the price."

"The big shots have arrived to save the situation."

Kees dismissed the possibility with a hand gesture.

"Have another glass, then, Kees. Enjoy what can be enjoyed." Miles raised his drink. "This red is delectable."

Kees wrinkled his nose. "You think so?"

"Do you really have a vineyard in South Africa, Kees?"

"Sold it. Bought a small one in the Okanagan Valley."

"What are you doing here?"

"What do you mean?"

"With a vineyard in the Okanagan, why work for Ludwig? Why work at all? And yes, why are you here at this thing?"

"Good question."

Vermaak stepped away and then returned. "That fellow who works for you, Mohan, I think. Yes, Mohan. What's wrong with him?"

"Nothing that I know of. Bit sensitive, perhaps."

"He was short with me. I asked a few question about your ESA studies, you know, the Ares Initiative, and he told me to get lost."

"Mohan?"

"Rude."

"I don't know, Kees. Bad day, perhaps, or the prima donna in him. He's talented, and wants respect. Likes smiling faces too."

"You mean it's a joke with him?"

"No, no. A smile would help, though. A smiling face, I mean, next time you approach him."

After the Champagne and four glasses of Geoff's vintages, being the designated gigolo for Ludwig Robotics seemed less absurd and definitely tempting. Anna Pripogurina was a kindred spirit, and a lovely one too. When Galya Shukin-Baker approached them, Miles was wantonly admiring Anna's figure. He was sure Galya didn't remember him and introduced himself. Galya smiled and said, "We've met before, haven't we? Somewhere, years ago. Our house?" Her wrinkled face was tanned. She and Ian had just returned from a cruise, she revealed. Taking cruises was their chosen way of travelling now, and they so much loved to travel. Always had. "Ian is still recovering. He's here, though not entirely. He can't keep up with me."

Miles was preparing to introduce Galya to Anna, but she stopped him. "No, no need. We've met. We were among the first to arrive, and I was put to work immediately. I think they invited us because I speak Russian. We've known Geoff since he was a boy. His father was a good friend of Ian, and we've kept in touch. Geoff has neglected us since Ian's stroke. In health, but not in sickness." She grinned. "Pay no attention to what I say. I'm bitter, and he's not married to Ian. I like speaking Russian. I shouldn't bitch."

Miles told Anna that the launch parties for all five volumes of Pavel Laukhin's journal were organized by Galya and her husband. "The Bakers have been the foremost supporters of Russian studies in Toronto for years," he added. "Galya is very loyal to Art Laukhin and his memory." He had the feeling he was saying things the two women had talked about already.

Galya's eyes filled with tears. "I couldn't put down the final volume. They were my last years in Moscow . . ." She looked at Anna and sighed. "You seem so young. Everybody seems young nowadays."

"Anna is a poet too," Miles said. "Did she tell you that?"

"No," Galya replied. "It was Moscow that kept us talking. People, places. I keep staring at you," she said to Anna. "You resemble somebody I used to know, in Moscow, a good friend of mine. Oh, well . . ."

Ian Baker was suddenly near them, somewhat unfocused. He made the appropriate noises in greeting them, though Miles wasn't sure the older man recognized him. Galya said, "Anna reminds me of Lyolya, Ian. You remember Lyolya, don't you?" Ian took a couple of shaky steps away and she grabbed his wrist. "Where are you off to? You just got here. Stay with us now; we'll go soon." She sighed. "Ah, you should have seen us, in Moscow, forty years ago." Without letting go of Ian, she turned to Anna. "Such a resemblance, uncanny. She was taller, though, my friend."

"What happened?" Miles asked.

"Ian Baker happened. I met him in Moscow and he swept me off my feet. Swept me out of the country too. Not easy in those days to marry a capitalist." She looked at her husband, who seemed to be paying no attention to her, and tugged his arm. "Swept me away, didn't you, Ian?"

Ian nodded. He was far from such gallant acts now.

"You lost touch with your friend?" Anna asked.

"Yes, of course. In those days, you know . . . She died soon after I married Ian. Cancer. We're leaving in a few days, Ian and I. Another cruise. Stepping on and off the tenders is a problem for Ian." She took Anna's hand. "We'll be able to chat longer the next time you come to Toronto."

Galya went away, pushing Ian ahead of her.

Pripogurina was talking with her husband again. Fowler-Biggelow approached Miles and said Louis Gandarax wanted a word.

A year before, Miles had made a brief presentation in front of Marc Garneau in Montreal, and Gandarax had been there too. Miles had not been included in the initial travelling plan, but at the last minute he was in and George Szetes was out.

"What happened?" Miles had asked Cecil when he found out.

"Garneau wants a few words on the European missions to Mars."

"Why is George out? Who's going to make the pitch for CMM?"

"Kees Vermaak."

"He's been here less than a month."

"Plenty of time. It's high level, Miles, and we'll jump in if he needs help." Lowering his voice, he added, "George gets on Geoff's nerves with his attitude."

"Everybody gets on Geoff's nerves. I'm one of the 'everybody.'"

It was Louis Gandarax who came down to receive the Ludwig party when they arrived at the Canadian Space Agency. They were early, and Gandarax, apologizing that the meeting room was still occupied, took them for a cup of coffee in the cafeteria. The talk, besides the polite banter around their flight and the unexpectedly fast drive from Dorval to Saint-Hubert, was about CSA's budget projections. Geoff and Cecil had many questions, and Miles had time to contemplate Garneau's assistant. A horizontal crease at the root of Gandarax's nose, more visible when he was making a point, marred a rather pleasant face. A thick neck, a round head with light, short hair, perhaps hiding incipient loss. Gandarax seemed to exude effort even while sipping coffee, like a trumpet player pausing between two solo sections. He excused himself when his cell phone rang and walked away from the table. Lowering his voice, Geoff said, "Probably from one of his mistresses." Gandarax's call was long, and Miles learned from a gossipy Geoff that there were many women in Gandarax's life.

The theme of the meeting was planetary exploration, with the emphasis on the Canadian Mars Mission and the collaboration with the Russian space industry. Everyone agreed that Russia was desperate for work from the West. Miles's talk on the studies done by Ludwig Robotics for ESA's Mars rover was mainly a report on how CSA's money was spent. He'd been given ten minutes and was told by Fowler-Biggelow to keep it low-key.

"Shorter than brief, Miles. And no gloating. Don't give CSA ideas on alternatives."

"Surely they are not that naive."

"Geoff's orders, and he'll be there. CSA's scientists don't like ESA's rover, anyway – it's engineering."

Cecil had been right. Miles felt it in the tepid response to his presentation. When he finished, Gandarax was the only one who asked a question, and Geoff cut Miles's answer short by clearing his throat and complaining about irrelevant details. At the end of the meeting, when they were leaving the room, Miles found himself walking beside Jean-Yves Cloutier, the head of robotics at CSA. Short, bald, his movements jerky, Cloutier was sometimes abrasive. He delivered his assessments with brutal candour briefly followed by squeaky laughter to soften the blow. Miles liked his direct ways, yet he felt, perhaps wrongly, that Cloutier had a visceral dislike of Ludwig. Looking around him, Miles wondered aloud whether increased funding from CSA for ESA's rover was a possibility. He dared it as no one else from Ludwig Robotics was within earshot. Cloutier shrugged and said, "What's in it for us, Miles?"

Uncertain of what he'd heard, Miles was considering another question when someone from behind spoke to Cloutier, something in French, and he gave up.

Gandarax had a glass of wine in his hand and was all smiles. "I hear your studies for ESA are going well," he said to Miles.

"I have good people."

"What do you hope?"

Miles looked at Cecil, who refused to take over. "Are you asking what are Ludwig's hopes long term with ESA's rover?"

"Yes."

"Cecil?" Miles pleaded.

Directly prodded, Cecil improvised. Challenging engineering. It kept Ludwig's people sharp. Rovers were a natural growth path for Ludwig Robotics. In space, of course. And although it was the rover Ludwig was working on, the company was exposed to other aspects of the mission as well, and that was a further gain. Landing systems, for example. Lidar was increasingly hot those days as a sensor for landing, and there was good work being done in that area in Canada, some of it in Quebec, in fact. Fowler-Biggelow realized he was straying. "Now, as you know, Ludwig is focused on the Canadian mission . . ."

Gandarax nodded. "We may find in ESA's Mars efforts a more affordable path."

Cecil played dumb. "Path? Much less visible than a Canadian mission."

"Is it?" said Gandarax. "Perhaps. Though the visibility would be pretty good if we were to be the prime contractor on the rover. A maple leaf painted on its chassis would do the trick, wouldn't it? Even without the maple leaf, everybody would know it was Canadian technology – we'd make sure of that. The world would watch the rover rolling along over the sands and rocks of Mars, and it wouldn't matter that the finicky instruments and the communications were at least as important, if not more so, and that the landing craft was a lot more challenging technically. What's the cost of the rover?"

"It depends on the mass budget and the tools and sensors selected," Miles said.

"Best guess on what's going to be approved."

"Two hundred million Euros."

"For the rover?"

"Rover vehicle and science instruments. It's the current estimate, and it's rough. Costs always go up, as you know. Frequently way up."

"What amount do you think will be needed to be prime contractor for the Rover System?"

Geoff Simmons approached their group. Miles hesitated, then said, "Hi, Geoff," hoping Gandarax wouldn't insist.

Gandarax kept staring at him. Eventually, he nudged him. "Well?"

"Sixty percent," Miles said. "A guess. ESA's ways are often arcane."

"That's a hundred and twenty million."

"At least."

"And the *vehicle*? What would be the amount to become the prime for the rover vehicle?"

"I don't know if they'll separate the vehicle."

"There are ways," Gandarax said. "Political ways. Countries understand these needs."

"Seventy million. Another guess."

"What are we guessing at," Geoff asked.

"Idle talk," Gandarax said. "Geoff, I see Marc has arrived. Let's get him and have another go at the Lavochkin fellow. He seems to hold all the cards."

Cecil's eyes followed the departing pair. "Things are not going well, I fear. I didn't like Gandarax's questions."

"Isn't the big Russian chief fixing things?"

"Pripogurin? He seems to float above it all. From what I heard, he bought the Myachkin Design Bureau as a favour to the government, and he's losing money. It seems it's a small leak for him; he can afford it. Perhaps a tax loss. He's into chemicals. That's how he made his fortune. Or pharmaceuticals. Both? He's not likely to put any pressure on Tamm. I found out he has other business matters to pursue in Toronto. In Vancouver too, with Ludwig Space, and mainly with Ludwig Corporation."

George Szetes sported a yellow bow tie. Yellow suspenders with a discreet blue stripe, barely visible under a long light-blue jacket, held up grey trousers.

The shoes were blue too. His powerful chest exuded contempt. With his dissatisfied air, moving slowly alone among the chattering crowd, he looked as if he'd just come down from Budapest to one of his Transylvanian domains for a surprise inspection tour, disdaining to mix with the locals.

"Colourful attire, George," Miles said. "Leaves an impression."

"I've seen you with the Plump Bully."

"Who?"

"Kees Vermaak."

"Ha. He's more big than plump."

"He's plump, and he's a bully. Although earlier his bluntness was refreshing."

"There was a meeting earlier? Here?"

"You should have seen them hiding behind half-truths. It came out when the Lavochkin chap, Tamm, told them the real cost. The launcher came close to what they said before, although still higher, but the spacecraft and the lander . . . Particularly the lander. I'll tell you, it created a shock. Should have seen Geoff's face. Tamm was very open. He didn't know how the previous costs were arrived at, but he was certain they weren't realistic. *Realistic* – I like this word. He liked it too. He repeated it several times. Disturbed minds contrived the earlier numbers, and disturbed minds believed them. He wasn't even apologetic, in spite of the fact that the costs came from the Russian industry. However badly they wanted our business, he said, they couldn't commit suicide. And then the usual crap began, with Geoff telling them we'd take another look at our numbers. Later, he took me aside and said, 'Cut the fat, George.' I said, 'There's no fat. The fat is long gone. I can cut functionality or instruments.' It was fun, Miles. You should be happy."

"Why?"

"Your ESA rover is on the up."

"What makes you think so?"

"We went into a separate huddle with the CSA chap, Gandarax, and he kept asking questions about the Ares Rover. 'That ESA mission, whatever its name is, has a rover in it, doesn't it? How are your studies with ESA?' Geoff would ignore Gandarax's question, or half answer them. Why do you think you are here, Miles?"

Anna hesitated and then said, "I also knew him, you know."

"Sorry? Who?"

"Laukhin."

"Ah."

She stared at him. "You don't seem surprised."

"Tell me more."

"There isn't much to tell. I met him five or six months before he jumped the fence. It was at a poetry reading. I lingered around afterward and talked to him. We were close . . . quite close for several months. I was young."

"There were others, from what I heard."

"Don't make it sound as if . . . *He* was the prey, not me. Believe me, he was such easy prey. He couldn't say no. He kept telling me we had no future together and that it would be better for me to stay away from him. It was only later that I understood what he meant." She smiled. "I'm not complaining, not at all. It wasn't a future together that I wanted from him, and I told him so. I have fond memories of my months with him. And it led to my one book of poetry – mostly about a departed lover. Rather bad. It was a miracle it was published at all in the Soviet Union. I can't look at it now. Last time I did, it was when I heard of Laukhin's death, fifteen years ago."

It was time to go and get Katelyn. Alas. To think that he had resented Fowler-Biggelow's summons.

"Would you join us?" Anna asked.

"Sorry?"

"Join us for dinner. There'll be dinner after this, from what I've been told. Don't worry – our host said it was fine."

"Geoff Simmons?

"You seem surprised."

"He doesn't like me lately."

"Oh?"

"It's a long story, and tiresome. Did you really ask him?"

"I asked my husband and he asked the host."

"Poor Geoff couldn't say no. It's kind of you to think of me."

"It's not kindness. It's not often that I meet someone I can talk to." She smiled. "Someone I like too."

"I can't . . . No, I can't join you for dinner tonight."

"Oh."

"I have to pick up my daughter."

"Would you change your mind if I insisted?"

"Her mother is going away tonight. Otherwise . . . We must meet again and speak, of course. I wanted to meet you at the symposium, but I didn't dare barge into your conversation with the two women you were with. And then I learned that you'd left for the airport. I was . . . And then, miracle of miracles, we meet here."

She didn't say anything.

"Laukhin talked about you," he said. "A lot."

"Ah, you knew."

"He was very fond of you."

She shook her head. "There's no need to exaggerate. You have my full attention. Are you saying he talked about me while the two of you were – what did you call it? – pub-crawling? I thought he'd been in love with that English woman, the one who died. . . . That's what I heard."

"He had no idea where you were. He tried to get in touch with you. It was as if you disappeared."

"Ben Paskow told me the same thing. I didn't disappear. I was in Leningrad, married, with a different last name. We were in Riga too for a number of years."

"He desperately wanted to find you, talk to you or at least write to you. He asked his sister to locate you. She couldn't, or wouldn't. He hoped Gorbachev's reforms would let him visit Russia and track you down."

"Why? It couldn't have been for old times' sake."

Hadn't Ben told her? Odd. "It may have had something to do with your stepfather too."

"My stepfather?" She seemed stunned. "Are you sure?"

Clearly, she knew nothing of what had happened twenty years earlier. But how would she if Ben hadn't told her? It wasn't as if Laukhin's cousin had rushed home to tell his wife or stepdaughter how he'd spent his time in Toronto.

"It's a long story," he said. "I'll tell it to you when we meet again. You're not leaving tomorrow – you can't do that."

"I can't see you tomorrow. Wifely duties."

"Monday?"

"We're leaving on Monday for Vancouver, and then we'll fly home. We may stop in Boston too, briefly. I'm not sure."

"Oh, no." He fished a card from his breast pocket. Luckily he had one with him. "Here is my office phone number, email. I'd like to see you again. Yes, I would. Very much."

"I may be back in November. I will be back. My husband has to return to Toronto for a couple of days, and I'll come with him. I might stay longer, too." She looked around and then she touched his arm lightly. "It will be just the two of us, and we'll talk about ghosts."

Was that a signal? He was bad at reading signals. Hopeless, in fact. He should carry ready-made cards for these kinds of situations, like the one left for him on a restaurant table several years ago: "I'm deaf, and if you want to speak to me, speak slowly, with full use of the lips and look at me while talking." His own card would say, "I'm inept at reading sexual signals. Make them loud and clear – forget subtlety."

"Ghosts?" he said.

"Laukhin. Well, either here or you'll have to fly to London or Saint Petersburg. London is closer. I spend much of the year in London these days."

She took a step away, then returned. "Your friend asked me to put down my memories of Laukhin."

"Are you? Ben's writing his biography. I'm sure there'll be a great deal of interest in your recollections – the Art Laukhin before the leap."

Chapter 9

October 2005

Lady Corolla was unhappy; one of her cylinders wasn't firing as it should. Did the old girl need new spark plugs? Were her groans and coughs grievances of neglect?

When he asked Katelyn on Friday whether she wished to come to Corby Falls with him for the weekend, she declined. "It may be one of the last times I'll drive there," he said. She shrugged, and Miles didn't insist.

It was Katelyn who had decided on the sex and social status of the now disgruntled vehicle. Four years old when Miles bought it, she had traced her finger admiringly along its shiny blue door and asked what car was that.

"Corolla," he told her.

"That's a girl's name."

"Do you like it?"

"Fancy."

Federica glanced proudly at her daughter. "Yes, a fancy girl. A lady."

Katelyn looked at both of them, unsure what to make of what she'd heard, and said, "Lady Corolla."

The roads were empty and windswept, and he drove fast. A cold October morning. The fine rain, almost a mist, stopped near Millcroft. As he left the highway, the low clouds disappeared and there was more light. On his right, Kennear Woods, or what was left of them, was a parade of reds, yellows, and greens. Like flags of Senegal, his father had commented once, to Miles's astonishment, on a fall drive to Millcroft.

Jim Cowley's phone call at the beginning of the month had not surprised him. "When are you coming up, Miles?"

"I don't know."

"I need to talk to you urgently."

"You are talking to me."

"Face to face."

"Come to the big city, Jim. I'll put you up."

"I'd rather you drive up here."

"I don't know, maybe in two, three weeks. There's Sarah's birthday in three weeks, and I might drive up for it, if she's there."

"What do you mean? I saw her the other day."

"Much of the time she's down here, north of Toronto. Mike wants her near him."

"Humour a friend and come up. It's important."

"To me or to you?"

"Both."

"What's it about, Jim?"

"I'd rather not say now."

Rather, and *humour a friend* – Jim's speech was getting gentrified.

Miles mumbled that Katelyn was unwilling to be dragged along to Corby Falls over a weekend and that he might come up for a night toward the end of the month. He knew what it was about, and had to face it sooner or later.

A Rueda had lived in Corby Falls for the last hundred and twenty years. One hundred and twenty-three years, according to Aunt Pearl. Four generations. Great-grandfather Ellis arrived in Corby Falls in 1882. He told the curious he was from the Black Sea. To those who pointed out that the Black Sea was not a country, he'd say, "My family moved around it. It was the sea that was always there." He told a story of how he almost drowned as a child in the Black Sea, and how he was saved by the servant of a young lady who was promenading on the beach. The first thing he saw when he came to was the young woman's worried look and her servant, whose clothes were soaked. It was a mystery why this particular story came out of him, because otherwise Great-grandfather Ellis never talked about his past or his family. Nothing of parents or siblings. If asked, he'd smile and say that he'd rather talk about the living, the here, the now. It was an ambiguous statement, since it could have meant that he had no family alive. No one ever knew for sure, not even Aunt Pearl, why or how he ended up in Ontario. She once heard him say he'd been eighteen months at sea, on a freighter, and got stuck in Veracruz because he didn't want to get back on a ship. Veracruz had been hard too. People were nasty, dour, and he was pressed into fights. He also said that it took him six years to get to Corby Falls from wherever he had started, but that was not a story, just a fact – a startling one, because of the length of the journey. A few other facts or vague impressions about Great-grandfather Ellis had reached Miles via Aunt Pearl. He had to get away. He'd always been able to eat more than what was put in front of him – an indirect way of saying he'd often been hungry. He never spoke the language he grew up with. Once he had lapsed into a foreign tongue, and when asked what that was, he said, laughing, Spanish.

Ellis Rueda arrived in Millcroft searching for work and moved to Corby Falls two years later. He married an Irish girl, Caitlin, and Miles remembered Heather once telling Joe that Caitlin had been the only one willing to marry him. Miles must have been four years old, and that stuck with him, because it was such an odd thing to say. Joe had kept a faded picture of his grandmother Caitlin – a worried, husky girl, with curly hair – probably taken before his grandparents got married. It had been a good marriage, Aunt Pearl said, until, of course, the tragedies of the last years. She remembered hearing that the locals had looked askance at Ellis Rueda at first, but the smile of the tall young man had been engaging, and he had not shied away from work. His light brown hair and blue-grey eyes helped, of course. One wouldn't keep grudges against a strapping young man with good colouring. "He fitted in," Aunt Pearl said. "That was his luck." Ellis Rueda was enterprising. He opened his own business, selling building materials, in Corby Falls. The railways had reached Millcroft in the late 1880s, and that led to a local mini-boom that stretched to Corby Falls, bringing mills, quarries, lumber, bigger homes, regional commerce. Ellis's store, in fact a large yard with a shack attached to it, did well. The hardware store was now on the same spot, with most of the yard long sold.

Caitlin and Ellis Rueda were married in the Anglican church, the one church in Corby Falls then, on the condition they stayed with it afterward. They did, Caitlin more than Ellis, and mainly for their young ones. Miles's father had treasured a photograph of what he called "the initial family," his grandparents and their children. They were all sitting behind a table, the couple in the centre, the children, some already grown up, on each side. And one grandchild, Pearl, under the table. Hesitant handwriting underneath: "Ellis and Caitlin Rueda, with their family. April, 1914." Everyone looked stern and serious – life was stern and serious in those days – except for Ellis, who was smiling. His hands were on the table and seemed huge. Not chatty by nature, he had carried around a jolly smile on his face and in his eyes. Especially in his eyes.

They were fairly prosperous and had a large family, and that was enough to pass for happiness in those days. Of the six children – the six that survived childhood – four were boys and two were girls. Three of the boys died in the Great War. Miles's grandfather, already married and with one child, stayed home. The worst part was that Ellis had encouraged his boys to sign up. Caitlin, of course, had been against it. Ellis had said why not, the country had been good to him, the country needed his sons, they wanted to go and fight, let them go. Nothing that the parents said would have mattered anyway, since the boys were caught up in the war frenzy. Yet Ellis had argued against even trying to stop them from going. It was her Irish roots that set Caitlin against them joining, he said to her. And then the three boys died. The first one killed was one of the twins, in 1915. The other two died on the same day in 1917. They weren't in the same unit, they weren't even fighting in the same sector of the front, but one of them had the unfortunate idea of visiting the other, and, under unexpected enemy gunfire, they were caught together by a shell. At least that was Aunt Pearl's version of the sad event. Caitlin followed them a year later. She had not said a word to her husband since that day in 1917 when she got the official telegram saying that two more of her boys had died. She wouldn't even say his name – he became "that fool who came from a sea." Ellis lived until 1921, his smile long gone. According to the doctor, the grief had weakened his heart. One of the daughters had also died, in child-birth, ten months after she got married. Of the six adult children, two were left when Ellis died: Miles's grandfather and the youngest sister, named after her mother. Grandfather got the store. It was he who slowly sold most of the yard and reshaped the business into a hardware store. "Downsized" was a better description than reshaped. He'd been a "boozer and a wastrel," in Aunt Pearl's words, and "had a woman in Toronto who pleasured him."

It began to rain again lightly in the late afternoon. He walked across the river on the new bridge, thinking he'd come back on the old one. "Doing the loop," he had called it as a child. An empty bus was parked across from the pub, with ads for hockey equipment along the side.

Bart's Alehouse was murky from smoke, and noisy. Jim was already there, at a table close to the men's. "The only free table," he said. "There's a hockey team here from Alverton. They stopped to unwind on the way home from Millcroft. Judging from how they are drinking, they must have lost. Did you walk here?"

Miles nodded. "It's a soft rain, almost pleasant."

"It'll get cooler tonight."

The smell of urine drifted toward them every time someone passed through the nearby door. The bar was crowded.

A young woman, rather bulky, brought their pints. Jim looked up at her and smiled. "Thanks, Norma." Norma inquired after Jim's older daughter and left without waiting for the answer. Jim took a sip and, leaning forward, said, "What the fuck's going on, Miles? What's this I hear?"

He knew what was coming and felt trapped in that smoky, piss-wafted corner. "I don't know, Jim. What do you hear?"

His friend looked around before answering. "I hear you have a wild tale, something that you saw thirty-five years ago," he said in a loud whisper. "A story that verges on the daft and ridiculous, except that it carries hurt with it. Something like one night, returning home, Dr. Biranek, now safely dead, found his first wife, Rose, near death on the ground floor of their house and drove away. Let her die. It reeks, Miles, this story of yours. It reeks like this corner here. And I hear it's a story you're keen to tell anybody who cares to listen."

"If you know everything, Jim, and if you've already made up your mind, why do you need to talk to me?"

"Talk some sense into you."

He took a deep breath. "Jim, do you want to know what I saw thirty-five years ago?"

"I know what you saw. You've told a lot of people what you saw."

Another deep breath. "I told it to a few friends."

"A few friends?"

"It was in a restaurant, a story to amuse the table."

"There's nothing amusing in it."

"Wrong word. To intrigue the table, to captivate them. Dinner, drinks, time for stories. It's a good story, Jim, gripping. The thing is, I had plenty of wine that evening and never thought there'd be complications. Biranek was dead; Rose was long dead. I didn't know Rose had had a daughter she gave up for adoption until Blanchard discovered her and told the world. And I didn't know Biranek had been that rich, or that he'd leave most of his money to the township."

Jim took a cigarette out of a pack and lit it. "I'd rather inhale smoke than piss," he said.

"You're doing both."

"Who was in the restaurant with you?"

"Our friend Ben—"

"Ben Paskow?"

"Yes. He got quite drunk that evening – you know how he is, two glasses are enough."

"Who else?"

"Ben's wife, Jennifer. And somebody who works with Jen, her boss, an older woman I've never met before, Lyn Collins."

"It's the Paskows, then. Ben, he's the one. He's from Corby. Somehow, he knew about Rose's daughter. He found her and told her."

"Why would he do that? Anyway, it wasn't Ben. He never believed my story to start with, the little he heard, half asleep at the table. It wasn't his wife, either. And I told the Paskows, afterwards, that I made up the story."

"Then it's that woman, Collins."

"Why do you think my story is the source? Someone else could have seen Biranek or his car that night in Corby Falls."

"What the fuck are you talking about? You just said you made it up."

"Jim, I saw Dr. Biranek that night in Corby Falls. He parked his car at his house and walked inside."

"You can't be certain."

"I am."

"Something you saw thirty-five years ago?"

"Yes."

"Not possible. You can't possibly remember that weekend after thirty-five years. No one could."

"No one? I bet you remember that weekend too."

"Me?"

"It's the weekend your father had his accident. He was hit on Saturday and died on Tuesday. For God's sake, Jim, I was at your house when your mother got the phone call that your father was in the hospital. There were two funerals that week in Corby Falls: Rose's and your dad's. I was there, at your dad's, with you."

"That was the weekend Rose Biranek died?"

"Yes, and my father drove to Devil's Elbow a day or two earlier to bring me home. Because, he said, I should be with my buddy Jim at the funeral."

There were screams near the bar and then general laughter. The Alverton boys were having a blast.

"We were good friends in those days, weren't we, Miles?"

He nodded.

"I mean, very good friends. The kind of tight friendship you have as twelve-year-olds. You wouldn't have kept such an extraordinary thing from me, would you? No. So how come, Miles, how come you never told me you saw Biranek that Saturday night?"

"I didn't know, Jim."

Jim stared at him and then repeated, "You didn't know."

"I didn't."

"What on earth do you mean, you didn't know?"

"I didn't know at the time he had murdered Rose."

"And now, after thirty-five years, all of a sudden you do."

"No, not all of a sudden. Haven't you been listening? I knew she was found dead by Biranek. I knew that he had returned to Corby Falls late Saturday night that weekend. I saw him, Jim, *I saw him*. Going to Devil's Elbow in the morning, skiing with my cousins, got me so excited that I couldn't sleep. I heard a car pull in, went to the window, and saw his car, his white Mercedes, parked at the back of his house, in the usual spot. I saw him getting out and entering the house through the side door. I went skiing the next day – my sister drove me to Devil's Elbow on Sunday morning – so I was away when Rose was found dead. When I returned for your father's funeral, four or five days later, I learned Rose had been found dead when her husband returned home and assumed it happened the Saturday night. *Assumed.* Anyway, it wasn't as if I was considerably affected by Rose's death. She'd always been a sick old woman as far as I was concerned, and her death seemed in the order of things. The recollection of that weekend stayed with me because of what happened to your father and because I had been looking forward so much to that week of skiing. The whole of Saturday and Saturday night passed so painfully slow that every detail was etched in my mind. And then I recently learned – let me repeat, recently, *in April this year*, to be precise, and only because of some nothing observation Sarah made – that Rose was found by Biranek on Monday morning. No one had mentioned it to me or said it in my presence before. I also learned that according to the inquest, Rose was alive until Sunday night."

"Alive until Sunday night. That's hearsay."

"My father was at the inquest, Jim."

"You heard it from him?"

"He told my sister, who told me."

"Ah."

"According to her, everybody in Corby Falls knows this. I mean, among the older people who are still with it."

"Fuck."

"Believe me, Jim, I told no one else what I told the Paskows and Lyn Collins that evening. And now, with the *Post* story, and with Blanchard's website, all I want is to keep my mouth shut."

Jim took a long sip of his pint and emptied it. "Well, it's you, Miles. Your story. You started all this shit."

"How do you know?"

"I know . . . Mary Lambert said that much when she warned Thula. She was clear: she knew of Biranek's role in her mother's death from the doctor's neighbour Miles Rueda."

"I've never met or talked to Mary Lambert."

"As I said, Lyn Collins."

"Did Mary Lambert say it was through her she heard it was my story?"

"I doubt it . . . I never heard that name mentioned before."

A shared childhood could not indefinitely sustain a friendship resuscitated by his infrequent and beer-sodden visits to Corby Falls. It was coming to an end now, with his father's death and his sister spending more time in Caledon. Nothing to bring him back here.

"This needs fixing, Miles," Jim went on. "You've got to do something."

"Do what?"

"Stop it."

"How?"

"What do you mean *how*? Deny the story."

"I'll deny it, sure. If anyone asks me, I'll say I made it up."

He thought he saw Jim's brother, Bill, at the bar, showing something on his cell phone to a younger man, or the other way around.

"Is that Bill there, near the bar?"

Without turning, Jim shook his head in dismay. "Yes, that's him."

"You two look more and more alike." He waved in Bill's direction.

"Leave him alone, Miles."

"Why?"

"He gets on my nerves."

Norma came to inquire how they were doing, and Jim ordered another round. He took off his black pullover, revealing a red plaid shirt. The effort put red on his face too.

"How do you know all this, Jim?"

"How do I know what?"

"Everything. You seem to know everything. Blanchard doesn't know my name, or at least he hasn't mentioned me on his website. He's just said someone may have new facts on Rose's death, and either Blanchard doesn't know who and what, or he's biding his time. But you, you know everything. You know more than Blanchard seems to know, and he knows a lot. So here's the same question: How do you know so much, Jim? How do you know this shit, as you so delicately put it, started with me? Your father-in-law?"

Jim nodded.

"And how does he know?"

"Think."

"Thula?"

"Yes."

"I thought she had no interest in making the whole thing public."

Jim shrugged. "She had to tell B&M Construction."

"B&M? The whole company?"

"She told Tom Bryson and Barry Matlock."

"Ah."

"She had to tell the owners. Didn't have a choice there. She had promised them the work and was basking in the glory. It was as if Biranek's will had been her doing. Funds for the hospital, for the church in Corby Falls. Work for the people of the township, who'd continue to pay taxes as a result. And then, oops, something went wrong. She had to explain why B&M would face layoffs and potential bankruptcy."

"And Tom and Barry talked."

"Tom Bryson did. Such a fool. He insists he didn't say that much. Obviously he did – I don't know . . . at the dinner table, worried sick about what was happening to B&M – and his dickhead son, Eddy, was there."

"And daddy-in-law told his own family what Thula said, didn't he, Jim, because you know too. You know, and Eddy knows, and God knows who else. It's out, Jim. And it's not just me. It's out because Tom Bryson and daddy-in-law Barry Matlock couldn't keep their mouth shut either."

"Barry told me, only me. And Tom doesn't talk to Eddy anymore."

"It's too late now."

"He says he didn't tell Eddy much to start with."

"Enough for his initial piece in the *Gazette*. Enough to get the *Post* and Blanchard going."

Jim didn't say anything.

"Did Tom Bryson tell Eddy my name?" Miles went on.

Jim hesitated. "He says he didn't. Bit of luck there. He's old, Tom, a bit gaga now, and who exactly the witness was got lost or he forgot. So he claimed."

"And you believe him?"

"What's done is done. Eddy will get his comeuppance."

"From?"

"From his father, to start with."

"He's an ambitious boy and has a good story. He won't stop. Not now."

"He will."

"How do you know?"

"Eddy will see the light. If he hasn't already."

That was the tone of somebody who was in the know and was enjoying it, and Miles began to think that in a way Jim didn't mind this whole mess. He had a role in it, and not a minor one.

"Meaning?" Miles asked.

"Let's drop fucking Eddy. Jesus, Miles."

Tom Locksley and Greg Moroney were near the bar too, each holding a pint, part of a merry group. "And there's Tom, Tom Locksley. And the Moose," Miles said. "It's like a high school reunion at Bart's Alehouse. Tom bulged up, didn't he, Jim? The premier athlete of the school. Thula said he's had trouble adjusting to her new status."

Jim took a quick look toward the bar. "Lay off the beer, that's the adjusting he needs."

Tom's back was now turned. Had Miles seen him since his and Thula's wedding? A younger man in a yellow waterproof jacket came up to big Greg Moroney and touched his arm. Greg turned around and said something to him. The younger man shook his head in an exaggerated way and then bent forward and to his left, as if in pain from his kidney, his hand placed on the area of discomfort. Greg said a few more words to him, which were met with another shake of the younger man's head. Greg shrugged and turned away, and Miles read in that gesture both exasperation and resignation.

"Who's the yellow jacket?"

Jim turned briefly again and sneered. "That's Greg's brother."

"The Moose has a brother? You don't say. He seems young. Looks a bit like the Moose, I guess. A lesser version."

"He *is* young. The parents had the last fuck of their lives and out plopped little Ronnie."

"What's wrong with him?"

"He's a bit simple. Always follows Greg. He can't get rid of him."

Greg Moroney had not changed much. He'd been a year ahead of them in high school. It should have been two, but he repeated a year. Was Greg with B&M too? Miles had seen him now and then in Millcroft. He was easy to spot, being so tall. With his massive shoulders and round, wide nose and protruding upper teeth and lip, everybody had called him the Moose. He didn't seem to mind, although he was unpredictable with his anger. Once, when Miles made a comment in the schoolyard – concerning Greg's appearance? – the Moose broke his nose. "That was discourteous," the Moose said, looking with pity at him, and Miles remembered being stunned both by the blow and the fancy word Greg had used. He was not a stupid lad, Moose Moroney, he was simply uninterested in what school had to offer. He'd say, "I don't want to be here, to learn new things. Fuck school." His voice had an odd sound, as if it were coming out of a cave. Ha, he remembered what he told Greg in the schoolyard. He told him that if a moose could talk, it would sound exactly like him.

"How simple is Ronnie?"

Jim rolled his eyes. "He's not an idiot, if that's what you're thinking. He's odd, the way he moves and the way he follows the Moose. His words are hard to untangle too."

"B&M Construction?"

"What? No, not Ronnie."

"What does he do?"

"I don't know, Miles, lines up shopping carts at IGA. Who the fuck cares? Why are we talking about Ron Moroney?"

There was no avoiding it. "What do you want from me, Jim?"

Jim lit another cigarette. "Tell me about the other witness."

"What other witness?"

"Mary Lambert told Thula there was another witness. Thula dismissed her threats. You know, twelve-year-old witness of something that happened so long ago. And Mary said it wasn't just you—"

"It was just me, Jim. I was embellishing my story, trying to dispel doubts."

"You're sure?"

"You didn't answer me. What do you want?"

"Keep mum."

"I am. It's Thula and B&M who're doing the talking. And Eddy Bryson talks to the *Post* and Blanchard. Maybe Mary Lambert."

"It's not Mary Lambert. She's not talking to Blanchard. Or the newspapers."

"Why not? What's she after?"

"She doesn't want Josef Biranek's name anywhere. No trace of him. No hospital name, no statue, no commemorative gathering, no biography, nothing."

"That's it?"

"Just about."

"No money?"

"She . . . she wants some money too. A month or so ago, Barry complained that they might have to give her some. I'm fuzzy as to whether she asked for money or an offer was made to buy her silence."

"What was the amount?"

"I heard a hundred thousand."

"That's modest."

"Maybe in your fancy big city."

"Out of twelve million? I'm sure Thula and the township could live with it, as long as the bequest money got to them. Hollie Biranek might not be happy—"

Jim interrupted him with bitter laughter. "You don't get it, do you?"

"Get what?"

"It's simple Miles. No hospital name, no bequest. The will is clear on that."

"The hospital will ignore Mary Lambert."

"She'll tell the story of Rose's death, your story, to the newspapers."

"They know it already."

"Tom Bryson swears he didn't tell Eddy or anyone the name of the witness and the details of what the witness saw. He merely mentioned Mary Lambert and that she was the cause of the funding delays."

"And you believe him."

Jim nodded.

"I won't corroborate her story, Jim. If journalists come to me I'll say I have nothing to say. The whole thing will go away in time."

"Thula says they won't be able to give a murderer's name to the hospital."

"No one is a murderer unless proven in court."

"In the public eye, Dr. Biranek will be a murderer. The fact that he forced Rose to give up her two-year-old daughter won't help either. Stories of him groping women patients seem to be creeping out too."

"Twelve million is a lot of money, Jim. Everybody will hold their nose."

"They won't have his name. Fuck. The board of trustees, or directors or whatever they are, got together and made a decision. They won't use Biranek's name until it's fully cleared."

"Meaning?"

"The township or Hollie Biranek, maybe both, would have to sue any newspaper that printed the story. And if the newspapers don't repeat the stuff Blanchard is spewing, they'll sue Blanchard. And you'd be the witness, Miles, the main witness."

Greg Moroney and Bill Cowley were now looking in their direction as they talked. What was Moroney doing over in Corby Falls? And Tom Locksley? And where had Tom disappeared to?

"I won't appear as a witness for Mary Lambert or whatever newspaper," he said, still looking toward the bar.

"You'll be subpoenaed. So you'll have to deny the story."

"Do what?"

"Deny the story. If it comes to that, you have to say either that you weren't sure what you saw thirty-five years ago or that what you told your companions at that restaurant was just a silly story you came up with simply to amuse them. Either would do, though the second option is better. You were tipsy and . . . You yourself said you were tipsy."

"It would make me look like a fool."

"You are a fool."

"You want me to lie?"

"Yes, lie."

"I can't do that, Jim."

"Why not?"

"It's not that I never lie, but this is different."

"Why different?"

"It's murder, Jim. And it's in court."

"So?"

"I won't lie in court."

"Everybody does."

"I doubt it. Anyway, I don't."

"Why not?"

How could he explain it? "Jim, that's why this country is still . . . decent. People – well, most people – respect the law. That's why this country is not, I don't know . . ."

Jim moved his chair back and repeated Miles's words. "That's why this country is still decent." He slapped his forehead. "I'm glad you told me, Miles. Really am. You'd know, wouldn't you?" He looked around as if to find other witnesses to Miles's foolish words. "He doesn't lie in court. Listen to that, people. Saint Miles doesn't lie in court." He nodded, slowly, as if finally convinced by what he'd heard. After a while, he leaned forward and asked, "Even if livelihoods depended on it?"

"Livelihoods depending on my lies? Whose livelihoods?"

"Mine, for instance. Another seventy people in Millcroft. Corby Falls too, by the way. More, much more, if you consider families."

"What are you saying?"

"B&M Construction. That's what I'm saying. Don't look at me as if you don't know. There's no work, Miles. None, period. The work at the hospital and the church, that's all we have right now – would have right now. I mean, big enough to get us over this hump."

"I won't lie in court, Jim."

"You'll have to."

"And if I don't?"

"Miles, there are some rough . . . some very rough people who are not happy."

"Is that a threat?"

"I know they are angry, and . . ."

"And?"

"It's not just you. You have a sister; you have a daughter."

Jesus. Miles was sweating now. Was it anger or fear? Both?

"You leave my daughter and sister out of this."

"It's not me, Miles."

"Your father-in-law?"

"Don't be daft."

"Are you their messenger?"

"I'm not anybody's messenger. I hear things."

"You hear things . . . You hear things that make you threaten my daughter?"

"I'm on your side, Miles. This is my own appeal to you. I don't want any harm to come to you."

Norma came by and they ordered another pint. He was hit by another waft from the door behind him. "God, they piss a lot in this town."

Jim nodded somberly. "We're good at it."

"Do you miss Corby Falls, Jim?"

"Millcroft is ten minutes away."

"Do you come back here often?" He was going through the standard questions he had for Jim whenever they met before the beer erased their awkwardness.

"Hardly. On Bill's birthdays, and not always then. I see enough of him at B&M." Everybody was with B&M.

"He stayed here, in Corby Falls, didn't he?"

"He can't afford Millcroft. I wanted to settle here too, when I married Jill, but Barry wouldn't hear of it. He wanted his daughter and future grandchildren near him. Money always wins. Our house in Millcroft is in his name. He keeps saying he'll gift it to Jill. Well, you know all this."

With his cell phone in one hand and a pint in the other, Bill made his way towards them. He put his glass on the table and tapped Miles on the shoulder. "I've just learned how to text. The things young people know. What brings you here, Miles?"

"Your brother. My sister."

"How is she? The best looking teacher I had, and by far. I see her now and then, still looking good."

"She's fine."

"Pity she gave up teaching."

"She did that a long time ago."

The Moose was observing them from the bar. It was quieter now. The Alverton lads had left.

"I should get back," Bill said. "Good to see you, Miles. Are you boys here much longer?"

"No, not really," Miles said. "Was that Tom Locksley I saw there with you and Greg?"

"You have good eyes."

"Is he gone?"

"I don't know."

"Goodbye, Bill," Jim said.

"I'll see you, boys," Bill said and went away.

He looked after Bill. "Why is he getting on your nerves, Jim?"

"Can't keep his dick in his pants. He's already paying alimony to one ex, and now he's headed for two. He's always hard up for money as it is, and he thinks my pockets are full. He has money for beer, though. A new phone too."

Norma came with their pints and Miles asked for the bill. When she returned with it, Miles waved away Jim's half-hearted attempt to contribute. Jim said he'd pick up the tab next time, but they both knew there wouldn't be a next time.

Moose Moroney was leaving. Bill was talking on his cell phone, or trying to; with his phone attached to his ear, he left his pint on the zinc bar top and walked towards the exit. Chatting up the next alimony claimant.

"Well?" Jim said.

"I'll keep my mouth shut, Jim. That's all I can promise. If it comes to a trial, though, I don't know . . ."

"You'll do it for the hospital, Miles. You must. For a good modern hospital in this township that would benefit tens of thousands; so that B&M doesn't have to close its doors and leave its employees and their families in the cold, including mine."

"Jim, that'll never happen. Matlock has enough money. He won't let his daughter and granddaughters go without."

"He doesn't think much of me, Miles."

"Since when?"

"Since always. He never loses an opportunity to ask why he employs me. He calls me Jimmy, like a houseboy. Jim is too dignified for his useless son-in-law."

"I've never heard you say that."

"I told Barry I'd solve this problem for him. I mean, this problem with you. I told him I'd sort it out with you. I told him you were my friend and I'd convince you."

"You said that to him?"

"Yes."

Why was he so irritated by Jim? Why was it so hard to say he'd do what his friend wanted him to do?

"I don't know, Jim."

"Will you give it some thought?"

"I'll give it some thought."

They parted outside. Jim said he had to get home because his in-laws were coming to dinner. Bill Cowley was not far beyond the door, still playing with his phone. Jim stopped and talked to him and they were soon in an argument. No doubt Bill was short of money again.

It wasn't raining anymore, but it had turned colder. Before looping back home, Miles decided on a longer walk. He went past the old bridge, up Ripple Road, which followed the bend of the river. Sarah had told him the township had designated that end of Corby Falls – close to the IGA and not far from the turn towards the highway and Millcroft – as the best area for low-rise apartment buildings for those seeking peaceful and affordable retirement. There were two light poles beyond the bridge, enough for him to see the road, and he did not intend to keep going for long. He needed to clear his lungs of the smoke and piss particles. Another childhood lesson from Bill, who'd told young Miles and Jim, pointing to his nose, "You smell it, you eat it." Was that before or after he taught them the mechanics of masturbation?

Clear his mind too. He had to decide. He should think things through again, with great care, maybe write everything down when he got home.

There was no doubt about what he and Sarah had seen that Saturday night thirty-five years ago. The white Mercedes parked in the usual place, Dr. Biranek getting out of the car and disappearing into the house through the side door. Once inside, the doctor switched the hall lights on and saw – must have! – Rose, probably unconscious but alive. And he left her there. Perhaps not even unconscious. She could have been looking at him, begging for help. He might have stared at her, might even have taken her pulse, then gone to fetch his spare pair of eyeglasses and left. Murder by omission. He didn't have to do anything. He was a doctor; he knew that when he returned on Monday morning she'd be dead.

Unless Rose had been lying at the foot of the stairs when Dr. Biranek went into the house and had crawled into the patients' waiting room later, after Biranek left with his spare glasses. Wouldn't he have noticed something was amiss? There would have been enough light from the waiting room to see the foot of the stairs, and the light on the top landing had been on as well. She'd have groaned too, if she was conscious, tried to make enough noise to catch the attention of whoever had walked in. *Unless* she didn't have enough strength? Nonsense. If Rose didn't have the strength to make enough noise to make her presence known, it was unlikely that, in terrible pain and dehydrated, she would then have had the strength to crawl on Sunday into the waiting room, hours after she fell. Undoubtedly, Rose had inched her way there not long after she tumbled down.

Dr. Biranek would have seen the lights on in his wife's bedroom, anyway, when he got out of his car. Yet he chose not to check on her. One o'clock in the middle of the night, and Rose's windows were lit. Clearly something was wrong. And even assuming he had somehow missed it, he had returned home after eight days away and chosen not to check on his suffering wife. That in itself was almost as callous as seeing her dying on the floor and doing nothing.

Of course, the other possibility was that Dr. Biranek had seen Rose lying there in the waiting room and she was already dead. In which case Dr. Biranek had not been a murderer. Why would he leave her there, though, and drive back to Toronto? Was it simply to see that show again? No, that was too silly. Maybe he was afraid he'd be accused of pushing her down the stairs himself. Perhaps she had fallen and died not long before he got there. He'd know that, as a doctor, wouldn't he? He'd have been asked by the police why he had driven back to Corby Falls in the middle of the night.

On the other hand he could have expedited her death. Not much, a nudge. Cover Rose's mouth and pinch her nostrils for half of a minute. She was barely hanging on, anyway. That was the case for Dr. Biranek having been, technically, a murderer by commission.

No, no, no! What nonsense! His father had been at the inquest and said it was determined that Rose died late Sunday night or early Monday morning.

Coming up with such a story now, after thirty-five years, about things he'd seen as a twelve-year-old – who'd believe his memories were not confused or outright wrong? And it was his story. No one knew that Sarah had seen what he'd seen, and she wanted no involvement. She'd screamed at him to keep her out of it. Everybody in Corby Falls would view him as the reason St. Anselm's roof remained in disrepair. And for the people of Millcroft he would be the self-important attention seeker who single-handedly left many of them jobless and halted the much needed modernization of the township hospital. And no doubt they'd point out that he, of course, lived in Toronto, where the best hospitals in the country were.

He should get back. The wet cold was getting to him, and he was too far past the last town light to be able to do more than guess the road. Anyway, he had his decision; the walk and the cold air had dispelled whatever doubts or second thoughts or delusions he'd been entertaining. In fact, he had long accepted it. It had grown inside him, burrowing into his innards, and heart, and brain. He'd just been irritated at having to explain himself to Jim. If the whole mess ended up in court, he would lie. He would perjure himself. He wasn't sure how seriously he needed to take Jim's veiled threats, but the thought of Katelyn made it easier for him, and for that he should be grateful to his friend. He might have played tough and principled if it were just his own skin, but he couldn't, and had no right to, if it involved Katelyn. Dragged into court as a witness, he'd say that the story he told his companions at Le

Paradis was an invention, the silly creation of an intoxicated brain. He'd had some alcohol – not some, plenty – and made it all up. Yes, for amusement. He'd had no idea it would spread like a virus. As to why would he think of such a story, he'd say that when, at twelve years old, he heard Elma Mulligan tell his father that Dr. Biranek had killed Rose, not understanding the figurative way she meant it, he imagined how it might have happened.

And if he lied – what then? No doubt he would look like a fool with his invented story and retraction. Looking like a fool sounded like the least bad option. A lie removed the threats to his daughter. A lie kept people employed. A lie allowed the building of a modern hospital, albeit with the name of a murderer on it.

A car passed going the other way, blinding him briefly. A couple finding an undisturbed spot to park near the river. He remembered walking with Thula Armstrong on that road leading practically nowhere with the same aim. In summer, though. The one night he'd managed to get his father's car for a short trip to Ripple Road, Thula didn't show up. Hard to get, Thula.

He didn't hear him, or them – later, he suspected there'd been more than one – not one ominous sound, and in a way that was his luck, because he had no time to feel any fear. And the blows to his back and head cut him off from the outside world until they were long finished with him.

When he came to, he slowly became aware of pain everywhere, of the fact that he was lying on the ground, of darkness around him, his wet clothes, the river nearby. His head was throbbing. Slowly, other sources of pain became better defined. The right side of his torso ached too, and his left knee and shin. He was cold and shivering, like a child who'd forgotten himself while playing outside in the middle of winter. He'd been like that the morning his father came to pick him up from Devil's Elbow for Bart Cowley's funeral. The temperature was close to zero – the old zero – and the Westbrooks had long returned to the main chalet for a break and hot chocolate, yet he had remained on the beginners' hill, going up by the short T-bar lift, then down the slope, and down a great deal in the snow as well, getting horribly cold, his ski pants all wet, and mad at himself for being so clumsy. His body had ached from the endless falls, though it was nothing like the pain he felt now.

Up there, between bare branches, he saw stars. A timid half-moon was somewhere to his right, or so he thought. He rolled slowly on his side. His whole head hurt. In the darkness, with only the stars to go by, he had to concentrate to convince himself he was seeing out of both eyes. The vision in one was hazy. The left one? Yes, the left one. Carefully, he began to get up. First he half rolled, then was on knees and hands, then, having blindly grabbed on to some branches, he pulled himself up, swearing, breathing heavily, using mainly the right leg, his knees painfully protesting. It had taken him minutes to achieve verticality, or some semblance of it. When he moved, agonizing pain emanated from his ribs, and he inferred that one or two were cracked. He was metres from the road. Shaking uncontrollably, he saw the lights near the old bridge to his left. He was soaked, and it was more than the wet from the rain. He had pissed himself. All that beer – three pints, or was it more? Jim was right, they were good at pissing, the Corby Falls natives, they could do it even when whacked on the head.

He dragged himself along, step by step, thinking he'd do a superb impersonation of a Hollywood hero, badly hurt, limping away alone to lick his wounds. He'd discover who his foes were and smite them. Harrison Ford came to mind, but Dr. Richard Kimble had jumped a hundred feet off a waterfall, floated away in the cold river, covered himself with dead leaves, and slept the night in the woods, while Miles, with some luck, would make it home in half an hour. If he had enough strength, he would slide into a hot bath. He could think of nothing more wonderful. He doubted he'd be smiting his assailants in the future, though. He wasn't as resolute as Dr. Kimble.

Judging by the emptiness of Market Street, it was late. Near the bridge, he looked at his watch: minutes past midnight. He had lain there at the side of the road for almost four hours. He leaned against a lamppost to gather his strength. What he needed was Dr. Kimble's determination. He felt a definite affinity with the fugitive surgeon, despite the obvious differences. He wasn't being pursued by a relentless marshal, but Kimble had not been as badly beaten as him. Mind you, falling a hundred feet, even with water at the bottom, would mangle one's body pretty effectively too. No doubt, the doctor had been more durable than him. And then? What did Dr. Kimble do after his shut-eye under the leaves? A blank. He couldn't recall what happened after that. The next scene he remembered was the renting of a shabby room from a – Polish? – woman in Chicago with a crooked fat son. Had Richard Kimble taken a hot bath first thing?

He moved on. A dog barked half-heartedly at him as he turned onto Second Street. He kept telling himself he was almost home, and then he was. He climbed the few steps, opened the front door, switched on the light, and willed himself into the small powder room. "Christ," he whispered, not liking what he saw in the mirror, "they were angry all right."

The boots took him a century. He thought long and hard about sitting down on the stairs to remove them, afraid he wouldn't be able to get back up, but saw no other solution. After that, the jacket took some effort too, and climbing the staircase consumed minutes. In the bathroom, he gazed again at his horrid mirrored self. He succeeded somehow in taking his clothes off, except for his socks, and the idea of soaking in the bathtub with them on amused him. He opened the taps in the bathtub and managed to climb in and sit down. He wasn't sure he'd be able to get back out, but there was no point fretting about it; he intended to lie there for a long time. He was pleased with himself and thought of sleeping there.

The taps were still gushing when Sarah barged in. "Are you drunk?" she shouted. "Taking a bath at this hour? And what are the slimy . . . Oh, my God, what happened to your face? And your . . . Jesus, you have blood all over the back of your head."

She wanted to drive him immediately to emergency in Millcroft. He touched his lips and whispered that he'd be in the bathtub for a long while and would then drag himself to bed and slumber a long slumber. In the morning, she could drive him to Toronto. He didn't think anything was broken, unless it was a rib or two, and there was no need to rush on their account. He'd fingered the back of his head and felt the clot. The bleeding had stopped; his uturdy skull had withstood the affront. He said he'd be grateful if Sarah could take his socks off and help him later, much later, to get out of the tub. It was a good thing, he joked, that she was used to moving her heavy artwork around. In his pained, soft way – he couldn't speak loudly for some reason, or he didn't have the strength – he was forceful, and Sarah didn't argue. She didn't even insist on knowing what happened after he said he'd tell her in the morning.

Chapter 10

October, November 2005

He fell asleep at daybreak. When he woke up, Sarah was in his room, touching his forehead. High fever. He mumbled that his head was hurting. She brought him a glass of water and put two Excedrin pills in his hand. She watched him swallow them, then helped him get dressed. "Your wallet is gone," she said. "I washed everything you were wearing last night, and I checked your pockets. Shouldn't we go back there and look for it? I'll do it."

"I don't know the exact place."

"There'd be traces left."

He tried to laugh. "Tracker Sarah. They took the wallet."

"How do you know?"

"I know."

As they were going out to the car, she said she didn't understand why he wouldn't call the police.

"I don't want them involved," he moaned.

"What are you going to say at the hospital?"

"That I was mugged."

"Miles, they'll tell the police."

"Maybe. It was a mugging, Sarah, and the wallet is gone. That's the story, if anyone asks. And for all we know, it was a mugging. I'm not calling the police, because there's nothing I can say that will help them find the culprits."

She wouldn't give up. "Where is your OHIP card?"

He couldn't think properly. "OHIP?"

"How do you think you'll be admitted without it?"

"Ah. In the wallet."

"What colour is the wallet?"

"Black."

"Better than brown. We'll take a quick drive along Ripple Road. You said you didn't go that far – ten, fifteen minutes past the last light, say a quarter of a mile. I'll stop there and look around. Not for long. Think of the hassle you'll avoid if you find the wallet with all your cards."

The hassle was the last thing worrying him. The Excedrin was making him drowsy and he fell asleep. Much later, he was woken by the car's sudden acceleration as they joined the 404. She thought she'd located the place on Ripple Road where he'd been assaulted. Couldn't be sure, of course, but it had seemed trampled enough. She'd searched that area but found no wallet. He muttered he was "in a pickle." He was pleased with what his confused mind had come up with, because it expressed, tersely, the absurdity of his situation. Sarah laughed. "In a pickle" had been their father's expression for any trouble – the entire range, from mild constipation to approaching tornadoes. A month before he died, Joe whispered to them, as they were gathered by his bed with Dr. Pogaretz, "I fear I'm in a pickle."

As they neared the city, he told Sarah what had happened to him, as best as he could, and who he thought had thumped him so thoroughly. It took him a long time, because he'd fall asleep during his account, and Sarah, annoyingly, would wake him up with questions. In Toronto, she drove to the house on Montgomery Avenue. He struggled to explain where his passport and SIN card were. It was lucky, he heard himself say, that he hadn't kept the SIN card in the wallet. "I'm a lucky bloke in a pickle." Sarah was a long time inside. Eventually she came out with a bag of personal things she thought he'd need at the hospital. "Got the passport," she said. "I couldn't find the card. Do you remember your SIN number?" He thought for some time, then nodded. "I hope you do, Miles. And I hope they'll take you in without an OHIP card." She shook her head as she started the car. "They might, once they take a good look at you."

The five weeks he was in bed, or not far from one, he thought of little else but his predicament. He didn't remember a great deal of his stay in the ICU. He learned he'd been kept there because of the head wound and the high fever he developed. When, on the morning of the fourth day, they moved him – to a distant wing, he gathered, because the ceilings seemed to be sliding above his gurney for ever – his mind was still foggy. At the end of the trip, he wondered whether he was awake. A nurse with a Jamaican accent told him he was confused because of the high fever and the morphine. Later, he heard her complain of overwork. "We're supposed to look after six patients. I have eleven today. Eleven! How do I do that?" Was she talking to him? Was he not alone in the room?

An intern came that afternoon – although it may have been the afternoon of the following day – and listed for Miles's benefit the ailments afflicting him. No doubt he was summarizing the consensus of a team of specialists. A blow to the head. Several blows, in fact, and the one at the back, on the occiput, was nasty. It had been the doctors' main concern at first. It was less of a worry now, as there appeared to be no complications. "You probably know already," the intern said, with a tired smile, "you have a remarkably sturdy skull. We had to shave it, unfortunately. Once we take the bandage off, in a few days, you'll feel surgical sutures at the back of your head. Stitches, that's what I should say. For some reason *stitches* sounds less alarming than *sutures*. You were lucky, you know. It was imprudent of you not to go to a hospital immediately after the incident." The intern gently touched Miles's bandaged head. "It'll grow better."

"Better? What will grow better?"

"Your hair will grow denser." The doctor seemed to ponder his statement. "So they say."

There was no internal bleeding. He was lucky again: sturdy skull, sturdy innards. Their main worry now was pneumonia. They believed at first the fever was due to an infection. The thought of pneumonia came to them late. Another tired smile, and a raised finger. "Not too late. Your sister said you were drenched and shivering when you crawled home. She said – what did she say? – that you fell in a river? No. Ah, that you'd been lying in soaked dirt for hours. Near a river, yes."

The intern handed him a small mirror as he went on with his report. On Miles's left side, a split brow, broken skin on the cheekbone, and a bruised eye. A couple of stitches for the brow. The eye wouldn't open fully, but it would be fine eventually, once the swelling went down.

"Eventually?"

"The contusions will take a while to heal. Cover you right eye. Good. Can you see?"

"Blurry."

"It will improve. The ophthalmologist will have another look at you later today. One fractured rib. Painful, yes? Avoid laughing for now and it will heal."

"They say a good laugh is better than any medicine."

"They shouldn't. You have bruises all over your body. A bad one on your left shin. It will hurt for a week or two. And you have a mild case of effusion in the left knee."

"What's that?"

"Water on the knee. It might grow before it seeps away."

Overall, an impressive list, he told himself. "Am I full of morphine?" he asked.

"Some. Why?"

"I feel, I don't know, ebullient."

"Now that's a word I haven't heard around here. The sick don't generally feel ebullient. Turn your head to the right. Hm. Now turn back to me. Hm." The intern stared at his face with mild interest. "Are you experiencing a diminished airflow? Your nose may have been displaced a tad. We'll know for sure once it's less swollen."

Miles gingerly touched his nose and didn't like the feel of it. "I'm not getting much air through my nose. It could simply be plugged, with the fever and everything."

"Repairing surgery, if needed, can wait. Besides, who knows, you may become fond of your new face."

The intern was blond and thin, with the wistful not-all-there face of an exhausted poet. Judging by the conversation, he was a user of morphine too. Or some other drug that kept him going.

"A mugging, Mr. Rueda? I saw it on your sheet."

"Yes."

"Nothing personal, was there?"

"Personal?"

"I'd say he went at it with more vigour than was needed. What did he hit you with?"

Miles shook his bandaged head. "I don't know. I didn't see him, or them."

"Anything taken?"

"My wallet. I had over nine hundred dollars in it."

Why on earth did he say that? The morphine? He may have had sixty or seventy dollars in his wallet. At most. He felt immensely proud of his lie. He wondered whether he was talking to a doctor or a cop. From the questions he asked, the tired young man in green could be a cop, a gentle, knowledgeable, undercover agent of the provincial police. Maybe he should tell the cop-doctor of his impossible dilemma, share his immersion in brine with him. No, too long a story, and he had no strength for it.

The intern kept talking to him, asking questions, while Miles's mind went back to Biranek. From his grave, with help from others, Biranek had him in a pickle. In a roundabout way, he had also rearranged his face.

Federica brought Katelyn to the hospital twice. The first time, he was in the ICU, and he only vaguely remembered it. The second time, in the semi-private room, he was still feverish, but his mind was clear. His roommate, wheeled in an hour earlier, had introduced himself as Randall, and Miles had not asked whether it was his first name or his last. Randall was a student at Ryerson, living with his parents. His elbow had been shattered into several pieces, but the worrisome injury was to his head. He had jumped on his bicycle to go to the corner store for soda water, he told Miles, and hadn't put his helmet on. He never did for short rides around the neighbourhood. His wheel somehow hit the curb – his attention must have been elsewhere – and down he went. Something had swollen up and was pressing on something else in his brain, and the doctors were worried.

"I'm not worried," Randall added.

"That's good," Miles said.

"The doctors keep asking me if I feel in any way different from the way I was before the accident. Mentally, I mean, because physically, of course . . . You know, I think I am different."

"Did you tell them?"

"The doctors? No . . . I don't know. I'm embarrassed." After waiting for Miles to show interest, Randall gave up and said, "You want to know the difference?"

"Sure."

"You'll laugh."

"Maybe."

"I'm funnier since the accident."

Miles thought he understood what Randall meant though wanted to be certain. "You find more things hilarious now than you did before."

"No, *I* am more hilarious than before. I make more jokes, and better too."

"You don't say."

"I'm telling you."

"There's no cause for alarm, then, is there?"

He feared he'd be asked by Randall to attest to his jocosity, but at that moment Federica and Katelyn arrived. Katelyn let out a little cry when she saw him. Later, she told him he looked worse than he had in the ICU. She stayed close to her mother and stared at him as if he were, if not exactly a stranger, someone she didn't know as well as she thought.

"It's just temporary, Katelyn," he said. "I may look worse, but I feel better. And one intern gave me hope for an improved face once I've healed."

Katelyn nodded, yet soon he heard her whisper to Federica, "Let's go home, Mom. Dad is tired, and I have some work to do for tomorrow."

His heart cringed, and it was a mindless, selfish reaction, a leftover from the custody battle.

"What happened, Miles?" Federica asked. "Sarah didn't say much when she called."

He told them about the beers he drank with Jim Cowley at Bart's Alehouse, and his unfortunate idea of getting some fresh air on Ripple Road afterward. He added, winking at Katelyn, that Jim had been one of her mother's favourite people in Corby Falls. Predictably, Federica rolled her eyes. He described his beating in joyous terms, a result of incompetent and jittery muggers, the whole thing an ungainly and comical ballet with him the star, and as he listened to himself, his pain buried under the morphine, he was impressed by his ability to put on an act. He mentioned how his doctors had marvelled at the thickness of his skull and ended his account by alluding to the potential benefits from head injuries, as illustrated by his new friend Randall. He made a vague gesture towards the other bed. Katelyn and Federica looked briefly towards Randall, who didn't look up from his magazine.

Katelyn said, "Martha was awed by what happened to you."

He thought he detected some irony. "You told Martha?"

"A wicked story, Dad. I'm sure you gave as good as you got."

Ah, his sarcastic daughter.

The second time Ben visited him in the hospital, Helen come along. "I never miss an opportunity to see a battered face," she explained.

"When I told Helen what happened, she insisted on joining me," Ben said.

A month after "the flattening" – Helen's words had stayed with him – he'd had a drink with her. She was drawn and moody. She was losing her hair because of the chemo. She and Bleidd had separated and were in the process of divorcing. It was not the most cheerful of evenings, Miles not knowing what was appropriate to say, or where to look. Helen snarled at him, "You can look at my ribs now and then, Miles. You know, it's not fucking natural to keep staring at my forehead." He laughed awkwardly and asked, "Are you going to, you know, replace them?" She shrugged, as if either it didn't matter to her or she had not made up her mind.

The replacements were there now, and she tried to hide her shock at his appearance by pointing to her chest. "Look, Miles. Not what they used to be, alas, rather a modest, demure duo now, but – the silver lining – less affected by age. Best surgeon in Toronto. The way you look, you could use him too. It's clear they go full force in that town of yours. No gentle mugging there, no. You're from the same town, aren't you, Ben? Village? What do they do there for settling scores?"

She was wearing a wig, and it didn't look bad on her. Randall sat up in his bed, facing them, as if ready to join the conversation. Helen looked at him and mumbled something about privacy, then proceeded to pull the curtain along the curved rail in the ceiling.

"How is *Studying with the Poet* going?" Miles asked. "Did you find a better title?"

"Those were Ben's first words when we met. Laukhin, always Laukhin."

Don banged on the open door of Miles's hospital room and waved a hand holding a brown paper bag.

"Your ESA team will be here tomorrow. George Szetes too. He said, 'Miles's face turned into hamburger – I can't miss that.' Even Geoff Simmons asked how you were doing the other day. Cecil wants to know if you are visitable. He whispered to me mysteriously that you were letting him down. The whole company is buzzing, Miles. I'm being told we haven't had such excitement since a young twosome were caught fornicating in the first aid room. That was before my time. It's not often that space pioneers are roughed up. One violent village, I say, Corby Falls."

He put his paper bag down carefully, fished a small camera from his coat pocket, and quickly took a picture. "I'm considerate, not asking you to smile. No, no, you should thank me; I had to promise pictures to keep the hordes away. You don't want everybody here, do you? Wild rumours are circulating, Miles." Don sat down and took a closer look at his colleague. He whistled with admiration. "Roughed up doesn't describe it. No, not at all. What on earth happened? Did you fight back? I must take another picture, then you can tell me the whole story. Will you take the gown off? I'll help. Are the body contusions as good? For my collection. No?"

"Don't be a piss, Donald."

Donald was a piss, and took more shots. "A star should want his picture taken. All you have to do is be absent, and things take a turn for the better. There are rumours that CMM is out and ESA's rover is in. Solid rumours – well, more than rumours. There are talks with Astrium, and I hear they may be visiting Ludwig soon. Cecil stopped me the other day and said, 'Airbus and Astrium, they're owned by the same parent company, aren't they? Who do you know at Astrium?' I said I knew chaps in Toulouse, and he was disappointed. The visitors would be from the UK, apparently. Your friends, aren't they, Miles?"

"When are they coming?"

"Not sure. Mohan will fill you in tomorrow. He's had a few rough days. Clashes with Kees Vermaak, I hear."

Don took a flask from the brown bag and pushed it toward Miles. "Want a taste? I need it. Hospitals depress me." He took a satisfied sip. "They don't do things by halves in Corby Falls. They get their coin and then they proceed with the contusion work. Bone-work too? Anything broken?" He was clearly cheered by the drink, or had already had a mouthful in the elevator coming up. "Alarming place, your village. A bequest mired in controversy, suggestion of a suspicious death, and now one of its foremost citizens, Miles Rueda, brutally assaulted. Guess who was I talking to about you recently?"

"Your MPP?"

"Lyle Blanchard. He was at my parents' place last night, plastered – so were my parents. God, at their age. And at some point the chat touched on the Biranek affair, and Lyle began to ramble on and on about how he disliked the buttoned-lip residents of Millcroft County and how he was going to get to the bottom of it, even if he had to move to Corby Falls, because" – here, Don shifted to a lower-pitched voice – "'No one stops Lyle Blanchard, you hear me, no one and nothing.' And I said, 'You know, a good friend of mine is a former resident of Corby Falls.' So I told him I knew you."

"You did."

"I also told him about your recent mishap and that as a result you were here at Sunnybrook. Blanchard took a sudden interest in you."

"Dear Lyle."

"He said he might pay you a visit. What did he say? 'I'll give him a box of chocolates, and he'll tell me Corby Falls tales.' He seemed pleased with himself."

"Fuck you, Don."

"Are you saying I shouldn't have opened my mouth?"

"That's what I am saying."

He walked slowly with Don down the corridor and through a few turns to the elevators. His left leg sent sharp pain signals to his brain, and so did his ribs. The therapist, a short woman with short hair and clipped sentences, had told him to move as much as he could, even if it was painful. "Though not too painful," she warned him. "You'll know. The knee is a joint. It mustn't freeze."

As they waited for the elevator, Don said, "I had an odd exchange with Geoff Simmons this morning. I bumped into him, and he casually wondered whether I'd be interested doing some work with Europe. The European Space Agency. He said, 'You worked in Europe for years. Give it some thought.' He was in a hurry and rather grouchy."

"I thought you were on your way out. Out of Ludwig and out of space. Failed to get an offer?"

"The opposite. Too many. Can't make up my mind."

Miles looped the longer way back to his bed, passing by the common room, where a large TV was tuned to a documentary about African wildlife. A man hooked to an IV stand was watching intently. His lips were moving slowly, as if he were summarizing to himself whatever he saw on the screen. Miles sat in an armchair to catch his breath. Miraculously untrampled, baby elephants hurried amidst dust and legs. Sprawling lionesses drowsily licked one another. He stood up and ambled on, thinking what a relief it would be to lie down, and hoping he could avoid Randall's chit-chat.

As he approached his room, he heard a loud voice coming from inside. A large, red-faced man, glaring at a supine Randall, was at the tail end of a forceful argument. "And I'll pummel your face into a marshmallow, you smartass." Sensing Miles's presence, he turned around and, after looking him up and down, asked rather abruptly, "Are you Miles Rueda?"

Miles nodded, and the big man pointed his finger at Randall. "This clown here is impersonating you."

Randall had a pacifying smile for Miles. "I thought, what the heck—"

"Randall has had a late calling to comedy," Miles said to the big man, "and now he's workshopping his material."

"You a comedian too?" asked the man.

He raised his hands. "No." Sitting down on his bed, he asked, "And you are?"

In one confident swoop – like something Miles had seen in movies – the big man took a card from an inside pocket. "Lyle Blanchard, journalist."

"Ah."

"Do you read the *Post*, Miles?"

Such informality. "Now and then. Mainly the *Globe*."

"Bland."

"My ex-wife left me a *Globe* subscription."

"I understand you were born in Corby Falls."

"I was."

"Have you read what I wrote in the *Post* about the bequests Dr. Biranek left to your township?"

"Someone brought it to my attention."

"Did you get to my website as well?"

Should he lie? No point. "I did, yes. A friend pointed it out to me."

"And?"

"And what?"

Lyle Blanchard seemed ready to settle his large frame into the chair in which Don had been sitting, then changed his mind. "Is there a place where we can sit down and talk undisturbed?"

"Are you interviewing me?"

"If you don't mind."

"About?"

"Corby Falls. Biranek and his bequests."

"Why me?"

"You're from Corby Falls, and you knew Biranek."

His first thought was to tell Lyle Blanchard politely to get lost. He was too tired and in too much pain to carry on a conversation. But Blanchard would return the next day or the following one. Besides, talking to him might allow Miles to gauge whether the journalist knew he was the source of the new information regarding Rose's death.

"Everybody knew Biranek," he said. "Corby Falls is small."

"How well did you know him?"

"Somewhat."

A lie, and not a good one. Blanchard probably already knew that the Ruedas and the Biraneks had been neighbours. He shouldn't appear too uncooperative or the journalist would suspect he had something to hide.

Blanchard looked at Randall and then back at Miles. "So, is there a place to sit down and talk?"

"Right here." Miles pointed to the empty chair near his bed.

The big man gestured towards Randall. "With him here?"

Miles shrugged.

"I see," Blanchard said with a sigh. He pushed the empty chair closer to Miles's bed and sat down without taking his raincoat off. He wasn't a big man; he was huge. Outside a hospital, he probably squeezed annoying men like Randall in one hand until the pulp seeped through his fingers. From a raincoat pocket he took out a notebook and a pen. He crossed his legs, a move which brought a size fifteen shoe to the level of Miles's eyes. "What did you think of Dr. Biranek, Miles?"

"He was all right."

"That's it?"

"I'm tired, *Lyle.*" Under other circumstances he might have liked Blanchard, but as it was, he was finding it difficult to hide his hostility. "The thing is, once I started university, my contacts with Corby Falls, hence Dr. Biranek, became sparse."

"You were his neighbour, weren't you?"

Aha. "Backyard neighbours."

"Was he your doctor?"

"My father's."

"What did your father think of him?"

"He liked him fine. It was convenient too, you know, as a doctor, being so close."

"Was your mother his patient too?"

"No."

"Why not?"

"I'm not sure. I guess she stuck with her old physician in Millcroft. She died when I was young."

"What of Dr. Biranek's relationship with his first wife?"

"With Rose? She was ill."

"Biranek had an open affair with his office nurse, didn't he?"

"Yes."

"While Rose was alive."

"Yes."

"He'd travel with his mistress, Hollie McGinnes, leaving Rose at home. Ill and alone."

"There was someone looking after Rose. Elma Mulligan. You mentioned her in your piece."

"Hollie McGinnes became, after Rose's death, the second Mrs. Biranek."

"Yes."

"What's your view of Rose Biranek's death?"

There it was, Lyle Blanchard getting into what he was really after. How much did he already know? Careful now.

"My view?"

"Yes. And what do you know of it."

"Why are you asking me?"

"I'm asking others too. Someone knows more about Rose's death, more than has been said in the past, new facts. Like any journalist, I want to corroborate what I hear."

"What do you hear? And who is this someone?"

"I thought I was the one asking questions."

"Do you know who this person is?"

"I can't answer that."

"You can't or you won't?"

Blanchard looked amused. "Let's leave it." He re-crossed his legs the other way. His brown brogues had thick rubber soles, probably cut from tractor tires.

"Yet you want me to answer your questions," Miles said.

"I can't force you, Miles. But why wouldn't you?"

"It's unlikely anyone would have new things to say regarding Rose's death after thirty-five years."

"We don't think so. Anyway, getting back to my earlier question, what are your recollections of Rose Biranek's death?"

"I have hardly any."

"None? You know nothing?"

"I know what everybody knows. Perhaps less." There it went, a big lie, *the* lie. Did he blush? Was Blanchard trained in reading mendacious faces? "I mean, what I know is hearsay. I was young then, not even a teenager, and was away when she died." That last part was true.

"Away?"

"Yes, I went skiing with my cousins the weekend she died. I learned what happened to poor Rose when I got back to Corby Falls, four or five days later." That was true.

"Are you sure?"

There were equal parts disappointment and disbelief in Lyle Blanchard's voice. The tip of the giant shoe, five or six feet away from Miles's face, was tracing a vaguely circular motion. Could it be that Eddy Bryson hadn't told Blanchard that Miles was the source of the story? Was Eddy keeping this final piece tight to his chest, or did he simply not know?

"Of course."

"How could you be? How could you be sure that was the weekend Rose died? As you said, it was thirty-five years ago."

He shouldn't insist. "You're right, I'm not absolutely sure. Fairly sure, though. That weekend stayed in my mind because . . . I was looking forward to the skiing trip. Very much so. That weekend too, or that week, my friend's father died. The best friend I had at the time."

A male nurse brought in the evening meals, a good opportunity to end the charade.

"I'd like to have my dinner now, Lyle."

"Two more questions?"

Miles sighed. "I'll walk you to the elevator. I need the exercise."

"This mishap you had in Corby Falls," Blanchard said, waving his hand at him, once they were out of the room. "What exactly happened?"

"I went for a walk and was mugged."

"Mugged?"

"Yes."

"You're sure?"

"I was there."

"It's just that mugging doesn't happen too often in Corby Falls."

"My luck. They took my wallet with hundreds of dollars in it, and my credit card, and bank card, and driver's licence. My OHIP card too. It made it harder to get admitted here."

"Why smack you over the head? Muggers don't usually do that."

"Maybe they didn't have a gun or a knife to threaten me with. I wouldn't have seen it anyway. It was too dark."

"They? Did you say *they*?"

"He, they, she – I don't know. I didn't see anything."

"Why the extreme brutality? You obviously got some obstinate pounding, and I heard you have a couple of cracked ribs as well."

Bloody Don.

"I wasn't bashed that badly."

"You've been in the hospital for eight days now. Three or four in the ICU."

"I had pneumonia."

"Your face and head show signs of heavy blows, not pneumonia."

"They were jittery, I guess, inexperienced. As you said, it barely happens in Corby Falls."

"*They* again. It was as if *they* didn't like you. Do you think *they* were locals?"

"I don't know."

"What did the police say?"

"I didn't go to the police."

"You didn't?"

"No."

Out came the notebook again, and Blanchard, propped against the wall, wrote a wordy note in it. Was its length meant to worry him? Additional remarks on his frosty demeanour?

"You didn't go to the local hospital either," Blanchard said, "as most people would. Instead you drove down here, or somebody drove you, and promptly checked yourself in. It looks like a flight. What were you running away from, Miles?"

"I'd rather be here, Lyle, in Toronto, where I live, close to my daughter."

He left Blanchard waiting for the elevator, but after a few steps he came back and asked, "Did you manage to talk to Mary Lambert?" It wasn't prudent of him; his curiosity might show he'd paid more attention to Lyle Blanchard's stories on the web than he'd casually admitted to earlier, yet he needed to know.

Blanchard stared at him before he answered. "Briefly. I ambushed her near her house."

"What kind of person is she?"

"The kind who doesn't talk. Or smile. She has a son who hasn't done anything with his life except be in and out of jail. Like her husband, apparently."

"Does she have a job?"

"Dental assistant. She struggles. She owns a shitty little house with a tenant in it in Leslieville. Bought it twenty years ago and is still paying the mortgage. I don't know how she could have afforded it, even so long ago. I don't think she's had an easy life. Easy or happy. Why so curious, Miles?"

Chapter 11

November 2005

The phone rang as Sarah left the house. It took him time to get to it.

"At last," he heard. "You're not easy to find." A woman's voice, a heavy accent he'd heard before.

"I just got home," he muttered.

"You're never in your office, or reading your emails. Some woman refused to give us your home phone number. We had to call Ted Ludwig – he had it in an hour."

The unmistakable inflections of Anna the poetess. "Who's *we*?"

"I asked Grisha to help me. I had to. Ted Ludwig couldn't figure out who exactly we were after. He couldn't place you, what *business* you were in."

"I made a lasting impression on him – footsteps on a beach."

There was a long pause before he heard her voice again – it was either the distance or she was shaping her next sentence.

"We'll be in Toronto the day after tomorrow, and I'll have some free time."

He struggled for an answer.

"Miles?"

"Anna, it's not a good time."

"Not a good time?"

"Not a good time to come. I'm not presentable."

Another lengthy silence. "I'm not sure . . . What are you saying?"

"I mean I've been rearranged, my face in particular, and it's hard to look at me right now. I met with some hostile fists and knees, Anna. A truncheon of some sort too. I'm not good for anything, and don't want to be seen this way."

It took her a while to process his explanation. "The police? Did they hit you?"

He laughed feebly. "Not the police, no, of course not."

"We can't . . . meet and talk?"

"There's nothing I'd like more, but . . . I was ten days in the hospital – more – and got home an hour ago. I have a shaved skull with stiches, two cracked ribs, a painful knee, a black eye that barely opens. I'm limping. My nose is askew. I'm not pretty to look at, Anna, and I'm vain."

"We'll play beauty and the beast. You can wear a mask, or hide behind a screen."

He laughed again, and his ribs protested. "It's not a good idea, Anna. Believe me, I'd love to see you."

"Are you all right?"

"I *will* be. I've been assaulted, battered. I'm finally home now, trying to heal. That's why you couldn't find me at work."

"Who did this to you? And why?"

"It's a long story. I'll tell it to you when we meet."

"This is the second long story you have promised me."

"Second?"

"Something about my late stepfather, remember?"

"We'll have to spend a lot of time together."

He found himself picturing Anna coming to the house. First, she'd take in the chipped front steps, and when he opened the door she'd see his barely opened left eye – the undissolved blue below, the scar above – and his shaved head. Following him inside, she'd spot his limp as he led her along the narrow hall and into the sitting room. He'd show her the incongruous drinks cabinet Laukhin had left him. She'd ask what had happened. He'd try not to bore her with Biranek and Corby Falls and his worries, and when he went to make, what, tea – not a drinker, Anna, he had noticed that – she'd follow him into the kitchen and wrinkle her nose at its size, the old-fashioned cabinets, the cracked tiles. Not at all like the kitchen in her well-appointed pied-à-terre in London, he imagined, or the huge apartment in Saint Petersburg. Would she explore the upstairs too? Out of curiosity? *Nostalgie de la boue*? Not likely. If bedding him was part of her plan, or a whim after hours of reminiscing about her old lover, it would be in her hotel suite, not on Montgomery Avenue. It would be where she'd be sure of clean bedsheets and a sparkling, comfortable bathroom.

Still, with Anna on Montgomery Avenue, he wouldn't dwell on Biranek. Here he was again, his mind returning to Corby Falls, like the axis of a gyroscope recovering its direction after a disturbance. He looked around him, hoping to find something that might distract his thoughts. Katelyn should be on his mind. She hadn't seemed eager to come by when he rang her with the news he would be discharged. She said she was glad and would tell her mother. Nothing about coming to Montgomery Avenue. Well, it was for the better; she shouldn't be with him until he'd found a way out of this mess of his.

He hobbled into the sitting room and poured himself a drink. It had worked in the past, a reliable source of gyroscope drift. Sarah would shake her head if she saw him, meaning, Not now, Miles. Not in your state. He sat down and switched on the TV. Manoeuvres to bring down the minority government. Paul Martin was in a fix too, perhaps pouring himself a stiff one as well. Politicians, at least, had people around them, always, advisers with soothing solutions. He switched off the TV and stood up with some difficulty.

He was painfully climbing the stairs when the phone rang again. Puffing by the time he picked up the phone in the small study, he heard George Szetes's deep voice. Work, Ludwig Robotics, that was what he needed.

"The man of the hour," George said. "What did I tell you at the hospital? Well? I said ESA's Mars rover was on the up, didn't I? And I said it before, too."

"How are things, George?"

"CMM is kaput and your rover is now the star. Flavour of the month. No, flavour of the year, of many years. It's what CSA will support. Garneau wants it, or feels it's the only reasonable option left for Canada. I was told to drop everything on CMM and catch up on ESA's mission to land a rover on Mars. They call it AEM, don't they, Ares Exploration Mission? Not a catchy moniker. Are you there, Miles? There are hints I'll be put on the proposal for the AEM work."

"Good, isn't it?"

"I'm on overhead again, Miles. It's not good to be on overhead at my age, no program or department to charge on. Older lads like me on overhead are two steps from the door."

George paused, waiting for a rebuttal, and Miles complied. "They won't turf you out, George. Geoff isn't stupid."

"Remember Brownian motion from high school science, Miles? We're all dancing every which way these days, like dust particles in sunlight. Zigzagging raised to a science. Reassessing and refocusing, that's the zeitgeist now. Blame everything around you, even swirls in the air. I hear Geoff blames Cecil for the CMM fiasco. He's not your friend either, Miles. We had a meeting yesterday in preparation for the switch to AEM. The room was full, and Kees Vermaak was there. And some troublemaker asked if Kees would simply be moved from being the proposed manager of CMM to the same position for the ESA work. There was a long silence, and then Geoff said, 'It's premature to talk of this, but it is, uh, um, not inconceivable, and since Miles is rather poorly now (yes, he said *rather poorly*), Kees may be named proposal manager. Mind you, no decision has been made. As to the program, we'll see.' Then Fowler-Biggelow cleared his throat a couple of times – classy, you know, the way the Brits do it, classier than Geoff, anyway – and said, 'Of course, Miles has done good work on his ESA projects, excellent, in fact, and his team is well regarded in Europe. We don't really know when the invitation to tender will be put out, but Miles should be back by then. He may have a shot at the program position too, as he knows the field and the players. Geoff is right, it's too early to address who'd be the program manager.' But Geoff got in again and, said that Kees has experience managing large programs. I don't know, Miles, which large programs Kees managed in his past, but Geoff was implying that you don't have the same kind of background. Cecil didn't say anything after that, but I have to give it to him: he did put in his two cents' worth on your behalf. Are you buddies these days?"

"He dislikes me less than he dislikes Geoff. And Kees Vermaak is an unknown quantity to him."

"No one knows Kees. And I worked with him for half a year on CMM."

"Come on, George. What's he like?"

"Correct, polite, few words. No jokes and no smiles, not a trace. Never a hello or even a nod. Nothing."

"Why is he here?"

"You mean, in Toronto?"

"Why did he move to Ludwig Robotics from Ludwig Space? Who in his right mind moves from Vancouver to Toronto?"

"I don't know. Got to go, Miles. Check your emails. When are you coming back? You *are* coming back, aren't you?"

"I need the money, George."

"You're both poor and poorly. Any news from Dr. Chu? Is he aware you are *rather poorly* these days?"

He wished Anna was there with him. Perhaps he should not have put her off. If nothing else, they would have talked. Anna the poetess, not Anna Pripogurina. Not the most fetching last name, Pripogurina. No wonder she kept Lyutova for her forthcoming volume. Anna Lyutova sounded much better, though *Anna the poetess* sounded best. There was a shade of dismissing irony in it, true, yet benevolent, and with an endearing, affable echo. *Poetess* was in disfavour now, Ben had told him. University professors must pay attention to correctness, he said, although Ben didn't at all mind *poetess*. It was close to *poetesa*, the Russian word for it.

In the growing shadows of the evening his romantic imagination took over and the impossible faded. A long, quiet dinner with Anna the poetess. Candlelight, the increased attraction of her reserved smile.

He logged in to the company system to read his emails. Gazillions, one even from Dr. Chu. Most recent ones first, or work his way up from the early ones? The latter; he had plenty of time.

Not much from Mohan. He'd always been a face-to-face communicator, not a writer of emails. It exasperated Miles. He once accused Mohan of "not wanting to leave a trace of how your mind works." Mohan erupted: "You're able to track my mind in technical memos and reports. Emails are for managers and big shots. That's what they fill their time with." Mohan had a good excuse now. He explained in an email sent the Monday after the incident in Corby Falls that he was upset by what had happened to Miles and saw no reason to clutter his in-box while he was away from work.

He had a point. Half a point. Cecil showed no such reluctance, and Miles decided to give priority to his boss. The first email had been sent while Miles was still in the ICU.

Date: 25 October 2005, 10:06

Miles,

On Sunday your sister left me a message you'd been assaulted in Corby Falls and that, as a result, you would not be able to come to work for some time. I'm shocked by what happened to you – the whole of Ludwig Robotics is. This morning Mohan said he called the hospital yesterday and learned you were in the ICU. He also said the doctors had been worried about your very high fever once they patched you up, but that you're likely to be moved out of the ICU in a day or two. We're breathing easier here, and everyone joins me in wishing you a speedy recovery.

I don't know when you'll read this. Of course, the sooner you do, and the sooner you're back at work, the better. You're missed here – the more so because eyes are now converging on your ESA studies and the ESA rover. Geoff and Ted Ludwig have had another chat with Garneau in Ottawa on Monday, and this morning Geoff sounded deflated. He said he had not fully given up on CMM. I wasn't sure whether to believe him or not.

Get well soon.

Cecil

His next email was sent six days later.

Date: 31 October 31, 2005, 15:22

Miles,

What a difference a few days make. The country's planetary exploration now rests with AEM – that's what Geoff told us on Friday. With the unexpected jump in the Russian cost estimate, CSA simply doesn't have the funds for CMM. Garneau refuses to ask the government for the "exorbitant" (his word) amount CMM now needs, and believes that the shocking hike in the cost of the program is just the first in many.

Garneau seems to be fully behind AEM now. No amount of money has been committed yet, but there is unofficial talk of $120 million Canadian. This is €80 million at the current exchange rate, and a major drop in Ludwig's projected income. Still, half a loaf is better than no loaf. Our much heralded political contacts, including a former CSA president, were unable to revive CMM, so we speak AEMish now. Sadly, Mr. AEM himself – that's you – is not here. Mohan is giving a crash course in AEMish. He's busy though, because two of your small studies are coming to an end and obviously need his attention. He's also impatient (we know that), has no ear for nuances, and leaves a confused picture of ESA's structure and leading players. I asked him to draw a list of the main actors in the AEM play – I have yet to see it. You've been in and around ESA's Ares Initiative for almost three years now, and I'm sure you have all that down. I wish I had paid more attention to ESA in the past.

In a teleconference last night Ted Ludwig had harsh words for Geoff and me. What was happening in Toronto was unacceptable, he said. Unless we had some new work coming in, and soon, we'd have to lay off people. The cows that we'd milked for years were exhausted – his exact words. On-orbit servicing was going nowhere slow, we were not nimble enough for terrestrial robotics, and now CMM was dead. We had to bring in a good chunk of ESA's work now. Ted, of course, conveniently forgot that he was the one who pushed us in the CMM ring. We did nothing else for a year now except dance CMM. But it's the prerogative of chiefs to forget their own blunders.

I hear you're out of ICU and doing better. Please email me as soon as you know when you'll be back.

Again wishing you a speedy recovery,

Cecil

He heard Sarah on the stairs. She came into the room, put her hands on his shoulders, and stared at the screen. "Work? That should keep your mind off other things. Good news from Ludwig?"

"Yes and no. Well, yes."

"Why the doubt? Problems? Knee deep in raccoon shit? The wheels don't walk?"

"No, no . . . Things are fine, technically. Too good, in fact."

"What?"

"Too much interest."

"Interest? Where?"

"At Ludwig."

"Isn't it good?"

"Not for me."

"What's happening?"

"The agency has wised up on the Canadian Mars Mission. I don't think they ever believed in it – I mean, it was at least several hundred million dollars – but bureaucracies need problems to agonize over. They don't survive if they just say, 'This is silly, not realistic, there's no money for it. Next.' They'd be out of work. So they kick everything down the road for as long as they can. Shows they're busy."

"And?"

"And now a contribution to the Mars rover that Europe is putting together – a significant contribution, although much less than the amount for the Canadian mission – seems the way to go."

"Is CSA falling in love with the *perambulator*?"

"One CSA person is, the president. Don't understand why, as he's a former astronaut. We didn't do badly in the concept studies and in Phase A, and there is a good case for Canada to get a visible chunk of the rover. Providing the funding is adequate, of course."

"*Visible* chunk?"

"Something politicians can grasp and show off. Something they can paint a Maple Leaf on."

"But you're not happy."

"No."

"Why?"

"I might be out."

"What?"

"They'll want one of the golden boys at the helm."

"And you're not one of them."

"You know I'm not. They gave me these small projects simply because they had no future. Somehow we did well; we worked fine with the European companies, and ESA like us. And now their rover is fashionable."

"The fruits of success are a fuckton of trouble. Could be the name of my first abstract sculpture. Still, better than brooding about Biranek and Jim Cowley and . . ." She patted the back of his neck, wary of the scar above. "I'm leaving now, Miles. I have to drive to Corby Falls – see to a few things – and Mike is threatening separation. I'll come back on Saturday and do more shopping for you. I'll phone every day. Call if you need anything."

"How is old Mike?"

"Not happy. He wonders why he bought a big house in Caledon if I'm hardly ever there. As if I asked him to." She tapped him lightly on the shoulder. "I'm going now, meeting a friend."

Cecil's next email was sent three days later.

Date: 03 November 2005; 9:15

Miles,

Things are moving ahead rapidly. We're in the middle of a two-day meeting here with Astrium. Old acquaintances from Stevenage are here – Max Tennant and Penelope Shore. Escorting them is a Robert Cintron, with international business development at Astrium. His card, now that I look at it, says Stevenage, Toulouse, and Friedrichshafen. Blimey. Max and Penelope seemed bewildered by what happened to you and they are uncomfortable with the idea of weeks before your return.

This may turn out to be a long email. I'll send you the minutes from today as soon as they become available. I'd like you to "hit the ground running" when you return. The question of who will manage the future phases of our involvement in ESA's AEM is a concern to me.

Geoff was in the meeting at least half of the time, in and out. (This will tell you how important AEM has become for him.) Mohan arrived late – he always is – and Max Tennant seemed relieved to see him. Kees Vermaak and George Szetes were there as well. Geoff introduced Kees as a potential program manager, mentioning your poor state and the uncertain date of your return. Need I say he has not properly discussed this with me? I'm not sure whether he thinks highly of Kees, simply likes him, or has instructions from Vancouver. This is a "heads-up."

Now the meat. Astrium think Ludwig Robotics are a good fit with them. They are keen to bid with us for Phase B work. We told them we are too.

The first information Astrium were after was the value of the Canadian commitment for AEM. Geoff said €80 million, and emphasized he had that number from Garneau himself. Unofficial number for now, he hastened to add, but as it came from the mouth of the CSA's president, there should be no doubts regarding Canada's commitment. There was another question Astrium were keen on having answered. Was Canada interested strictly in AEM, or were there other aspects of the Mars missions being contemplated by ESA that were of interest too? Geoff said AEM – and strictly the rover. (I don't disagree, but we are on rocky ground here, as the CSA's scientists might object.)

Astrium expect the UK government to commit some €240 million to the Ares Initiative. The UK priorities are: science instruments and tools, €115 million; Ares Rover, €85 million; entry, descent, and landing system technologies, €40 million. They want to be prime for the Ares Rover. On the rover subsystems they expressed particular interest in data handling, telecom, operations centre. It's not clear whether the Rover Operations Centre (ROC?) will come under the Ares Rover proper or under AEM.

We agreed it is a good thing there is no major overlapping of interests in subsystems. Astrium said they are perfectly aware that both they and Ludwig want to be the Rover System prime. They expect to be the prime. It is sensible, they argued, as their commitment to AEM is much bigger overall if consideration is given to the science instruments and the entry, descent, and landing system. (Their interest in the latter stems, I think, from the failure of the Beagle mission to land.) They expect Phase B to be divided into a Phase B1 (short, kind of a consolidation of Phase A) and a stretched Phase B2, which will be the real Phase B. Astrium proposed to carry on during B1 with the same Phase A arrangements, and re-address the issue of who will be the rover prime at the start of the real Phase B. Smooth. I couldn't argue with the logic. Geoff said nothing, and the matter was left there.

The team Astrium have in mind includes, besides Ludwig Robotics, Färber & Feldt in Munich, with which both Astrium and Ludwig have worked in the past, and the Italian company Galileo Aerospaziale. They may have to consider more than one Italian company, and may bring in a Swiss and/or a Spanish company too. It depends on the financial commitment each ESA member makes. Astrium consider Alenia their main competition, because the Italians have said they would contribute enough funds to be the prime of the rover mission to Mars. Alenia is a great concern to Astrium.

The rest of the day was spent with Astrium explaining to us – mainly Geoff and Kees and George – ESA's pie-splitting principle that each country gets work proportional to its financial contribution. They emphasized that ESA tries to adhere to this rule in each program, and when that turns out to be impossible, they "balance the books" on other programs, ongoing or subsequent. ESA recognize it's nightmarishly complicated trying to balance the technical requirements of a program with industrial competences and geopolitical financial commitments. An almost impossible task, yet they do it and have done it in the past, by means of compromises which inevitably lead to cost increases and schedule slips. Geoff kept scratching his head.

When are you coming back to work? Your absence is felt.

Cecil

PS: What's the likelihood of a split Phase B in your opinion?

He'd never received such a long email from Cecil. There was a chatty nervousness about it, and the language was curiously tame.

Sarah was right: reading Cecil's emails and concentrating on work, he'd forgotten Biranek. Well, almost, because with that observation the late doctor and Corby Falls were back in his mind.

Should he answer Cecil's email now or in the morning? A cup of coffee before deciding? No, too late for coffee. A drink? With all the pills in him? He imagined his painful trip down the stairs, then having to clamber back up. Elma Mulligan said Rose had found going up the stairs easier than going down. He pictured himself tumbling down and being unable to move at the bottom. Like Rose. Sarah did say she'd ring every day, didn't she? So had Elma; she said she'd ring Rose later, and then she forgot her. He should insist Sarah phoned twice a day, and come immediately if he didn't answer. He should ask Katelyn to do the same, tell her mother to drive here if there was no answer.

He answered Cecil's emails in the morning, after he'd cautiously taken a shower and spent five minutes staring at his face in the mirror. No wonder his own daughter had been put off. He'd been right to delay Anna. She would have taken one look at him and run away screaming.

Date: 07 November 2005, 8:55

Cecil,

I got home yesterday from the hospital. I'm reading my work email now, and answering them one by one. Here are some comments in response to your email from Nov 3.

I heard rumours of €400–500 million from the Italian government, and with that amount Alenia could choose to be prime for any element, not only the overall mission. It explains the jitters Astrium has regarding Alenia. The creation over the summer of Thales Alenia Space, with the merger of Alenia's space segment with Alcatel's, has created a large French-Italian competitor of a size that can battle Astrium on equal terms. It is the Italian division which will get most (all?) of the work, as the French, with a large of investment in Ariane, will be less generous to the Ares Initiative. Until now DLR has kept quiet about the level of the German commitment to AEM.

It's more than likely that a Phase B will be split into a short B1 and a much longer B2. To date, the financial commitments to the mission are uncertain. Furthermore, two teams are now (Phase A) working on concept definitions. Unless one is way better than the other – hardly ever the case – they'll have to be reconciled somehow. Finally, the mission prime (Italy?) needs to buy into the chosen concept and firm up the requirements. Therefore, a Phase B1 as a consolidation of Phase A is eminently reasonable, almost a must.

The €80 million from the government will not get Canada the Rover System prime role. It is smaller than the UK's amount (never mind Italy's). An opening for us would be to insist on the prime role for the Rover Vehicle, although its definition will always be an arcane argument.

The date of my return to work is Nov 21. Not sooner – doctors' orders. It might be later if my appearance doesn't take a quick turn for the better. Because, Cecil, I look a fright right now. There's a limit to my willingness to play the monster. I'll wear headgear of some sort and sunglasses when I get back.

I'll read emails, answer the phone – if I get to it in time with my swollen knee – offer opinions, read documents. If needed, you can hook me into teleconferences.

Thanks for the good wishes,

Miles

PS: Thanks for the "heads-up" too.

The third day at home he called Federica and asked her to come over. "Without Katelyn," he added. "I need to talk to you alone."

"About?"

"It affects Katelyn in an indirect way. It's a long story, Federica, and I don't want Katelyn to hear it. Come tomorrow, when she's at school."

"I'm working, Miles."

"It's important."

"Is Sarah there?"

"She's gone up to Corby Falls. She's had enough of me and hospitals."

"Are you all right by yourself?"

"I have everything I need and Dr. Time is healing me."

Federica came the following day around lunchtime with sushi and a bottle of white wine. Under a fur coat, she wore a V-necked black dress with a belt detail at the waist. Black suede boots. An appreciative sound escaped him when she took off the coat, so she did a pirouette and said, "A cashmere wrap dress for the Brazilian business woman. I dashed on some Brazilian perfume too – a little heavy but sensual. Greg was in Brazil last week. He sends his best. Can't get over your mishap." She offered him the crook of her neck. "Here, smell."

Ah, Federica, she knew how to get a man's attention, always did. She brought plates and glasses from the kitchen and they sat at one end of the dining table.

"Poor Miles, look at you," she said. "Do you have to wear those hideous sunglasses? That baseball cap?"

"I got myself into trouble, Federica, by opening my mouth. And it's not just me."

It took him a long time to tell her what had happened and the bind he was in, and she became quieter as his long chronicle went on. When he finished, most of the sushi and the wine was gone, though Federica had hardly touched either. At the end, she got up and walked to the window. He stood up too and joined her. The day was dull, with low clouds. They looked at the uneven backyard lawn with the surge of withered oregano and weeds in what used to be the herb patch.

"I don't remember Ripple Road," she said.

"Past the old bridge. We used to take walks along it in the summer. The road follows the river, more or less, and it's pleasant on a nice day. There's a small point, after half a mile or so, where there are trees and picnic tables, and there's a shallow little bay that Katelyn waded in sometimes."

"I understand where it is and can place it, but I don't have any picture of it in my mind."

His knee was still hurting. He had felt low the entire morning, and the wine was failing to cheer him up. He missed the hospital morphine. They had weaned him off it before he'd gone home. He missed Katelyn too.

"Well?" he asked.

She didn't answer, and he repeated his prompt.

"You don't have a choice," Federica said softly, without looking at him.

"You mean, if it gets to court, I'll have to lie."

"Yes."

"Surprising advice from a lawyer."

She nodded.

"It bugs me," he said.

"It's Katelyn, Miles."

"I know."

"In Europe, you know, she'd be safe."

"Don't do this."

"It's the logical thing to say."

He left her at the window and sat down.

"You can't take chances with Katelyn," Federica went on. "You can't take chances with your sister either. Or with you, again. Look at you. There isn't anything to decide."

He couldn't think why lying in court was so hard to contemplate. On a whim he had lied about his wallet being stuffed with banknotes. He had told lies before – small lies – time and again. Everybody did. He'd lied to Lyle Blanchard: he'd said he knew nothing about Rose's death.

"I dismissed Jim's threats," he said. "I told myself that was just him talking big. But even before we parted, I more or less decided I was going to tell anyone who asked me, court or no court, that I made up the story. Jim was right: the good citizens of Millcroft Township have every right to a modern hospital. The walk along Ripple Road and the fresh air helped. And then they fucked me up. They could've killed me, Federica. I wonder if they didn't think I was dead when they left me there, or hope I'd die. It bugs me to give in to Jim and his goons. Jim, my buddy."

Her face to the window, Federica said, "There's something wild, out of control, about what they did to you. Jim met you to give you a warning, yet they got to you the same evening."

She was right, of course. And lying in court, or to whomever, led to the best outcome. There was no escaping the soundness of that logic. Murderer or not, Biranek had left most of his money to the township hospital. Should the money be burnt? Wasn't tainted money best spent on a good cause, and wasn't the hospital in Millcroft the best cause?

The news from Ottawa and Europe remained by and large encouraging. Cecil's last email, four days before Miles's delayed return to work, confirmed things were on the right track.

Date: 23 November 2005, 13:50

Miles,

It's disappointing you've postponed your return for a week, but I'm sure you and your doctors know what's best for you.

The overall news on ESA's rover is fine, inasmuch as there haven't been any nasty surprises and things are moving along the expected course.

We had a telecon with CSA yesterday morning. Louis Gandarax was on the other side, and so was Paul Arsenault. Gandarax brought him along at the last moment for his insights into ESA.

Gandarax said that the CSA's Executive Committee met on November 16 and 17. On the participation in ESA's AEM, the consensus was that Canada would pursue this unique opportunity. Garneau stressed the importance of a *visible* role, and they all agreed that the AEM rover was the most visible element of the mission.

Financial aspects of AEM were discussed around a sheet distributed by Lysiane Monast, the senior VP. A cash flow problem was identified – matching CSA's cash availability with ESA/AEM needs. Gandarax reported he had a long talk with the manager of AEM at ESA who said ESA would be flexible in this regard.

There was opposition too. Alain Joubert, CSA's Director of Strategic Planning and Development, said AEM was not in the recent CSA ten-year plan. He was of the opinion that CSA, with its small budget and large Space Station and manned programs commitments, should concentrate on Earth observation. This (as per Gandarax) was received with a glare from Garneau, and no one else followed Joubert on the road of explicit dissent. There were voices of implied dissent though, expressed in the worry that other programs would have their budgets cut to make room for AEM, and that, as with CMM, one should go to the treasury for the funding. Garneau assured everybody that there was no need to go to the treasury, because AEM's financial needs were significantly smaller than CMM's. With ESA's avowed flexibility, a way to finance Canada's participation in AEM would be found without disturbing an already besieged government.

Toward the end of the telecon Paul Arsenault mentioned the upcoming ESA's Council of Ministers meeting in Berlin on December 5–6. Most countries would make definite commitments re AEM in Berlin. Was the CSA ready to do the same in such a short time?

There was another telecon in the afternoon with Astrium. Your friend Max Tennant was in a bad mood – Italy seemed set to get a high profile role in the rover. Other countries were preparing large commitments to AEM as well. There were rumours, Tennant said, that minnow Switzerland would contribute €40 million to AEM, and that Spain would commit twice that amount. Can this be true, Miles, €80 million from Spain? Let's hope Spain is not interested in the rover.

I'll see you on Monday.

Cecil

Arsenault was CSA's lead delegate to ESA's program board under which planetary exploration fell. He was also in many working groups and spent part of his time travelling to Paris and various ESA centres. Miles found Arsenault cagey, not always willing to share the latest material or information from ESA. It was a conclusion he reached following discussions with Astrium and Färber & Feldt in which he realized that Ludwig's European partners were much better informed of the goings-on at ESA. Miles had complained about it to Fowler-Biggelow, who shrugged and said it was being on the continent that made the Europeans better informed. "They're all a one-hour flight from each other, Miles. They smell every one of ESA's farts."

Chapter 12

November, December 2005

He went back to work on the last Monday of November. His colleagues at Ludwig Robotics were clearly startled by his appearance: the way they looked, or avoided looking, at him; the awkward insistence on learning the significance of *Camp Kitchi* on his green cap; the attempts at humour ("Creepy shades, Miles.").

Geoff Simmons put on a compassionate face when they met. Miles was pondering which coffee beans were best suited for a late November morning.

"You should have stayed off longer," said Geoff. "Psychological recovery from an incident like that is as important as the physical recovery. More important, even. The Ivory Noir is freshly ground." He took a few steps away, then turned back. "Corby Falls, isn't it? Your home town. That's what Cecil said when he mentioned your mishap."

"Corby Falls, yes."

"I read something about Corby Falls in the *Post* two or three months ago. Dorothea pointed it out to me. A bequest was in trouble. A doctor who left his money to the local hospital, isn't it? Troubles with the bequest . . . or with the doctor. I don't remember. Same Corby Falls?"

"Same one. Our few minutes of fame."

"How many souls live there, Miles?"

"Under a thousand."

"Huh! The things that go on in your little town. I'll tell Dorothea that Corby Falls is where one of our engineers was badly bashed. She'll be delighted. She's been obsessed by the *Post* story, bombards my ears with it. There were further incidents on some website, I understand, with added drama and promises of more. I don't remember the doctor's name, though. Did you know him?"

"Oh, you know, it's such a small place."

Geoff didn't insist. "Wait till I tell Dorothea." Then he made a show of reconsidering. "On second thought, perhaps I won't. She might invite you to dinner, and we don't want that, do we?" He left, laughing, pleased with his remark.

Miles had hoped he could forget Biranek and Corby Falls at work. Now, walking gingerly back to his office with his mug of Ivory Noir, a feeling of dismay set in at the thought that even Geoff Simmons knew of the Biranek affair. And if Geoff was not fully apprised, his wife was, and she'd keep him up to date. Surely Geoff had talked to Cecil about it, at least in passing. Had Don said something to Geoff too? Had he shared what he knew with a delighted Dorothea at a recent dinner at the Simmonses'? Don was a third or fourth cousin of Dorothea's, and once told Miles about a superb meal he'd had there. At least Don would not be a problem for much longer. These were his last weeks with Ludwig – he'd already given notice.

He spend most of the day listening to Mohan, answering emails, trying to guess what was next for the fragile AEM. The launch in 2009 was impossible, everyone knew that, although, as always, no one was willing to be the first to state the obvious. And this was just the beginning; nothing had yet been built, or tested. Schedule slips were complicated by the launch windows, which came every two years or so. Knowing the way ESA operated and made decisions, even 2011 seemed tight. It was chaotic, dependent on yet-undeclared geopolitical commitments, the whims of whatever governments and responsible ministers were in power, the passing fads of various committees, ad hoc industrial teamings, elastic political notions like visibility or leverage coefficient. A Level 2 chaos, no doubt. He was a shaman reading bones, fooling himself that order might be predicted from disorder.

When he left, he found Fowler-Biggelow outside the back door, brooding and uncertain of the best way to navigate past the ambling geese separating them from the parking lot.

"It's here that we need hazard detection software, not on Mars," Miles said. "The flock is getting bigger and bigger. Exponentially."

"Gaggle."

"Sorry?"

"Gaggle, for non-flying geese. Skein, for those flying, the V-shape."

"Wow."

"Learned that from Geoff. He says two-thirds of Canada geese don't fly south, and so far none of these have. He's become obsessed by them, end of his wits. Nothing seems to work. He's given up on swans and dogs. We had a goose-whisperer while you were away, and he's talking of death-rays now, something that will vaporize the geese without a trace. The shit is the worst part. They do it every twenty minutes or so. Also from Geoff." He fished a cigarette out of a pack with his long fingers and lit it. "There's shit in Ottawa too." He inhaled deeply. "Terrible news, Miles, with the Liberals' fall."

"Martin lost the confidence vote?"

"Just found out." Cecil sounded distressed.

"They'll be back in a month."

"I don't know. If they're back, it will be a minority government. Not good for Ludwig Robotics or Ludwig Space. Not good for CSA's budgets. Almost as bad as a Conservative government. But worse for us is that Marc Garneau has resigned."

"What?"

"He'll run as a Liberal in the forthcoming elections."

"You sure?"

"Ted Ludwig sent around an email. Well, Garneau has never hidden his political ambitions. It's his time now, a safe Quebec Liberal seat." He regarded Miles's cap and sunglasses. "When is the disguise coming off?"

Paul Arsenault was at ESA's headquarters in Paris that week. He sounded cheerful when Miles and Mohan reached him in his hotel room. It was early evening in Paris, unusually mild, Paul told them. He wasn't sure if he'd need a coat going out. He would stay put through the weekend to recover, then was off to Germany for ESA's Council of Ministers meeting. As expected, AEM had been the main focus of the board, and the last two days had been a grind, with rumours and side-meetings and manoeuvrings outside the formal proceedings. Germany was under the same constraint as Canada: they needed a visible role, and that meant the rover. Much energy was spent on arriving at the exact definition of, and difference between, the Rover System and the Rover Vehicle. The UK acted during the meeting as if the Rover System was theirs for the taking. Canada, of course, coveted the Rover System too, but – and here Paul's voice acquired a low, melancholy tone – based on what he'd heard from Astrium, and also on some informal discussions at CSA, it was the Rover Vehicle which seemed more attainable. There had been strong hints, though, that Italy would announce a huge contribution to AEM in Berlin and that as a result the Rover System lead belonged to them. Them being Alenia. In which case, the UK would insist on the Rover Vehicle lead, and Canada, that is, Ludwig . . . Paul paused to let the implication sink in. Coming down in the hierarchy of systems, Paul went on, the next best thing was the Chassis and Locomotion Subsystem. But, again, it was a question of how one defined that subsystem, and much time was spent on it too. Leaving its exact content aside, Germany was now demanding the Chassis and Locomotion for Färber & Feldt. Amusement in Paul's voice. There they were, playing at a kind of a musical chairs. If Astrium pushed Ludwig Robotics from the Rover Vehicle, then Ludwig would be clashing with Färber & Feldt. Was the Chassis and Locomotion Subsystem truly visible? Visible at all?

"Hard to see how," Mohan said, and then laughed happily at his own joke.

Miles shook his head at him and hastened to say that one could make a case to the politicians that it *was* a visible element; after all, one could always see the chassis and the wheels, particularly the wheels, though most people would yawn uncomprehendingly. No politician would understand the difference between the Rover System and the Rover Vehicle either.

Paul went on. In a long dinner with his UK and German counterparts, the DLR rep had got quite heated and reminded Paul that Canada was only a tolerated member of ESA. Common sense quickly prevailed, and they agreed that until the politicians stated exactly how open their purses were it made no sense getting overworked. Germany's position was not driven by the Ares Initiative only. Like France, Germany had a heavy investment in Ariane as well. Following the DLR rep's outburst, Paul reminded the table that the Rover Operations Centre was also a visible element of the mission. All eyes would be on it – or in it – once proper exploration was under way. The centre went along fittingly with the German expertise in space operations. Paul knew the UK was eying it too, but it was worth making the point to calm the waters. It helped. Paul paused to allow Miles and Mohan time to comprehend the calibre of his diplomacy. He had them on speaker, and his voice seemed modulated by how far he strayed from the phone in his hotel room. Still deciding on the appropriate attire? Moving back and forth to admire himself in front of the mirror? He had a tête-à-tête with the UK rep afterward, Paul went on with a sigh. The agreement with the UK, ironed out at the earlier meetings between Astrium and Ludwig, remained solid. The last piece of news was that Switzerland had been aggressive both in and outside the meeting and had pestered everybody about their interest in either the Chassis and Locomotion Subsystem or in the Navigation Subsystem. Yes, the Swiss were in the picture, and not shy about trumpeting their interests and expertise before the hard commitments were made.

Before he hung up, Paul told them that Garneau had indeed resigned and was off into federal politics as a Liberal Party candidate. "It's going to make everything more difficult," he said.

"Everything?" Miles asked.

"The support for AEM."

Did he hear a mild giggle in Paul's voice?

Somehow Miles was left with the impression that Paul Arsenault's modest interventions had been timely and decisive. It was only later, when he recalled Paul saying, "I'll spend the weekend in Paris to recover, then I'm off to Germany," that he felt a mounting resentment. Indignation too. Recover? What from? The long dinners? Outbursts of irate agency reps? What the fuck had Paul actually done there? What did Paul tell him that was new and substantial? That the Swiss were elbowing in?

The difficulties with CSA became clearer a week later. Miles had heard unsettling noises from Berlin, but with Cecil away on a sudden three-day trip he'd been unable to get a straight story. When he learned from Denise, Cecil's secretary, that the boss had returned, Miles went to his office. Kees Vermaak was just leaving and walked past Miles without saying a word.

"A disagreement?" Miles asked Cecil, as he shut the door.

"That man has the charm of an airport washroom. He came with a message from Geoff, but the way he delivered it . . . I told him to bugger off. Of course Geoff will be in my hair soon."

Cecil looked greyer and thinner than ever, his nose acquiring the profile of a woodpecker's beak. He and Geoff had been to Saint-Hubert, then Vancouver, then back to Saint-Hubert and finally Ottawa. He said that he'd read Miles's querying emails, but he needed to make sure of certain facts before he could answer. Yes, there were problems with the Canadian commitment to AEM, and the trip had been very difficult, but things were being worked out at the highest levels. He raised a nonbelligerent hand. He knew that usually such a cliché meant either nothing or trouble. However, he'd heard Ted Ludwig call his father in Vancouver and there was no reason to be down. All the same, it would be best if Miles didn't spread the word in the company. Not even to his team. They were on a roller-coaster ride – unexpectedly down at this time, but up would follow for sure. Ludwig was a big company, influential, with friends in the highest places, and contacts and lobbyists. Furthermore, Marc Garneau, although gone, still had some pull. If the Liberals won, he would be back as the responsible minister.

"You think so?"

"No doubt."

"What happened?"

Cecil gave a lengthy sigh. Bad news from the most recent CSA executive committee meeting, the first since Garneau's departure. With Garneau gone, voices were raised against AEM and its rover. Many voices, a majority. Joseph Courant, a satellite man named acting president soon after Garneau bolted, had in the past cautiously followed Garneau's lead. Now he was wavering. Geoff and Cecil learned on their trip that Garneau had never briefed the minister about his enthusiasm for ESA's Mars efforts. And now many on the executive committee told Courant that he couldn't commit increased funds to ESA without getting the minister's nod. With the election looming, there was no point in seeing the minister. And that was not the worst. There was a new stance at CSA regarding the Ares Initiative: they would support it, yes, but only with new money. In other words, no other projects or undertakings would be quashed to finance AEM. Garneau might have followed that path, but not Courant.

"And Gandarax?" Miles asked. "Louis Gandarax was keen on AEM as well. Kept his mouth shut? Nothing from him?"

"Gandarax's gone too."

"What?"

"This election came at a bad time."

"Is he running for a seat as well?"

"He's taken a leave of absence to work for a candidate."

"For Garneau?"

"Perhaps."

Cecil raised his hand to signal there was more. Like a speaking semaphore tower, he used his long arms to underline or convey a message. Alain Joubert, the brain behind CSA's ten-year strategic plan, had been the loudest voice. No wonder, as there was nothing noteworthy in it regarding ESA. This meant that it would take some time now to get significant funding for AEM from CSA. The next ascent on the roller coaster would be long in coming.

"How long? What happened at the Council of Ministers? Arsenault wouldn't return my calls or answer my emails. Neither would Max Tennant."

Another long sigh from Cecil. Arsenault was likely taking his usual added-on vacation. In Berlin, Courant had explained that the Canadian government had fallen and the agency had to wait for a newly elected government to sanction the full Canadian contribution. Courant confirmed the existing €6-million contribution, and reaffirmed the intention to commit another €59 million within a few months, for a total of €65 million.

"Sixty-five?" Miles said. "It was eighty million before. What happened?"

Cecil frowned and said it was the number Courant told the meeting, and the number ESA was now counting on. "Games were played with numbers. The Canadian position was accepted by the other member states. Well, the Europeans were well-mannered, and they didn't have much choice. No doubt some countries rejoiced in the Canadian hiatus; less competition for the craved visibility."

"Who committed what?"

Cecil looked at a piece of paper on his desk. There was both distress and disgust in his voice as he listed the numbers: Italy, €250 million; United Kingdom, €105 million; France, €95 million; Germany, €85 million; Spain, €40 million; Switzerland, €32 million; lower amounts from other countries; Canada, €6 million.

"We're fucked," Miles said.

"No, no. For now, perhaps. Briefly buggered, short term. Given the fall of the government, what Courant said at the Council of Minsters was encouraging. The challenge before us now is to ensure that Canada makes good on the additional €59 million once a new government is in place. Say, within three months. At the same time, of course, agitating for a rover-visible role. Our position remains that Canada has made a strong commitment, almost as strong as those of the other countries. The interregnum is a technicality."

Did Cecil believe his own words?

Astrium rang in the early afternoon. When he heard Max Tennant's voice, Miles wished he hadn't picked up the phone. From the long delays in Tennant's replies and an irregular background noise, Miles knew Max was on speakerphone and that others were in the room with him. More minds to assess the damage. And, no doubt, calls from Astrium were made or would be made at higher levels. The highest levels, and not necessarily to Ludwig Robotics.

Max sounded tired. He had not returned Miles's messages because they were busy re-evaluating their plans at Astrium based on the outcome of ESA's Council of Ministers. They'd been in endless meetings since, but Max wanted a quick exchange on Miles's views after Berlin.

Best to sound a note of moderate optimism without sounding silly, Miles told himself. True, he began – in what he hoped was a clear, measured tone – on the Canadian contribution things in Berlin hadn't gone as Ludwig Robotics had been led to believe they would. But it was just a matter of time, an interval, until a new government was in place. The fact that CSA's president had resigned to enter politics was not of great help either. A permanent replacement would be found soon. He threw in the word *interregnum*, somewhat ashamed and unsure of the proper pronunciation. A double-inter-regnum.

AEM, Max said after what seemed an interminable lag, had had a good meeting in Berlin, a proper birth, and it was now oversubscribed. The set budget of €595 million was surpassed. Even with Canada's puny contribution, the countries had committed €650 million. The windfall had led some delegates to dream of a mission with a larger rover launched with Ariane. Back-of-the-envelope calculations were carried out amid whispers to check whether the switch from the less powerful Soyuz launcher was at all feasible. (Max himself didn't think so.) With the weak Canadian contribution, the Germans were already telling everybody that the Chassis and Locomotion Subsystem was theirs. The Swiss were making similar noises. Germany might be easier to deal with, because they were also interested in the rover payload and in the Rover Operations Centre. Canada would have a fight on their hands, and at least in the short term they would be under a lot of pressure. The UK's position had not changed, and it depended on how quickly Canada could sort out its mess. A Färber & Feldt with "sharpened claws" would be making new demands at the three-party teleconference next week. "Be prepared for grief from them," Max said.

After what Miles guessed was a brief consultation with someone in the room, Max carried on. Near-term programmatic decisions had been taken in Berlin as well. The partition of Phase B into B1 and B2 had been confirmed. It had been Italy all the way, and, yes, they would run the circus. Phase B1 would give Alenia, the clear lead company now, time to grow into the role of mission prime. All requirements and concepts would be readdressed. Because B1 was short in duration and scope, Max added hesitantly after a small break in the connection, the €6 million from Canada would go a long way, and Canada would still be "in" at the end of it. Good news for Ludwig; it offered a respite. The additional €59 million ought to be officially committed by Canada by the end of B1 for Ludwig to properly claim a visible role on the rover at the start of the real Phase B. No, he had to correct himself: the commitment must be made before, by the time the invitations to tender for B2 were out.

He drove east on Dundas to Hamilton Street. Turning right, he proceeded slowly, glancing to his left, until he saw the number he was looking for. It was a crimson vinyl-sided house, one of several semi-detached houses, narrow, three-storeyed, rather run down. A blue-grey house on one side, a yellow one on the other. Such exuberance of colour seemed more appropriate to a hill town perched over the Ligurian Sea. Squashed under the sloped roofs, the third floors looked like afterthought additions for penurious, child-sized tenants. Leslieville. Didn't they have strip joints in Leslieville? Jilly's? Yes, that was the name, one of them. In the very old days he was once dragged along to Jilly's – not that he needed much dragging – by Ben and a colleague of his who, unexpectedly, had won at Woodbine and claimed to be a connoisseur of the finer points of exotic dancing. Even Helen had gone along with them that time. "It's on me, don't you three worry," the punter had said. "There are things to learn, especially you, Helen. You'll dazzle that boyfriend of yours. What kind of name is Bleidd?"

On his third loop around, going back up north on Munro Street and then down south again, he found a space that had just opened up and squeezed the Corolla into it. From here he could keep an eye on the crimson house ahead. Mary Lambert's house, if the ancient phone book was to be trusted. The wooden porch in front was shaded by a striped white and green awning, torn in places. A thin young woman came out of the blue-grey house next door with an anxious dog, which had to be pulled down the few steps to the street level. An older man in wrinkled pajamas put his nose out and said something to her from the doorstep. The woman stopped, nodded, and continued on her way with the dog, while the man stared after her. He then coughed, leaned over the porch rail to spit a night-long accumulation of phlegm, and disappeared inside.

The good thing about displaying such visible evidence of his mauling was that Miles could at any time claim a day off in order to see the doctors monitoring his recovery. The day before, he'd told Fowler-Biggelow he needed at least the morning for a medical assessment. Might be the whole day, he'd added, as an entire team of doctors had put him back together after the assault. Necessary lies, and also training in case he ended up testifying. He got out of his car and stretched. Seven thirty – he had time to walk up and down the street before he began his watch. The sky was lighter now. It wasn't that cold, considering it was already early December. Walking north, he passed a large red-faced man who was crouching to gently chastise a small grey dog on a leash. A plastic bag was attached to his wrist, and it wasn't empty. Already past them, Miles heard, "A creature your size, it's against nature . . ."

The leafless trees made him feel melancholy. Mary Lambert's was a street of mainly row dwellings and, it seemed, countless dogs. He had an impression of understated poverty and of pennies carefully counted. Closer to Dundas, the brick houses were in better shape; in Leslieville, gentrification proceeded cautiously, north to south.

He caught sight of her at eight thirty-five, just as he was thinking of getting out of the car for another stretch. He wasn't entirely sure the woman who came out of the crimson house was Mary Lambert. She appeared to be the right age, at least from a distance and from the back. Anyway, he was fed up with the waiting and watching. She headed south toward Queen Street, and he followed her. Not a short woman, rather bulky. Grey hair, a blue coat of many years, a neck scarf, a large brown purse, sensible flat shoes.

On Queen Street, she turned left. Miles, who had hurried after her once she turned the corner, had to pass her, because just a few doors down Queen she had stopped in front of a dental office and was looking into her purse. A couple of stores beyond her he faked interest in the window of a pizza outlet. He turned and looked back, delighted it had been so easy to find where she worked. But she resumed her walk, and Miles sighed with disappointment. He let her pass him and resumed following her. There was Jilly's, on the other side. He feared she'd take the streetcar once across Broadview. She didn't; she walked on past the streetcar stop. Was Mary Lambert – if she *was* Mary Lambert – simply out for an early walk? Yet she wasn't exactly strolling. She wasn't walking fast either, as most people going to work would, and that was a good thing, because his knee was beginning to hurt. Past Boulton Avenue, she glanced in the window of a small store that sold women's apparel. Did she look back toward him? If she did, she would have noticed him, with his silly sunglasses. She stopped briefly in front of another window, which turned out to be a travel medical clinic sharing space, oddly, with a criminal lawyer. Was she thinking of a voyage somewhere exotic? Did her son need a defender?

The presumed Mary Lambert went on. A railway underpass with gaudy murals, a recreation centre promising the opportunity to stretch both body and mind, a bicycle store, a public house. When she crossed Logan – she'd been walking for more than twenty minutes already, and his knee was getting worse – he began thinking that Mary Lambert was simply out for some exercise and fresh air. She stopped and seemed to peer through the window of the Starbucks café on the far corner, and Miles caught her wave a brief hello to one of the customers lined along a counter facing the street. He was forced to pass her again. How far was she going? Not to the Beaches, was she? Another medical office, a community donation centre, a thrift store. And then, a miracle, another dental office, and the woman he'd been following for half an hour disappeared inside. She was Mary Lambert, no doubt now.

He walked past the dental office and then back and forth, undecided. A dental *centre*, not an office. Everything was a centre now – dental centres, medical centres, fast food centres, centres for performing arts. Formerly modest bank branches were now banking centres. He retraced his steps to the Starbucks – a coffee centre? – and had an espresso. Afterward he returned to the dental centre and walked in.

The sparkling clean surroundings and furniture were not congruent with that rather shabby part of Queen Street. The lighting was discreet, indirect, *Star Trek*–ish. One patiently waiting patient. Two women sat behind a high, rounded counter, looking at, he assumed, hidden screens. Both wore dark, tight suits. Uniforms? We'll do your teeth, they seemed to say, that is why we are here, but why not come along on a brief interstellar trip meanwhile? The younger one, blond, with a glinting pin on her lapel, smiled at him and said, "Mr. Boyden?"

"No, no, I . . . I wonder when would Mrs. Lambert finish her work today?"

"Mary Lambert?"

"Yes."

The older woman looked up at him. "Why are you asking?"

"I'd like a word with her. I don't need to disturb her now, it's not that urgent." He read doubt in their eyes – no wonder, sunglasses in December – and added, thinking he was getting fluent at lying, "It's . . . her son."

"Are you police?" the younger woman asked.

"Please tell me."

The older woman shrugged and nodded at the younger one, who tapped at her keyboard. "Today she'll be done by three o'clock. Unless she has a last-minute appointment, or Dr. Greenlock gets an emergency."

Miles was back outside the dental centre at half past two. He was lucky he got there so early, because she came out five minutes later.

"Mrs. Lambert? Mary Lambert?"

She looked suspiciously at him. A puffy face, not unattractive. There was a weariness about her, the general air and posture of someone who has not had a lot of breaks in life.

"What now with Derek?" she asked.

"Derek?"

"What's my son done now? What do you want?"

It crossed his mind she'd left early to avoid him. Dr. Greenlock would be used to Mary Lambert dodging the police. "It's not your son, Mrs. Lambert, and I'm not a cop."

"No?" She glanced back towards the dental centre, as if thinking of going back in. "What then? You're with that newspaper, aren't you? Leave me alone. I have nothing to say."

The blond woman with the glinting pin came out of the dental centre and approached them.

"I'm not with a newspaper, Mrs. Lambert. My name is Miles Rueda."

She knew his name, of course. She'd based the demands she made of the township on his story, after all.

"Are you okay, Mary?" the blond woman asked.

Mary Lambert turned to her and then back to him. "I'm fine, I'm fine, Lianne," she said slowly, as if trying to figure out what to do next. "I know who he is."

"You're sure?"

Reluctantly, the young woman went back in. Miles suggested a cup of coffee at the Starbucks, but Mary shook her head. "We can talk here. If there is anything to say."

She looked ready to take off at any moment, and he decided to get directly to the crux of what he wanted to tell her. "Mrs. Lambert, I sympathize with your wish to have Biranek's name and memory erased. Yet I feel I must tell you I saw nothing the weekend your mother died. I made up the story. It was stupid of me, of course . . . Do you understand what I'm saying? I made up the whole thing. I did."

She seemed to struggle with her answer. "Lyn and I thought you'd say you made it all up. She told me it's of no import."

Lyn? Lyn Collins, of course, the well-dressed banker, Jennifer's new boss. He'd been right, Jim; it was through Lyn that his story got to Mary Lambert.

"Lyn is wrong."

She shook her head without saying anything.

"The hospital name, Mrs. Lambert, why don't you drop that demand and instead ask for more money?"

She kept staring wordlessly at him.

"As compensation for what Biranek did to your mother, forcing her to abandon you," he went on. "As compensation for what Biranek did to you."

"Money?" she said with contempt.

"The hospital in Millcroft is poorly funded, Mrs. Lambert, and needs Biranek's money. And you too—"

"As if I care about Millcroft or their hospital," Mary said, barely containing herself.

"Mrs. Lambert, surely, you can use—"

"It's not the main thing. Don't you get it?" she shouted.

Ah, not the main thing. Part of it nonetheless. He had wondered why she hadn't done it yet, got it all out in the open, talked to Lyle Blanchard of suddenly finding herself with strangers as a two-year-old, of Rose cruelly left to die. There it was, the confirmation that she also wanted a cut of Biranek's wealth for her silence.

"Money, only money," she said. "You're like Reg."

"Sorry – like who?"

"My husband. My good-for-nothing husband." The thought of Reg seemed to renew her anger. "He smelled money, Reg. Somebody must have shown him the newspapers with my name in it. Reg can smell money all right, even from far away. It's the one thing he's good at. He says he'll leave me alone for good if I get him some money. He says I can get a pile of it from the township if I'm smart. Ha! He's smart, Reg. Smart for jail."

"He's right, Mrs. Lambert."

"You're smart too, aren't you? Everybody's smart. Lyn is smarter than you all."

"How do you know her, Lyn Collins."

"I'm going now. Lyn told me to keep to myself."

"Don't go, Mrs. Lambert. Give me a little more time."

He reached for her forearm, hoping to keep her there a while longer, but a strong hand grabbed his wrist.

"Let her go."

Blue eyes were looking at him with fury. A big man in an old winter jacket, his grey hair pulled tightly back in a thin ponytail. Miles had a feeling he'd seen him before, not long ago, and then recognized the red-faced man who'd been talking to the little dog on Hamilton Street. The man seemed to have spent months of sunny days on a windy shore. The ear Miles could see, rather large and purplish, was missing a bit of its upper helix, as if a caterpillar had nibbled at it. Miles moved back a step and, unsure of what to do next, mumbled something about simply trying to talk to Mrs. Lambert.

"Get lost, scum," the man said.

"Reg," Mary said, "I thought you left this morning. Why are you here?"

Ah, Reg, the circling husband. She didn't sound happy to see him.

Reg ignored her. "You hard of hearing?" he said to Miles. "Scram."

"Don't do anything stupid, Reg," Mary said.

"This man followed you this morning, Mary. I know, because I followed him."

"I wasn't sure it was you," Miles said to Mary. "I just wanted to be certain before I talked to you."

Reg pushed him away. "Get lost, do you hear?"

"He's doing you a favour, Reg," said Mary. "He thinks I should get the money and forget everything else." She looked unhappily around her, then said to Miles, "You better go now. Go."

He walked slowly back to his car. Reg was the kind who could do more rearranging of his face. Anyway, it was Lyn he needed to talk to. Mary Lambert either wasn't that smart or didn't think she was, and Lyn seemed to be the one she listened to.

It had not been easy to get Lyn Collins on the phone. After Miles tracked her down at the bank, he kept getting her secretary. Ms. Collins was away or in meetings. Yes, his earlier message had reached Ms. Collins. Then one morning Lyn herself answered, and after some hesitation she agreed to a late lunch close to her office the following day.

"Another medical appointment," he told Cecil the next day. "The orthopod is puzzled by my knee." He left work at twelve thirty. More lies, although last time he saw him, the knee specialist had indeed seemed baffled. He drove home, then took the subway to King and walked west from there. The cold rain was turning into sleet. Shouldn't there be real snow in December? A nasty wind had picked up, amplified by the towering buildings. At home, realizing it was early, he had made himself a huge sandwich, almost half a baguette, and what he needed now was a drink to warm up. The eatery, reached that time of the year through a second-level food court, seemed more a bar than a restaurant. A room-length window overlooked a deserted terrace. The bar ran parallel to it. Tables where lined up against the window. He was engulfed in monotonous dull brown – the tables, the chairs, the floor, the exposed pipes on the ceiling, even the table mat in front of him. The place was empty except for two young men in business suits at the far end of the room and a woman three tables away, thoughtfully sampling a bowl of soup in front of her.

He sat down facing the window and ordered a double whisky from a waitress with a black apron. King Street was on his left, so he was facing west. Staring at the cold, wet, grey outside, at the sleet-battered terrace, at the crown of a leafless tree beyond it, at the concrete building blocking his view past the tree, he felt miserable.

Lyn Collins, without a coat or an umbrella, appeared beside him, and as he stood up, she said, "I took the underground walkway. What's with the sunglasses when it's raining out there? What's with the baseball cap? It took courage to approach you."

"That's how I ingratiate myself to the aliens I meet in my work."

She remembered the pleasant dinner they'd had at Le Paradis with the Paskows.

"I wish that dinner never took place," he said. "You must help me."

"Help you? In what way?"

"Mary Lambert is your friend."

She didn't answer immediately, as if contemplating the meaning of his words. Yes, she had known Mary since they were children, she began. They'd been in school together, and friends, good friends, in fact. Not now. Time had a way of slowly breaking up what once seemed unbreakable. It was like plate tectonics, unseen creep, unhurried, steady, and then, before anyone knew, there was a chasm that before had been unthinkable. They'd kept in touch, though, on and off. Because she hadn't been the friend she should have been, she put more effort in it than Mary. She had even switched her dentist for that reason. Mary's boss was her dentist now, although that *centre* on Queen Street was not conveniently located for her. She saw Mary twice a year or so, whenever she had a dental appointment, and they would have lunch or an early dinner somewhere nearby and catch up. It wasn't very genuine on her part, of course, and Mary knew it. She would emphasize the gap between them with bouts of illiterate speech. "You's the fancy lady now, can't be friends with your old friend Mary no more." A few times they ate right there, in First Canadian

Place, or in the Scotia Plaza tower, where Lyn's office was, in order for Lyn to show Mary she didn't mind being seen with her. Mary would come in her worst clothes, just to embarrass her. "She's manipulative, Mary, and clever at it. She knows I feel guilty."

The aproned waitress, her hair in a tight bun, had a coloured tattoo below her nape. Lyn ordered a salad and a glass of white wine. He asked for water and another whisky.

Lyn went on. Mary was the outcome of a brief liaison before the boy soldier, who never knew he'd become a father, was shipped overseas. The boat he was on was sunk by a German submarine. When Joseph Biranek met Rose Reaney, she had been a single mother for more than a year. They became lovers – he was completing his medical studies then – but he had no patience for children. After a year of being together, Rose gave Mary away for adoption and Dr. Biranek – he was a doctor now – married her. Years later, Mary's adoptive parents, the Lamberts, told her about her natural parents and that Rose had married and returned to her home town of Corby Falls with her doctor husband. For a long time Mary thought of contacting Rose. Then, thirty-five years ago, she learned of Rose's death, and that put an end to her indecision. She went on with her life and tried not to think of her. *Tried*, because it had been hard for Mary not to think of her birth mother. "You see, Mary hasn't had an easy life, and she blamed both her mother and Biranek for it. Especially Biranek."

She was Mary Lambert's age, early sixties, yet she looked younger than her friend. Much younger. It helped to have a well-paid job, and self-esteem, and image consultants.

"And?"

"And *you* came in. You, with your story of what Dr. Biranek did, or didn't do, thirty-five years ago."

That part, he knew.

"Jen Paskow asked me along that evening. Unknown to anybody at the table, I happened to know Mary Lambert. I also knew that Rose Biranek was her natural mother. Unlikely, yes, I admit. I didn't say anything about Mary. I'm not sure why. Later, I told Mary what I'd heard. Understandably, it had a strong effect on her."

On him too, he thought bitterly. Especially on his skull, and left eye, and ribcage, and knee.

"A few weeks later, Mary read about Biranek's bequests in the newspapers and found out about the millions he'd left to the hospital in Millcroft, which would acquire his name. And she found out about the statue that would be raised in his honour. It drove her batty. She bombarded me with phone calls.

I told her a thousand times to forget it and began to regret telling her what I'd heard. After a month of brooding, she decided she had to erase Biranek's name and memory. It's like a religion to her now."

Yes, a chain of most unlikely occurrences. What were the odds of such a sequence of events? That Rose Reaney, unknown to anybody, had a child out of wedlock she gave up for adoption? That as a twelve-year-old Miles accidentally saw Dr. Biranek briefly returning to his house in Corby Falls on a Saturday night more than twenty-four hours before Rose died? That thirty-five years later, because of some harmless remark his sister made one day, he realized the significance of what he'd seen that Saturday night? That he failed to keep the story to himself and following many glasses of wine told it to others at Le Paradis. Last, what were the odds that a friend of Rose Reaney's abandoned daughter would be there, at his table, and hear his story? Multiplying all these small odds would lead to a result vanishingly close to zero.

"You shouldn't do this," he said.

"Do what?"

"You're helping her, advising her."

"She asked for my help."

"She swears by you. I tried to talk to her, to reason her out of it. She barely listened to me. To anything I said, she answered with your name, that you knew better than anyone else. 'Lyn says this. Lyn knows that.'"

"Don't be fooled by that. She knows what she wants."

"You're the one who can steer her, make her see some sense."

"Sense?"

"Surely bringing an old hospital into the modern age is a worthwhile use of Biranek's money. Or fixing a crumbling church."

Lyn remained quiet.

"You think I'm wrong?"

"Mary's fine with the money going to the hospital. She doesn't want Biranek's name out there on the hospital walls and letterhead."

Ah, the hospital letterhead. "Biranek's will is clear: no name, no money."

"Josef Biranek has caused her endless pain and suffering. She doesn't want his name—"

"Endless pain and suffering? Lyn, we're talking months at most. It's been, what, six months since you told her the story of her mother's death. The death of a mother who gave her up for adoption. It's half a year of . . . at worst sorrow, *mild* sorrow."

"Biranek forced Rose Reaney to give Mary up for adoption. He would not have married her otherwise."

"That's what Mary wants to believe. How would she know?"

"Her adoptive parents told her. They weren't exactly thoughtful or sensitive. I knew them; I was her friend. I often wondered why the Lamberts adopted her in the first place. I think they enjoyed telling that to Mary. Don't ask me why, I don't know."

"Were the Lamberts mean to Mary?"

"They didn't beat her, if that's what you're asking, or no more than a spanking. They weren't, I don't know, warm, loving parents, and Mary felt it. She was two years old when Rose gave her away. It must have been heartbreaking and confusing for Mary to find herself without the mother she knew. She didn't have a happy childhood and hasn't had an easy life, and it has made her bitter. She has a son, Derek, also born out of wedlock, who has problems. In and out of jail too, like his father. She's been a good mother to him, but he's a bad seed."

Should he have another drink? Something to nibble? "What do you know of Reg?"

She sighed. "Reginald Bent, her husband and Derek's father. It was Mary's misfortune to meet him."

"You said her son was born out of wedlock."

"She married Reg later, three years after their son was born. I have no idea why she did it. I asked her more than once why she married him, and she always laughed and said because they both loved dogs."

"What?"

"That was the only thing she could come up with. She does love dogs, Mary, always had one, even growing up with the Lamberts. Small, ugly mutts rescued from the humane society, except her current dog, a miniature Schnauzer, her pride and joy these days, a gift from Reg. That's how Reg reappeared in her life after twenty years, with little Buddy on a leash for Mary. Her previous dog, a smelly creature she'd drag everywhere, had been put down a few months earlier. Reg truly loves dogs – well, that's what Mary says – and is good and gentle with them. And dogs adore him too, all dogs. That's how they met, walking their dogs in some park." Lyn laughed. "Odd creatures, dog lovers. A sect. Mary thinks Reg got Buddy by stealing him, because he didn't have that kind money, or, if he did, not for her. She knows Reg well enough, and Buddy wasn't a puppy anyway when she got him. The vet said Buddy was between two and three years old. Reg claimed Buddy had been his dog and that he simply gave him to her. She didn't believe him and was afraid someone would come and claim Buddy back. She didn't take Buddy to the vet for that reason at first. She shouldn't have worried – Reg is a careful operator. I'm sure he grabbed the dog somewhere in the Maritimes, not near Toronto."

"She didn't change her last name when she married him."

"Reg may have been in jail when Mary gave birth to Derek. Or in Nova Scotia; he's from somewhere there. So, no, she didn't change her last name when she married him, figuring the marriage wouldn't last. They never divorced. He was back in prison soon after they got married, and when he got out she told him she didn't want him near her anymore. He left, but he beat her before going, so that she'd remember his face and fists. She didn't have the energy to divorce him and was afraid he'd show up if she started the papers."

"He wants money from her."

"Reg has always wanted money from Mary."

"He's circling around her, telling her to get a cut of Biranek's money and drop her other requests. I saw him. I saw Reg. I waited for her on Queen Street in front of the dentistry office, to talk to her, and when we were talking he showed up and told me to get lost. I did. He looked like someone it was unwise to go against. I'm on his side, the fool."

She raised her hands in a helpless gesture.

He turned around to look for the waitress. She was behind the bar, under a wide colour photograph of the Toronto skyline taken looking south from a plane or a helicopter.

"Reg is right, you know," he said to Lyn.

"Reg is a horrible man."

"Have you met him?"

"Yes, twice. It was enough. Got away as fast as I could. There was a period when I had no patience for Mary. I had a husband, a young child, a career. I was rather abrupt with her once or twice. That was the time of Mary's disintegration, when Reg appeared, and she got pregnant and had Derek, and then three years later, when she married Reg during one of his spells out of jail." She sighed. "I didn't go to her wedding, you know. Mary might not have ruined her life with Reg if I'd have had more patience for her. I feel guilty about it now, I told you. Mary knows it, and in her stubborn, manipulative way, she exploits it. Exploits me. We are not friends, Mary and I, not in the usual sense. Friends have common interests, enjoy similar jokes, like to be together; they feel comfortable with each other. None of that applies to us, or not since high school."

The waitress came by, and Miles asked for some bread and cheese and a glass of red wine.

"In the end it'll amount to nothing," Miles said. "Mary should take the money. I'm sure the township will agree to a handout provided she's not too greedy. They'll find a hush-hush way to do it. You should tell Mary that."

"That's extortion. I'll never tell her that. I won't be part of it."

"She won't get anything any other way. It may take longer, but a modern, expanded Josef Biranek Hospital will be a fixture in Millcroft for decades. Twelve million dollars is a lot. Over twenty, with the government contribution. Such a large sum is a spot-remover. The lawyers will find a way to clear Biranek's name, or the trustees will hold their nose. It'll take longer. There's always a way."

"How? The story of Mary's mother's death will appear in the newspapers."

"The first newspaper to publish it will be sued by the township or by Biranek's widow. Possibly both. And the newspaper will lose. The same thing holds for Blanchard's blog. He will be sued."

"No. You'll be subpoenaed and you'll tell your story."

"I won't."

"What?"

"It was a made-up story to amuse you people that evening at Le Paradis. I was tipsy and told a tall story."

She stared at him. "Did you?"

"That's what I'll say."

"You'll lie under oath?"

"It's not a lie."

"There'll be my testimony, and Jen's. Her husband Ben will testify too. Three against one."

"I'm the source."

"Why won't you tell the truth?"

"It is the truth."

"It isn't."

"You don't know that."

"It's the texture and the details. It doesn't sound like a cock-and-bull story made up by a middle-aged engineer simply to amuse his dining companions in a restaurant. Besides, it all fits with the coroner's report."

"You've seen the coroner's report on Rose's death?"

"A copy of it, yes. That was the first thing I told Mary to get. It wasn't that easy, because she had to prove she was family, and it took time to get it officially documented that Rose Biranek was her natural mother."

"Do you have it?"

"Mary does."

"Would you make a copy for me?"

"What for?"

"Let's say curiosity."

She seemed unsure of what to say and left his request unanswered. Instead she returned to what interested her. "Why would you insist that the story was invented? Why would you lie?"

"*If* it is a lie, it's a good lie. I want Biranek's money to go to the hospital. I want the church in Corby Falls to be safe."

"You'll have a murderer's name on the hospital. It's like having, I don't know, the Paul Bernardo Memorial Hospital in Millcroft."

The waitress returned with his order and said, proudly, "A Spanish cheese with a Spanish red."

The tall and generous wedge of cheese had a brownish rind with an embossed pattern that reminded him of a smelly herringbone tweed jacket his father had been fond of.

"Talk to Mary. Please. Tell her to get a slice of Biranek's money and forget everything else."

"I won't do it."

"It would be Mary's belated compensation. What better revenge on Biranek than getting a chunk of his money? She'd have an easier old age."

"I already told you, I won't be part of any extortion."

A big word, *extortion*. To his mind, passing some of Biranek's money to Mary Lambert for injuries past was sensible.

"You already are."

"It's the name of the hospital that matters to Mary," Lyn said. "She's not asking for any money."

"She is."

"She told me she wasn't."

"Don't you wonder why she doesn't tell the newspapers what she knows? Why hasn't she had a chat with Lyle Blanchard from the *Post* and given him my name and the details of my story?"

"She wants the hospital to be built."

"When I talked to her, I urged her to take money from the township and drop everything else. Her answer was that money was *not the main thing*. Her exact words, She's seeking money too. Reg is as well. She said that money was all that Reg was interested in. And Reg is a persuasive man."

"I sat beside her when she had her first phone call with the township's mayor."

"I'm sure she's had other conversations with her. It's easy to dial a number. She went to Millcroft too, and more than once."

It was now properly snowing outside – small, wind-blown flakes. He sighed and said, "They threatened my daughter."

"What?"

"They threatened the safety of my fourteen-year-old daughter. I can't have anything happen to Katelyn."

"Did you tell the police?"

"No. I don't want them involved. I'm scared, Lyn. They threatened me and my sister too."

"What are you saying? Who are *they*?"

"Everybody wants the hospital in Millcroft to be rebuilt. And there are some for whom this is, how should I put it, a matter of life, of life carrying on as before, of preservation. It's a huge sum: twenty million dollars. And much of it would be pumped back into the township."

"You're not telling me who *they* are."

He dismissed her words with a wave of his hand.

She took a deep breath. "I don't know what to make of all this. I don't know what to make of you, hiding behind those impossible glasses. It's like a bad movie. Are you saying they, whoever *they* are, will try to kill you?"

"They already got to me. I was attacked and badly beaten, Lyn."

"I don't believe you."

With a slow, theatrical gesture – almost enjoying it – he took his cap off, turned in his chair, and traced his fingers along the stitches in his skull. Hair might have grown around the scar, but it was still visible. Then he took off his sunglasses. At the sight of his half-open left eye, the blue patch underneath it, the scar on his brow, she gasped.

"The doctors assure me the eye will go back to normal in time," he said. "Maybe it won't fully open, not the same as the right eye, but it won't be obviously noticeable. No one's eyes are exactly the same as each other, they tell me. There's cosmetic surgery too; it seems they can fix things if I'm unhappy with my appearance once it stabilizes. More troubling is that the eye is still a bit blurry now and again. I'm told time will fix that too. Stabilize it. My entire body has been stabilizing for a month and a half, and I'm sick of it. I'm walking with a limp too, a hint of one. I'll demo that when we leave."

The tattooed waitress was resetting one of the tables not far away from theirs. She was looking at him. He put his sunglasses back on.

Eyes on her empty plate, Lyn said, "Put your glasses back on, please."

"I already did."

"You fell or something."

"That would be a hell of a fall. You're right in a way. Most of the damage was done while I was down."

"I don't believe you."

"I spent twelve days in a hospital and three weeks at home in November."

"What did the police say?"

"I didn't go to the police. At the hospital I said I was mugged. *They* were smart enough to take my wallet."

Chapter 13

January, February 2006

The copy of the coroner's report came with a brief note from Lyn Collins: "It wasn't easy to talk Mary into letting you read this, because she couldn't see how it would advance her demands. I can't either, but I don't think it will do any harm. That is not a good enough reason for sending you the report, of course, yet Mary is now dragging me to where I do not want to go. I have only myself to blame. Perhaps, who knows, you'll see a way out."

Miles sat down in his small study upstairs and read the report twice. Afterward he ambled down and poured himself a drink. The findings were specific and clear. The body of Rose Biranek was found by her husband on Monday, December 28, 1970, at eight o'clock in the morning. Dr. Biranek had driven to Corby Falls from Toronto that day. With him was Hollie McGinnes, his office nurse. They had spent a week in Mexico, with a weekend in Toronto at the end of their trip. Adding two days in Toronto was a spontaneous decision, as they initially planned to get back to Corby Falls on Saturday. The medical examiner found that Rose Biranek had suffered several fractures: the left hip, both bones in the left forearm, two ribs. She had contusions on her face and all over her body. Everything was consistent with an accidental fall down the stairs from the second floor to the first. The fall was a result of her poor condition, as Rose Biranek had been suffering from multiple sclerosis for years. The immediate cause of death was cardiac arrest. She was dehydrated, and died between eight o'clock and eleven o'clock on Sunday night, some nine to twelve hours before she was found. She had not eaten or drunk anything for thirty-six hours or more. A glass in her bedroom containing a residue of whisky pointed to an intake of alcohol shortly before her fall.

Elma Mulligan was the last person who saw Rose before her death. She told the inquest that she had phoned Rose on Saturday afternoon and had visited her shortly after. Rose had seemed fine. They had tea together in the kitchen. Rose complained about her husband, who had phoned earlier to let her know he was delaying his return and would be back in Corby Falls on Sunday morning. Elma left Rose around two o'clock. She accompanied Rose upstairs and saw her into her bedroom. Rose had gone up the stairs without needing help. Asked whether she had called Rose on Sunday to see how she was doing, Elma said she hadn't. After all, Rose had seemed fine on Saturday afternoon and her husband was driving home in the morning.

The inquest arrived at the following sequence of events. Sometime on Saturday afternoon, likely between three and five o'clock, Rose attempted to go back down, probably to get something from the kitchen. She fell and ended up at the bottom of the stairs, in what the Biraneks called the "central hall." The fall resulted in fractures and contusions. The lights on the landing at the top of the stairs were on, so there was some light in the hall. Rose might have been unconscious at first. Eventually, she came to, and slowly – she must have been in excruciating pain – crawled into the room that served as a waiting area for Dr. Biranek's patients. The folding doors leading to it were open. Rose may have been attempting to reach the phone on Hollie McGinnes's reception desk. Perhaps she hoped to pull it to the floor by its cord. Unfortunately, she couldn't find the cord on the floor in the semi-darkness or was unable to reach it. Rose was found there, in the waiting area, near Hollie's desk, not far from the side door used by Dr. Biranek's patients. She was lying on her right side, her torso pitched downward somewhat. From the hematomas on her body, it was determined that she had not moved for some thirty-six hours before she died. That is, Rose had reached the waiting room by late Saturday, between seven and ten o'clock.

It was unfortunate, the inquest concluded, that Dr. Biranek postponed his return to Corby Falls a second time and didn't get back until Monday morning. Had he arrived on Sunday morning or afternoon, he would have found his wife alive.

The report was disappointing. He had hoped either that Rose had died earlier, only a few hours after she fell down the stairs, in which case Biranek found her already dead and, callous but not a murderer, simply left her there and drove back to Toronto with his second pair of glasses, or, if she was still alive when Biranek returned, she had remained where she'd landed, at the bottom of the stairs, and Biranek picked up his glasses after stepping directly into the examination room from the waiting area and never saw or heard her. No such luck. If anything, the coroner's report made things more difficult for Miles, because now there was no doubt in his mind that Dr. Biranek had seen Rose alive that night. The doctor had left her there to die.

He slumped on the dusty sofa under the bay window and stared at the liquor cabinet Laukhin had left him. The poet's other bequest, Chemakoff's ink and watercolour depiction of a group of half-mannequins, half-birds, was hanging above it. Miles had insisted they belonged together. The two things of value in the house. It was Don who told him the liquor cabinet had some worth. He'd run his hand across the shiny wood and said, whistling, "Burr walnut, Miles. Do you know what burr walnut is? And these fluted doors, some workmanship. Art deco, isn't it?"

That was how he spent his evenings now, drinking, eyes glued on Laukhin's absurd liquor cabinet, thinking of the Biranek affair and of Anna the poetess, now likely back in cold, windy Saint Petersburg. Or in London. Or on a yacht floating on the balmier waters of the Mediterranean. That was what oligarchs and their wives did.

The house was oppressively quiet. To think that he would ask Katelyn to turn down her music when she was with him. The day before, he had phoned Federica's house and talked to Katelyn on the silly pretext he couldn't find the scissors. She had come to the phone panting, and he inquired if there was anything wrong.

"I was on the treadmill."

"Ah."

There was a whole gym in the basement of Palazzo Greg. Irritated, he asked, "Does Greg ever use it?"

"Sometimes. Mom does."

Katelyn had cleverly surmised why he was calling and said, with the directness of youth, "Scissors? Poor old Dad, you miss me, don't you? I'll be back, don't worry, and soon. Why don't you come here for dinner on Saturday?"

He'd had dinner there once and had left early and in a bad mood. "You shouldn't invite people like that without talking to your mother."

"She won't mind."

"How do you know?"

"There's always too much food. Maria cooks for a regiment. She's a fabulous cook, you know – a real *chef*."

"No skiing this weekend?"

"No."

"Greg will mind."

"A friend of Greg's is coming to dinner with his wife. The wife gets on Greg's nerves – Mom told me. Your presence will distract him."

Such astute dissection of social dynamics from a fourteen-year-old. "I can't this Saturday," he lied. "Going out with some friends."

Katelyn had also invited him to spend New Year's Eve with them. She'd said that Federica had asked her to convey the invitation.

"Your mother should be the one asking me."

"Don't be so sensitive, Dad. Mom said you love parties. Or used to."

"Will you be there?"

"Of course. I invited some friends too."

"Ah. A large gathering then."

"Three of my friends. Mostly Mom's and Greg's friends."

"How many of them?"

"I don't know, twenty, thirty. Does it matter, Dad?"

He'd lied to her then too. He said he'd already decided to have a quiet New Year's Eve with the Paskows. It wasn't an outright lie; he'd been invited by Ben to celebrate the New Year with them – Helen and two other couples, colleagues of Ben's, were coming as well – but he'd had no intention of going. What happened to him? He'd always enjoyed gatherings, crowds, group drinking, brainless prattle. "The reason I'll marry you," Federica said, when he proposed to her, "is that you are functional at parties." He was a lone drinker now. Sarah had picked up on it, and since his divorce she often rang late at night to check up on his state.

What had Katelyn said? "Does it matter, Dad?" It mattered, of course. It meant seeing Katelyn with thirty other people around, disappearing with her own friends into some other part of the house at the first opportunity. He missed the weekends with his beautiful, ironic daughter, the quiet breakfast or lunch hours, her stories about teachers and friends, her efforts at improving his monotonous cooking, watching silly shows together on TV, the consoling way she said "poor old Dad." He missed telling her to use earphones if she really felt like ruining her eardrums, hearing her chatter on the phone in her room. He surmised that, at his age, he was allowed only bursts of happiness, often triggered by little things, like wondering whether his daughter was talking with a boy or a girl. She was growing up, Katelyn, and their togetherness, sporadic and frail anyway, was coming to an end. Fourteen, not far from fifteen. She increasingly valued spending time with her friends. Before long she'd be dating. Most Fridays, he'd leave work early to pick her up from school, and he dreaded a Thursday phone call: "Dad, don't pick me up tomorrow, because . . ." Once she was in the car with him, he prayed for clogged streets. The traffic gods rarely disappointed. Weekends, he'd drive Katelyn around, and he'd choose the longest routes. She had caught on quickly and seemed to understand his need to do it. How easily she took to living in the large house in Rosedale, with her spacious bedroom and ensuite bathroom, overlooking the backyard pool and flowerbeds, with the well-appointed basement gym, and with Maria's "fabulous" cooking. She was now issuing invitations for dinner. How deftly she had pushed him into weekend duty – and not every weekend, because there was skiing at Greg's club, and the cottage in the summer, and visiting friends for sleepovers. He was a duty, a parents' deal, soon to become a drag.

He doubted that keeping Katelyn away from him made her safe, but he kept reminding himself that while Jim Cowley had visited him on Montgomery Avenue and knew that Katelyn spent the weekends with her father, he didn't know where Federica lived. And Maria was a daily presence at Greg's house, and a gardener was there often throughout the summer. Anyway, Miles and Federica had agreed that for now, until this whole thing was over one way or another, Katelyn would avoid Montgomery Avenue. He was irked by the thought that he was giving in, but if he wanted his daughter back on weekends, he should precipitate things, send the message that he would keep his mouth shut and that, if forced to appear in court, he would say his story had been an unfortunate fabrication. It meant, of course, calling Jim Cowley or Thula.

Midnight. He should file the copy of the coroner's report in the blue folder. Sleep was not coming easily to him now, and lately his ordinary nightmare was showing up with a horrifying new twist. Years ago – they were on Prince Arthur Street then – Federica, awakened by his groan or shriek or whatever aggravating noise he'd made, scoffed at his description.

"Your ordinary nightmare? What do you mean?"

"Always the same."

"Never different?"

"Not really."

He would be crossing the street near their apartment building and see the bus approaching – not worried, because he had looked carefully both ways before crossing. There was nothing coming except that red and white TTC bus, still far enough away, and he would calmly hasten – there would be no point in overdoing it – and then the troublesome part of the dream would begin. The bus would widen its already broad, flat front, and he would start running to avoid the monster bearing down on him, and it would grow wider and wider, as wide as the street, and when he reached the sidewalk and think himself safe, because there were trees on the sidewalk, and lampposts, and hefty poles with cables and transformers, the bus would be there too, crushing the flimsy obstacles in its way, King Kong–like, and he would wake up.

He first had the nightmare after he'd almost been run over by a bus on Bathurst Street. He was an undergraduate student at the time, and was saved by a metal pole standing between himself and the bus, which had careered onto the sidewalk.

"Why Prince Arthur Street, then?" Federica asked. "There are no TTC buses on Prince Arthur."

He had got used to his recurring nightmare, accepted it the way one accepted a nagging parent or a non-life-threatening illness. And anyway, in time it became less frequent; months would pass before he'd have another one. Sometimes he had the impression he was half awake already by the time the bus was crumpling trees and lampposts on the sidewalk. It was as if he knew he'd already been through what was coming, that he'd get out of it somehow. Lately, though, there had been a twist to his nightmare, a horror-filled twist, because Katelyn was with him – a younger Katelyn, eleven or twelve, the age she'd been during the custody battle – gripping his hand as he crossed the street.

Fuck sleep. He glanced around for the blue folder, annoyed it was not on the desk. He found it in one of the drawers. With a sigh he reread the first column on the fledgling Biranek affair his sister had shown him the day of their father's funeral, and then Thula's letter, the letter he never answered, in which she formally asked him to help honour the doctor's memory and given him her home phone number.

It was Thula herself who picked up the phone.

"I give up," he said directly. "There's no story, and Biranek can rest in peace. I'll keep my mouth shut, and if it ever comes to court I'll say I made up the story."

"Miles?"

"You can begin or restart the work on the hospital – the planning, I don't know, whatever you or the hospital have been doing. You win, Thula, you and your henchmen."

"Jesus, Miles, do you know what time it is?"

"Of course I do. I have a fucking horologe on my wrist."

"Are you drunk?"

"I'm not drunk. I'm not Tom."

She didn't reply, and he wasn't sure how to continue. "Did you hear what I said? There is no danger – I've capitulated. Handy word that, *capitulated*, and a mouthful too, don't you think? It implies a negotiated surrender, ha, although Millcroft's style is bodily harm and threats to daughters. Your millions are safe. Biranek's millions, I mean. His millions, and the millions the province eventually adds, will be available. You and the township and B&M Construction have won. I don't want anything happening to my daughter."

There was no immediate answer from Thula. "What are you saying, Miles?" she eventually asked. "I don't get it."

"You know damn well what I'm saying. I'll cause no harm to your plans, but what happened to me must not happen to my daughter. Make sure you send the order down the ranks."

"You don't think I . . . Miles, it's terrible what happened to you. I had nothing to do with it, believe me."

"How else would you know, Thula, how else would you know what happened to me?"

"People talk," she said, after a pause.

"People in Corby Falls? In Millcroft? How would they know?"

"It's not what you think."

"I saw Tom at Bart's Alehouse that evening."

"What evening?"

"The evening they left me there, broken bones and all, near the river."

"Tom was there?"

"Yes. You didn't know? Ask him. Surely by now he's awake too – just whisper the question into his ear."

"He . . . he's not here."

"Out drinking?"

"Tom wouldn't do such a thing. He's not violent."

"He was there, at Bart's Alehouse, and so was Moroney and Bill Cowley. I haven't seen Tom in Corby Falls in years – come to think of it, not since high school – and then, what do you know, he's there the evening I get clobbered. It wasn't a coincidence, Thula."

"Miles, believe me, I had nothing to do with it."

"I can picture it. Tom comes home that night, slips into a warm bed, whispers, 'Don't worry anymore, Thula dear, it's all looked after.' Have I missed anything? Perhaps a long embrace?"

"How could you think I would condone that?"

"Call off your dogs, Thula. I'll say nothing provided my daughter is left unharmed. If anything happens to her, I'll tell the police and the newspapers what I know. Everything. I want a promise that my daughter will not be touched."

"What kind of a promise, Miles? A piece of paper with signatures?"

Jim Cowley phoned him two days later. "I've been wanting to call you for a long time, and I didn't know how. Didn't know what to say. And there's nothing I could possibly say, is there? But you must believe me, Miles, that I had nothing to do with what happened to you. Miles? Are you there? Please say you believe me."

Thula had had nothing to do with it. Now Jim claimed innocence too. Pretty soon Miles would have to accept that no one had left him battered and bloodied on a cold, rainy night on the bank of the Corby River, or had threatened Katelyn.

"I do not," he said with difficulty.

"You can't mean I was complicit in it."

"I do."

"We've been friends for so long. How can you?"

"You threatened my daughter."

"No, no, not me, Miles. I wanted to make sure that nothing happened to her."

Miles said nothing. He wondered why he didn't hang up and end the farcical conversation. In the silence, he thought he heard another voice in the background, as if someone was whispering in Jim's ear, yet it might have been an impression driven by the dislike he now felt for his former friend.

"It was a good thing, Miles. I mean, your decision."

So that was why Jim called. He'd been told to check on him, double check, make sure that what Miles told Thula wasn't a drunken impulse to be disavowed on sober second thought. A directive passed on via his father-in-law.

"I meant what I said." He had found it easier to say that to Thula for some reason, although both Jim and Thula had been in on it, one way or another. Perhaps because Thula had never claimed to be a friend. "I meant what I told Thula."

"I knew you'd do it, Miles. Hell, you almost told me as much at Bart's Alehouse, didn't you? I told them, Miles, I told them you'd come around to our way of thinking. I told them all you needed was time. That's why I don't know why they . . . did to you what they did. It was harebrained, Miles, crazy."

"Fuck you, Jim," he said, and hung up.

For two weeks afterward, he blamed himself, his stupidity and stubbornness, and wondered if he should call Thula again – Thula, not Jim – to make sure his intentions were well understood. He carped and moaned in a long call one night to his sister, during which he felt she was getting impatient and prickly, and calmed down only three days later, when he received an envelope with a clipping inside from the *Millcroft Gazette*. It was another Township Alert column, this one signed by D. Brown. There was no note in the envelope or sender's name or address on the outside.

We've learned from informed sources that the planning for the modernization of the Millcroft Regional Hospital is back on track and that the work will soon be open to bidding. We know too that B&M Construction has teamed with a large construction company and a major architectural firm, both based in Toronto. Which ones these two are, we've not been told, but we've been assured that both have significant experience in the expansion and renovation of hospitals. The township and its business community are keen to get this work going as soon as possible, and there is great relief everywhere that things are moving again.

The plans are more advanced at St. Anselm's Church in Corby Falls, the beneficiary of Dr. Biranek's smaller bequest. Long overdue repairs on the church structure and roof will start in early May. We talked to Barry Matlock, one of the owners of B&M Construction, and he told us that his company would handle that work. He said too that the St. Anselm's repairs are welcome work for his firm. He has great hopes for getting a sizeable piece of the hospital work in Millcroft; if that does not happen, and soon, they'll have to lay off people at B&M, because they've been going through a rough patch lately.

There was more in the column, including a brief interview with Peter Burlington, the director of the hospital in Millcroft. The last ten months had been testing for the hospital and its planning committee. He was thrilled that things were moving again, and also frustrated, because the provincial government had not yet indicated the exact amount of money it would add to the bequest. It would be between six and ten million, and everybody in the township hoped it would be closer to the upper limit. Since they were in a hurry to start the work, they might have to ask the bidders to assume two levels of available funding, and that, of course, would slow down the bidding process.

There it was: he had got what he wanted, the proof that his promises had reached the right ears and were taken seriously. Katelyn could spend weekends with him again.

Toward the end of January he rang Enrico Viale to assess ESA's mood after Canada's catastrophic inability to commit above the token €6 million. Everyone expected Viale to be the manager at ESA directly responsible for the Ares Rover. His tone alone could tell a lot. He might shed some light too on when the invitations to tender for Phase B1 would likely be posted on ESA's website. A window at least, an earliest and latest date. Fowler-Bigelow wasn't pleased with Miles's vague guesses. "We can't keep people on overhead, waiting months in a row for ITTs which might or might not result in a winning proposal."

Six weeks after Berlin, ESA's mood was still good. Viale sounded upbeat on the phone, and didn't seem disappointed by Canada's flaky stance. The European Space Agency, he said, was used to political setbacks. He laughed, accepting of ESA's ways. There was always an election coming somewhere among ESA's twenty-two member or cooperating states, and they could surely cope with Canada's delay, which was, everybody knew, technical in nature.

"Do we know more on B1 now?" Miles asked.

Viale sighed. He had hoped the top ITT, the one for the mission, would come out before Christmas, but, alas, there had been too many glitches. Right now, his best guess was the end of January at the earliest, and it would be directed to Alenia. No choice there. In turn, Alenia would issue ITTs for the elements of AEM. There would be a delay there, of course. It would take Alenia at least two months to issue the lower lever ITTs, longer if there were big issues to be ironed out between them and ESA. The rover itself would be directed to Astrium. The Rover Vehicle, yes. Again, no choice, with no other country coming close in matching the UK's commitment and interest in the rover. The payload instruments and tools would each have their own ITTs. The rover ITT would be issued first. Earliest date? End of March, beginning of April.

"Latest date?"

"Latest?"

"Most realistic."

Viale laughed. "Miles, you're a smart man. *Sei un uomo intelligente.* You make the guess. I tell you earliest, you do the rest. Alenia has a lot to do in a short time, and at ESA we are doing our best to support them. As Astrium is in a directed contract for the rover, they may start discussing the Rover Vehicle early. Might be already doing it. The rover, while a first for ESA, is not the most critical element of the mission. The Entry, Descent and Landing System is, and by far. Everybody knows this. It's the element which has ESA, and now Alenia, worried. My boss will talk of nothing else. For him the rover is a toy – true, a highly visible and useful one. Astrium will issue competitive ITTs for various subsystems of the rover a month after receiving the rover ITT from Alenia. Well, say two months. With an oversubscribed program – more oversubscribed than officially acknowledged, because of the additional €59 million from Canada everyone is counting on – some critical subsystems might afford two winners in the coming short phase, with the thought of carrying on to the next phase with the best concept."

"Would the Chassis and Locomotion Subsystem be among them?"

"Likely. The Germans are quite keen on it. Which reminds me: it would be a good thing to offer DLR some work on wheel flexibility and wheel–soil mechanics. DLR has been active in these areas for years – well, you know that. A small consulting contract, Miles, ten thousand at most, not more. It would grease a squeaky wheel, between me and you. Yes, it makes DLR more amenable."

"You mean, during B1?"

"Yes. A thought, you know. If you win the contract, of course. Well, perhaps even before . . . Did I already mention this to you?"

"Sure, yes, good advice. Back to the dates, Enrico – it seems tight to me."

"Miles, tight is good, isn't it?" Explosive laughter, and Miles tried his best to join in. Was Viale's jollity due to the unexpected popularity of AEM? Had his new position been confirmed? Merely a sunny day in Noordwijk? Perhaps

Miles was a fool, and the Canadian arguments in Berlin had been both forceful and plausible. Viale's timetable was silly, of course. It would be a miracle if Alenia released the Rover Vehicle ITT in March.

Another depressing teleconference in Cecil's office. Paul Arsenault, in Saint-Hubert, was the disseminator of the bad news. The next meeting of the board in charge of AEM, Arsenault began, would be in mid-February. He'd be there, in Paris, of course. Although after the federal election, Canada would not be able to commit new funds to AEM by then. CSA's position had not changed: the Ares Initiative was a great opportunity, but every dollar of the additional €59 million would have to be new money approved by the new government. In other words, there would be no appropriations from ongoing or approved programs. An executive committee meeting held a day earlier at CSA did not change the policy adopted soon after Garneau's resignation. Existing programs would not be pilfered.

Miles glanced at Fowler-Biggelow. Cecil's face had turned grey. It wasn't just the stinging "every dollar," it was also the tone of Arsenault's voice, his clipped, clear words, as if he'd rehearsed to make sure the message was not muddled.

The roller coaster was hurtling down.

"What is the likely sequence and timing of events for getting new money approved?" Miles asked.

There was no immediate answer, only unintelligible background talk, and then a voice Miles could not identify said they needed a moment to talk it over. In the ensuing silence, Cecil stood up and began to pace, his lips whispering audible obscenities. Miles stood up too. The view from Cecil's office was the desolate parking lot behind the building. A thin layer of snow had fallen overnight. In the gloom of the cloud-covered morning, a few stragglers were making their way from far-off parking spaces, avoiding the unsettled geese and the small islands of green droppings in the untrodden snow.

Arsenault's voice came back on. The current minister would not have the time or the inclination to engage – never mind decide – on a long-term policy issue before the election. The acting president, a new one, since Joe Courant's days at the top were coming to an end, would meet the future minister in charge of CSA, whoever he or she would be. A team at CSA was currently working on a "transition package" for the new minister. AEM would be in the package. If the minister liked the mission, then, presto, there for his approval was the additional amount needed. CSA anticipated a longer wait for a decision if the Liberals failed to return to government and the Conservatives won instead. Much longer. The meeting with the new minister would be within a month or two after the election. Reaching a decision afterward would take additional months. It might be that the minister would want to designate a new CSA president before deciding. Whichever way, if the minister was favourable to the idea, it simply meant CSA could carry on talking about a future commitment. No more than that, nothing firm. Then it would be up to the Treasury Board to approve the new funds. Overall, five to six months, if approved expeditiously. Nine months was more likely.

"Nine months from now?" Miles asked. "*Nine* months?"

"If we have to wait that long we are dead," Cecil said.

Arsenault's response was curt. Ludwig must use all the levers they had for the speedy release of new funds.

A dense silence followed Arsenault's words. Cecil whispered "knobhead" and waved his hands to indicate he'd had enough.

"Anything on the length of B1 and the budget?" Miles asked. "Likely start? We'll take guesses, rumours, idle chit-chat if nothing else. It would confirm our own speculations and what we've heard."

Arsenault believed the budget for the short Phase B1 would be around €13 million. He couldn't shed light on the duration or the start. He doubted B1 would start soon.

Afterward, Cecil and Miles sat without a word, each hoping the other would find something even vaguely encouraging to say. CSA – the CSA without Garneau – was clearly against ESA's Ares Initiative. They were fine with providing modest support, as they'd been in the past, but nothing substantial. Drops, not a flow. Not even a trickle. Cecil grumbled that it was Arsenault's tone that shocked him the most. The message itself simply confirmed what Cecil had heard earlier from Geoff. There'd been a side meeting at CSA on Tuesday regarding AEM. Ted Ludwig, who was at CSA on other matters, had asked Geoff to join him. The meeting achieved nothing. Joe Courant was adamant CSA wouldn't be able to commit the €60 million – gallantly, Courant had rounded up by one million – for AEM without a new government infusion. Lysiane Monast was among the most aggressive, and Geoff heard she'd replace Courant as acting president in February.

At the door, Miles turned around. "The silver lining is that B1 won't start any time soon. Arsenault confirmed what Viale said. And if B1 is more than a few months in duration, well, who knows, that's the nine months."

Around noon, Miles rang Jean-Yves Cloutier and left word that he wanted a chat. If anybody could tell him what was happening at CSA regarding AEM, it would be Jean-Yves.

Cloutier called back ten minutes later. Miles asked him straight away what was at the root of CSA's dislike for AEM. Perhaps startled, Jean-Yves didn't answer immediately. *Dislike?* That was a harsh word, he said, not entirely fitting. He had always had mixed feelings regarding AEM. On the fence. Surprising, wasn't it, for the head of robotics at CSA to be lukewarm toward a program in which a rover was by far the most visible element. Yes, a great program and opportunity – though not for CSA and its employees. Entirely managed by ESA. CSA had no role in it except mailing the cheques. That was *the* major objection to it. Garneau had liked AEM, but Garneau was a politician already.

Exactly what Cloutier had said to Miles in Saint-Hubert almost a year before. "What's in it for us?" Jean-Yves had asked, when Miles sought his opinion on AEM. A question in answer to a question, deciphered with Cecil's help on the flight back. Ludwig's mistake was that they hadn't thought of a role for CSA. True, at the time of that presentation at Saint-Hubert, the Canadian Mars Mission was all the talk, and CSA had a major part in CMM. AEM was background noise, a few minor studies, and Miles had ignored Cloutier's reply. He should have remembered it, though, once AEM came to the forefront. That was not a mistake; that was a blunder, their blunder. Well, Miles's mainly. The fall of the government was their misfortune, compounded by the hurried Garneau. A former astronaut who couldn't leave the space agency fast enough.

"Is Arsenault dead set against AEM?" Miles asked Cloutier.

Paul Arsenault was a scientist, Jean-Yves said. The small projects he was in charge of would be in the greatest danger of being cut if funds were to be reallocated to AEM. It affected Arsenault directly. And there were others like him. They'd go for it, for AEM, sure, why not, if new money found its way into CSA's coffers. The larger the budget, the better for all. After all, CSA was a bureaucracy – a glamourous one, with hundreds of scientists and engineers, but still a bureaucracy. And bureaucracies defended and enhanced their turf.

Cloutier wasn't finished. For many people at CSA, planetary exploration was not, and never should be, a major focus. Canada's space budget was pitifully small, and a large portion of it was spent on the attention-getting astronaut program. Canada's efforts in space should be Earth related – communications and Earth observation. The former had once been their main effort, and the latter should be now. Earth observation, yes, and that was what CSA's ten-year plan said. Miles's own colleagues in Vancouver, at Ludwig Space, had said so too, when Ludwig made inputs to the plan. And Jean-Yves, in spite of his position and leaning, could find little fault with this thinking. Miles hadn't expected to hear *that* from the head of robotics at CSA, had he?

Jean-Yves had an odd question toward the end. "What makes you think that Ludwig is fully behind AEM?"

"I'm not following you."

"It's not about Ludwig Robotics. I'm wondering about Ludwig Space, the Vancouver bosses. Their livelihood is Earth observation."

"What are you saying, Jean-Yves?"

"Silly words I pick up here and there. Perhaps . . . It may be nothing."

Long after the phone call was over, Miles remained in his chair. Except for the remark about the Ludwig bosses in Vancouver, which he dismissed as a nasty dig, there was nothing unexpected in what Jean-Yves had told him. Though hearing it stated explicitly, all in one go, from the one person at CSA who should have been an unconditional supporter of the AEM rover, told him he was fighting a battle already lost. ESA's willingness to wait for a firm commitment from Canada would not last long. The patience of Ludwig's industrial partners would not either, especially now that AEM was oversubscribed. The picture would be simpler without Canada, and juicier subsystems – like Chassis and Locomotion, or Navigation – less contested. Earlier that morning, he'd already seen an ominous comment on the ESA website about the success of the Council of Ministers meeting: "As far as the financial shares in the programme are concerned, Italy has confirmed its leading role, followed by the United Kingdom, France, and Germany. This will also be reflected in the selection of the industrial consortium that ESA will task to build the first European rover for the exploration of Mars, along with a carrier and a descent module. Encouraging were the larger-than-expected contributions from other countries, like Spain and Switzerland, and an oversubscribed AEM program." No mention of Canada at all.

The Friday before the Monday election, Mohan joined him in the tri-party teleconference. It was brief, Färber & Feldt saying hardly a word. Max Tennant sounded hurried or dismissive when he brought up the two points he wanted to make. The first was parcelled as a question: What steps, exactly, was Ludwig taking to speed up the Canadian commitment? Miles was taken aback by the question, especially by the presence of the word *exactly*, which intimated that Astrium now had serious doubts regarding Canada. Miles looked at Mohan and mumbled a few words, then recovered and said he'd talk with his bosses and get back to him. "The more effective steps are taken at a level higher than mine, Max, and that information may be too sensitive for my ears or for outside consumption. Still, I'll try. I'll claim I need to calm down our industrial partners." As he said it, Miles shrugged his shoulders at Mohan. Mohan silently clapped in mock approval. Max said he had to rush into another meeting, but the other thing he wanted to say was that the additional Canadian money – the €59 million, if the amount ever materialized – would not suffice to get AEM to an Ariane launcher. It was the latest he'd heard from Viale. AEM would have to carry on within the constraints of the lesser launch mass of Soyuz.

It was, no doubt, a hint that Canada's increased contribution was not desperately needed. The message was the same: Ludwig should precipitate a Canadian decision, one way or another.

The election results added to his gloom. "It may not be that bad," Mohan said the following day, trying to lift Miles's spirits. "It would be different if the Conservatives had got a majority. Minority governments are cautious. And, who knows, Stephen Harper may be a secret space buff."

In late February Miles told Cecil it was time to manage Astrium's expectations.

"Manage?" Cecil said.

"Manage down. Reduce. I'm tired of sounding falsely upbeat, hearing myself say an increased Canadian contribution is just a matter of time."

"They're not stupid, Miles. They've guessed. They know more than we do, an hour from Noordwijk, and with Brits working there."

"Exactly. Why make fools of ourselves?"

They were talking in the cafeteria, both holding cups of Sumatra Mandheling Dark Brew. Fowler-Biggelow gestured to him to sit at one of the tables. After a swiping look around, he whispered, "Don't be so dejected, there may be a way out."

"Out?"

"A way forward. I'm not sure I should tell you. I mean, don't spread it."

What now?

Cecil leaned toward him. "Maxime Bernier is the minister of industry in Harper's new government. CSA is in his fief."

"So?"

"We have somebody at his court. An assistant."

"So?" He was sounding like Zhelenin at the Laukhin symposium. "I'm sure he has many assistants."

"This one is advising him on space policy. Among other areas, I'm sure."

"Friendly to Ludwig?"

Cecil seemed to weigh his answer. "Yes. To Ludwig Space, in general."

"And he likes Mars and rovers."

"He does."

"How do you know?"

"I know him. You know him too."

"I do?"

"Louis Gandarax."

Now that was a surprise. A pleasant one. "Was he with Bernier in the election?"

"Yes."

"Not a Liberal, then."

"Conservative, it turns out. He's a friend of Ted Ludwig too. Better than liking rovers."

"And money will flow."

"Not immediately. Still, a friend at the court is better than a penny in the purse, as the saying goes."

"And there will be pennies, yes?"

"Why have an adviser if you don't follow his advice."

A vertiginous ride up, all of a sudden.

Chapter 14

March 2006

He was cheerful at breakfast, and even managed some work after Katelyn had gone back up to her room. He'd been in a good mood since Cecil told him about Louis Gandarax's role as adviser to Maxime Bernier. He made jokes about the "Gandarax effect" with Mohan, and in a teleconference with Astrium and Färber & Feldt he alluded to Ludwig's mysterious ways in influencing Canada's space policies. Mohan had looked at him and raised his thick eyebrows. "Aren't you making too much of it?" he whispered.

But Miles was convinced that things were finally turning around. And not just at work. There had been no new disclosures about the Biranek affair on Blanchard's website since September. And, while he still checked the website daily, he no longer got the *Post* every morning on his way to Ludwig Robotics. He allowed himself the hope either that Mary Lambert had given up or some arrangement with the township had been reached. Having Katelyn on weekends again had a lot to do with his jolly mood, and so had Anna's call the night before. Katelyn had answered the phone, and she gave him a funny look when she put the handset on the kitchen counter, saying it was "Somebody who speaks with an odd accent." Anna had suggested "Trooflz" as the place for lunch. He'd heard about Truffles before, most recently from Federica, who liked to tell him about posh places and people, invariably adding, "You should go out more, Miles."

He'd have something to placate Fowler-Biggelow with, let him know he was keeping in touch with the Pripogurins. He hadn't forgotten being accused at the Simmonses' gathering of having a "criminal lack of interest" in the wealthy Russian couple. Cecil was wrong, dead wrong. Miles was more than interested in Anna Pripogurina. He'd been tempted to say as much a week earlier, when Cecil had told him the Pripogurins were in Vancouver and wondered what they were doing there. Miles had shrugged. "Ask Ted Ludwig. Aren't he and Pripogurin buddies? Geoff might know too." Fowler-Biggelow shook his head, irritated. "Geoff doesn't know much. Sometimes I wonder if he knows anything. Ted keeps him in the dark, and that's not a good thing. Ted was in Italy and Russia recently. In Italy he talked to Alenia.

And before you say anything, the trip was not about AEM or rovers but satellites and Earth observation. At least, that's what Geoff thinks. He wasn't aware of the trip, and when I mentioned it – I still have some connections on the continent – he got upset. And now Pripogurin is in Vancouver. Geoff is beginning to think the buggers in Vancouver are quietly screwing us – not the first time – with CSA's help. Yes, the knobheads in Saint-Hubert love Earth observation."

Katelyn was planning to see a movie with friends that afternoon. She was at her laptop when he knocked and entered her room. "I'm going out for lunch," he said.

"Who is she?"

"Who?"

"The strange woman on the phone"

"Why *strange*?"

"It's her accent. A stranger, isn't she?"

"Ah. Someone I met a while ago."

"Where?"

"At a symposium."

"Oh yeah?"

"Last summer. The Laukhin symposium. Ben told me to drop in, and I did."

"You don't usually go to things like that, do you?"

"Ask your mother. She and I were at the first symposium too. Quite enjoyed it, if I remember. Your mother more than me."

"You met her, the stranger, there?"

"It's more that I saw her there. I met her, properly, in the fall, at a—"

"Are you a couple?"

"Don't be silly."

"Do you like her?"

"Katelyn, I met her once, and there were other people around."

"Why are you meeting her now?"

"To reminisce. We had a common friend, Laukhin."

"Can I bring my friends here after the movie?"

"Sorry? Yes, sure. Why here?"

"The movie's at the Cineplex. We'll be two steps from Montgomery. When will you be back?"

"Two to three hours."

"Depends on how approachable she is?"

"You are silly."

Truffles was not the kind of restaurant he could afford often on his pay, but Anna had insisted. It was on the ground floor of her hotel, and on the phone she'd said enigmatically, "It makes everything simpler." He could interpret that to mean either easier for her to come down from her room for lunch, or more convenient for them to go back up afterward. On the subway heading downtown, lustful images appeared in his head simply because he'd be having lunch with an attractive woman who had a room – no, a suite – an elevator ride away. It had been a long time since he last had lustful thoughts in a subway car, perhaps when returning with Federica to Montgomery Avenue, late at night, him intoxicated.

He had never been in bed with a Russian woman. Come to think of it, he'd never been in bed with a foreigner. A *stranger*, as per Katelyn. He'd been monotonously provincial. Ben Paskow had bedded a Russian woman, having decided that not doing so would be a gap on the resumé of any professor of Russian literature. He'd had a tumble or two with a colleague of his, frizzy-haired Olga Tamanova – who taught the nineteenth-century Russian novel – or, more truthfully, as Ben told him one of the few times he'd had too much to drink, Olga had a tumble or two with him. Although, confused that night by the alcohol, Ben wasn't completely sure he'd met the resumé prerequisite. Tamanova's parents were Russian all right, and she'd been born there, in Tula, but she was one year old when they left the Soviet Union and grew up in Upstate New York.

When was the last time he had gone on a date so eagerly? He shouldn't jump to calling it a date. It was – how had Anna put it at the Simmonses'? – an occasion to tell stories and talk about ghosts.

Anna synchronized an exaggerated sigh of relief with a flutter of her right hand. "I feared you'd be harder to look at." She wanted to know what happened to him, and asked questions, especially toward the end of his long story. She seemed mystified by his hesitations. Surely lying was the answer. No need to agonize, even if it meant lying in court. Uttering falsehoods – and Russians weren't bad at it, she implied with a smile – was acceptable, "even a duty," if it was to avoid a bigger harm. Could he live with himself if something happened to his daughter? She mentioned the obvious too, that his lies would benefit the township and his village. As to his telling of a creepy story concerning a dead neighbour who had been a respected pillar of the community and then changing his mind – there Anna raised her narrow shoulders and smiled again – he'd survive the ordeal. There was a softness about her, the softness that middle age brought to bodies and eyes.

He'd ordered what she had. When he finished his story, there was only one other couple left in the restaurant, a fat older man and a young woman.

"Enough of Biranek and Rose's death, and enough of Mary Lambert," Miles said. "I desperately need a break. I want to look at you, and talk to you. I need the illusion that I'm a mid-level engineer again in an irrelevant company, and that life is back to normal."

She couldn't stop gazing at the scar above his left eye. "It's still red," she commented. "In time, I'm certain, it will acquire the right pallor. What exactly did it?"

"A boot, I'd say. I was on the ground and not aware of much."

She stood behind his chair and, with Miles's hand guiding her, touched the area at the back of his head where sparse hair was timidly regrowing. "Oh, yes, I feel it," she said. "It's long for a boot." Her hand lingered on his skull, a delicate and clear message. "It's very Russian to have scars. Laukhin had a scar on his belly – he wouldn't say how he got it. You have a budding air of thuggery, although plenty of catching up to do. Fledgling air of thuggery? Do you say *fledgling*? What's the pronunciation?"

Afterward he settled in a chair near the dressing table and told Anna an abbreviated and, as Laukhin would have insisted, comical version of the events in Toronto involving her former lover and her stepfather. He knew the story well, had heard it time and again from Laukhin, and at various levels of intoxication. It became a teary story after the poet's first stroke. Lengthier too, as Laukhin strove to find the right words. Miles began by explaining the idea of compiling bundled excerpts from Laukhin's father's journal for publication in literary magazines as a way of keeping the public's interest in its long-awaited first volume, and how Laukhin and Ben Paskow worked on a Tsvetayeva bundle for *The New Yorker*. The choice of the Russian *poetesa* – Miles used the Russian word – had been careful. The journal entries relating to Marina Tsvetayeva were gripping, novel, and self-contained, a coherent narrative of sensible size. Pasternak's presence in many of them had been a strong consideration too, as he was much better known in the West. His tangled relationship with Tsvetayeva, and remorse after her death were added bonuses. Miles then moved to the Bakers' soiree in support of the Soviet dissidents, the first time Laukhin had set eyes on Audrey Millay, and described Laukhin's efforts to win her affection. He talked at some length about an opening night at Jean Lezzard's gallery, where some ghastly sculptures were admired by the guests, a huge dog ate everything thrown at him and licked everybody's shoes, Audrey's formidable mother refused to pay any attention to celebrated poet Laukhin – causing a row with her daughter – and a drunk Lezzard made asinine remarks while watching Laukhin and Audrey tidy up the gallery after everybody had left. The opening night at Lezzard's gallery had been the episode Laukhin returned to the most in his reminiscing; he had even worked on a poem about it, called "Vernissage," his one attempt at writing poetry after the stroke. Lezzard, Miles warned Anna, would turn out to be a central villain in the story, the source of the tragic streams beginning to gather, although not yet visible, in the comedic flow. He told Anna that Laukhin went to bed with Audrey Millay after the vernissage, the first of only two nights they spent together. He told her what happened during their second night, the one in which the comedy reached its acme with the middle-of-the-night phone call from one of Laukhin's students pleading to be rescued from a pub downtown, where, unable to pay for a rather large consumption of beverages, he was being kept prisoner. He told her about Laukhin's return later that night, when he found Audrey on the floor, unconscious, the ambulance trip to the hospital, and, of course, the disappearance of the green folder which contained all the work on the Tsvetayeva bundle of journal excerpts. The tragedy arrived unexpectedly. It crept in, stealthily, cowardly, with disturbing, and later haunting, medical terms: extra-axial hemorrhage, epidural hematoma, pressure buildup, lucid interval, craniotomy, surgical aspiration. He rushed his story at the end, after he told Anna how, on the morning of her second day in the hospital, Audrey recalled what had happened to her and identified Cornilov, Anna's stepfather, as the burglar and the other villain of the story. That same day at noon, Miles went on, the doctors, baffled by the unusually slow and late buildup of pressure on Audrey's brain and her atypically long interval of lucidity, ordered a procedure to relieve the pressure. Audrey's mother, who had been phoned by the hospital before the surgery, arrived at Toronto General in the late afternoon, and Laukhin saw her when he came back to the hospital in the early evening. Audrey, conscious although getting worse, was being watched by nervous, worried doctors. She died that night.

Two long stories in one afternoon. This time Anna didn't interrupt him, not once. She didn't smile at the beginning, despite his light tone, and didn't make any sound betraying surprise or shock at the end. The bedcover had fallen on the floor. She lay on her back under the top sheet, staring at the ceiling, her arms exposed. Miles was impressed by her ability to listen and be still for so long. He couldn't take his eyes of her.

"Your friend asked me to write down my recollections of Laukhin," Anna said.

"Ben is asking everybody. He asked Joan-Geraldine too. English, older, you met her at the symposium. A lover of Laukhin's long before you."

"Did he ask you?"

"Me?"

"Why not? From what I gather, you spent several years drinking with him and listening to his stories. You could call it *Drinking with the Poet.*"

It then crossed his mind – assuming, of course, he'd ever write of his boozing with Laukhin – that he might be an author who'd slept with the same woman as his subject. Had there been others? One research topic Ben could undertake, or ask one of his students to pursue. Could he call himself an author without being published? *Drinking with the Poet* had a good ring to it. *Blotto with the Poet? Legless with the Poet?* Perhaps as a subtitle, to attract literary winos. Make a copy for Ben and send the manuscript to publishers. He imagined a romantic blurb: "As he was writing his recollections of the poet, the author fell in love with the woman who, twenty-seven years earlier, had been the great passion of his book's hero." That would sell copies galore. Was he falling in love?

In the silence that followed, Miles said that a large part of Laukhin's reminiscing, particularly after his stroke, had been about the women in his life. It wasn't that he boasted about them, nothing like that. He simply enjoyed describing them, their likes and dislikes, the way they dressed and undressed. Above all he remembered their bodies. He could speak of each one for a long time, tears streaming down his sunken, unshaved cheeks. "It was as if he had high-definition pictures in his mind."

"Oh, God."

"I never heard him say anything bad about a woman he'd slept with. After the stroke, he'd sometimes switch to Russian without realizing. I didn't understand a word, but I carried on listening."

"What did he say about me?" she asked, after a long pause.

"He said the timing had been terrible, just as he was preparing to leave, and that you could have been the great love of his life. You're making a face, but it's true."

"Except that I wasn't."

Perhaps Varlamov had a point. "You don't know that. One of your countrymen is convinced that *Poems for A* were written with you in mind. You were the *A*, not Audrey Millay. Do you know what I think? I think he had both of you in mind."

"Don't do that."

The alarm clock on the bedside table showed half past five. Would Katelyn be home by now?

"He was with a woman when he had his second stroke," he said.

She looked at him incredulously. "You mean he died during . . ."

He smiled. "I didn't mean that. A young woman called 911 and opened the door of his apartment to the ambulance crew. Laukhin never regained consciousness. He died that night."

"Who was she?"

"She was Russian."

"A friend?"

"Not exactly. Maybe they became friends. She worked part-time for an escort service. I talked to her afterward. She'd been to his apartment regularly, once or twice a month for half a year. She said she'd undress and climb into his bed. He'd rarely achieve an erection. It didn't matter to him, or not that much. He liked to lie there with her, smell her, touch her, look at her. He was specific as to the perfume she'd have to put on before slipping into his bed. Loads of it. He always had that perfume in his bedroom, ready for her."

"What kind of perfume?"

"I don't remember. Something that sounded Japanese. She said Laukhin was sweet and overpaid her. He told her he didn't know what to do with his money and that he was dying."

"Was she good looking?"

"Very. She worked part-time at Holt Renfrew."

"Where?"

"A fancy clothing store. It was there that I talked to her first."

"How did you know of her existence?"

"He told me. Not much, but enough to find her afterward."

"How did they . . . get together?"

"I didn't ask."

"What was her name?"

"Alya."

"Another *A*."

She turned on her side, her back to him, the sheet only partly covering her now. From where he was sitting she seemed so young. The thought must have come out aloud, because, without turning, she said, "I'm older than you. I mean, scaled against our expected lifespans. Russians don't live long, as you know. What do they say about a dog's years: multiply by seven to find its age on a human scale? A friend of mine said the coefficient for Russians is one and one-third. We are one-third older than our calendar age. I'm not forty-seven, I'm sixty-three." He stared at her delicate neck, her back, the curve of her haunches, places that an hour or more ago he'd been kissing. Places Laukhin had kissed twenty-seven years earlier.

He got up and went to the window. The suite was high up. The sun was going down somewhere to his right, and clouds were gathering to the south, far out on the hidden lake. His eyes swept the view below him. The brutalist hotel building wrapped around a church, the grey, leafless Queen's Park, the pink-stone palace of the legislative building, the university campus, the tall structures of the financial district, the dim, silly arrow of the CN Tower, the anodyne west. He thought of telling Anna that the bricks used in the legislative building had been made by prison inmates, but decided against it. No Russian would be impressed by such mild-mannered use of forced labour.

"Audrey's death changed Laukhin," he said. "He couldn't get over it, became difficult and irritable. He insulted his colleagues. Nothing pleased him. People said the money had changed him."

"The money?"

"The first two volumes of his father's journal were bestsellers. Not only here, elsewhere too, especially in Europe. It wasn't the money, though. Audrey's death took a terrible toll on him. He drank a great deal."

"He always did."

"Much more. And he started smoking again. It was almost as if he wanted to do himself in. He kept drinking even after the stroke." He turned from the window and looked at Anna. "I could do with a drink too."

The sitting room had a vaguely Indian air. He searched through the whisky offerings in the bar. Glenlivet, Blanton's, Jameson. He mixed the bourbon with ice, took a sip, and returned to the bedroom.

She seemed lost in thought, then asked, "This Audrey, the woman Laukhin mourned after, what was she like?"

"I didn't know her. Younger than him – twelve, fifteen years."

"Young women liked Laukhin. Beautiful?"

"She was – at least in the photo he always had with him."

"He did love her, didn't he?"

"He did, yes."

She turned to face him, expecting more.

"He loved you too, Anna. He thought often of you."

"You keep saying that to make me feel good."

"He said you were special, different, a blessed creature."

Her eyes were suddenly tearful. She sat up and pulled a tissue from the box on the night table. She said, "It's not Laukhin. I got over him long ago. It's the times that are gone, youth, I don't know, innocent daring. Naive enthusiasms, the belief that . . ." She wiped her eyes.

A good thing Ben hadn't told Anna of Audrey's death and Cornilov's role in it. He might not have had time. She was not at the symposium long, and it wasn't the kind of story one told quickly in a break with other people around. Yes, a good thing, because Miles had her undivided attention now.

He was under no illusion – Anna's interest in him was built around Laukhin. He should have told Audrey's story in pieces, one at every get-together. A to-be-continued story to keep her captivated.

"Ben Paskow had been close to Laukhin, hadn't he?"

"Yes."

"Would he know more of Cornilov's role?"

Careful here. There was, perhaps, a need for constructive exaggeration. "Ben knows more about Laukhin's life here in Toronto, of course. His work, his poetic output, which was meagre, his efforts with his father's journal, the literary and the department intrigues. As to Audrey's death . . . I told him details he never knew. Laukhin wouldn't talk of Audrey unless plastered, and I saw him in that state a lot more than Ben did."

"More material for *Drinking with the Poet*."

"Ben will soon squeeze out of me all I know about Laukhin. There's at least one other author already writing a biography, and Ben is worried and seriously into it now."

She said something unexpected. "I'll talk to my stepbrother."

"Cornilov's son?"

"That's what Ben would want, isn't it?" She smiled. "For the biography."

He nodded.

"It'll have to wait until I get back to Saint Petersburg. I don't know when that will be."

"You could phone him."

"It's not something for a telephone conversation."

He found that curious, such caution after so many years.

"On the way here, I hoped we'd end up in bed together," he said.

She didn't answer him immediately. When she did, she startled him again. "Do you think we're attracted to each other because of our connection with Laukhin?"

His fear confirmed. "You should have enticed Ben, not me."

"You know what I mean."

"Not on my part, Anna." He picked up a pillow lying on the floor and lobbed it gently at her. "This is the perfect way to commit adultery, with the husband away on another continent. No fear of awkward—"

"Grisha would not be awkward, even if he knew."

Should he find out what she meant? Did he really want to know? "Where is he now?"

"He flew back."

"Back where?"

"London first, then Saint Petersburg."

"Were you in Vancouver with him?"

"I was. I have a good friend in Vancouver."

"What was he . . . your husband, doing there?"

"Business, of course."

"What kind of business?"

"Some satellite I think, among other things . . ."

"Did he visit Ludwig?"

"He knows the bosses there, the Ludwigs. He's close to the young one, the son. A friend, he says. As friends in business are. Beautiful home, overlooking the ocean."

"What was the purpose of the visit? Did you say satellites?"

"Miles, what is this?"

"I'm asking because, hard to believe . . . it may affect my work."

She seemed startled. Lines appeared on her forehead. "I don't know. From what I understand, Grisha likes the young Ludwig but prefers doing business with the senior. Grisha is a chemist, a scientist. He's into space by accident, as a favour. Tamm was with us for a day – Mikhail Tamm, the Lavochkin designer, or whatever he is – so, yes, they talked space. But not only . . ." She shook her head.

A brief email from Max Tennant touched on rumours of a recent meeting between Ludwig and Alenia. Was Astrium worried about a secret understanding between the two companies now that Alenia, after the windfall from the Italian government, was the uncontested AEM lead? It couldn't be, not with ESA's clear and unbreakable contribution constraints. Even assuming Canada would come through in time with the additional €59 million, it would still be a significantly smaller contributor. Was Alenia bluffing in an attempt to make arrogant Astrium more amenable?

He walked to Cecil's office. On the phone, and clearly having an irritating conversation, his boss pointed to one of the chairs lined against the wall. The call seemed to be about painting and colour choices, and Miles surmised his boss was talking to his wife, who had plenty to say and, judging by Cecil's somber nodding, none of it happy.

"Another domestic cock-up," Cecil said, after he put the phone down. "Wrong shade, to start with. Wrong make too. And not enough, but that turns out to be good, because a different paint is needed."

Miles told him what he was after. Cecil raised his thin shoulders and said it must have been the meeting in Vancouver he'd talked to him about the previous week. He'd learned recently that, besides Pripogurin and one or two other Russians, people from Alenia had been there too, and that the meeting had been on HEOS, the Hyperspectral Earth Observation Satellite. Vancouver had long promoted HEOS, and Alenia's satellite people had worked with Ludwig Space on several feasibility studies. They might be thinking now of more than just the hyperspectral payload. As far as Cecil knew, it had been a get-together prior to a four-way meeting in Saint-Hubert, with CSA and the Italian Space Agency also involved. The two agencies had long been supporters of HEOS, or whatever new name the satellite would end up having. Forest inventory was one of the original missions of HEOS, perhaps the main one. Russia was considering getting involved in HEOS as well, hence the Russian presence in Vancouver. There was a lot of Earth to observe in Russia. Forests too. Siberia was one huge forest.

"This smells, Cecil."

"I'm hardly in the loop myself."

"CSA is against AEM and not being entirely open with us. Max Tennant is always surprised at how little Ludwig Robotics knows about what happens at ESA. He's never been impressed by my information on Ludwig's intentions either. And now I learn, from Astrium, that our chiefs at Ludwig Space are hiding things from us and possibly abandoning AEM. Plotting in secret with Alenia and CSA."

"You're exaggerating."

"Am I? You're the one who first stirred doubts in me."

Cecil sighed. "There are priorities which are beyond our spheres."

"In Stevenage they think I'm a fool."

"You're paid to play the fool. So am I."

It crossed his mind that it might be a glorious feeling to flatten Cecil's pointed nose. He took a few steps toward the window. The geese were not there. Had Geoff and the plant manager won their battle with the birds? A temporary respite? Likely the latter – the big *Branta canadensis* were resilient neighbours. More pertinent, though, was the question of what it was that had made him so upset. So what if Ludwig's work on the AEM rover came to nothing or very little. Only, what, six months ago, it had been a tiny program left in his care, someone on the slow track at Ludwig Robotics. The collapse of the Canadian Mars Mission made AEM prominent simply because the agency's president-astronaut, recently turned politician, had briefly taken a fancy to the idea of a Canadian-built Mars rover. It was understandable that the big shots at Ludwig Space were now having second thoughts. Even thoughts of canning it for something better, with the astronaut's party losing the election. For Ludwig Space, AEM had no immediate or obvious leverage. No future.

Still looking at the parking lot, he said, "It's not work that makes sense for Ludwig Space."

"What isn't?"

"AEM."

Cecil tried to laugh. "This entire division, Miles – Ludwig Robotics – doesn't make sense to Ludwig Space."

"They have a good gig going, our Western masters. They get government dough to build a satellite and then charge customers, including the government, for the data gathered by the satellite."

"They do."

"Would Geoff know more than you?"

"Geoff is currently very busy with NASA. Trying to keep them and CSA happy on the big old program."

"Is HEOS a go?"

"No definite decision has been made. It's Earth observation, though, and, from what I understand, in CSA's plan."

"Funded?"

"In part. Better funded than AEM is right now."

"Any words from Gandarax?"

"Too early to get the minister's ear on something as inconsequential as space."

Miles stood up. "Who knows, perhaps Bernier played with rovers as a child."

"Don't go yet, Miles." Cecil got up and approached the window. "Where are the geese? Could it be that I miss them? Didn't geese save a city once? Sometimes I think they are the only creatures that make sense around here. We need them to save us. Lysiane Monast is the acting president at CSA now. Joe Courant was at his limit of three months. She's an administrator who will strictly follow the ten-year plan. Not a friend of Ludwig, as you know. Paul Arsenault rang me an hour ago. He said that with Courant replaced, support for AEM is weaker than ever. He also said our credibility has eroded with ESA and perhaps with our partners in Europe. Canada will look ridiculous if the contribution does not come through soon, and there are countries and companies ready to pounce. It's an impression he's gathered here and there on his trips, around the proverbial water coolers. 'Why,' Arsenault asked, 'why aren't Ludwig's big shots putting more pressure in the right places?' I asked Arsenault about the meeting with Bernier. It seems Bernier is still getting organized. He's a novice, and with industry, trade, and commerce on his lap, he has scores of portfolios to look after. CSA is just one of them, and it barely registers. The agency wanted an early meeting with him and were told it would be within the next four to eight weeks. That was a while ago. CSA has prepared the meeting carefully and will ask for additional money for both HEOS and AEM."

HEOS again, genuine Earth observation. What chance did AEM have?

Katelyn was skiing that weekend with Federica and Greg and a couple of friends she'd invited along. He left work late, a mistake on a snowy Friday. A long, aggravating drive to an empty home and weekend. On the ramp connecting the 409 to the 401, he felt the old Corolla slide to the left as he was inching his way ahead. The car closest to him was sliding too – another cheapskate unwilling to pay for snow tires – though less than his, and their side mirrors may have touched. An old woman in the passenger seat of the other car was staring straight ahead, oblivious to minor worries. To make matters worse, he needed to pee.

As he navigated the Corolla into the narrow driveway and got out of the car, he noticed a Land Rover idling across from the house, the interior light on. A large man got out and waved to him, then bent to saying something to the driver. He waved again as he crossed the street.

"Finally," the man said, and Miles recognized Lyle Blanchard. "I feared you were gone for the weekend." Blanchard had a manila envelope in his hand. "My son in there," he added nodding toward the car, "is bored and resentful. I have something for you."

Miles looked at the yellow envelope without touching it. "What's this?"

"There's an explanatory note inside."

"Tell me."

"The draft of a piece that will be posted early next week on my website. We'd like your comment."

"Who's we?"

Blanchard hesitated. "The *Post* might print it too, or a version of it. They are not sure, though, not yet. And they want some changes. They don't like my style, you see. Too combative – too, how did they put it, *novelistic*." The last word came out bundled in sarcasm and disdain. "They don't understand that the rules of the game have changed, with the internet elbowing to the top." He thrust the envelope toward Miles. "Another condition is to let you read it and comment."

"Me?"

"Yes. It doesn't much matter to me – it will be on my website next week."

He should stop his silly acting. "What's it about?"

"The death of Rose Biranek."

"And you want my input. Mine in particular."

"You had me fooled at the hospital, Miles. You're something, you know, a thespian manqué. Better than the punk that tried to impersonate you."

"Look, it's been a long drive and I need a piss."

"Just read it."

"It doesn't concern me."

"Oh, it does, very much so. Mary Lambert told me that you know – in fact as a direct witness always knew – that Dr. Biranek was implicated in her mother's death. It was from you, indirectly, that she became aware of his role. It's reasonable to give you the opportunity to comment on the story before we print it."

"Mary Lambert talked to you?"

"Yes, but you won't hear me say that anywhere else. That was Mary's condition. As far as you or the world knows, my source is my secret."

"Why would she tell you this?"

"You know why. She doesn't want a hospital with Biranek's name."

He looked at the envelope. "I don't know if I want to read it."

"It's your decision. I'm offering it to you, and my son waiting there, who desperately wants to get away, is witness that I did. He might even have taken a picture of the two of us talking, although in this light . . . The *Post* was of the opinion we should do it, given that it all started with you."

He took the envelope, might as well face the harm.

"You don't have much time, Miles. I want to put the story up on Monday. I was hoping the *Post* would print it in the weekend edition, with time for readers to absorb the story at leisure, but the editor had this harebrained idea of giving the protagonist the opportunity to comment. Bah, they'll likely need more time to think this over. A fearful bunch, hiding behind lawyers. I'll phone you later tonight. Have a drink or two. No more, though. We want sober comment."

He sat in the small living room and opened the envelope. It was surprising how unsurprisingly events followed one another sometimes, almost as if, for brief stretches, and particularly when one hoped for an unexpected twist, life seemed dismayingly coherent and sensible. The note enclosed with the printout was typed, with Lyle Blanchard's elaborate signature in blue ink under his name. That day's date was at the top.

Dear Mr. Rueda,

You'll find enclosed a draft of the article that will be posted on my website on Monday. It's about the Biranek affair, of course, and it concerns you. It's only fair to give you the opportunity to comment on the story in advance.

    With best regards,

Lyle Blanchard

PS: The *Post* mulls printing this article as well, or a version of it.

The piece was long, and he was the protagonist, appearing as Miles or as Mr. Rueda, depending on whether it was the child of thirty-five years earlier or the grownup of today. There was a long description of his physical condition in the hospital, as Lyle began his article with his visit there, cheaply squeezing every drop of drama out of the place and the initial impression his protagonist made on him: "I first met Mr. Rueda at the Toronto General, and his face . . ." The Ruedas were introduced next, a respected family in Corby Falls and neighbours of the Biraneks. Miles's father was described as an early patient of Dr. Biranek, and Heather Rueda had somehow become a childhood friend of Rose Biranek. Blanchard's text implied that the Ruedas and the Biraneks had been close. A long paragraph was dedicated to the township of Millcroft, its hospital, and its mayor.

Lyle Blanchard got right most of the story of the weekend Rose died. That was unexpected, considering the number of people the story had gone through to reach him. Significant details were missing, of course. He didn't mention that Miles had always thought it was common knowledge Dr. Biranek and Hollie McGinnes had returned to Corby Falls late Saturday night, or that Miles learned the official version of events only thirty-five years later. Also missing was what Hollie had told him about someone breaking Biranek's glasses in the hotel bar after the show that fateful Saturday night in Toronto, and how the doctor was so unduly upset he almost came to blows with the clumsy man, only to be cheerfully wearing his spare glasses when Hollie got up the next morning. He *had* mentioned the aside about Biranek's glasses at Le Paradis. Had Lyn Collins missed or forgotten that important coda to his story? Could it be that Blanchard was keeping it for later?

Less relevant details, though, had found their way into Blanchard's draft. Among them, embarrassingly, the fact that Miles would climb down from his bedroom window on summer nights, cross into the Biraneks' backyard, skulk around the windows of their ground floor living room, and watch, mesmerized, Dr. Biranek's sexual trysts with his office nurse. How on earth did Lyle know? From Jim? Jim had been his companion, an apprentice voyeur, once or twice. Jim could have boasted to others about their childhood forays, and somehow the story reached Eddy B and, through him, Lyle. Blanchard introduced that bit of titillation with an oily sentence: "Little Miles had long been fascinated by the Biraneks and by what took place inside their large house." His colleagues at Ludwig Robotics would love that. It was a good thing Don was gone; he would have been unbearable. Little Miles. Besides accusing a former family friend of murder, Miles Rueda was a voyeur. Jesus. He could imagine Martha's parents exchanging glances while asking Katelyn questions about her father. How to explain to Katelyn that one is not a voyeur at the age of eleven or twelve but simply curious about the adult world? He imagined Katelyn staring silently at him.

In closing, to bookend his story, Lyle returned to his first impression of Mr. Rueda at the hospital and the impact of the savage beating he suffered in Corby Falls. "Barely able to walk, with his head bandaged and the left side of his face reminding me of visits to military hospitals, Mr. Rueda claimed he'd been a victim of an ordinary mugging getting unusually violent. Oddly, he didn't report his beating to the police. His sister drove him to Toronto and he got himself into Toronto General. According to OPP records, muggings are not common in Millcroft Township. The last recorded mugging in Corby Falls was in 1997. Did the assault on Mr. Rueda have something to do with what he saw as a child thirty-five years ago, the weekend Rose Biranek was left to die?"

As to how the incendiary revelations in the article had reached him, Blanchard was guarded. He wrote that Mr. Rueda had told a few friends one evening about what he'd seen. Nothing of Mary's friend Lyn Collins hearing Miles's story at Le Paradis. Mary Lambert's name was mentioned only to further blacken Dr. Biranek's. He had forced Rose to give Mary away for adoption. He'd behaved horribly to the suffering Rose. Either Lyle was keeping his word to Mary Lambert or he planned to reveal later how Mary had played a role in the story of her mother's death becoming news.

Lyle Blanchard called at nine o'clock and then every half hour afterwards. Miles watched the call display and didn't answer. At midnight, telling himself it was better to get it over with, he picked up the phone.

"At last. Lyle here, Lyle Blanchard. Have you read what I wrote?"

"I have."

"And?"

"And nothing."

"No comment at all?"

"It's silly tales, Lyle, and you'll definitely be sued for libel. The *Post* too, if they publish it or anything resembling it."

"What's silly tales?"

"All of it."

"Are you saying that the entire story was a fabrication?"

"Yes."

"You're saying you lied?"

"I told you – it's all silly tales."

"You're back where you started."

"I am."

"That's all you have to say?"

"It is."

"It will be on my website on Monday. I'm still struggling for a title."

"You're making a mistake."

"Ah, the libel."

"Yes."

"You'll sue?"

"Not me. I have no interest in this thing dragging on in the courts and in the news. Biranek's widow will, and she's been left well off. She'll have the support of the township too."

"The courts will find that I believed the story to be true when I posted it."

"They might not. Anyway, you know very well that's not enough."

"You're a legal expert now."

"What you have is hearsay, which went through sundry mouths and ears, and which I, the source, am now dismissing."

"You'll be subpoenaed. You won't lie under oath."

"That's what you'll hear from me in court – all silly tales. And it's not a lie. I'll also say that I had the same message for you when you asked me to comment on your article in which my name first appeared, and that despite my warning you still posted it."

Lyle chuckled. "You mean you'll say you told a fib."

"You figured it out, Lyle."

The journalist was quiet for a while. "It's a good story," he said. "What's more, a court challenge will make it last longer and add another aspect to it. And the *Post* will milk it for all it's worth."

"The *Post* won't publish it if you tell them what I just told you."

"It will be on my website, whether the weaklings at the *Post* publish it or not."

"As I said, you'll be the one sued."

"I'll have more readers. More clicks – isn't it what they say? Gazillions. My website will be more popular than ever. And even if a jury finds me wrong in the law, they'll also learn Biranek was an absolute shit: forcing his wife to give up her daughter, living openly with his mistress in the house he shared with his suffering wife, being away with his mistress while his wife, alone, died. Other things will come out, I'm sure. I've heard his hands strayed to women's delicate areas. What damage, Miles, will the jury award? One dollar? Two dollars? Five?" He chuckled, happy with himself. "The perplexing fact that a serious, reasonable, educated man comes up with a story that accuses a neighbour of murder will delight our readers. And, in turn, they'll wonder, Is the man lying under oath? And if he is, why? Because, you see, Miles, I think you're lying. I don't know why, yet you are."

Chapter 15

April 2006

He checked Blanchard's website first thing on Monday morning. There was nothing new that early. On his way to Allen Road he stopped for the *Post*. He spent ten minutes in the car carefully scanning every page. No part of Blanchard's dreaded exposé was to be found. At work he returned to Blanchard's website whenever he was back at his desk. Nothing, again and again. Perhaps Lyle had decided to hold off for a few more days in the hope that at least portions of his piece would appear in the *Post* as well. Miles didn't dare think he had given up. It was the same on Tuesday, but when he arrived at Ludwig on Wednesday and checked Blanchard's website he saw the new entry. Its title, "The Witness," left no doubt what it was about.

Only the ending seemed to have changed from the draft he'd seen, and not much. "I gave Mr. Rueda the opportunity to comment on the facts presented here. I waited in front of his house in the winter storm of last Friday and, as he drove in, I handed him a typed draft. Both in the brief discussion we had then and in a telephone conversation held after he read the draft, Mr. Rueda maintained that his story about what he saw as a twelve-year-old was made up. An invention of his, a fantasy, a fib. The mind whirls at such a startling claim and then turns to the assault Mr. Rueda was a victim of in Corby Falls in October. An ordinary mugging turned unusually violent, he told me. Oddly, he didn't report it to the police. His sister drove him to Toronto, and he got himself into Toronto General. According to the OPP records, muggings are not common in Corby Falls; the last reported one was in 1997. Did the assault on Mr. Rueda have something to do with what he'd seen as a child thirty-five years earlier, the weekend Rose Biranek died?"

Miles was jittery the entire day, but no one said anything to him. A relief to realize that there were not that many readers of Blanchard's blog. Not yet?

The following Monday Hollie Biranek issued a statement printed in the *Millcroft Gazette*. Through her lawyer, Joe Montanari, she threatened to sue Lyle Blanchard for defamation unless a quick retraction of his blog story "The Witness" appeared on his website and in at least one of the major newspapers. All entries regarding the Biranek bequests and the death of Rose Biranek were to be erased from the website as well. In a brief interview on the same page, Montanari said he was certain Mr. Rueda would deny the ridiculous allegations attributed to him. He described Blanchard's blog as wild, desperate journalism.

Sarah rang late that Monday and read him both the statement and the interview. According to one of Sarah's friends, the regional CBC Radio station in Peterborough had mentioned the spat in their local news.

Three days later the *Post* printed an interview with Lyle Blanchard. He was introduced as a contributor to the *Post*, and a reference was made to his website and the extensive writing in it about Biranek's bequests. Blanchard said he had published his blog material on the Biranek affair in good faith and believed it to be true. Several people had heard Mr. Rueda tell what he'd seen thirty-five years earlier, and he doubted Mr. Rueda would claim in court it was a made-up story. There was a difference between a casual lie and perjury. Blanchard said he would not retract or delete anything on his website and would vigorously defend any legal action against him.

There it was, Miles's name out there for all to see, not just the obsessive readers of Blanchard's blog.

He put the newspaper down and considered the sheer brilliance of it all. Had Blanchard and the *Post* come up with that strategy at the beginning, or did they stumble into it? It was a story newspapers dreamt of. It had everything: a will with a large bequest left to a rundown township hospital in dire need of funding; a township that would do anything to get what they thought was their due; a local construction company in desperate need of new work; a neglected sick wife and an abandoned child; a benefactor who was both a respected doctor and possibly a murderer; a mysterious witness to the murder. It was a story, or a series of stories, which would sell many newspapers but couldn't be printed, because it was based on what the *Post*'s lawyers surely described as conjectures of an unreliable witness who, meanwhile, had changed his mind. There was also a distinct possibility of the newspaper being sued. The murderer himself was dead, but his second wife was still alive and quite well off. The township could threaten legal action too. Initially undecided, the *Post* had assigned a journalist to the story who was not in their current employ but a frequent contributor. The journalist, an old hand, had done a superb job and uncovered many juicy side stories, but little of it was publishable in a reputable paper. And then the brilliant thought must have come to them. The journalist could have it all, the whole story, for his personal website. In a blog. References to the website would be made in whatever bland, inoffensive articles the newspaper could publish about the bequest, and many readers would visit it. If the journalist was sued for libel, so much better. Because the facts around the threatened action and the eventual court proceedings would have to be conveyed to the readers of the newspaper. In detail. And the names and the damaging facts that the website contained would be repeated in the reporting pieces. Inevitably. The readers needed to understand what all the kerfuffle was about. Part of any good reporting.

Yes, simple and brilliant. Going to court was probably fine with Blanchard. His website would explode, and he'd be at the centre of it all. The newspaper would likely pay for his legal expenses and whatever damages he'd suffer if found guilty.

He wondered who had a say in Hollie's decision to go after Blanchard, besides Joe Montanari. Mayor Thula, of course, and maybe someone from B&M Construction. Barry Matlock perhaps, since Tom Bryson had been compromised by his son. Could be someone from St. Anselm's too, ensuring the Almighty would not forget their side was the righteous one? Perhaps not, they'd want to keep their war council small. Would they meet in Joe Montanari's office or in Hollie's house? Did they have a name for themselves? Biranek's Defenders? The Save the Millcroft Hospital Committee? Would Jim Cowley be part of it too? No, Jim was low rank. Yet he seemed well informed. No doubt his father-in-law kept him abreast of the council's thinking and Jim then translated it into direct orders for the army wing, like teaching loose-tongued Miles Rueda a lesson he wouldn't forget. Jim would undertake more delicate tasks too, such as pointing out to the same Miles Rueda that his daughter was an easy target.

He poured himself a drink and rang Federica. It was Greg who answered. "Ah, the man of the hour. I'm more popular than ever now – telling everybody Miles Rueda is my wife's ex and I know him well. A mild exaggeration. Working in taxation, one yearns for a bit of notoriety."

Miles repressed a sharp remark and repeated what he'd told George and Cecil.

"Whatever, Miles. Yes, Federica is here."

Whatever, Miles? Had Federica told him? Spouses told each other many things in bed or at the dinner table. Still, Feds was a lawyer and knew better.

Federica came on the line quickly. Blanchard's interview in the *Post* had sent her to his website. She'd read what he wrote about Biranek's bequests. Devoured, not read. Twice. Yes, Katelyn had read it too, and wasn't sure what to make of it. She was amazed her dad was suddenly the subject of a much-talked-about blog. The fact that he'd told a whopper in which a doctor, now dead, had committed an ancient murder had not yet registered, or not fully. It would, especially when her friends asked questions, some prompted by their parents.

"Feds, how much does Greg know?"

"Oh . . . whatever is out there."

"He sounded as if . . . I'm a bit wound up these days."

"You should take a holiday, Miles. A long one."

She sounded concerned, and so did Sarah when he called her. As always, his sister tried to make light of it.

"It will be over in a few weeks."

"It won't, and you know it. Hollie will sue, or the township. Maybe both. It's twenty million dollars, Sarah."

"It will die soon if you tell everybody it's a made-up story. You'll look like a fool, true, but in a month . . . well, perhaps longer, it will be forgotten."

Big sister Sarah cleverly switched the subject. She was in Caledon half of the time now. Hilly grounds, woods, the Humber River somewhere, also a famous moraine. There were only gentle people around them, and horses and church were big things. The gentle people, when visible, liked to drink, which was good. A famous sculptor had lived nearby, so she was in a fertile location. Artistically fertile. One annoying thing was that the closest hardware store was half an hour away. Nothing like Corby Falls.

The following evening, Katelyn, no doubt prompted by her classmates, asked a lot of questions on the phone. He told her he'd concocted the story to regale some friends. He'd been slightly tipsy, and she knew about Dad being tipsy and talking nonsense. He swore her to silence, whatever her friends asked. She was intrigued by his request, and by everyone's interest in him, a father who might be, after all, less conventional than she had thought.

"Say nothing?" she asked, animated. "That's not easy, Dad."

"Look mysterious."

"How do I do that?"

The first to comment among his co-workers was George Szetes, at lunchtime. He saw Miles looking around with a tray in his hand and waved him over.

"Well, well, well. Here's the witness himself," George chuckled happily, as Miles sat opposite him.

"I'm not in the mood, George," Miles whispered.

"That bad?"

"Worse."

"Thirty-five years is a long time."

"Who else knows? No one has said anything yet."

"I heard Denise say, 'Miles? Our Miles? I don't believe it.' And if a secretary knows . . . It was a shock, I have to say."

"I was drunk and told a daft story. I tried to amuse the people I had dinner with at a restaurant. Before long the *Post* got interested in Biranek's bequests, and the contributor assigned to the story has been laying it on thick on his personal website."

"You made it up? That's not like you, Miles."

"I have flaws."

"You'll be famous soon."

"How is the family, George? Any trips planned? A Danube cruise?"

"You told the blogger it's a fabricated story."

"Yes."

"And he didn't believe you."

"He didn't."

"There's more to it than you're saying. The battering you received in your village makes more sense now."

Miles looked around to check if the neighbouring tables were paying attention to George's insinuations. "George, my life is very hard right now."

"The website made the connection first."

"There isn't one. None. How can there be when the whole thing was a fantasy of mine?"

Toward the end of the day Cecil alluded to Blanchard's website. They were in his boss's office. Miles waved his hands, expressed his embarrassment, and told him what he told George.

Cecil seemed amused by Miles's predicament. "A tall story told to amuse a group of friends while intoxicated – any Brit understands that. Never mind. It will be forgotten in a while. Geoff had a giggle too, by the by. I learned about all this over lunch with him. His wife, Dorothea, had shown him the website."

"Everybody's so droll."

"Here's something to put you in a better mood, Miles. Word is that Gandarax's advice is getting some traction."

"Anything concrete?"

"Bernier is beginning to open his mind to ESA and AEM. On Monday they spent almost an hour talking Mars and rovers. Some dollar numbers have been thrown around too."

"Did you hear this from Gandarax?"

"From Ted Ludwig."

"Ah."

"It will take some time. Don't pass it around."

Geoff happened to walk by as Miles was leaving Cecil. "Come with me, Miles," he said, without turning or stopping.

Miles followed him, wondering if Geoff had been tasked by Dorothea to get more juicy details from his employee. They reached Geoff's office with Miles ten steps behind. Geoff sat at his large desk and pointed to a chair for Miles. "I guess you know what this is about," he said.

"Not in the slightest. Unless it's about what was said about me today on some blog, and which—"

"It isn't. Dorothea is thrilled, by the way. No, it's about AEM. Managing the program."

"Ah."

"It's a big program."

"Yes. Well, biggish. As it would stretch over a long period, the yearly intake would be fairly modest. If we get it, that is."

"We'll get it. The question I have is, do you aspire to be the program manager?"

"Aspire? Good word. Yes, I hope to be the program manager. I think I deserve it."

"You've never been in charge of such a sizeable program."

"There's always a first time."

"It's not the best time for experiments. We've lost a much larger CMM and there isn't much else immediately on the horizon."

Miles didn't say anything.

Geoff waited and then nodded. "Okay, I see how things stand." He sighed. "I thought it would be easy. I guess we'll have to make a decision."

"Who else is in the running?"

"Kees Vermaak for one."

"Ah, the Vancouver boy."

"A *risible* candidate, Miles? You see, that's the other drawback with you, arrogant lips which run ahead of your brain. That's how you got into this mess of yours with the doctor, isn't it? Yeah . . . There is, also, the lack of experience with larger programs."

"I have worked on larger programs."

"I mean manage."

"Does Kees have the experience?"

"I was told he does."

"Which program?"

"I don't know the details."

"Does he know the ESA crowd and the European space companies?"

"Perhaps not like you. But dealing with the Europeans there is need for . . . I don't know, finesse."

"Finesse? Did you say finesse? That's the last thing I'd associate with Vermaak."

"Finesse and firmness. Finesse in a firm way."

The nightmare stretch began a week later. As Miles was contemplating the wall above the urinal and reminding himself to keep an upright posture, Fowler-Biggelow filled the space to his right.

"Geoff had a difficult meeting with CSA yesterday," Cecil said.

"Meaning?"

"Tense, disturbing. He doesn't understand what's going on. Everybody was smiling last week. Even Lysiane Monast had friendly words. She said she'd see Bernier this week and that Ludwig had an influential friend near the minister, meaning Gandarax. And now only tense faces. Ted Ludwig is flying to Ottawa next week."

"To see Bernier?"

"That's what he was hoping. He's not sure now."

"Gandarax, then?"

"Perhaps. He'll still try to see the minister, if things don't go sourer meanwhile. I don't get it. Dealing with neurotic politicians."

Fowler-Biggelow carried on while they were dutifully washing their hands. "I'll let you know as soon as I hear anything new. The important thing is to do well during B1. If ever that fucking phase starts. Dazzle them, Miles, dazzle ESA and Astrium and Alenia with Ludwig's technical prowess."

Such silliness. Cecil, like him, was paid to be silly. Play the fool, that was what he'd said.

The following Wednesday, as Miles was preparing to go home, Cecil's secretary, Diane, rang to summon him to Fowler-Biggelow's office. After carefully shutting the door behind Miles, Cecil said that the news from Ottawa could not be worse. Ted Ludwig had met that morning with the minister, and Bernier told him that, based on the advice he'd received, no additional funding would be made available for the Ares Exploration Mission. Nothing significant, that was – perhaps a few more million from existing funds, but no new money. Not for a couple of years, anyway. HEOS was another issue, and on that Bernier would need additional input. Looking tired, Cecil told Miles to keep what he'd just heard quiet. Ludwig wanted the Phase B1 work on Chassis and Locomotion, and there was no point in alarming Astrium or ESA. Anyway, with the AEM program barely moving, in two years things would not be much further ahead. Miles should go on claiming to ESA and the industrial partners that no definite decision had been made, that the minister had not made up his mind. This would be the official position of Ludwig Robotics until B1 work was secured. The only concession Ted Ludwig could get was that Bernier would say the same thing: his government was still considering the pros and cons. Yes, Gandarax had been in the meeting, and he had said little. Ted and Gandarax had agreed to have a drink later that evening.

His phone was ringing when he got back to his desk. A number in Europe. France? He was tempted to let it ring, then thought better of it and answered. The excitement in Don Verbrugge's voice told him what his ex-colleague wanted to talk about.

"Where are you, Don? In France?"

"Toulouse, my friend. Everything's forgiven and I'm selling airplanes once more. What a relief, Miles, what a relief. Things around me have colour again. Anyway, that's not why I called."

"I couldn't possibly be news in Toulouse."

"No, not yet, although I'm telling everybody your story. My parents clipped Lyle's interview and sent it to me. I read his blog too, of course. What a shock. Lying to your pal all this time."

"I'll come and visit you, Don. Always liked that part of France. Foie gras, fries in duck fat."

"A fancy story you told around a restaurant table? Fiction? The assault on you in Corby Falls, and now this. I don't know, Miles, you're not just a pretty boy able to hold his drink, there's a bit of, what, *darkness* and—"

"Invite me to Toulouse if you want more details, or an insight into my dark side. We'll take a barge trip on the Canal du Midi, eat, drink, and tell stories, fiction or otherwise. Not now, though. You don't ask a drowning man for comments."

The explosion was the following day. He was in the cafeteria, hesitating between a cup of Bom Dia or one of Kona Reserve, and thinking over what Cecil had told him the day before, when George Szetes passed by.

"Is it between elephant or puma piss that you are trying to decide on? Puma, trust me. By the way, Miles, everybody's looking for you. Fowler-Bigelow wants you, sooner than soonest, and he's in a rage. What did you do? Try your excuse with me – workshop it. More revelations on the web? Social media?"

"George, fuck off."

"Diane asked me where you were. She said Cecil screamed at her, 'Get that knobhead in here!' Cecil doesn't scream at secretaries – first time it has happened. Slammed the door afterward. Cecil doesn't slam doors either. There's a reward for locating you, Miles, and I want it. Can I tell Diane you'll be coming?"

Miles walked slowly back so as not to slop his cup of Bom Dia. Diane waved him into Cecil's office with a curious stare. Fowler-Biggelow made an odd squeak on seeing him, closed his office door carefully, sat down in his chair, and, trying to control himself, said, "What the fuck's going on, Miles?"

No wasting time on small talk. Even Jim, who had asked Miles the same question at Bart's Alehouse, had frittered away a minute talking about rain and the pissing lads from Alverton.

"Cecil, I'm not sure—"

Cecil's eyes bulged. "Not sure?"

"I don't know—"

"You don't know what this is about? Could it be – hold steady, heart – could it be that I'm not being *explicit* enough for you?" Cecil raised his gaunt body halfway out of his chair, and for a second Miles feared his boss was looking around for a weapon. "I'll give you *explicit*. An engineer who masquerades as a manager, a complete tosser, comes up with a story of murder. He accuses a respected doctor – who, already dead, can't defend himself – of killing his first wife. Our engineer – he's ours, alas, works here at Ludwig Robotics – remembers he saw something as a twelve-year-old boy that looked like murder. Twelve, Miles, twelve! I don't recall a fucking thing from that snotty age, and most people don't either, but our tosser does. He remembers it thirty-five years later, *thirty-five*, and everything is as fresh to him as his morning wank. And he tells some friends around a restaurant table what he's all of a sudden summoned up. The story of the murdering doctor spreads like ink on blotting paper. A blogger learns of it too, and, after some further digging, his website has everything in it, and then some. A huge bequest the doctor made to a local hospital is now in jeopardy. Newspapers – it's good copy, after all – get hold of the narrative too and want to print it. Of course. Now, what I don't entirely understand, Miles, is why our engineer – a respected one, yes he is, though I fear not for long – why he came up with such a ridiculous story. The answer I've settled on after some soul searching is that he's a knobber, a fucking fool. I hope you heard me: a *fucking fool*. It does explain everything. It makes *us* fools too, his employers—"

"Surely, Cecil—"

"I'm not done with the *explicit*. You're a voyeur—"

"I wasn't even twelve."

"Don't interrupt me. You're badly beaten up in Corby Falls, the seat of the scandal. So badly, in fact, that you miss work for six weeks. You scamper off to

Toronto and don't tell the police. A mugging gone pointlessly violent, that's how you explain it to us, and we believe you—"

"It was."

"Shut the fuck up. Ted Ludwig has been on the phone with Geoff. He wants to *contain* the scandal. He's told Geoff to come up with a strategy by the end of the day. Now, how the hell do I do it? Huh? Because I have to do it. Not Geoff. He doesn't want to talk to you, he says, because he's afraid he'll break your neck. If only. How the fucking hell do I *contain* the scandal, Miles? Tell me. Come on, don't be shy."

Something was amiss, clearly, something he wasn't aware of. "I don't understand, Cecil. I don't . . . You seemed amused by the story ten days ago. Why now the rage?"

"Why now the rage? Sounds Shakespearean, or almost. I'll tell you *why now the rage*. That doctor in your village, Biranek or whatever, he had a wife, a second wife, didn't he?"

"Huh? Yes . . ."

"And she's alive, isn't she?"

"She is, yes."

"That's why the rage, you fool."

"Cecil, I—"

"Still not explicit enough? What's her name?"

"Her name? Why?"

"Well?"

"Hollie. Hollie Biranek. Hollie is from Héloïse."

"What do you know of her?"

"I know she's from Quebec originally, from Montreal."

"Ah, good, good. This is progress. What else?"

"Worked in a hospital in Montreal, St. Mary's, or something like that. Trained as a nurse. Her first husband, McGinnes, was a cop. He called her Hollie. Couldn't say Héloïse, it seems."

"She has a sister, did you know?"

"She has several siblings."

"One sister married and had a son."

He shrugged.

"The husband's last name was Gandarax."

It couldn't be.

"Gandarax, Miles, Gandarax. It's not a common last name. Hollie Biranek is Louis Gandarax's aunt. That's what Gandarax told Ted Ludwig. They had a drink last night, after the meeting with the minister. He also said AEM was a lost cause."

It was farcical. Absurd. *Risible.*

Katelyn spent Friday evening and Saturday morning on Montgomery Avenue. Around lunchtime he drove her to Martha's place.

When they got there, Katelyn asked him, "Would you come in?"

"Come in where?"

"Martha's."

"Why on earth?"

"She wondered if you'd come in."

"What for? A cup of coffee? A slice of apple pie? Is it Martha who's asking or her parents?"

"Does it matter?"

"Jesus, Katelyn."

Back home he opened a can of tuna and ate it distractedly. He needed something before he applied himself to some serious thinking about what was happening to him. And that kind of thinking meant drinking.

He went to the liquor cabinet and took out the bottle of bourbon. Back in the kitchen he poured himself a generous amount, and dutifully thought of Laukhin. Federica was right, he should take a long break. Wait for the summer, then get away. He had eight weeks of accumulated vacation, and with that year's four weeks, he'd have almost three months. With AEM returning to its minor status at Ludwig Robotics, he'd easily get two or three months of additional unpaid leave. He wasn't popular with his bosses, especially now, and they would be glad to see as little as possible of him. Perhaps he needed more than a long breather. A real change. Something dramatic, like leaving Ludwig Robotics. Or, verging on the extreme, giving up engineering altogether. What else could he do, though? Run a hardware store, a return to his tranquil roots? Perhaps a store close to Mike Ancona's place in Caledon. He'd put an ad in the local paper: "Builder of space hardware is now selling home hardware in the neighbourhood." He'd have one sure customer: Sarah. Two, with Mike. It would be tranquil, no doubt. He could scribble *Drinking with the Poet* at the store counter. Ben would love him for it, and he'd get some brownie points with Anna the poetess. A mystery why she wasted her time with him. It was awkward enough for her to come to Toronto, but would she seek him out in the wilderness of Caledon? Perhaps once, out of curiosity. See the moraine – she'd look around and ask where exactly it was – and read his manuscript. No, not Caledon. Katelyn would find visiting him there gruelling. The attraction of the Montgomery house for her was its location, with everything, including the subway, nearby. Her mom's place in ritzy Rosedale had no such amenities.

A job in Europe – that would indeed be drastic. Something in Paris, close to Katelyn if . . . If? Yes, he'd let Katelyn go with her mother and Greg. He'd already made the decision – he knew that – he just hadn't said it out loud. It was the way his mind worked, sometimes much the worse for him. He had already made up his mind to perjure himself in court if called to testify, and because, mulishly, he wouldn't tell Jim of his decision, his former school buddies had a go at him.

Yes, he'd do that, let Katelyn be with her mother in Paris. The solution was staring at him, simple, all he had to do was follow his daughter across the Atlantic. Near Katelyn. Near Anna too. Would a move to the UK be easier than France? The language, of course, otherwise . . . France as a first choice, but the UK would be near enough too. It was a one-hour flight to Paris from just about anywhere in the UK. The train was an option as well, and likely faster without the hassles of airports. Move to do what, though? He couldn't be a tourist for three years. An immigrant? A temporary resident? Even if allowed in, he wouldn't have a work permit, not immediately. He needed the advice of someone who knew how such things worked.

What could he do in Europe if he resolved to make his radical break with engineering? The people he knew over there were all engineers or somehow linked with engineering. Space too, which was worse. Only Don Verbrugge . . . A salesman of Airbus planes, like Don. Why not? A job with Airbus in Toulouse. From there, he could hop to Paris to see Katelyn. By TGV it would be a few hours. It was a quick hop to London too, if *Grisha* wasn't around and Anna's call came. Not engineering, yet his technical background might help. Not that he knew anything about airplanes or selling them. Don would mentor him, and he'd shadow Don until he learned the ropes. Was such a thing possible? Would a less wobbly command of French be needed? Clients would be from all over the world, after all, and English would be a plus. To think that he'd had five years of French in school, several years of on-and-off classes at U of T's School of Continuing Studies, learning to "express original thoughts using an ever-expanding vocabulary," and four months of being lectured on the wonders of Proust in a crowded apartment which smelled of onions and baby feces. What one did for love. The lecturer, Tsvetko – what was his last name? – had been a student of Darius Milo with Federica, and, unlike Feds, carried on. He'd been applying for academic positions and did some part-time teaching. Most of the lectured – friends, or friends of friends, of Tsvetko – looked as if they longed to be elsewhere. The child, there was a child, yes, never seen but heard and smelled, would sometime start crying, at which point Bolena, Tsvetko's wife, would put her head into the room and say, "I'll look into it – he'll be quiet soon." Miles never understood why that notification was needed. He complained to Federica about the stuffy air and the smells. "They have a child, for God's sake," she snapped. "What do you expect, the scent of violets?" Tsvetko was short and pudgy, with short black curly hair. He perspired while he imparted Proust's wisdom and beauty. He looked like a sweaty Karakul lamb. He made his students learn the original of Proust's famous *pensées*, or aphorisms, or whatever they were, by heart. "It will come in handy," Tsvetko would say at the mildest signs of rebellion, and it made Miles think of Bill Cowley's words of assurance. He once heard Bolena say to Federica as she and Miles were saying goodbye, "What can I do? He likes onions. Yes, with everything. It can be trying. But he's a good man, Federica, such a good man."

His mind was off again. Liquor got one outside the box, and, frequently, far away from it too.

Letting Katelyn live in Paris with her mother was the key decision. Everything else followed. That was the beauty of addressing dilemmas while imbibing; obstacles looked minor and could be ignored. He'd sell the Montgomery house, pocket his half, and fly to Europe, preferably France. Work in a restaurant until something more lucrative came up. And if a customer baffled him with a torrent of French, he could always say, with his disarming pronunciation, "*Je ne comprend pas, madame/monsieur, mais 'les plats se lisent et les livres se mangent'.*" One of the shorter Proustian insights – less likely to evade him under pressure – and fitting in a restaurant. Food for thought too, and the Frenchies would forgive him for maltreating their language. He remembered plenty more aperçus, thanks to kind, sweaty Tsvetko, though he could only hazard a guess at the meaning of some of them.

He'd quickly forget about Biranek in Europe. But would they find him and drag him back if Hollie's threat to sue Blanchard ended up in court?

Chapter 16

May, June 2006

Sarah, sitting in the middle, called the two of them "the men in my life." An irksome bit of jollity. Mike was in a cheerful mood too. Near Millcroft, he announced with triumph in his voice that the truck he'd rented came with a pneumatic column lift and a dolly.

"Your boyfriend is getting emotional," Miles told Sarah.

When Sarah phoned two days earlier asking for his help, Miles had demurred. "I don't want to go back to Corby Falls."

"A trip to Corby would be a break from your drinking and brooding."

"I'll be lynched."

"You won't."

"How do you know?"

"Mike will back up into the driveway. You'll be in the house or in the backyard helping us, and once we're done, you'll hop back in the truck and we'll be on our way. No one will know you've even been there. I mean, unless you walk down to Market Street and begin greeting people."

"I don't like it."

"There are some big pieces, Miles, and Mike and I can't do it alone. We're counting on your muscled youth."

"Hire movers. I'll pay for it."

"I don't trust them."

As they approached Corby Falls, he voiced what really rattled him. "It's Hollie."

The sale of her house had fallen through somehow, although Sarah had heard she'd found another buyer.

"What of her?"

"What if she's there and comes out? What on earth do I tell her, Sarah?"

"You won't see her. She's hardly there these days."

"How would you know? You're in Caledon most of the time."

"I still have friends in Corby Falls."

Hollie turned out to be at home that weekend, and to his horror she crossed her backyard and came into theirs to confront him. The three of them were debating how best to load Sarah's bull on the dolly and wheel it out without tipping when Miles realized Sarah was looking apprehensively beyond him. He turned around, but it was too late. Hollie was already closing in on him. She made a soft growling sound, like an animal who at last had caught the long-coveted prey, and slapped him. He covered his face without moving away and she continued to hit him. Her slaps and punches had no strength. She was an aged, exhausted Fury, and knew it, yet she didn't let up, a way of showing what she thought of him.

When she stopped, she could barely speak. "How could you? How could you say such things?" She was close enough that a sour morning breath reached him.

"Hollie, it's not what you think . . ." he mumbled.

"What's not what I think? What should I think?"

"I'm so sorry."

"You're sick."

She had withered since he saw her after his father's funeral. She was in a nightgown, over which she'd thrown on a rust-coloured housecoat so deeply creased it must have lain for days under something heavy. In bed, perhaps wondering what the day, or what was left of it, would bring, she'd heard their voices and rushed out, unwashed and dishevelled.

"I don't know what got into me, Hollie. I had too much to drink . . . and, you know, the . . . It was too much, I mean, the alcohol . . . I came up with that story."

"You're wicked. You're evil. How could you?"

"I . . . I have no excuse."

"He loved you, Miles. Josef loved you, talked about you. You were like a son to him."

"I'm . . . I'm so sorry, Hollie."

"Who found you a French tutor in Lindsay when you were failing French? Who paid for the lessons?"

"My father did," he whispered, and immediately realized his mistake.

"You, you . . . ignorant scoundrel. It was Josef who found that teacher, and the lessons were twice the amount he told your father. Josef paid him on the side. Yes, that's what the *murderer* did for you."

"People say anything when they think no one . . . A rotten coincidence, Hollie, such an unlikely—"

"He lent you his books. His precious books. Josef told you to strive, to make something of yourself. And as thanks you drag his name through the mud. Why? What kind of monster are you?"

Sarah took a step toward them and said, "Hollie, he didn't know, couldn't—"

Hollie ignored her or didn't hear her. "And then, that morning in the backyard, after your father's funeral, you had the wickedness to ask me what we did in Toronto the weekend Rose died. As Josef was dying, and you knew it, because I told you. You villain. Revolting little man. You were preparing your horrible lies then, and, like an idiot, I . . . I just talked. What did Josef do to you, in God's name? What kind of a poisonous snake are you? Well, we'll see you in court soon. Yes, we'll see you there."

There was vengefulness in her words, and it occurred to him that in her anger she had forgotten he was on her side now – her main witness, in fact, if her suit ended up in court. She took two steps towards her house, then turned around and said, pointing somewhere behind her, "They should have killed you there, down the road. I wish they did." She walked slowly away, bending near the line of sumacs.

The dolly was leaning against the beech tree, and Miles rolled it to the sliding door leading to the family room. Mike, who had watched the entire scene from there, touched Miles's shoulder and exhaled noisily, concisely expressing his relief and sympathy. Sarah approached them and said, "Made up the story. What was that, Miles? Trying to make her feel better?"

"I made up the story, Sarah. It's as simple as that."

"What?"

"I made up the story. You won't hear anything else from me."

"I was there too, remember?"

"Do you want to be able to come back to this house? Do you want to be kept out of all this? You screamed at me to keep you out of it."

Mike said, "Let it go, Sarah. Miles knows better than you do."

"What's that supposed to mean?" Sarah said.

"Let it go."

Briggs Leaman Honecker was a medium size, respected litigation firm. Leaman, in particular, had a solid reputation. Rhona Honecker specialized in defamation law. Mike actually said "defamation and reputation management," and Miles couldn't suppress a chuckle.

Mike had asked around about Rhona Honecker and heard she was a "straight shooter." He began to reminisce long distance. "I worked with Harry Briggs for several years. He's not active these days, old Harry, but he was an earthmover once. He had a difficult temper, and I remember—"

"I'm supposed to see Honecker tomorrow," Miles said quickly. "I have no desire to go. I sent her a statement the other day, and we can haggle over it on the phone."

"Drop the sour mood, Miles. Try to like her, or at least understand what she needs from you, because she's going to be in your life until a decision or a settlement."

Rhona Honecker had sounded annoyed that she needed to explain herself. "We'll have to see you, and more than once, Mr. Rueda," she said on the phone. "And if we get to trial or into discovery, you'll be a regular visitor here." She told him what examinations for discovery were, and he found the whole conversation long and irritating. Was it her tone? It was as if she were addressing a bizarre creature, interesting to poke and study if wearing gloves. Did she know or suspect he was a coerced witness? The "bequest council" must have advised her one way or another, a delicate procedure of hints and innuendoes, he imagined, because the manner of coercing, the means by which they turned him into their witness, was best left untold.

"It's the simplest of cases," Miles protested. "The statement I sent you said it all: the story I told one evening in a restaurant, and which eventually reached Lyle Blanchard, was untrue, something I made up. I'm the witness for you, the plaintiff, and I'll say the same thing in court. What else is there to discuss?"

Rhona Honecker chuckled and said that, if nothing else, his affidavit must be properly signed, sworn, and witnessed. "A Word document attached to an email will not do." She refused to argue the simplicity or complexity of the case.

Rhona Honecker's office was in one of the towers of the TD Centre. He walked west from the King subway station, then turned left and crossed the TD Centre's vast inner courtyard. The south tower was across Wellington Street. It was lunchtime. Like fancily dressed prisoners taking their hour of fresh air, the office workers were out en masse, eating and chatting in the sun, crowding the stone benches, the lush lawn, Fafard's cows. Four-year-old Katelyn had climbed up and down the sprawled bovines one summer Sunday for close to an hour, waiting under his watch for her mother to finish something urgent at the office in the days Federica had worked in the east tower. After a while, his clever daughter said, "I don't know, they're all the same."

The sign affixed to a massive oak door was discreet, with LAW CHAMBERS in the middle and the surnames of the three principals across the top. In a surprisingly small anteroom the receptionist smiled at him from under an Arctic landscape.

He was shown into a room with a huge oblong table. It reminded him of Emma Levitsky's boardroom, only on a grander scale. A bookshelf on one wall, with heavy tomes, probably untouched in years. On the opposite wall a series of prints depicted horses in various gaits, each with impossibly thin legs. A line of explanation was at the bottom of each print, the cursive lettering faded. Tame Victorian illustrations. No naked cellist, nothing to trouble the fragile clients.

The straight shooter walked in, and a young woman with a laptop followed her. Not that Rhona Honecker – she introduced herself and shook his hand – was old. In her forties, tall, big boned, round faced. She wore glasses, and she examined him from behind them with open curiosity before mentioning that Adelle Choy – she pointed to the younger woman, already sitting down and opening the laptop – an articling student, would take notes. Adelle joked that somebody had to do the menial tasks.

He sat across the table from the two women and asked, "When will the trial be?"

"There may not be a trial," Honecker said. "We'll try to reach a settlement before getting to court. A settlement involving a full and public retraction, of course."

"Do you think they will settle? I mean, knowing what I'll say if it comes to a trial."

The two women looked at each other. "We have a strong case for our libel action," Honecker said. "Still, things are often less simple than they seem, and we lawyers are good at muddying the waters. Unexpected things come out if one pokes long enough, and examinations for discovery are ideal for that."

"Will I be involved?"

"In discovery? If I were the lawyer on the other side, I'd ask for you. Judges in Ontario are not that keen on allowing third-party witnesses, and that's what you'd be, Mr. Rueda. But because the whole case depends on your testimony, I think the judge will agree."

"Can you fight it?"

"I'm not sure I want to. My client wants this over as soon as possible, ideally without a trial. I expect that a discovery in which you are examined will tell Mr. Blanchard he'll lose, pushing him to settle out of court. Coffee, Mr. Rueda?"

"Sure, milk."

Adelle stood up and went out of the room.

After she made a brief note on a green pad, Honecker raised her eyes. They sat looking at each other, the din of an espresso machine reaching them from beyond the door, Honecker clearly feeling no need to break their silence with useless chatter. Was she taught in law school that by letting a potential witness steam in awkward silence one learned more about him or her than from a hundred questions? She continued her visual examination of the curious new insect impaled in front of her. This engineer, meant to address the design of mechanisms bound for Mars, had come up with the story of a neighbour, no longer alive, who years earlier had murdered his wife. Could he be trusted as the key witness?

He offered to sign his affidavit in her presence. Honecker shook her head gently, as if dealing with a child with slow comprehension, and explained that he'd have to rewrite his affidavit before having it signed and witnessed. "You must provide details in it, not simply refer to what Lyle Blanchard posted on his website. You must use your own descriptions, detail your recollections as accurately as possible. It wouldn't be wise, anyway, to rely on the words of the person we are taking to court."

Adelle brought in a tray with three small cups. She set it on the wide table between the two parties and returned to her laptop. She looked inquiringly at Honecker, who shook her head, and Miles couldn't decide whether it meant that nothing of importance had transpired while she was out of the room or that she'd tell her later.

"Do you frequently have such flights of imagination, Mr. Rueda?" Honecker asked.

"Sorry?"

"Inventing stories about your neighbours, as an example."

"Look, I'm not paid by the hour. Let's keep this short and relevant."

"It's one of the questions the defence lawyers are going to ask you."

"During discovery?"

"Either discovery or trial."

He took a deep breath. "No, not frequently."

"Now and then?"

"Almost never."

The two women exchanged looks that told each other his answer should be improved.

"Did you come up with the story extemporaneously? I mean, there you were, having a meal with friends, and you just came up with it?"

"Is this another question the defence will ask me?"

"I would."

"I came up with the story as a child, soon after Rose Biranek's death. As I said in my statement, the feverish imagination of a twelve-year-old boy."

"When exactly did you come up with it?"

"Weeks or months after."

"What triggered it?"

"Triggered it?"

"Mr. Rueda, it's not common to start imagining your neighbour a murderer."

"I don't remember."

"Nothing?"

"It was thirty-five years ago, Ms. Honecker, and I was twelve."

"Did you tell anyone else this story of murder?"

"No."

"Yet it stayed with you for thirty-five years."

"Yes."

Honecker sighed, clearly unhappy with his answer.

"Who's the defence?" he asked.

"They are with a big firm here in Toronto."

"They?"

"I say *they* because there might be more than one."

"How many lawyers will you have handling Hollie's side?"

She smiled, a stretching of the mouth. "You're looking at her. Adelle will help me too. As you said, our argument is simple. Theirs isn't."

"What's their argument?"

"They will try to show your story to be true. That you, for whatever reason, have changed your mind and are pretending to have imagined the story."

"How will they do that?"

"It's too early to say."

"That's it, their only line?"

"They'll also say Blanchard believed your story to be true and that there was no malice on his side. Did Lyle Blanchard talk to you about the Biranek affair and his interest in it?"

"Twice. The second time, briefly, just before his last blog."

The two women looked at each other again.

"When? Wait, never mind that now, we'll get into the details later. Did Lyle Blanchard ask you to comment on what he wrote?"

"He did."

"And?"

"I told him it was all silly stories and that he'd be sued for libel."

"You said to him that what you'd told your friends at . . . where was it now . . . ah, Le Paradis, was a fabrication?"

"That was the gist of it."

"When was that?"

"Five or six days before it was posted. He handed me a draft in front of my house and phoned me later for comments."

"Interesting. Lyle Blanchard wrote that you refused to offer any."

"Or say anything substantial," Adelle added, looking at her screen.

"Blanchard lied," he said.

"You talked to him earlier, didn't you?" Honecker asked.

"Yes, once."

"Did he contact you?"

"He came to see me."

"When was that?"

"November."

"Why you? How did he zero in on you?"

He sighed. "From a colleague of mine who had met him at his parents' house. Don, that's my colleague – well, *was* my colleague – likes the sound of his voice, always did, and in the middle of some idle chat around the Biranek affair, he heard himself say his friend – that was me – grew up in Corby Falls."

"So Lyle Blanchard showed up at your door."

"He visited me in the hospital."

"Were you sick?"

"I was mugged."

They stared at him, waiting for more, and he added, "Roughed up a bit. Let's not make a big fuss. It was written up on Blanchard's website. Surely you read it. Miles Rueda in the hospital was how he began and ended his last entry. Ending with the innuendo that I'd been assaulted *because* of the story I told about Biranek."

Honecker looked at Adelle Choy, who nodded. Could it be she'd not read Blanchard's blog? Relying on an articling student?

"We won't make a big fuss," Rhona Honecker said. "Though if it gets to trial the other side will. Anyway, what did Lyle Blanchard want from you?"

"He was on a fishing expedition. He might not have known then that I was the source of the story."

"You didn't tell him."

"No."

"Why not?"

"I hoped it wouldn't come out."

"So when he came to see you in the hospital, he knew little about you."

"It turned out he knew more than I thought he did. When he questioned me at the hospital, he was somehow aware I had been a neighbour of the Biraneks in Corby Falls and had known the doctor."

"He learned it from your colleague."

"I never told Don that."

"How did Blanchard know, then?"

"I'm not sure. From a local reporter, or on his own."

Adelle Choy's fingers were flying on the keyboard.

"What's the name of the defence lawyer?" he asked.

"The lead one? Bakker. Al Bakker." She spelled the surname. "Al is short for Alvard. A Norwegian name."

"Tell me more."

"Good lawyer. Tall, intermittent charm. Aggressive when he feels it helps his case, with rehearsed, well-acted displays of anger. Likes to make witnesses feel ill at ease early on."

"Expensive?"

Honecker hesitated. "I'm not privy to his hourly charges. I presume he doesn't come cheap. He's effective, and the clients pay."

"Can Blanchard afford Bakker? Bakker and his team? I mean, if things get stretched. I know Hollie can, and the township might chip in, but Blanchard?"

"We don't want this to stretch. Mrs. Biranek wants a resolution as quickly as possible. The township too, of course. As to whether Blanchard can afford Al Bakker, you should assume the *Post* will cover Bakker's fee."

"Why would the *Post* do that?"

She nodded as if she expected that question. "Adelle and I were chatting about it earlier. Perhaps they asked, in exchange, for access to everything related to the case, spicy details included. It's rich newspaper material, this affair you have started. Sorry, that was uncalled for. But I can see the *Post* going for it. Blanchard may write a book about the affair afterward, and the *Post* may want to publish excerpts. Or he may write a series of long articles about it. I'm speculating, of course. Perhaps the *Post* feels they owe it to Blanchard. He's worked for then for, what, thirty years?"

"Have you been opposite Al Bakker before? Do you know him well?"

She smiled. "I know him well."

As he was leaving, he asked Honecker, "Will it be a jury or a judge deciding the outcome?"

"Again, there may not be a trial. Cases like this are usually settled."

"And if it gets to court?"

"It's too early to say, but we'll probably want a jury. Among other things, it's faster. Judges often reserve their verdict and then agonize over them because they think they are great legal minds and superb stylists."

Walking back to the subway, he wondered what Rhona Honecker really thought. He felt she wasn't convinced he was telling the truth and had sensed danger in the story of his mugging.

The discovery was held in Briggs Leaman Honecker's boardroom. Hollie, in dark glasses and already seated, refused to acknowledge his hello. Al Bakker was fairly tall, though it wasn't obvious why Rhona Honecker considered his height worth remarking on. With his combed-back dark hair, wide nostrils, and bountiful moustache, he didn't look particularly Norwegian. He reminded Miles of a dartboard with a portrait of Maxim Gorky on it that Laukhin had in his apartment and repeatedly aimed at. The poet claimed he had acquired the novelty dartboard for one dollar at, oddly, an estate sale near Gravenhurst. A not-so-young junior or assistant in a grey suit arrived rolling a fat case behind him. Bakker and Honecker were conferred in whispers in a corner, then Bakker put his hand on Rhona's upper arm and kept it there until they separated. Miles sat near Adelle. Al's assistant took the seat almost directly across from Miles. A moment later the assistant stood up and stretched his hand toward him and said the name Fred followed by something with a *stein* ending. A thin woman with dark patches under her eyes sat at the near end of the table in front of a machine that looked like a small computer with a simplified keyboard. On either side of her were two open laptops. The stenographer.

Rhona Honecker sat between Adelle and Hollie, and Al Bakker took a seat across from her. Lyle Blanchard arrived last, and after a curt node to Al Bakker he sat opposite the stenographer, away from everybody else.

Al Bakker coughed, looked around him amused, then turned his body towards Miles. "Miles Connolly Rueda, engineer."

Miles nodded.

"The one at the root of this frivolous libel suit."

Like the previous statement, this was not framed as a question. Miles leaned back and looked at Honecker, who shook her head. Miles interpreted that to mean *Don't let it bother you, because there'll be worse.*

"Well, we'll get to the bottom of it," Bakker said. "And we'll do it together, won't we? Yes, you and I, Mr. Rueda, we'll figure out the scam."

"Get on with it, Al," Honecker said.

Miles moved his chair back so that his view of Rhona Honecker wasn't blocked by Adelle. *Al?* Shouldn't it be *Mr. Bakker?* Could it be that Rhona and Alvard knew each other better than one might expect? Current or former lovers? It would explain the hand on Rhona's arm and her generous assessment of Alvard's height.

They spent almost two hours on Miles's affidavit. He tried to keep to the wording he had used in it, having been warned by Rhona Honecker it was best. Minor deviations, even different words with similar meanings, would provide opportunities for the examining counsel to poke his nose in. He felt he did reasonably well. Around eleven o'clock, immediately after a break, Al

Bakker asked, "Connolly, that's an unusual middle name this days. In the family, Mr. Rueda?"

"My great-grandmother's family name."

"Hm. Mr. Rueda, I understand you're working for a company whose products end up in space."

"Some of them."

"What company?"

"Ludwig. Ludwig Robotics."

"That's exciting, isn't it?"

"There are moments."

"What exactly do you do there?"

"Studies of rovers. That's what I've been doing lately."

"Studies?"

"Prior to the launch of a difficult program, studies are often done. I mean technically difficult, and the studies are meant to remove some of the risks."

"What program is that?"

"An ESA program. That's the European Space Agency. They want to land a rover on Mars."

"Studies. Not bad, like being in school." Alvard looked around him, happy-faced.

"We did get into the program proper, the initial phase, Phase A, though that's kind of a study too, meant to come up with concepts and specifications. This is tiresome, Mr. Bakker, you don't want more details."

"Rovers for Mars – that's something. The planet Mars, right?"

"Yes."

"Do we know a lot about Mars, Mr. Rueda?"

"Some."

"But not everything."

"No."

"So the rest you have to imagine. I mean, what you don't know."

"It doesn't work like that."

"How does it work?"

"Engineers don't invent or imagine what they don't know, at least try not to. When uncertain, as they would be regarding many things on Mars, engineers make conservative calculations and assumptions so that their designs fall on the safe side."

"Engineers don't invent, don't imagine things. Yet you imagined the story you told your friends at Le Paradis. The murdering Doctor Biranek was an invention, a story entirely made up."

Miles looked at Honecker, who was watching Al Bakker intently. "Yes."

"When did you come up with it? The affidavit is not clear at all."

The room was too warm. His body began to betray signs of discomfort – armpit perspiration – although he had expected that question and was prepared for it. He took a deep breath and immediately knew it was a mistake. "Not long after Rose Biranek's death."

A loud sigh seemed to emanate from Hollie, and Miles glanced in her direction. The dark glasses were fixed on him. Rhona turned to her with an air of disapproval. She likely had told her to keep quiet, no reactions of any kind, no histrionics.

"As a twelve-year-old?" Al Bakker said after staring briefly at Hollie.

"Yes."

"That is, thirty-five years ago?"

"Yes."

"When exactly? Was it one week, two weeks, two months after Rose's death?"

"I can't be precise."

"Let's try to bracket it. Would you say between two weeks and two months?"

"Possibly."

"Would between two weeks and six months be better?"

"Possibly."

"*Possibly* again. If it's more than six months, wouldn't you agree that 'not long after' is not the right description?"

He looked at Honecker, who didn't seem troubled. "You may be right."

Al Bakker sighed. "If I say between two weeks and two years, would this interval satisfy you?"

"Two years is too long."

"You tell me, Mr. Rueda. Tell me the window you're comfortable with."

"Between two weeks and one year. A good guess would be between two weeks and two months."

"I see. Hallelujah. Did it happen regularly, Mr. Rueda?"

"I'm not following. Did what happen?"

"I mean, as a twelve-year-old, did you regularly imagine that one of your neighbours was a murderer?"

"No."

"Was this the only story of this genre you've concocted?"

No doubt, Al Bakker was having a good time.

"Yes."

"Did you come up with other stories? Say, not of murders, but, oh, I don't know, other compelling stories."

He looked toward Rhona Honecker, who kept her eyes on Bakker. She had asked Miles the same question during their first interview.

"We had a lot of wine that evening. My friend's wife was late and meanwhile—"

"Yes, yes, I know you were drunk that night. Give me an example."

"An example?"

"Of another story you came up with."

Honecker said, "Al, really."

"It's a reasonable question, Rhona. I'm curious. Mr. Rueda?"

"I told my daughter stories."

"Everybody tells stories to children. I mean stories you might tell an adult, like Biranek's, stories to take our breath away."

"Told my future wife about my sexual prowess. Took *her* breath away."

There was laughter in the room, Al Bakker's the loudest. "Good, very good, Mr. Rueda. You have a happy wife."

"We are divorced."

More jollity, and this time the lead came from Lyle Blanchard, who included his entire body in the act. As before, Al Bakker seemed to savour the levity around him. "Good, very funny, very funny indeed." Fred handed him a tissue and Alvard wiped his eyes with it. "Since you can't come up with another story, let's go back to Biranek's. Why him? What made you imagine Dr. Biranek a murderer?"

"I don't know."

"You can't explain?"

"It was thirty-five years ago. I don't remember."

"Yet you remembered the story you imagined thirty-five years ago, and with remarkable details too. How can that be?"

"I can't explain."

"It's an unusual story, wouldn't you say?"

"Al, please," Rhona said.

"What I mean, Mr. Rueda, is that it's not a typical story a twelve-year-old would come up with."

"Alvard, really," Rhona said. "How can Mr. Rueda answer that?"

"A guess, Mr. Rueda? Surely you must have wondered yourself."

He took the plunge. "People in the village whispered at the time that the doctor had been cruel to Rose. Ghastly to her, said many. Elma Mulligan, a woman who helped in our house after Mother died – well, before too – was even more outspoken. I heard her tell my father more than once that Dr. Biranek killed Rose. She must have meant he had killed Rose by not coming home the day he was supposed to. I, though, had a more literal mind.

It would have been a short leap for me to imagine that he did come home briefly, unknown to anybody else except me, found Rose, alive but too badly hurt to be saved – he was a doctor, after all, and would know – and went away." He sneaked a look at Rhona, who met his gaze, deep furrows on her forehead. This was all news to her, and she'd be concerned about where he was going. "Strictly a guess, Mr. Bakker, since you insisted. Anyway, I didn't really think of Biranek as a murderer then. To a twelve-year-old a murderer shoots, or slashes with a saber, or pushes his victim off a cliff." He'd had time to ponder this, but he was improvising too.

Al Bakker grinned at Rhona Honecker then returned to him. "That's exactly my point, Mr. Rueda. You're right, and it's hard to improve on what you said. A twelve-year-old would come up with, oh, I don't know, that he'd seen Dr. Biranek getting out of his car waving a handgun, and that later he heard shots—"

"Rose Biranek was not shot," Rhona Honecker said.

"Or that he saw lights on the second floor soon after Dr. Biranek walked in and heard a woman scream and the sound of a body falling down the stairs. What I'm trying to say, Mr. Rueda, is that your story does not fit the mind of a child. The details of your allegedly concocted story are too realistic and plausible, and events might easily have happened the way you described them. There is nothing in the coroner's report that would contradict what you told your friends at Le Paradis. Absolutely nothing. Furthermore, Dr. Biranek was in Toronto then and could easily have driven to Corby Falls and back, exactly as your story implied. This is not a story invented by a child."

He had a point. Honecker, who had herself shaken her head and said "That's quite a story for a twelve-year-old" when she heard it, had not dwelt on her comment. Miles had decided to say he dreamt up the story soon after Rose's death so that he stayed close to the truth. He had not wanted, either, to seem ridiculous claiming he'd invented it as a mature man.

"I came up with it not long after Rose Biranek died," he said.

Al Bakker shook his head. "No one would believe you, Mr. Rueda, neither judge nor jury." He looked around the table, smiling. His assistant passed a piece of paper to him, and he spent some time contemplating it. "This Elma Mulligan," he went on, after nodding, "she's not in your affidavit, is she?"

"No."

"Why is that?"

"I didn't think it important."

"You didn't? The only explanation you have for the story you concocted, and you didn't think it important?"

"It was a guess, Mr. Bakker, not an explanation. I said I couldn't explain it, and, as you pressed me to guess, I obliged. A guess as to how I could have ended up with my story."

Al Bakker conferred in whispers with his assistant and said, "Is Elma Mulligan the same Mrs. Mulligan who appeared in one of Mr. Blanchard's earlier blog posts?"

"Yes."

"She worked for the Biraneks, didn't she?"

"My mother was not a well woman, and Elma came to help once a week. She worked the rest of the week for the Biraneks. Until she was let go."

"When was that?"

"Not long after Rose died."

"Why was she let go?"

"I don't know."

"So after Elma Mulligan was dismissed by the Biraneks, she continued to come to your house and do some work."

"Yes."

"Still once a week?"

"Yes."

More whispers from the assistant. Al Bakker nodded and went on. "Would she come during the day?"

"I guess so."

"You guess?"

"I don't remember exactly when she came. All right, yes, during the day."

"Was your mother alive then?"

"No."

"You father worked, didn't he?"

"Yes."

"What did he do?"

"He had the hardware store in the village."

"Was it open during the day?"

"The store? Yes, of course."

"Elma worked during the day in your house, while your father was at the store. Yet you just said you heard her tell your father, time and again, that Biranek killed his wife. When could you hear it, Mr. Rueda?"

He shouldn't get flustered. He should lick his wound, a minor one, nothing major, and contain the damage.

"It's what I remember, Mr. Bakker, can't be helped. Sometimes she didn't leave our house until after my father came home. She cooked for us when she came. Now and then she helped us with dinner and then she left."

Al Bakker looked at his watch and whispered something to Fred, who handed him a piece of paper. Bakker looked at it, nodded, and smiled. "One more question before we break for lunch, Mr. Rueda. Who is the second witness?"

"Second witness?"

"Another witness who saw Dr. Biranek that night in Corby Falls."

"Mr. Bakker, I told you, I made up the story. There can't be another witness."

"But when you told your story at Le Paradis, and someone questioned the weight of a story from a twelve-year-old, you said there was another witness, an adult."

"I told you, it was a made-up story."

"Mr. Rueda, we have a witness, Ms. Collins, who heard you use these words, another witness, an adult. Come now, are you denying that?"

He was a fucking bastard, Al Bakker. Miles looked around the table, trying to think of the best way to reply. Probably a mistake – showed he'd been unsettled. Rhona Honecker was staring at him, no doubt thinking, Why is it that I don't know about this? How could you be so daft, Miles Rueda?

Nothing came to mind. "I invented this second witness too."

He had lunch in a nearby Japanese restaurant, a long, narrow room a few steps below street level. It was dark inside, or so it seemed to him, coming in from the noon sunshine. The tables, separated by partitions, were lined up in two rows, and in the aisle between them, thin young women smiled and bowed busily. Following one of them, he passed by a table shared by Hollie, Rhona Honecker, and Adelle Choy. The two lawyers nodded at his wave. At the back, there were six chairs at a counter, five of them occupied. Behind the counter, two chefs, shoulder to shoulder, bent over their delicate tasks. A flat green samurai pasted on a blue background watched their quiet, precise toil. Miles took the last chair and ordered a twelve-piece sashimi board, rice, and half a pint of beer. Eating moderately would keep him sharp for the afternoon bout. Except for the minor hiccup at the end, he felt that so far he'd done fine. He wanted to talk about it; having one's own lawyer had at least the advantage of an immediate analysis of what had transpired. Rhona Honecker wasn't his lawyer, but shouldn't she have invited him to join them? He was their main witness; their case depended on him. He should be shown more consideration. Rhona should tell him what he did right and what he should expect next. True, she had spent an hour with him at the beginning of the week. Although he had resented it at the time, now he felt pumped up and keen to hear her opinion on how he had handled Alvard.

As he drank the last of his beer, Hollie, looking purposefully straight ahead, passed by him on her way to the ladies' room.

He got up and walked to their table. "How did I do?" he asked.

"You did okay," Honecker said.

"Only okay?"

"Mr. Rueda, I can't talk to you during examination."

"It's lunchtime."

"And then we continue."

After lunch, Bakker returned to Miles's story. "Why this yarn, Mr. Rueda?"

"I beg your pardon?"

"Why this story about Dr. Biranek?"

"I'm repeating myself here, Mr. Bakker. We had a lot to drink – this friend of mine and I – and he was falling asleep. Wine does that to him. He's from Corby Falls too, and I thought I'd keep him awake with a hometown story, and—"

"Yes, yes, I understand. You wanted to wake him up, entertain him. Am I right?"

"Yes."

"The thing is, Mr. Rueda, the story you told your companions that evening, well, it's not an amusing story. Not at all. Quite the contrary. Why not tell, say, a joke, an anecdote. That's how one entertains, how one amuses, people, isn't it?"

Sly bugger, Bakker saying "entertains" and "amuses." Miles couldn't think of a reply.

"Slander Dr. Biranek, that's what you did," Bakker went on. He took a sip from a glass of water and lent his ear to whispers from his assistant before nodding and saying, "Mr. Rueda, in October last year you were assaulted in Corby Falls, weren't you?"

He'd expected it sooner or later. Still, he frowned, opened his arms, played the innocent, glancing around and looking at Rhona Honecker. She acted along, sighing and looking up as if praying for help with this examiner who'd lost his mind. "Is that relevant?" she asked.

"We'll see," Al Bakker said. "Mr. Rueda?"

"I was mugged," Miles said.

"You were severely beaten and spent weeks in hospital."

"I spent two weeks in the hospital."

"You were at home recovering after that for another three weeks."

"Yes."

"So you were severely beaten."

"Yes."

"Muggers don't usually do that."

"I don't know."

"Could it be that mugging wasn't uppermost in the minds of those who attacked you?"

"They took my wallet, and I had money in it. At the hospital I couldn't show my OHIP card. I had to replace my lost cards."

"Tell me exactly what happened, Mr. Rueda. Where and how were you mugged, and what did you do before and after?"

Rhona Honecker said, "What's this for, Alvard? How could this be relevant?"

"I have some leeway in discovery, Rhona."

"Not too much, though."

"Look, either Mr. Rueda tells us all we want to know and the court reporter puts it down, or we request an affidavit and he goes home and writes one, swears it, and signs it, and then I ask him questions about it. It will be slower, of course, but, hey, more money in my pocket." He patted his side and laughed, delighted by the alternative.

Honecker frowned and said, "Mr. Rueda, please indulge him so we don't have to come another day."

He kept it short. He'd had a drink with an old school friend at Bart's Alehouse, always did whenever he went back to Corby Falls. Afterward, to clear his head and lungs – there had been a lot of cigarette smoke in the pub – he went for a walk along the river, past the old bridge. He was attacked, hit on the head, didn't remember much afterward. He came to hours later, cold and wet, near the road. Somehow, he managed to crawl home. The next morning, his sister drove him to the hospital. It was she who discovered his wallet was missing.

"You had a couple of broken ribs, didn't you, Mr. Rueda?"

"Cracked."

"You could barely walk or open an eye afterward. Your left knee was busted."

"That's an exaggeration."

"You had stitches on your head and on your forehead."

"Yes."

"You had bruises all over your body."

"Yes."

"Mr. Rueda, that was not a mugging; that was a vicious assault, an execution almost."

"They took my wallet."

"So you say, Mr. Rueda. Muggings aren't frequent in Corby Falls, are they?"

"I don't know."

"Have you heard of other muggings in Corby Falls?"

"I haven't lived there for thirty years."

"I'll tell you: there aren't many. According to the OPP, the last one was nine years ago. So how do you explain being mugged in peaceful Corby Falls on a rainy, cold night?"

"I can't."

"A rainy, cold night in October, Mr. Rueda, on a road leading nowhere, and which, even in more clement weather, has hardly any strollers? Why would muggers stalk a place with no prey?"

"My bad luck."

"Your bad luck. We'll see whether it was luck or not. What did the police say?"

"I didn't go to the police?"

"You didn't report the assault to the police?"

As if he didn't know. Al Bakker's question contained both perplexity and outrage. Shouldn't he keep the histrionics for the trial?

"That's right."

"Why is that, Mr. Rueda?"

"There was no point."

"No point? No point in reporting a crime?"

"I couldn't have told the police anything about the attacker or attackers. It was a mugging, during which things got needlessly violent. There was nothing the police could do, and I wasn't keen on writing affidavits and answering questions just for the sake of it."

"And you didn't think anyone needed to know that there were violent criminals at large in the community?"

"I wasn't in a state to think clearly."

"But afterward?"

Miles found nothing to say.

Al Bakker waited for an answer, then smiled. "You don't think much of the OPP, do you?"

"I don't think about them."

"You see, Mr. Rueda . . . On second thought, this can wait. Who was the friend you had a drink with that evening?"

"Jim. Jim Cowley."

"Good friend?"

"Since primary school. Even before."

"And you kept in touch with him after you moved to Toronto."

"Yes."

"What did you drink?"

"Beer."

"You'd have a beer or two with Jim Cowley whenever you drove to Corby Falls."

"Yes."

"Every time?"

"Most times."

"It was a ritual, wasn't it?"

Miles shrugged. "If you like that word."

"Did you have a beer with Jim the last time you were in Corby Falls?"

"The last time?"

"Yes."

That was when Hollie Biranek had come into the yard and slapped him. He looked briefly at her, and her dark glasses seemed to tell him she'd never forgive him.

"I didn't have a beer with him then, no."

"Why is that, Mr. Rueda?"

"I drove there with my sister and her companion to pick up some heavy things she left there. We had to drive the load to Caledon, and there wasn't time."

"Going back to your friend Jim. You're saying you didn't have the traditional drink with him?"

"That's right."

"When did you talk to him last?"

"With Jim Cowley?"

"Yes."

"Several months ago, on the phone."

"What did you talk about?"

"I don't know, the usual nonsense."

"You don't know?"

"I don't remember. Nothing that stands out. How are things? How's the family? Recalling school days . . ."

"Who called whom?"

It was Jim who had called him, but he decided to keep it vague. "I don't remember."

"All right, when did you last have a drink with your friend Jim?"

"October."

"Was that the time you were assaulted?"

"Yes."

"And you haven't had a drink with your friend since."

"That's right."

"It's been, what, seven months?"

"I haven't been back to Corby Falls since then, except the quick trip with my sister."

"Has he visited you here in Toronto since?"

"No."

"Any reason?"

"He doesn't drive to Toronto often."

"Rather odd: good friends and haven't seen each other for seven months. Good to know, good to know. Now, Mr. Rueda, Jim has a wife and two daughters, am I right?"

"Yes."

"He lives in Millcroft, doesn't he?"

Al Bakker was worryingly well informed.

"He does."

Rhona Honecker said, "Are we fishing, Al?"

"Let's go back to the drink you had with your buddy Jim," Alvard said, ignoring Rhona. "Besides families and recollections, did you discuss work?"

"Possibly. I don't remember."

"Your work?"

"We might have."

"Is Jim Cowley interested in space? Rovers, colonizing Mars?"

"It's his favourite topic."

Al Bakker laughed heartily, and Lyle Blanchard smiled. Rhona said, "A flippant question, a flippant answer."

"Did you discuss his work as well?" Al asked.

"I don't remember. I'm not sure we did."

"He works for M&B Construction, doesn't he?"

Christ, how much did he know? Lyle Blanchard and Eddy Bryson had clearly spent hours with Alvard. Others must have had his ear too, because someone had told him about his last visit to Corby Falls, the one he made with Sarah and Mike. Hollie must have mentioned their backyard encounter to somebody and it had reached Al Bakker.

"He does."

"His father-in-law, Barry Matlock, is the owner of M&B Construction, isn't he?"

"Half owner."

"He's the M in M&B."

"He is."

"How's M&B doing, Mr. Rueda?"

"I'm not following you, Mr. Bakker."

"How is it doing, as a company?"

"I doubt they're rolling in cash lately, but I'm really not privy to their finances."

"Not as much work as they'd like?"

"So it seems."

"And Jim complained about it?"

"He said they could do with more work."

"He'd know, wouldn't he? I mean, working there, and also from his father-in-law."

"Yes, he would know."

"Was Josef Biranek's bequest ever discussed between the two of you?"

"Sure. For a while, that was the only topic in the township."

"Was it a topic that evening, the one when you were later assaulted?"

"It's possible."

"Possible. Not certain, though. You're not certain about anything you discussed with Jim that evening. Not sure if you chatted about work, his or yours; not sure if you talked about Biranek's bequests. How can that be, Mr. Rueda? Never mind. Did Jim Cowley ever express concern that the township seemed to have run into problems with the bequests?"

Miles considered the direction in which Alvard was taking him and decided to follow. "Yes. M&B hoped for a significant share of the work on the hospital in Millcroft. The church in Corby Falls as well, I think. I've heard it from others too. Heard it from my sister, Sarah."

"When did Jim Cowley tell you all this?"

"I'm not sure. As I said, I may have heard it from others. The *Millcroft Gazette*."

"You read the *Millcroft Gazette*, Mr. Rueda?"

"Now and then, at my sister's urging."

Al Bakker took a sip of water. "Mr. Blanchard's blog about the bequest must have caused considerable concern to your friend, don't you think?"

"It's likely."

"The last blog entry, early April, the one identifying you as the witness, must have distressed him no end."

"It's possible."

"You're not sure?"

"I haven't talked to him since."

"Haven't talked to him. Now this is odd. Your good friend, a best friend, reads an account in Mr. Blanchard's blog in which your story damages M&B's

chances for badly needed work, never mind a renovated hospital in Millcroft, yet he never calls you. How can that be?"

"I don't know."

"Come on, Mr. Rueda. You must have asked yourself this question."

"Perhaps he heard from others that I made the story up."

"And that was enough for him?"

"Maybe."

"He wouldn't have felt the need to give you a piece of his mind? 'What's this rubbish you're coming up with, Miles?' Something along that line?"

"I don't know."

"And you didn't feel like picking up the phone and talking to him, making excuses for the fact that you put the work of numerous people in Millcroft, including your friend, in jeopardy? No?"

"It would have been awkward."

"Awkward, indeed."

Al Bakker and his assistant left first, and Lyle Blanchard hurried after them. From behind her dark glasses, Hollie, who had not addressed one word to Miles the entire day, seemed to expect him to leave as well. As if guessing what was on Miles's mind, Rhona Honecker approached him and said that the transcripts would be available in a day or two. Al Bakker and his team would pore over them before deciding whether more discovery was needed before the trial. She figured they had gathered enough material to chew on for now. She was troubled by Bakker's insistence on the mugging. She was also troubled by the fact that Miles and Jim Cowley hadn't talked after the last piece in the *Post* appeared. She should have considered it, she said. It seemed that Al Bakker was building a case for threats against Miles forcing him to change his story, and that the mugging in Corby Falls, which Bakker insisted on calling an assault throughout the examination, was the threats materialized. She looked hard at Miles and said she hoped Al Bakker wouldn't be able to miraculously discover a witness to any threat or to the assault. Of course, she added, the *Post* might also decide to settle, although she didn't expect it to happen soon. Most settlements were reached shortly before court proceedings were due to start, and the trial date was still to be set.

The room had emptied. Rhona took a step toward the door, where Adelle and Hollie were waiting for her, then turned back to him. "I thought for a moment you were going to change your mind and say you made up your story later. It's a good thing you stayed the course."

Stayed the course. "You doubt me too," he said.

"You don't know that, and anyway it's not important. If we get to trial, Al Bakker will keep you a whole day on the stand with this. He'll hammer the point that your story couldn't be the fantasy of a twelve-year-old and won't let go. What you heard this morning is nothing, an appetizer. You must stick to your recollections and be brief in your answers. And talking about being brief: Elma Mulligan's part in coming up with the story was new to me. You didn't mention her name in our discussions. Well, it was not that bad. It was Al who insisted you take a stab at an explanation."

She stopped, seeming to be of two minds again, then went on. "What you also failed to mention in our discussions was the other witness Al Bakker asked you about. This deeply troubled me, and, if it gets to a trial, Bakker will flail you on it."

"I hardly remembered it."

"But you did say at Le Paradis that there had been a second witness, an adult, didn't you?"

"I . . . Yes, I did."

"You see, Mr. Rueda, this also-invented other witness stretches credulity. I mean, a juror's credulity. Al Bakker got you to acknowledge it and moved on. Bad sign – he'll spend a long time on it at the trial. We may have to talk more about this."

Chapter 17

June 2006

"Where to?" Federica had asked when Miles rang to tell her he'd be going away for a week.

"London."

"Job related?"

"In some way."

"Have you had an offer?"

"It's not easy. I wish I had European roots."

"You do. Great-grandfather Ellis."

"Ha. The Black Sea is not a country."

"Let me talk to Greg. He has countless connections in Europe."

"No, no. I'll find something."

"Katelyn says you have a sentimental liaison, someone with a strong accent she can't place."

"How does she know?"

"Oh, Miles, it's Katelyn; she doesn't miss much. She answered the phone a few times – once when you weren't home. And one weekend she caught some of your long-distance chatter. Perhaps more than once. You have lengthy telephone conversations, it seems. You want more? Twice you disappeared for hours and returned home wearing a smug face. She saw a trace of lipstick too. Katelyn is convinced you changed your mind because you have a girlfriend overseas."

He arrived in London tired but exhilarated. It wasn't only the majestic city or the anticipation of seeing Anna; it was also the escape from the Biranek nightmare. Fleeting escape, true, short-lived, a week to breathe freer and, he hoped, evade obsessing about it. He'd been in London before, mostly passing through. He played tourist once with Federica, a trip marred by a mammoth row between them, but he wasn't that familiar with the sprawling city. Anna said she knew London well. The irony of it, a Russian showing a Canadian the heart of the Empire. A pity Fowler-Biggelow would never know of his visit to London. Cecil would have vigorously approved of Miles's assignation with Anna Pripogurina. To think that he was following to the letter Cecil's injunction to "keep in touch" with her.

They were to meet somewhere between Victoria Embankment and Whitehall. She would be visiting a friend's flat, Anna had said, when she gave him the address. She added that it was not far from his hotel and that he could walk there if he felt so inclined. He decided against it. The traffic got slower as they approached the river, and the cab driver was muttering to himself as Miles paid him and got out. He waited in front of the huge, castle-like building. It was a warm late afternoon, with the sun still strong. A bus in pink and violet stripes stopped near him with a regretful sigh. An older man in a grey uniform, the guardian of the castle, rushed out onto the sidewalk and, with slow, delicate hand motions urged the garish monster to back off. The bus obeyed and began disgorging shouting teenagers.

Anna came out just as the grey-uniformed man went back into his castle. She was wearing an off-white short-sleeved dress, and were it not for the bold heels of her sandals, he would have thought a high school student was approaching him. They faced each other awkwardly, not embracing or touching hands. He told her she looked wonderful and that he'd missed her. She had a frowning smile for him, undoubtedly expecting words less trite. He glanced up and down the street, not sure which way to go. "A walk?" he said. "I think the Thames isn't far." Anna looked at her feet. "I can't walk in these shoes, Miles, not for long anyway." She suggested they take a cab to her flat – not a long ride from where they were standing – and then, after slipping her feet into something more sensible, walk back down to the Embankment, stroll along the river, and stop somewhere for a bite.

They were quiet during the short cab ride. The driver's presence had something to do with it, but it was also as if they were taking stock of each other. She didn't allow him to pay when the cab stopped. Pointing to the building across the street, she said, "That's it." A flat, light-grey façade, French windows and intricate false balconies, a narrow frieze at the top adorned with what may have been, years earlier, golden leaves and flowers. "Built by a Belgian investor at the turn of the last century, or so we've been told. Rubber money. He might have skimped on quality. We all seem to pay through the nose to keep it from falling apart. A friend advised us to sell and find another place. Grisha bought the apartment years ago and can't be bothered to move now. We both like this area, anyway."

Grisha again. "My husband" – even Grigory – would be less irritating. Before midnight, he'd be in bed with Anna, yet *Grisha* alluded to a continuing fondness and intimacy between her and Pripogurin, and to Miles's acknowledgement of and complicity in it. He felt ridiculous, naive, unworldly, a proper dweller of Corby Falls. Her life was different from his, and he knew nothing of it. Grisha had bought an apartment in the centre of the most expensive city in Europe. The Pripogurins didn't have a mansion in London now only because Grisha couldn't "be bothered." No doubt they had a palace in Saint Petersburg. Plenty of palaces there. That he was ridiculous had not been obvious to Miles in bland, familiar Toronto; now, though, in this strange and overwhelming city, it was. No wonder Pripogurin seemed unconcerned. Miles was a distraction for Anna, a novelty, a way of remembering an episode of her youth still precious to her. Nothing more than that. He should simply enjoy the moment, the hours she deigned to bless him with.

They crossed the street and he followed her into a cool foyer with a dusty blue and white floor. A mobile scaffold was pushed against the wall to his left, and tools and debris scattered around attested that renovations, or at least patch-ups, were afoot. Grey tarpaulin was bunched in a corner near a narrow wooden crate. There was a faint smell of fresh paint, although nothing seemed to be newly painted. Wide stairs ascended in a rectangular spiral. He tilted his head and stared upward through it. Five or six flights above them, a cupola of glass and ironwork filtered the daylight into a pale column reaching down.

In the tightness of the elevator his nostrils filled up with her scent, and it crossed his mind that perhaps the walk had not been an inspired suggestion.

She said she'd make coffee. From the entrance hall, narrow and rather long, she led him into a large room and then disappeared through another door, which she left open. Soon he heard noises of tap water running and of cups and plates being set out.

Terracotta-coloured walls, tall windows, high ceilings. The Belgian investor might have skimped on quality but not on space. The furniture, rather sparse, was not modern. A fireplace, giving the room an air of restfulness. A large number of paintings, on display in planned disorder. The Pripogurins were collectors. Ambling toward the windows, he thought he recognized a Chemakoff oil from the artist's less coveted exile period, a typical scene of waterways and squeezed, narrow houses, which the artist had found, toward the end of his life, on frequent trips to Amsterdam and Harlem. The Dutch cities with their waterways had reminded Chemakoff of his native Saint Petersburg, and he had seriously considered resettling there. Miles had read this in the thin monograph on Chemakoff he acquired in a Bloor Street bookstore days after he was told of Laukhin's unexpected farewell gifts to him. Laukhin's father had been an admirer of Chemakoff, the poet told Miles once, at the Duke of York. It was late, Laukhin had reached the stage of near physical collapse, and Miles was preparing to drag him across the street, when the poet set off jabbering about the painter. An early Chemakoff oil, large, "very large, Miles, huge, or so it seemed, because the rooms in Lavrushinsky Lane were moderate in size," had hung in their apartment in Moscow. It depicted a soiree of Russian rulers and doers before the revolution, perhaps a masked ball, with an odd person here and there, odd in the sense of incongruous, not belonging, anachronistically sporting a Soviet *militsiya* uniform, or a leather jacket over a gown, or holding a pneumatic hammer. A *zek* too, a patron of the gulag. Chemakoff had done many such oils; in fact for close to ten years he painted hardly anything else – now by far his most prized work – and there was always a *zek*. Coming home or leaving the apartment, Laukhin would often make a detour and stop in front of that painting and think what a risqué masked ball Moscow was. He had described it in one of his poems as toxic, lethal drollery, a carnival of suicides, but he was too drunk to remember which one or the exact lines. Staring at the Dutch scene now, Miles reflected that Chemakoff's work had always been nearby Laukhin, not in the immediate foreground, yet somehow affecting his life, like a minor moon circling a planet and disturbing its trajectory. In some unconscious way, the poet had felt it. He'd slashed one of Chemakoff's masterpieces, after all, in a furious and impotent act.

Anna came back into the room balancing a huge tray. A blue bottle of water boasted purity and sponsorship of British athletics. She laid the tray on a long, low table and made herself comfortable on the sofa facing the fireplace. She had already changed her shoes and now took them off, placed a pillow between herself and the arm of the sofa, and leaned on it as she brought her feet up, legs bent at the knees. She tucked her dress under her knees and smiled at him. It was something she did frequently, he realized. Her lips would form the required shape, and her eyes would shine for a second or two, yet it was always a restrained, somewhat melancholy smile, one that precluded ensuing laughter. She had hazel eyes, a touch slanted, and their green flecks seemed to vary with the light.

His sights rested on a photograph on the mantelpiece. A young Anna with a thin man in his early thirties, the two of them surrounded by summer and rows of grapevines curving up a gentle hill behind them. To the right of the fireplace he noticed an oil portrait of a seated man, seemingly the same man as in the photo, only older and thicker.

"Your husband, isn't it, posing stuck in an armchair?"

"Horrid, don't you think? His colleagues forced him to sit for it, and because he couldn't bear to look at it every day, he shipped it here from Saint Petersburg with the armchair. I'm thinking of dumping both. Grisha won't mind. He hates the painting and hated the process leading to it."

He wondered where Pripogurin was. Should he ask her? They would come back here, after their walk along the river and dinner, and make love, and he had no idea where Anna's husband was.

"How far is the river from here?" he asked.

"Half an hour. Perhaps less."

A stylized orange lion stared at them through Corinthian columns. *Lyceum Theatre*, he read under the pediment. Past it they crossed a busy street, the famous Strand, according to Anna. He learned that in the old days the best families had their houses on the Strand, with their own river gates and landings. Of course, the Thames ran freely and its banks were closer then. Humbler houses were built later, and then the Embankment, which changed everything.

"Where is the river? I'm telling myself that I can smell it."

Anna pointed ahead of her. "You seem to have avoided London."

"Federica would rather travel to France."

The view opened up at a nondescript bridge ahead of them. He was delighted by the sight of the Thames, even if its brownish colour was a disappointment. They walked to the middle of the bridge for the view. Up the river, the intricate parliament building seemed to be growing out of the water, like a huge Venetian palace. A man holding a sign with *Nantes* written on it in heavy italics was leading a slow-moving group of tourists. He stopped not far from Miles and leaned his back and elbows on the railing. His French had English roots. Without following what the guide was saying, Miles guessed they all were on Waterloo Bridge. There was something in the guide's address about the original bridge – not the bridge they were standing on, an earlier one – and something about the famous battle. Shouldn't tour companies skip this bridge with French groups? There seemed to be no resentment among the good people from Nantes, only tired apathy.

They retraced their steps and he followed Anna down to the Embankment and then along the river toward Westminster. They passed under a footbridge, and Anna stopped by a pier where a low, white boat, RS *Hispaniola*, was moored. She said, "Tapas and drinks on-board. What do you think?"

They sat outside on curved iron chairs at a table set against the rail on the bow's port side. A timid candle was fluttering in a round bowl. Anna claimed they were lucky to find seats on the deck; it was, after all, Saturday, and a beautiful evening.

"Do you come here often?" he asked.

"I don't know if you are aware that we're back were we started." She pointed to her left. "That's Whitehall Court, there, behind the garden, the building in front of which we met earlier today. I come here with the friend I visited this afternoon. The trees are hiding her windows. Some days we climb aboard for tea or a drink."

An aged waiter whose face told of battles with the bottle came out with menus and asked if they wanted anything from the bar. They agreed on a bottle of white wine, and Anna suggested a name which made the waiter nod. Miles, thirsty, said he'd start with a beer. The waiter raised a pair of overgrown eyebrows.

"What kind of beer, sir?"

"I don't know. Something on tap for a foreigner, and cold."

"Foster's? It's a lager."

"A half, please."

He looked briefly at the menu, and then at her. God, she looked lovely. "*Langostinos a la plancha*? Their translation says grilled prawns in garlic butter."

"Sounds good. Yes, let's have that, twice."

"*Aceitunas en anchoa*. Green olives marinated with anchovies."

"Yes again."

The drinks arrived and they ordered. He told her how happy he was to be there, in London, with her. As the words came out, he knew he should have left London out. Again he had the impression she had expected better from him. She was a poet, after all, and had had an affair with one of the world's foremost contemporary poets. There may have been others too, and, who knew, perhaps Grisha Pripogurin had – *had* had? – a way with words of courtship. Her restrained smile resurfaced, this time twinned with a chuckle. "I've been tinkering with a poem," she said. "I'll add a riverboat, a table on the deck, two lovers, and Spanish-sounding dishes. I have the title for it now, 'The Pub-Crawler's Fling.'"

There was endearing irony there, nothing more. "Fling? That's all this is?"

"It sounds better in Russian. 'The Pub-Crawler's Romance'?"

Darkness was falling over the river, and lights were becoming visible. The cold beer was having a soothing effect on him. He needed to relax and enjoy the moment, accept that her attraction to him was temporary, a whim, a fling. He took a sip of the wine too, and it was delicious. Would life henceforth offer him a better moment? A warm evening, a shimmering river, a glass of splendour from the Loire Valley, the anticipation of being in bed with the beautiful woman facing him. A woman who might allude to him in a stanza or a few lines in a poem of hers.

He asked what she had learned from her stepbrother. She shook her head. She had a peculiar way of doing it, without hurry, smiling too, but mainly with her eyes, and giving the impression of perfect anticipation of whatever he'd say next. Nothing that he didn't know, she said, just details. He imagined that what happened to Laukhin twenty years earlier had sounded to Anna rather tame. Of interest, no doubt, because Laukhin had been, briefly, her lover. Of interest too because her stepfather turned out to be the main villain. But tame, because she could tell him stories with real drama, tragedies old and new, not this mild fluff about the disappearance of a green folder and the accidental death of a young Englishwoman.

"I put down on paper all that my stepbrother told me," she said. "Censored by him, of course, but the gist of what he said is there. I'll give it to you later" – she searched her purse and retrieved a photograph – "with this picture of Cornilov. I prepared an envelope for Ben, but I wanted to show it to you. I stole it from my stepbrother. Not a good photo. I looked for one that was close to the time Tsvetayeva was killed, and it was the best I could do."

"Your brother, was he not, I don't know, taken aback?"

She shook her head slowly, closing her eyes briefly and sighing at the same time, the way one does with hopeless children or Westerners. "It's been a while, Miles, and he knows his father was not a saint. Anyway, he's certain Tsvetayeva killed herself. It's the accepted view nowadays. Of course, Cornilov did what he could to erase a terrible rumour about him." She handed him the photo.

The candle was of little help. He stood up hoping for more light from the lamps above them. The photograph was faded and grainy. A tall, broad man, in his late twenties or early thirties, military uniform, bareheaded. A gaunt, tired face, turned, almost in profile, probably unaware his picture was being taken. Writing in Cyrillic on the back. When he sat down, he pointed at it, and she raised her shoulders.

"Hard to decipher, even in good light," she said. "I think, '1943, September,' and perhaps 'Smolensk.' He'd requested a transfer to the front at the end of 1941."

"Priceless. Ben would want more photographs, and definitely one from his later years. A picture of you too, I'm sure, preferably from the time you were with Laukhin. I'm saying this because I'd like to see it too."

"I can see the caption underneath: 'Laukhin's last fling before defection.'"

The tapas arrived, and with it some bread. The anchovies were inside the olives. The brown-grey *langostinos* lay resignedly on scattered slivers of lettuce with lemon wedges. From across the river, the London Eye watched disinterestedly their tentative steps with fork and knife. It didn't look like an eye to him, more like the unicycle of a giant who, newly arrived in the neighbourhood, got tired of the contraption and took off on foot, stepping over the Thames. Though not before propping his wheel upright. A careful colossus.

"I wrote about Laukhin too, you know," she said, "our brief time together, our fling." She smiled. "As the demanding Professor Paskow asked me to do.

Strange. It was so long ago, more than twenty-five years, and lasted, what, five months? I thought I'd have two or three pages, and already I've written more than twenty. What I have now is enough. He doesn't need details of how the rumpled bedsheets looked as moonbeams fell on them. Or pillow talk, or a young woman's silly dreams. I'm going to write more. I reread the poetry I wrote then, and almost each line triggered another recollection. I'm thinking of finding a journal for it, who knows. If it came out before my new volume of poetry, it might create some interest. Grisha's advice. It might lead to a reprint of my other book too. But enough of me. Tell me what's new with you."

"There isn't much that you don't know already."

She knew what was happening to him. They had been exchanging emails, and two weeks earlier, a Sunday morning, Anna had rung and mentioned, again, she'd have a free week she could share with him if he came to London. This time, he said he would. The conversation that day had been long. He'd told her that Katelyn would be moving with her mother and stepfather to Paris for three years and that he had plans to find a job in Europe and be close to her. "Closer to you too, Anna," he'd added, and there'd been a disheartening silence at the other end. He'd told her that ESA's Mars rover, the program he'd been working on for several years and for which he'd had many hopes, was now dwindling into insignificance for Ludwig Robotics because of the unexpected government decision to curtail further funding. He mentioned Louis Gandarax's role in that decision, the adviser to the minister in charge of the space agency, who happened to be the nephew of Hollie Biranek. Anna had become confused when he first named Hollie as the reason for Gandarax's change of heart, and it took him a while to clarify the connection. He wasn't sure how much Anna had retained from his complicated explanation that morning, but the next thing she said to him, stabbing the last of the green olives, proved she'd been a good listener.

"This story, with the aunt and the nephew, Miles, I don't know. I mean, how do you know for sure?"

"My boss. I was screamed at. He'd heard it directly from his boss. And his boss heard it from Ted Ludwig. You've met him, Ted, your husband's friend. You met all of these actors at Geoff Simmons's home in November."

"Well, it's odd," she said.

"What's odd?"

"I'm not to repeat what I see or hear at my husband's business dinners, you know, and anyway I hardly ever participate, but he wanted me there, and it couldn't have been that important or confidential . . . You see, I saw Ted Ludwig several days ago. Your minister, Mr. Bernier, was there too, and so was his adviser, Louis Gandarax. Gandarax mentioned I'd met him in November in Canada. Perhaps. He was the reason I was asked to join, because his wife was there too. No, I don't think it was his wife. Anyway, he was with a rather tall woman, pleasant, or so she seemed, as I hardly had a chance to talk to her. A Signor Bataloni Italian, kept us company too. It was a French restaurant, near Covent Garden, and it got noisy as the evening went on. The talk, I mean the business talk, was about, I'm not sure, a satellite of some sort. The Canadians were probing my husband about Russia's interest. Charming man, Louis Gandarax. The conversation was mostly in French. Good wines were drunk, and everybody had a good time. Lots of amusing stories about becoming the party in power. Ted Ludwig is quite nimble in French, did you know this?"

"No."

"He and Bernier seemed on the best of terms."

"Ted Ludwig is no fool."

"Best of terms with Louis Gandarax too. Pals. Laughing their heads off toward the end, with several glasses of brandy in them. And all this time Signor Bataloni was pestering me."

He wasn't entirely sure what Anna was driving at, though it hardly mattered now. And Gandarax made him think of Hollie, and Miles didn't want to think of the Biranek mess. He wished Anna spoke French to him. He might not understand much, but it would help him improve, which might help land a job close to Katelyn.

"Salad or potatoes?" he asked, looking at the menu again.

"What kind of potatoes?"

"*Patatas bravas*, whatever that means."

"Both. Let's be wild."

They were quiet until the waiter came. The sun had gone down, and lights had surged around them. The ones on the nearby bridge, behind him, were like modest fireworks frozen mid-flight. Ahead and to the left, the London Eye was a circle of delicate fire. Farther upstream, the Houses of Parliament were so gloriously alight that it gave the impression of a palace built for no other reason. The waving reflections, the castle-like Whitehall Court to his right, floodlit and half hidden by trees, beautiful Anna in front of him, the whole composition had a fleeting, fairy-tale quality.

As always, each sip tasted better than the previous one. Anna said something in Russian that sounded like a line or two of verse. She followed it with what he took to be the English version: "'Let us wait by the river that / rinses the coloured beads of street lights . . .' That's Tsvetayeva's. I read an English translation the other day. The flickering lights reminded me of her poem and of Saint Petersburg. She had a fling with another poet and a wonderful poem

was born. I had a fling with another poet and . . ." She made a face to show
what she thought of it.

"Who's the friend who lives in the castle," he asked, pointing to his right.

"Someone I've known for a long time. She was nice to me once, during
difficult days."

"She can afford a flat in that castle?"

"She had a good divorce."

The waiter brought the salad and the *patatas*, yellow cubes wading in pink
oil in a dark green bowl. He moved two of the cubes onto his plate. Anna was
playing with lettuce leaves on hers.

"And the search for work here?" she asked.

"Difficult."

"No luck?"

"Not yet."

She moved a cube of potato to her plate too and slowly proceeded to cut it
in half. "I could talk to Grisha."

"What?"

"He needs somebody here, in the West, to look after things, mostly space
matters. He's not interested in space. He was kind of forced into it and doesn't
think much will come out of any Russia–West collaboration. So he needs
someone who'd let him do what he wants to do."

"You're not serious."

"I am. It would be somewhere here or across the Channel. You'd travel a lot
to North America, of course, with the base in Europe."

"Anna, you're sleeping with me."

"Don't be so provincial."

Like Federica, Anna was proposing assistance from her husband. Grigory and Gregory volunteered by their wives to help helpless Miles. Feckless
Miles. Why was it that the Gregs of this world were between him and the
women he loved?

Nothing would disturb his good mood, not even shocking propositions.
He was pleasantly intoxicated, no doubt, but it was also the *fête-au-château*
surroundings, the river and the barely rocking boat, and Anna the poetess in
front of him. Anna of delicate body. He could not remember when he'd last
felt like this. It was happiness of some deluded sort, the kind assisted by alcohol and a deliberate effort to parcel London away from his Toronto worries.
Momentary, men's low-grade happiness.

It was getting cooler on the river. Increasing noise – an argument getting
out of hand? – was coming from right behind him. Evenings like this should
be without disturbances. He turned. A woman was trying to pull a man away

from the foredeck, saying, "That's enough, Ronald, enough." Ronald wore a checked jacket and seemed absent, trying to resurface from whatever alcoholic bath he'd been immersed in. He protested, "I like it here." A horrible jacket. Perhaps they'd come from the aft deck, or had been inside and stepped out for fresh air and the view. "Sure, sure," the woman said, "I like it here too. We have to go now, though. We'll come back soon." Reluctantly, Ronald turned around.

Miles felt an affinity for Ronald, although not for his sartorial judgment. He forked the last prawn and put it on his plate.

"Is the libel case going ahead?" she asked.

"No, no, I beg you. I came to London to forget about it for a few days, and to see you. Especially to see you."

"Please. Briefly."

His subjective well-being was under siege. "There's nothing new, Anna. It's going ahead, yes."

It was worse than simply "going ahead." That expression implied things were, even if not taking a favourable turn, advancing without unexpected and adverse surprises. Yet before Miles left for London, Al Bakker had requested one more day of questioning. Less, he'd promised – half a day. Miles found out about it after Rhona Honecker told him the trial date had been set and that Mary Lambert was now talking almost daily to Bakker and willing to be a witness for him. A sequence of three pieces of bad news, and he couldn't make up his mind which was the worst. It ended his hope for an out-of-court settlement. Rhona had told him not to despair; he wasn't in the witness box yet.

"A trial, then," Anna said.

"I fear so."

"When?"

"September. Two more months of pretrial shenanigans, and then on to the big show to shame Miles Rueda."

He woke up late, confused as to where he was and thinking he had to make a phone call he didn't want to make. He had dreamt that someone who looked like Fowler-Biggelow was forcing him to ring Jim Cowley to tell him . . . Tell him what? The Fowler-Biggelow lookalike glowered with anger and shouted that Miles knew very well what. And there were more bad things coming his way. Miles was to move back to Corby Falls; in fact, he was to drive there immediately after he'd called Jim. Miles protested – his work, his daughter, were in Toronto. Cecil – it was him, no doubt – sneered that Miles no longer had work in Toronto after the scandal. Miles cried that his daughter,

Katelyn, wouldn't visit him in Corby Falls. (A nightmare within a nightmare, he thought later.) By this point he was on his knees, begging, as Cecil glared down at him with lordly contempt. It was then that he woke up.

The clock on the night table showed twelve minutes past twelve. When he'd said goodbye to Anna the night before – she was leaving in the morning for Saint Petersburg, summoned there by her husband – he mentioned he'd have an entire day free before returning to Toronto. Well, half a day, although he felt he'd barely slept. He'd take it easy, lunch, stroll, wander here and there, nothing ambitious.

On the way to the bathroom, he noticed the blinking light telling him he had a phone message. From Toronto, obviously, as no one in London except Anna knew he was here. He hurried his morning ablutions, worried that the message was from Katelyn, or from Federica about Katelyn, the two souls he told he'd be in London. He imagined something troublesome. To his surprise he heard Rhona Honecker's voice, recorded the day before, asking him to phone back. He got her voice mail and left a message with his cell phone number. Rhona must have rung Federica to get the name of the hotel he was staying at. It couldn't be good news. Shit. He'd managed to forget his troubles – almost – while he'd been with Anna.

He had a late lunch alone, in a pub near Seven Dials. He hesitated between the slow-braised pork belly and the succulent lamb bhuna. A Punjabi dish, he read. The bartender, a man with a walrus moustache and sloping shoulders, was glaring at him, irritated by his indecision. The curry, he decided at long last, more exotic and with the promise of aromatic spices. And whatever beer went best with it. He watched the long glass-filling process and carried his drink to an empty table. He sat not far from the entrance, facing the wide bar. To his left, the room extended quite far, along the street. There were two other tables taken, one by three elderly couples, obviously tourists, and one, at the other end, by a pair clearly in love, because they were holding hands and giggling into each other's ears. The man, with sunglasses, was wearing a suit. Miles had hoped for a busier scene. Perhaps he should have sat at one of the tables at a window and watched the street.

The woman at the other end of the room stood up, pointing at her watch. The man stood up too, a tad shorter than she. An embrace ending in a long kiss. The man sat back down, and the woman made her way out past Miles in a hurry. Not as young as the fondling had intimated.

Between sips, he found his mind travelling to the awaiting ordeal in Toronto. Rose's death was a play in three acts. The death itself and what he'd seen as a boy was the first one. There was an intermediate act, the key one, relatively recent and brief, in which he became aware of what he'd seen thirty-five years earlier and which ended with the story he told a small group of friends in a restaurant. The third and final act was ongoing, stretched over more than a year now, with him unwillingly dragged toward centre stage and henchmen slowly setting up the pillory for his public humiliation. He'd be captive there, scorned good and long by all, and there was nothing he could do about it.

A familiar voice said, "Miles?"

He looked up. The man took his sunglasses off and he recognized Louis Gandarax. A smiling Louis Gandarax. The last person he expected to see at that moment. The last one he wanted to see, too. Embarrassed, Miles rose and shook his hand.

"I wondered, Louis, who the happy person was holding hands with the lovely woman. Now I know. Sunglasses inside – are you hiding?"

"What are you doing here? There are rumours you're on extended leave."

"I'm trying to figure out what to do next."

"Midlife uncertainties?"

"That too. My midlife seems to have started in my teens." He hesitated, and then decided to go straight into it. "The disappointment with the ESA's AEM is a big part, of course. But then, I kind of caused it."

"You did what?"

"Look, Louis, I'm really sorry. I didn't mean it, didn't expect it, too much liquor, my blabbering mouth, and it happened."

Gandarax seemed unsure what to make of his words. "Come again?"

"I tried to apologize to Hollie, more than once . . . She wouldn't talk to me."

"Hollie?"

"Hollie, yes, your aunt. Héloïse, your mother's sister."

"Ah, yes, yes, that. Of course. Hollie, if you wish, fine. You are in it, aren't you? I didn't know about it at the beginning. There was little in the Quebec newspapers, and who has time for newspapers these days? My mother might have said something – well, you know, she's old and gets mixed up, and I might have paid less attention than I should have. It was Ted Ludwig who reminded me of it four or five months ago. We had a drink one evening in Montreal, and he told me the details of your sudden fame. I was the one who told him that the Hollie from the paper was my Aunt Héloïse. Ted seemed quite amused by the coincidence. Amused and fascinated. Yes, an aunt I haven't seen in fifteen years. Ted Ludwig was carrying on about you again not long ago, here in London in fact, and we had a good laugh. Well, not just about you – the entire story of the bequest, and Aunt Héloïse, of course. Mind you, we were both tipsy. Several glasses of Cognac will do that. It was from him that I heard you were on extended leave. Anyway, good to see you, Miles. I've got to be somewhere, otherwise I'd stay and chat. Are you here for a few days?"

"Leaving tomorrow morning."

"We'll have a beer another time. They have good beer here."

Gandarax grabbed Miles's hand and shook it. He turned to leave, and Miles called him back.

"Louis, hold on, what are you saying? You're not upset?"

"Upset?"

"Angry, mad, furious."

"Should I be? Why?"

"Because of what happened to your aunt."

"Ah. Look, as I said, I haven't seen her in years. I'm not sure I'd even recognize her."

"Then . . . The government support for AEM . . . You didn't change Bernier's mind?"

"Miles, I didn't change anybody's mind. The economic case for AEM is simply not there. Nothing, zero, compared to Earth observation."

"I thought you were behind AEM."

"It was less of a disaster than CMM. I mean, I like Mars, and I like rovers; they are fine, though not for Canada, with its limited space budget. Shouldn't say limited – ridiculously small is more descriptive. Garneau was for AEM, yes, but you know how astronauts are: they like toys and spending money. It was a whim, nothing sound. It collapsed on its own, with Garneau leaving and CSA's cold shoulder . . . Miles, really, I've got to go."

He watched Gandarax walk out. Another tender rendezvous? What Louis had said was startling. Not that it mattered anymore. Still, was Fowler-Biggelow part of the intrigue to make everyone at Ludwig Robotics think that the collapse of the government's support for AEM was Miles's fault? Cecil's anger had seemed real, and Miles couldn't see him as a conniver. Was Geoff Simmons in it? Was it strictly Ted Ludwig's plot? The big boss who found it difficult to explain why Ludwig Space had switched their support from AEM to HEOS. Which meant work in Vancouver, but not in Toronto. And when Gandarax mentioned his aunt, Ted Ludwig found a way not to antagonize Ludwig Robotics: blame it on Miles Rueda.

Rhona Honecker called as he was finishing his curry and considering another beer. The pub was empty now, and he could hear her clearly.

"Mary Lambert is dead," she said.

"What?"

"She's dead."

Rhona wasn't into small talk. She delivered facts, no explanations or context. There was so much more she could have added to her dramatic statement.

"Had she been ill?" he asked.

She ignored his question. "I think Blanchard will settle and publish a retraction."

"Ms. Honecker, you've been saying that since we first met."

"It's different now, without Mary Lambert."

He still couldn't see why Mary's death would make the newspaper settle.

"The *Post* is having second thoughts about covering Blanchard's legal fees through a trial," Rhona went on.

"Did *they* say that?"

"They wouldn't."

"How do you know, then?"

"We had a talk with Al Bakker and his assistant yesterday, a long talk, and that's our assessment. Al couldn't believe what was happening. He seemed upset, then despondent, and then enraged. He was toying with carrying on pro bono. Not likely, since he has tax problems and in arrears with payments to his divorced wife."

An assessment. Alvard was upset. It was all speculation. He probed, still hopeful. "So . . . no court case?"

"I didn't say that. But there is a good chance we won't end up there. A lot better than before."

"The discovery . . . the last session Al Bakker wanted, is it off?"

"Afraid not. Al insists on it."

"Fuck, fuck, fuck. Why?"

Rhona didn't reply immediately, either gathering her thoughts or startled by his serial profanity. "He's hoping for some dramatic findings that will mean Blanchard doesn't need to settle. He thinks the newspaper's doubts are daft – his words to me. Keeps saying you are a liar and that he has a witness lined up who'll testify that you were assaulted so that you would retract your story about Biranek."

"A witness? Someone who was there as they were having a go at me? One of the participants?"

"He didn't elaborate. Often it's threats and bluster with Al Bakker."

Someone who'd been there, watching, without landing a punch or a kick, while the Millcroft boys were pummelling him? Someone feeling a pang of guilt? Laughable.

"Mary Lambert, out of the blue, she just . . . died?" he asked.

"She was killed."

"Did you say *killed*?"

"Yes."

"You mean somebody did her in?"

"Seems that way. Murder or manslaughter."

The bartender was staring at him, and he realized that in the empty pub his voice was travelling.

"When did it happen?"

"Two nights ago. I called you yesterday afternoon, as soon as I heard. It wasn't easy to get your former wife to tell me where you were."

"Did . . . did the police contact you?"

"No. Not yet, anyway."

"You think they will?"

He heard a sound, like air blown through tight lips, and took it that Rhona didn't know and found his question irrelevant. The bartender was clearing a nearby table. Miles turned away and lowered his voice. "How did you find out?"

"Al Bakker. Mary Lambert was supposed to come to see him in the morning, and when she didn't turn up at his office, he phoned her. It was a cop who answered. All this happened yesterday."

"Was she killed at home?"

"In a small park not that far from her house. Hubbard Park, or something like that. It seems she went there with her dog every day, often twice a day. A jogger stumbled upon her body yesterday morning. Her purse was missing. I don't know how they identified her so quickly."

"Who . . . who did it?"

"The cop in charge wouldn't tell Al anything. His first guess is hoodlums, high on crack." She paused and then added, "Leslieville," and he almost heard the shrug.

The walrus was back behind the bar, staring curiously at him. Miles walked over to him with his glass and gestured for another beer.

"It's a good thing you're away," he heard Rhona say.

"Is it?"

"You're not a suspect."

"Ms. Honecker, really."

"I mean, the police can quickly eliminate you from their inquiry."

No doubt Rhona was enjoying this.

"According to Al Bakker," she went on, and Miles had the impression of a long-distance chuckle, "they weren't sure of your whereabouts. Goodbye, Mr. Rueda."

The police weren't wondering very hard, because they could have got through to him on his cell phone. Would they call Ludwig Robotics – in fact, had they already? He imagined Fowler-Biggelow getting wind of the news that the police were tracking Miles and rushing to tell Geoff Simmons.

Chapter 18

June, July 2006

Miles wasn't looking forward to more hours with Al Bakker and his sneering face. Malicious Alvard. Since the call from Rhona Honecker, Bakker – nasty, shifty, manipulative, demanding another discovery session simply to taunt him – had been constantly on his mind. On the flight back to Toronto, Miles consoled himself that he'd at least learn the name of Alvard's much-touted witness, the one who'd been there on Ripple Road and watched his hammering. He had struggled for hours to figure out who he could be. Rhona herself, despite having told Miles she thought Al Bakker was bluffing, had asked him to write down three possible names, even if they were wild guesses. Someone who secretly resented B&M Construction? Ill-treated there, perhaps laid off? Someone with a grudge against the township? For a mad second, Miles considered Mike Ancona, not as a presence on Ripple Road but as someone who was aware of what happened to him. Daft. He was beginning to dismiss Al Bakker's claim. It wasn't as if tickets had been sold to the show on the right bank of the Corby River and – by sheer bad luck – one of the spectators was having second thoughts. A passerby? He'd seen not one soul that cold, rainy night. Someone driving by? What could he or she have seen in the dark? If there was a witness, it would have been a participant, somebody who, after throwing a few punches, got cold feet. A guilty conscience? A self-incriminating fool? No, Alvard had no witness. His snout in the air, he was simply sniffing.

What if there was such a fool, though? He had pictured Bill Cowley, Tom Locksley, and the Moose coming at him from behind. Others? Hard to say. Three were more than enough to make mincemeat out of him, especially if the Moose was one of them, and the more they were, the more likely word would get out. The Moose wouldn't talk, and neither would Tom – the mayor's husband – or Bill. No one, no . . . Unless tongues got loose drinking, or Bill Cowley bragged about it while attending to the needs of his dick. No . . . There remained, of course – it was a stretch – Moose's little brother, Ronnie. Hadn't he been at Bart's Alehouse that night? And didn't Jim say he was "a bit simple"? Ronnie could easily be the *fool* he was looking for. Would they have let him tag along with their posse? Maybe they couldn't get rid of him. But if he was uncontrollable they would have made sure he wasn't there. Had Ronnie followed them, or somehow got wind of what happened? Had he followed Miles, having overheard what his brother and the others had in mind? And? How would Ronnie or what he knew reach Al Bakker? Through Eddy Bryson? Was Eddy still nosing around? Was he a friend of Ronnie? Did Ronnie shoot his mouth off about what happened to the Toronto dude near the river? No, Ronnie wouldn't be a witness for Al Bakker. He'd be pressured, coached to lie. Unless Ronnie was, on occasion, stubbornly uncoachable. Fools often were. In that case, though, he wouldn't be a good witness for Al Bakker either. Which, perhaps, explained the threats Al Bakker kept making and his inability or hesitation to name his witness.

Ronnie's testimony, if it was him, might convince the judge that Miles had been scared into saying the story he told at Le Paradis was invented. Still, it wouldn't mean Biranek killed his wife. The judge would not put much trust in the recollection, thirty-five years later, of a witness who had shown himself to be unreliable. And the hospital would eventually get Biranek's money after more years of lawyerly arguments and compromises. Miles Rueda, however, would be fucked. Thoroughly, comprehensively.

A day earlier, he'd called Rhona Honecker to find out whether Al Bakker had revealed the identity of his new witness.

Rhona scoffed. "Not yet, and he better hurry."

"Would he reveal his name during the examination tomorrow?"

"I don't know. He doesn't have to. He's the one asking the questions."

"He'd have to reveal it before the trial starts, wouldn't he?'

"Yes."

Early in the morning he had a phone call from Don. Miles should not raise his hopes of a job too high, Don said quickly. It wasn't easy, as Miles had never worked in sales. He wasn't familiar with airplanes either, commercial or otherwise, although along that line there was room for exaggeration if Miles promised to do some cramming meanwhile. It helped to know what flaps were for. Getting in some flying lessons might help too. And French. Yes, English was the language of sales nowadays, but speaking French to Frenchies always left a good impression. His desire to be located in Europe, preferably in Paris or as close as possible, was another obstacle. They'd give Miles an interview, but . . . He'd be wise to keep his expectations in check. Don stopped to catch his breath. He had rung the previous week too – no one answered – and was in a rush now. Where had Miles been? He'd call the next day to give him more details. Learn more of Lyle's latest mischief-making too.

He went for a walk in Sherwood Park. He followed the familiar route, down the hill and across the little stream, turning left to follow the leafy path through the park, veering just before Blythwood Road, returning on the other bank. He passed by the area where dogs were allowed to run free, and as always the number of dogs and the devotion of their owners startled him. It must have been in a similar enclosure that Mary Lambert met Reg. A romance kindled by the love of canines. Katelyn had been nervous near dogs. The first years after they moved to Montgomery, he and Federica would often walk to Sherwood Park with Katelyn riding on his shoulders. Those had been their best years, when they believed things would somehow settle. And they had the wonder of Katelyn, old enough to amaze them and still enthralled by her parents.

Back home, he thought of having something to eat, keep his energy level up for the forthcoming battle. He warmed up the remains of a jar of pea soup bought the day he landed back in Toronto and gave up after two spoonfuls. He took the subway, got off at King, and, despite taking his time about it, arrived at Briggs Leaman Honecker ten minutes before two o'clock. Somewhat hesitant, Rhona's secretary showed him into the empty boardroom. He sat in the same chair he occupied at their previous session. The stenographer's paraphernalia was already there, in its usual place at one end of the table. Adelle Choy put her head in briefly and said they might be a little late. She disappeared before he had time to say anything. No explanation, just a fact.

Annoyed, he got up and began walking around the large oval table, thinking stupidly that he was ellipsing or ovalling, not circling, it. He paused at the windowed corner of the room. The view was south and west, and he guessed that a just-visible bit of steep copper-green roof belonged to the Royal York Hotel. Past it there were stretches of the Toronto Islands. A propeller plane taking off from the city airport reminded him that, with some luck, he might soon be selling such technical wonders. An elevator was crawling up the pointed structure of the CN Tower, one of the parasite insects the edifice had to bear for its existence.

As he turned away, the boardroom door was pulled open by invisible hands and an older woman pushed a trolley through with fresh coffee on it. When she left, he resumed his irritated ambulation. The room needed some dramatic art, not the barbiturate drawings of thin-legged horses that once were the pride of paddocks in Victorian England. A naked woman playing the cello would do, like the painting in Emma Levitsky's boardroom. That large oil – he'd always sat across from it – had stayed with him like none other, and he remembered going to his lawyer's office during the protracted battle with Federica with fewer misgivings because of it. Emma Levitsky, older and inclined to treat him like a defective son, had noticed his fondness for the cello player and once asked, "You like ugly naked girls?" In London, Anna told him she'd taken cello lessons as a child, hadn't been talented enough, and had to give it up. Her demanding and expensive teacher – a famous name he'd forgotten because it meant nothing to him – told Anna's mother that her daughter was too small for such a large instrument, a polite way to get rid of a less gifted pupil. Anna's face somewhat resembled that of the cello player in Emma Levitsky's painting, attuned to an inner music or inspiration. He wouldn't mind owning a portrait of a naked Anna playing the cello, perhaps by the same artist, a large painting, like the one in his lawyer's boardroom. He didn't have the proper space to hang it on Montgomery Avenue, though, and a smaller one wouldn't make such a strong impression. He'd ask the painter for a slight change in the viewpoint, more from the side and downward, allowing a hint, a surmise, of pubic hair. It would be a focusing detail, and, of course, make the portrait far more sensual. He should call Emma Levitsky and find out the painter's name. He remembered she had mentioned the Toronto gallery she got it from, so the artist might be contemporary and local. What would the painter say if Miles insisted on that inkling of pubic hair? Try to convince him it was impossible, given the size and position of the musical instrument? How much would it cost, and would Anna agree to pose? She'd say no, not at her age.

Now why had his thoughts drifted into such drivel? Anna had emailed him to say she would be spending three days in Toronto toward the end of August. He wished he could spend more time with her.

Would Rhona Honecker pose naked with a cello? Would she then place the painting in the boardroom of Briggs Leaman Honecker? Ha. She was not too small for the large instrument. He imagined Rhona walking into the boardroom with one of her clients, showing him to a chair opposite the painting, and sitting across from him beneath it. Would she expect a comment from the client? Allude to the painting behind her if none was forthcoming?

Damn, where was everybody? Almost half past. Outrageous. He stepped out of the room and asked the first person he saw, a young woman sitting at a small desk, where Ms. Honecker was. She made a brief phone call, and Rhona's secretary materialized nearby. Her face was red. She apologized and said that Rhona and Al Bakker and all the others were in Rhona's office. "There has been a development," she added, "and Mr. Bakker likes to hear himself talk, and the surprise of it—"

"What development?" Miles asked.

"I . . . I can't say."

"Ms. . . . Ms. . . ." In his fury, he realized he'd forgotten the secretary's name. "Tell Rhona, tell your boss, that unless she's in the boardroom in five minutes, I'm off. No, make it two minutes. Two minutes, you understand?"

He went back in the boardroom and slammed the heavy door, which wasn't easy. Rhona Honecker showed up almost immediately.

"Finally," he said.

"Sorry, Mr. Rueda. I should've come earlier and explained, not sent Adelle."

"What's happening?"

"There was an argument. Al Bakker argued we should go on with the examination. Al is posturing, letting off steam, whatever, and we're being polite. Besides, it's a good show."

"While I'm left waiting here."

"It took too long. Sorry again. You should go home now, Mr. Rueda."

"Look, I'm already here and might as well—"

"There won't be a trial, Mr. Rueda."

"No trial?"

"Yes. Al has been instructed to seek a settlement. He's seething, furious." A smile crossed her face. "We were right in our earlier assessment," she added, with a hint of pride.

"Why then does Bakker still want to go through with the examination?"

"He's certain he'll be able to quash the instruction he's received, and, since we are here already . . . It's nonsense. Bluff and nonsense."

"That's it, then?"

"It saves you a lot of bother, Mr. Rueda," she said. "Lucky you."

Irony. Somehow, Rhona Honecker had never believed he was telling the truth. Lucky? After what he'd been through, he didn't see it that way.

"You mean your client is lucky," he said. "The residents of Millcroft Township too. Particularly them."

"Of course. Everybody, except Mary Lambert."

He took a deep breath and there seemed to be less pressure on his chest. A crime had, unexpectedly, saved him. That was the way with nightmares, they built up slowly and came to an end abruptly.

"Why would Mary's death make Blanchard settle?"

"I can only surmise, Mr. Rueda. The *Post*, paying Blanchard's legal fees until now, has had a say in this too. Perhaps the decisive one. Blanchard counted on Mary Lambert as a witness. Her story of early abandonment and her dismal life would have painted Biranek as being heartless and might have persuaded the jury that he was capable of leaving Rose to die, and that, therefore, you might not have fabricated your story, or that it was reasonable for Blanchard to believe it despite your insistence that the story was made up. Personally, I saw little merit in this assessment, but perhaps Al Bakker made much of it, and it boomeranged on him." She paused and shook her head. "Even without you as our witness, Mr. Rueda, their case was hard. Convincing a judge or a jury of the veracity of what a twelve-year-old had seen thirty-five years earlier would not have been easy at all. Blanchard was willing to mortgage his house and contribute to the legal costs provided the *Post* would pay at least half of them going forward, but I think the *Post* executives had had enough. Mary's death precipitated the decision."

He was halfway through the door when he turned around and asked, "Do you play the cello, Ms. Honecker?"

"Sorry? The cello? No. Bizarre question. Why do you ask?"

"Pay no attention – crazy me."

The sky was without a cloud, the way festive skies should be. And for the first time in more than a year, his life was without a cloud. Ludwig was barely in his mind now. The fact that he didn't have a job or an income was a temporary inconvenience. He'd follow his daughter to Europe and find a job there. He'd be near her, and a simple hop to London would take him to Anna. He crossed the street and sat on one of the cows in the courtyard of the TD Centre, something he'd always wanted to do, a subdued celebration. He considered doing a little victory dance around the animal, then thought better of it. In a way, Rhona Honecker was right to call him lucky, although he'd been due a break after the unlikely sequence of events which led to the shit he'd been in for more than a year. Mary Lambert was the unlucky one, as Rhona had pointed out to him. Reginald Bent was unlucky too, because he wouldn't get any money now, but Reg was a villain.

Relief and elation. Katelyn was safe, and he wouldn't have to lie under oath, make a fool of himself, give satisfaction to the Millcroft thugs. Champagne corks would be flying at M&B's offices and Millcroft Township Hall. At St. Anselm's too, perhaps a cheaper, cautious crémant, more in keeping with that solemn institution. There'd be work for everybody, a modern hospital in the township, a safe roof over the prayerful at St. Anselm's. With Mary's death, everything was as it should be. Mary, the saviour of all. She'd never had much luck in life and had no one to mourn her. Her son was in jail, and, from what Lyn had told Miles, he wouldn't grieve much. Reg would curse his luck and head back to his maritime province. Lyn? She'd be sad, of course, wax philosophical – as he was doing now – about a wasted, dull, dismal existence, and she'd be relieved. No more grim lunches, and she could switch to a dentist who was more conveniently located. Mary would be quickly forgotten, and the police would not bother a great deal with her case. If they couldn't find the killer or killers quickly, well, their resources were limited, and they had other cases to resolve.

Two weeks later, unable to wait longer, he called Rhona Honecker to make sure the out-of-court settlement had been agreed on.

"Not yet," Rhona said, "at least not officially. It's a matter of sorting out some minor points in Blanchard's retraction."

"Was the *Post* chosen as the newspaper it will appear in?"

"It was."

"No further surprises?"

"I'm the one looking at the wording. There will be no case, because my client is satisfied. You're off the hook, Mr. Rueda. Mary Lambert's death is a relief that way."

That was really it, then.

"How did she die?" he asked.

"She was savagely beaten."

"Jesus."

"She may have been alive when he was done with her, but barely."

"He?"

She hesitated. "A way of speaking."

"Are the police getting anywhere?"

"The cops have suspects."

"I'm not one of them, I hope," he said, and instantly regretted it. The asinine banter of a carefree man.

"You are. You had something to gain by her death – at least judging by the *Post*'s change of heart."

"I wasn't to know."

She ignored his reply. "The hospital in Millcroft, the whole township, in fact, are suspects too. The rector of St. Anselm's is not on the list simply because it would be a sacrilege."

More irony from Rhona. "That's a lot of suspects," Miles said.

"Yes. Though I wouldn't fret if I were you, Mr. Rueda. The main one seems to be Mary Lambert's husband."

That was unexpected. "Reginald Bent?"

"Yes."

"How do you know?"

"From Al Bakker."

"How does he know?"

She hesitated again. "Al Bakker . . . He was a Crown attorney once, you know, and he still has connections with the police. The investigators had many questions for Al – he'd seen and talked to Mary Lambert often during her last few months – and they were most insistent on the whereabouts of Reginald Bent. I doubt Al could help, though."

"Why Reg Bent?"

He heard her talk to someone, muffled words, her hand covering the receiver. When she returned to him, she rushed her story. It was all hearsay, she wanted to be clear, yet it made sense. Mary's upstairs tenant, a young woman, told the police she'd heard shouts and threats whenever Reg dropped in on Mary. That is, since he'd reappeared. The tenant was afraid of him, and so was Mary, because twice she ran upstairs to hide from him. The young woman wanted to call the cops, but Mary wouldn't let her. The first time the tenant heard screams in Mary's apartment, she knocked on Mary's door – brave of her – and Reg almost hit her. These were the details the cops gave Al Bakker, hoping he'd know were Bent was spending his time when he wasn't harassing his wife.

In the ensuing silence he ruminated that Mary's violent, estranged husband had saved him from lethal embarrassment. The savage attack seemed to fit the image he had of Reg, though why kill her? She was his ticket to some easy money. Perhaps – upset at things going too slow, trying to make her see the same urgency he did – he'd lost control. Had he got wind of Mary's talks with Al Bakker and, seeing his windfall evaporating, attempted to change her mind and gone too far?

"I met him once, Reg, briefly, and he's scary all right. But kill Mary . . ."

"I'm saying he's the police's prime suspect, and there is a good possibility they'll charge him. If that happens . . . you might as well know, Al Bakker will be defending him."

There was no escaping Alvard. "Are you sure?"

"I talked to Al yesterday."

"You said there were no more twists."

"It's of no concern to you or me, Mr. Rueda."

The pause that followed was filled with renewed uneasiness. "Reg must have some emergency money stashed away," he said with difficulty.

"Al will do it pro bono. He seemed excited by the prospect."

"Has he solved his tax problems? Paid the arrears to his ex-wife?"

"Oh, it's a murder trial, and Al gets all aroused. Can't resist it."

Rhona was wrong. It was of concern to him. In court – because there would be a trial if Reg Bent was charged – Alvard would leave no stone unturned, and that would include the matter of Rose's death. It was another reason, no doubt, for Alvard's willingness to take the job pro bono.

Detective Ralph Janusi came to Montgomery Avenue for a chat the following day. That was what he'd said, "A simple chat," when he rang to make the appointment.

"About?" Miles asked.

"The death of Mary Lambert."

"Am I a suspect?"

On the phone, Ralph Janusi had sounded young and easily amused.

"No, no. They wouldn't send me if you were a suspect. No, just dotting the i's, crossing the t's, you know, the hoops we cops must go through."

Detective Janusi, in his early thirties, thin, polite, confessed to being only temporarily involved in Mary Lambert's case because of a colleague's recent illness, although he seemed prodigiously well informed about it. He knew all there was to know about the Biranek affair, Miles's inadvertent role in triggering it, the various interests at play, the names of the main actors. He appeared entertained by the "whole rigmarole," that's what he called it, and Miles surmised that having been given a folder of already gathered facts and statements, he'd read it as a diverting puzzle. He implied, or at least that was Miles's distinct impression, that the police had already made up their minds as to who had killed Mary Lambert. When he asked for details about Miles's whereabouts the night Mary was killed, the detective smiled and said it was a formality they had to go through.

The young detective's amused detachment receded when he mentioned the severe beating Miles had suffered in Corby Falls. "It was serious, Mr. Rueda, and you could have died. I've read the medical reports and seen the pictures. I think you were a lucky man. I understand that there's some long-term damage to one of your eyes and that you were not far from losing it. What we don't understand is why you didn't report it to the police."

"I barely managed to crawl home."

"And afterward?"

"I was in the hospital."

"We'd have come to you."

"I wasn't entirely ready for an interview. Or able to drive back to Corby Falls and point out to you exactly where the mugging took place."

"And afterward?"

"Too much time had elapsed. Weeks, in fact."

Ralph Janusi shook his head. "We'd be the ones to judge that."

"How many muggings do you solve, detective? And how many do you solve if they are reported three or four weeks after the fact?"

"It wasn't a mugging, Mr. Rueda; it was an aggravated assault. The person or persons who attacked you purposefully and recklessly caused you harm."

The detective tilted his head as if to signal his next question had a different orientation. "Could it have been Reginald Bent?"

That came out of nowhere, and he was stunned. "Reg, Mary's husband?"

"Yes."

No doubt Reg was capable of doing serious harm, even enjoying it. "You mean, could he have followed me to Corby Falls and pummelled me as I was getting some fresh air?"

"Something like that."

"But why would he?"

"Maybe he tried to kill you. Make sure you wouldn't change your story. With you saying it was a tall tale, a fabrication, Millcroft Township and those behind the hospital would have had less concern about Mary Lambert, and Reg would have seen no money coming his way."

The thought that, either way, he wouldn't have been left unscathed now crossed his mind. He could have picked the agent of his battering, or the reason: either the B&M thugs pounding him to change his story, or Reginald Bent so that he stuck to it.

"But Reg wouldn't have had any inkling at the time that my story was made up and that I'd change it," he said. "Not at that time."

The detective shrugged. "He didn't want to take a chance. A man out of the way can't change his story. You were lucky, Mr. Rueda. Mary Lambert didn't have your luck."

"What happened to her?"

"At first we thought it was drug addicts or drunken hooligans, one of those unfortunate occurrences, Mary Lambert being in the wrong place at the wrong time. But they clobbered her little dog too, you know, so badly, in fact, you could hardly recognize what sort of animal it was. Muggers don't usually do that, do they? Her purse wasn't found, but we think there was another reason for her death."

The detective closed his notebook and stood up. He took a step toward the door, then faced him again and asked, "What do you think of Reginald Bent?"

"I don't think of him, or not much."

"Your impression of him."

He lied. "I don't have one."

"Bent says you two met briefly, that you were harassing Mary one day as she was leaving work."

"We were together, what, two or three minutes. I was telling Mary that the story I told my sister was fiction. Bent appeared and told me to get lost. I did."

"Did you get the impression that he was capable of sudden rages, of losing his mind and beating his wife to death?"

"You have qualified people to offer you such opinions, detective."

"Still."

"He seemed rather abrupt and unsettling. As to whether he could have impulsive rages, that I don't know."

"Do you think he beat Mary Lambert to death?"

"That's what the police think?"

"The evidence points that way. Witnesses too. A couple saw him arguing with Mary that evening in Hubbard Park, not far from where she was found dead the following morning. Bent says he didn't touch his wife. He says he's slapped her once or twice in the past, perhaps more than slapped her, and he agrees he's shouted at her in the park because he was 'angry with the cunt' – his expression. But he says he left her there without touching a hair on her head. Unfortunately for him, he can't give a good account of what he did afterward, except that he walked the streets – being angry, you see, and trying to cool off. That's what he says he does when he's worked up, he walks. It's what he keeps telling us. He doesn't know where he was the evening of October 22 last year either." Seeing Miles's puzzled face, he added, "The night you were assaulted in Corby Falls. Says he couldn't possibly remember that far back."

Ralph Janusi was halfway out the door when he stopped. "I was an engineering student once," he said, sighing. "I liked it. Like you, I dreamt of space, trips to the Moon, Mars. I lasted two years."

"What happened?"

"My parents wanted me to be a priest. Wouldn't support me. So I became a cop. I was good at math, you know."

"I didn't dream of space, detective."

"Oh?"

The younger man stood there, staring past Miles, as if trapped by the door frame and his recollections.

"Detective, did you say the dog, Mary's little dog, was badly bashed too?"

"You should see the photos."

"Could it have been an accident? I mean, the dog."

"I doubt it."

He called it an *inconsistency* at first. That word had a lightness which precluded qualms, and not long after, he began to bundle it together with *minor*, hoping that paired that way it would stop niggling at him. He tried to convince himself that *minor inconsistency* was the proper description of what had been bothering him. Because he'd been uneasy since Ralph Janusi's visit, unwilling or afraid to think things through properly. Each day that passed made him more irritated, more annoyed with himself, and he felt he had to reach a decision. Not doing anything – not saying anything – was one decision, of course. He told himself he couldn't be sure at all, it was a mere conjecture, he was putting so much on so little. And furthermore, what made him think the police were not aware of the *inconsistency*? If he was aware of it, why wouldn't the trained minds of the police be too, minds that made a speciality of identifying and explaining inconsistencies? And yet . . .

He could live with the image of Reginald Bent in jail for something he didn't do; thug, thief, scoundrel, wife beater, irresponsible parent, he'd done enough nastiness in his life, and the world was better off with him behind bars. It wasn't a few months or years, though; if convicted this time – for a crime he had not committed – Reg would be in jail for years, perhaps a lifetime with his past record. Worse, the actual murderer or murderers would remain free.

His call to the police would be greeted with condescension. Detective Janusi would tell him he'd pass on his "valuable information," and Miles would hear the sarcasm in his voice, Janusi's way of telling him, "What makes you think we're not already aware of this?"

He knew it wasn't the *inconsistency* he should talk to the police about, or not only that. It was the mauling he'd got in Corby Falls and the threats to Katelyn which should be the core of his statement to the police. Included also should be the names of those he was certain thrashed him on the bank of the Corby River, and of the others implicated in it. The difficulties at B&M Construction too. The desperation of the township to retain Biranek's money and the provincial government's contribution. And, of course – simply thinking about it made him gag – he'd have to change his mind *again* and state that the story he told at Le Paradis was *not* a fib, that he'd seen Biranek in Corby Falls that Saturday night, when Rose was still alive. He'd have to involve his sister, acknowledge she'd been with him and seen Biranek too. He imagined himself at the trial, seeing Fowler-Biggelow's apoplectic face among the spectators. He'd be a witness for Al Bakker, and, oh, how Alvard would savour the moment, draw it out, watch him squirm in the stand. "Let me hear that again, Mr. Rueda, just to make it clear. You're now saying that what happened to you in October last year in Corby Falls was a deliberate assault, not a mugging. And that the assault was meant to change your mind about what you saw thirty-five years ago. You lied on both these accounts before, didn't you? You told the hospital, and later the police, that you were simply robbed a year ago in Corby Falls. And you lied during discovery about

what you witnessed as a twelve-year-old boy. That's perjury, Mr. Rueda." He'd
have to admit he had perjured himself – was it perjury if the lie was recorded
during discovery? – and he'd have to live through the entire nightmare he had
tried so hard to avoid. Katelyn would be in danger again. And this time she'd
really be ashamed of him.

Lyn Collins phoned him an hour after he'd left her a message to return his
call. "These meetings will be the end of me," she said.

"Isn't this what bankers do all day long? Meet? They meet with customers
who need money; they meet among themselves to assess the lending risks;
they meet with customers again to give them the good or the bad news."

She laughed. "It's clearly something you have given plenty of thought."

"Reginald Bent was charged with Mary's murder, Lyn."

She seemed to hesitate, and then he heard unclear words, a younger female
voice, and Lyn said to someone in the room, "You heard me, the emails to
him and from him from January onward, printed and on my desk. Yes, I need
them before I leave." She came back on the line. "Sorry, a crazy day, full of
drama. You were saying . . . Ah, yes, yes, Reg Bent. I saw his name in the
newspaper."

"What do you think?"

He heard her exhale. "I'm not surprised."

"I am. A young detective came to my office for a chat. The one time he
appeared mildly interested in my answers was when he admonished me
for not reporting the beating I got in Corby Falls. He asked my opinion of
Mary's husband and wouldn't let it go when I said I had none. I think the
police had long made up their minds that Reg was the one who did Mary in."

"Poor Mary," Lyn said.

He walked to the window. The wind had picked up and black rain clouds
were bringing darkness into the day.

"Lyn, she was Reginald's chance for some easy money. He'd been hovering
around Mary, more or less patiently, for almost a year, telling her what was
good for her – good for him too, of course – trying to sway her. Why kill her?"

"He didn't mean to."

"She was savagely beaten, from what I heard. If he didn't mean harm—"

"He's a violent man and lost it. He's beaten her before."

Maybe. Maybe Reg just lost it, but he doubted it. "Lyn," he said, "did the
police talk to you as well?"

"Yes. Shortly after Mary's death."

"Who contacted you?"

"I forget his name, an older cop. He said he was in charge of the case."

"What did he want to know?"

"Lots. He seemed to have plenty of free time and was interested in every-thing. In Mary, naturally, and in the Biranek affair. In you too, and what you said you saw – which he thought was preposterous, a twelve-year-old and a gap of thirty-five years – and in your mishap in Corby Falls. Quite taken by it, by what he called 'Rueda's battering.' Almost amused. He was most inter-ested in Reg Bent, though. Wherever our conversation went, he kept return-ing to Reg. Three hours, that's how long he kept me. He was disappointed I didn't know more about Reg, given I was Mary's friend. I kept telling him I never liked Reg and that I avoided him even if it meant seeing less of Mary or not at all."

How could no one see what he saw? How could the police miss it? Lyn had talked for three hours with the police about Mary's murder, and – she said it herself – Reg was uppermost in their minds. Surely she told them. Was the evidence against Reg so airtight that it didn't matter?

"Lyn, did you tell the police about the dogs?"

"The dogs?"

"Yes."

"Tell them what?"

"That Reg liked dogs."

She sounded both puzzled and amused. "No, I didn't. Why would I?"

"It's odd, Lyn, very odd."

"Odd? What's odd, Miles?"